PRAISE FOR TAHOE AVALANCHE

ONE OF THE TOP 5 MYSTERIES OF THE YEAR!
- Gayle Wedgwood, Mystery News

"BORG IS A SUPERB STORYTELLER...A MASTER OF THE GENRE"
- Midwest Book Review

"TAHOE AVALANCHE WAS SOOOO GOOD... A FASCINATING
MYSTERY with some really devious characters"
- Merry Cutler, Annie's Book Stop, Sharon, Massachusetts

"EXPLODES INTO A COMPLEX PLOT THAT LEADS TO MURDER
AND INTRIGUE"
- Nancy Hayden, Tahoe Daily Tribune

"READERS WILL BE KEPT ON THE EDGE OF THEIR SEATS"
- Sheryl McLaughlin, Douglas Times

"TODD BORG IS ON A ROLL"
- Taylor Flynn, Tahoe Mountain News

"WORTHY OF RECOGNITION"
-Jo Ann Vicarel, Library Journal

"INCLUDE BORG IN THE GROUP OF MYSTERY WRITERS that
write with a stong sense of place such as TONY HILLERMAN"
- William Clark, The Union

PRAISE FOR TAHOE SILENCE

WINNER, BEN FRANKLIN AWARD, BEST MYSTERY OF THE YEAR!

"A HEART-WRENCHING MYSTERY THAT IS ALSO ONE OF THE
BEST NOVELS WRITTEN ABOUT AUTISM"
STARRED REVIEW - Jo Ann Vicarel, Library Journal

CHOSEN BY LIBRARY JOURNAL AS ONE OF THE FIVE BEST
MYSTERIES OF THE YEAR

TAHOE NIGHT

TAHOE NIGHT

by

Todd Borg

THRILLER PRESS

First Thriller Press Edition, August 2009

Library of Congress Control Number: 2009900722

ISBN: 978-1-931296-17-5

Cover design and map by Keith Carlson

Manufactured in the United States of America

For Kit

ACKNOWLEDGMENTS

I am indebted to Truckee Police Officer Marty Schoenberg for taking me on a long ride-along one late, dark, fall night. In addition to seeing police work in action and touring the jail and other facilities, I also met other officers who, like Marty, were good natured about having a mystery writer in one of their patrol units and under their feet.

Marty was endlessly patient as I badgered him with countless questions. Many details from what he taught me found their way into this story.

I owe a great deal to Liz Johnston, who found so many mistakes in my manuscript that I need to buy her a new box of pencils. I am many times blessed to have such an observant, helpful editor.

Jenny Ross's legal expertise once again saved me. Owen, Diamond, Mallory and Agent Ramos would get many of the law-enforcement details wrong were it not for Jenny's fixes. She is an amazing gift.

Eric Berglund tackled the manuscript like a doctor doing arthroscopic surgery. Without leaving telltale scars, he managed to slice and dice until the patient was able to leave Intensive Care and breathe on its own.

Keith Carlson produced his best cover yet. As clean of line and sleek of message as the sailboat in the story, the cover of Tahoe Night is superb.

Special thanks to my parents, Helene and Hal, for creating a family culture of reading and pointing me toward mysteries at a young age.

Kit is always first and last in my life and in my writing. She took that first hopeless jumble of words and helped me shape the story elements. Later, she found the loose threads I'd forgotten and tied them off. Without her I'd have no choice but to find employment at the 7-Eleven.

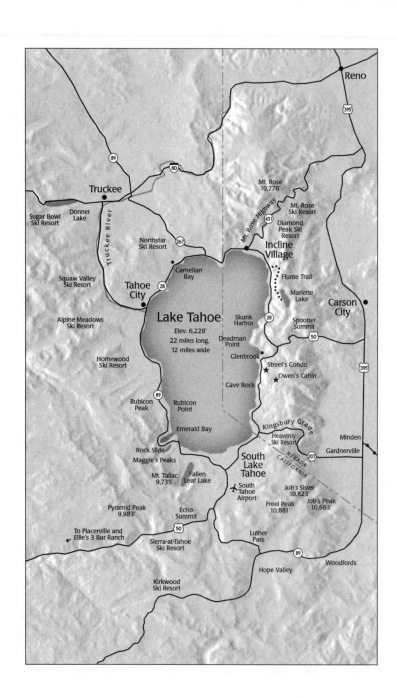

PROLOGUE

Reggie Deckman pricked her finger and squeezed her fingertip, milking another drop of blood out into the depression in the little white plastic watercolor palette.

The aspirin she'd taken would keep her blood from coagulating. But not from freezing. The bitter wind sang in the tall Jeffrey pines. The March weather was out of sync with the early June calendar. Three weeks before, when Reggie stepped off the bus from Sacramento, Tahoe locals had been celebrating a long stretch of glorious spring, sunshine so intense on the mountain snowfields that when Reggie stood in town and turned toward the sun-glazed slopes, she could feel the reflected heat on her face.

Now winter had returned for a final assault. Reggie shivered. The drop of blood fell, but it missed the depression she was aiming for and hit the tiny pool of orange paint next door. Deep red swirled into the orange, ruining the mixture.

Reggie squinted at the palette as the darkness came back, crowding in from the edges of her vision. It happened every time something went wrong. Her vision narrowed to a tunnel. The sounds around her became distant. Her heart thumped. It was difficult to get air into her lungs. Confusion overwhelmed her. She couldn't think straight. She didn't know what to do next.

Reggie tightened her hands into fists. Focus. Concentrate on a color. Not the paint or the palette. Not the worry, not the fear, not the confusion. Just a color. Take a deep breath and visualize.

It had helped her for fifty years. Maybe sixty. She couldn't remember. Ever since she was a young girl. When the darkness came, she had learned to focus. The doctors had different names for it over the decades. They put her on drugs, enrolled her in talk therapy groups, prescribed special diets and exercise.

But thinking of color worked better than all of the drugs, better than the psychotherapy. In color was comfort. It pushed back the confusion, the fear.

This time, Reggie thought of permanent green light. The color of young grass. The color of summer. The only cool color that felt warm to her, permanent green light felt like it was mixed with sunshine. She took a deep breath and held it.

Focus.

Gradually, her tunnel vision widened. Her heart slowed. The darkness went away.

But the cause of her new confusion was still there.

It had been decades. But they'd met and talked. He was worried. He told her what he'd like her to do if anything happened to him.

Reggie realized that he still cared for her. Maybe he still loved her. So she said yes, she would do it.

Reggie knew that she still loved him. She'd always loved him. Of course, he'd been the one who was willing to try to work it out. She was the one who had insisted on the divorce. It was a favor to him. She would never get better. She knew that even if he didn't.

The worst was her daughter. What kind of a woman leaves her young daughter?

Reggie worked another drop of blood out of her fingertip. This time she got it into the right place on the palette.

For painting watercolors, cadmium yellow and ultramarine blue provided two of the primary pigments. Many painters used cadmium red for the third primary, while some preferred alizarin crimson for its cool deep tone that mixed into better purples. Mix a little alizarin with the yellow and it produced a fine sienna. But Reggie knew that no commercial pigment worked like blood. Dried, it produced a burnt sienna with the smallest hint of umber undertones. Most important, it produced *verisimilitude*, the quality of making her images more like reality.

Reggie Deckman hunched over her tiny watercolor block as the cold spring wind pulled on the sign that was duct-taped to her knees. The letters on the sign were printed with black marker, surprisingly uneven and jerky for a talented artist.

Will Paint For Food

God Bless

Reggie reached into her bag and took out her brush holder, her most precious possession. It had always held her brushes. Now it held something even more important. Something from him and something from her. In a way, they were together again.

The brush holder was woven of tiny wooden reeds, thin parallel pieces held together with red thread. When the little mat was unrolled flat like a place mat, it showed a painting of a spectacular lotus flower. On the inside of the mat were loops of thread aligned in rows so that paintbrushes could be inserted. At the top and bottom edges of the mat were stitched green beads. When the mat was rolled up, it held the brushes inside, protecting them. The green beads all came together at the ends of the roll, still sparkling all these years after he'd sent the brushes and brush holder to her when she was stationed overseas. A birthday present. The best gift she'd ever received. A magic wand with emerald ends.

Reggie felt that her brushes were like her. Fighters. Witnesses. Survivors. If they were safe, she'd be safe. She protected them above all else.

Reggie slipped her brush back into the two vacant loops of thread and pulled out a smaller brush, the double-aught sable, its tiny hairs delicate and fragile. She stuck the end of it into her mouth for moisture, then flexed the brush across her lower lip to gauge the snap of the hairs. With delicate precision, she dipped the brush into the blood.

Quickly, before the blood could dry, she brought it to the watercolor block and made several tiny marks. Sand blew across the paper as she worked. She was close to finishing the painting. It was an important milestone, for she'd decided that she was going to the cops when she finished.

Reggie had always done that when she faced a dilemma requiring guts. She'd make a deal with herself. When her current painting was done, she'd do the task. She could not avoid painting. Painting was as inexorable for her as breathing. Linking an onerous chore to finishing her painting was a way to ensure that it got done.

He'd told her not to, of course. He'd stressed that no one could know unless he had an accident. But it wasn't right. Sometimes, you have to go against a person's desires to do what's right. The cops needed to know. She'd talked to the minister at her new church. He agreed with her. She'd talked to the ladies who ran the bake sales.

They agreed, too. She should tell the police.

A gust of wind pulled at her sign, threatening to rip the duct tape off and hurl the sign into the traffic. Reggie grabbed at the cardboard and turned her chin up toward the white snow plume blowing off the summit of Mt. Tallac. Behind the plume was an angry, roiling mass of gray clouds. The weather report predicted that this last winter storm of the season would pound Lake Tahoe with freezing rain and dump another foot of snow on the mountains that surrounded the basin. Reggie turned back to her painting.

The watercolor block was new, a gift from the woman who drove a polished black Audi and came by every weekday at 8:40 a.m. She would pull up at the intersection and nod at Reggie from the plush interior, then roll down the window and hand Reggie a large cup of organic yogurt with fresh fruit. Or carrot juice blended with minced wheat grass. Or an apple and a banana. And just once, a Starbucks coffee and raspberry scone. Each time, Reggie gave her a tiny painting. Emerald Bay. Mt. Tallac. A meadow with wildflowers.

Reggie loved the scone and coffee. But she always gave the other food away.

One day the window whirred down and the woman handed her the watercolor block and the new white palette she was using today.

Since taking the bus up to Tahoe, Reggie had scraped out a meager living selling miniature watercolors. She'd wondered if her ex-husband would ever drive by. She'd told him about selling paintings at the intersection when they met at the motel she rented by the week. He'd hinted about helping her. But she would have none of that.

Reggie didn't want to even think about their daughter. It was too painful. The guilt made it hard to breathe. Made the confusion come.

She worked on her painting.

But the thoughts kept intruding.

He'd said that their daughter was the reason he'd come to the mountains. Reggie didn't tell him that it was both of them that drew her up to Tahoe as well. She didn't say that they were all she had. But he probably knew that. He was smart. And he wasn't confused. Where the world was a murky fog to her, it was clear to him.

Reggie focused on her work.

A car came toward her and veered off onto the shoulder. It stopped, and a girl of 15 or 16, young enough to be her granddaughter, got out. The girl carried a backpack. The driver left, and the girl walked over toward the spot where Reggie sat. She stopped just twenty feet away and raised her arm toward the traffic, her thumb out.

Reggie frowned at the girl. Despite the bitter wind, the girl was wearing a bright green beach top that snugged up tight around her breasts. More permanent green light. Reggie's color. Eight inches of bare midriff showed above low-rider jeans that were so tight that Reggie didn't see how the girl could sit down.

Reggie was astonished at the audacity of the girl. Not because of her exposed skin, but because she upstaged Reggie's place at the intersection.

I should tell her to get her own place, Reggie thought. I should explain to her just what kind of risk she's taking, hitchhiking in such a skimpy outfit. Then Reggie remembered her own youth. She'd been a rebel, too. A provocative rebel. In fact, it was how Reggie had met her ex-husband, three months before the army shipped her halfway around the world. He was walking across the Berkeley campus and Reggie was sunning herself on a blanket on the commons. Wearing very little. Nothing like the old tried-and-true for getting a young man's attention. If an adult had attempted to tell the young Reggie that she shouldn't be so provocative, it would only have made her more determined.

Reggie decided not to say anything. Displaying her young body might get the girl into trouble, but it would also get her a ride. And Reggie would soon have her roadside spot to herself again.

Another gust of wind grabbed at Reggie's sign. Snowflakes hit her watercolor paper, melting into tiny drops that turned the color of the paint they struck. Reggie worked faster, trying to finish her image. This one was a special painting, a present for her ex-husband.

A huge pickup, the kind with four doors, approached and slowed. It had dark windows. Reggie watched as it came to a stop halfway between Reggie and the girl. Both front doors opened. Two big men got out. One man walked to the girl. He spoke to her. Reggie couldn't make out the words. She leaned toward them to hear better. She knew she might be witnessing a terrible event.

Reggie saw the man grin at the girl, more of a leer than a smile.

She heard the girl force a nervous laugh.

Reggie looked to see where the other man had gone. He was nowhere to be seen. The confusion was back. Darkness coming in from the sides of her vision.

Reggie tried to breathe, tried to focus on her color. What was the color? She couldn't remember.

Reggie wanted to call out. The girl was in grave danger, Reggie was positive. But Reggie couldn't make her voice work. She thought of waving at a passing driver, but there was a lull in traffic, no vehicles anywhere near.

Hands suddenly reached around Reggie from behind. Under her armpits, lifting her up, picking her clean into the air. Reggie was astonished. Her feet bicycled in the air. She tried to cry out, but no words came. The man carried her toward the truck. Her paints spilled onto the asphalt. The watercolor block fell face down into a slushy puddle of melting snow. Reggie was shocked into submission. She wanted to yell, tried to yell, but she couldn't make her voice work.

The other man opened the pickup's rear door, and they shoved Reggie inside. Reggie's head hit a hard cupholder as they pushed her down onto the floor. Her chin scraped on the floor mat. She felt the skin rip open, blood pour down. She was bent nearly in half. One man put his heavy boots on Reggie's head and shoulder as the other man got into the driver's seat and raced off.

The darkness overwhelmed Reggie's vision. She couldn't breathe.

Reggie still gripped her brush holder. In her confusion, just as she was about to pass out from lack of air, she pushed the little rolled mat with the green beads under the front seat, tucked it into a fold in the carpet.

If her brushes were safe, she would be safe.

ONE

"Ms. Casey told me you were discreet, Mr. McKenna." The woman sitting in my office chair was probably 80, but she looked more fit than most 50-year-olds.

"You know Street?" I asked.

"I just met her last week. She came to our yoga class. She said she had never tried yoga before. But she'll be great. She's got that focus. And posture. But she didn't come to class today, so maybe she didn't like it and dropped out of class."

"She had business out of town," I said.

"Oh, that's right. She said she had to go to an entomology conference. At any rate, you came up. I had heard of you, so I asked her."

"If I was discreet," I said.

The woman nodded. "Ms. Casey's answer was affirmative."

"Affirmative," I said.

"Yes." The woman was apparently unaware of how patrician she sounded. But it went with the tailored black wool skirt and jacket, the Roman nose, the small, elegant, leather purse with the faint embossed logo of an expensive brand, the sensible, plain black pumps, the short silver hair brushed to a high sheen, the fingernails cut modestly short and coated with clear gloss, the subtle hint of lipstick. She sat straight as a two-by-twelve and crossed her slender ankles, as she was no doubt taught at finishing school the better part of a century ago. She glanced down at Spot, my 170-pound Harlequin Great Dane, who was lying near the window in a shaft of morning sunlight, the ear stud he'd gotten during the avalanche case sparkling like the diamond it pretended to be. Something made the woman frown. The ear stud, maybe.

"About what or to whom would you like me to direct this discretion?" I asked.

The woman cleared her throat and swallowed. "My neighbor and his daughter. I'm worried. I'd like to pay you to look after them. I would prefer that they didn't know that I'm making this request of you."

"If I agree to work for you, I won't advertise it, but I won't hide it, either. Transparency is often best when dealing with neighbors."

"Meaning?"

"Meaning that they will be less likely to resist my efforts to look after them, as you put it, if they understand that it is the result of your caring and appreciation for them. We should try to convince them that you are in fact really concerned for their well-being and not just worried about how their situation will affect you."

She was affronted. "But I *do* care for their well-being! That is my *only* concern!"

I studied her. She seemed sincere.

"You said your name is Mrs. Phelter?"

"Yes. Lauren Phelter. My husband was Peter Phelter, the antitrust attorney. I'm sure you've heard of him. He passed away six years ago. It's been difficult, as I was very fond of him. But one must carry on. I sold the house in Marin two years later and moved up to our house here at the lake."

"What did you do while your husband was anti-trusting?" I asked.

She frowned at me for a moment. "You're rather rough around the edges, aren't you," she said. She sounded sarcastic, but I detected a tiny appreciation that I'd asked after her career.

"Yes, I wasn't just a dutiful wife," she continued. "I studied acting in college and at graduate school at UCLA. My career on stage wandered about Southern California until I met my husband. When I settled down, I realized I had more talent for off-stage work than on-stage.

"I founded the North Coast Playhouse in Marin. I ran it until my husband died. A little over thirty-two years. I should have stayed at the helm, but after Peter was gone, I..." She paused and took a deep breath. "Running a theater takes enormous energy. We did dinner performances Tuesday through Saturday and a matinee on Sunday. The theater business is all-consuming, and mine was no different. When Peter died, I simply didn't have it in me to continue. I sold the company to my protégé, Michael Dundee Washington. You've probably heard of him, too. Of course, I still own the building."

"Of course," I said.

"Our lake property is really two houses, the main house and the guesthouse. I rent out the guesthouse to Dr. Gary Kiyosawa. He is the neighbor to whom I refer."

She paused.

I waited.

"I don't know him well," she said, "and he's very private. It took a long time for him to open up to me. Although to say he opened up overstates how much he's spoken to me. Anyway, I'm worried about them."

"The man and his daughter."

"Yes."

"Who is his daughter?"

"Leah Printner. You do know of her?"

I nodded. This time I did know the name, as did most Tahoe locals. Probably a million tourists knew her name as well because Printner created and hosted the Tahoe Live TV show that was on the local cable channel and was the go-to source for news about Tahoe.

"She was in that car accident a month or so ago," I said. "The hit-and-run rollover by Cave Rock that killed her husband."

"Yes." Mrs. Phelter took a deep breath and let it out slowly, trying to calm herself. "From what I can gather, I think the death of her husband caused her so much emotional trauma that she can't work. I checked the TV. The talk show is no longer on. No surprise there, I guess. The show was her creation. No one else could fill her shoes. She's been living with Dr. Kiyosawa in my guesthouse while she's recuperating. I've never spoken to her. I believe the accident also scarred her face, because I saw bandages the night she came home from the hospital a week or so after the accident. I've only heard a few terse comments from Dr. Kiyosawa in the last month. I've caught him a couple of times as he comes and goes. I inquired after his daughter. He just mutters that she is fine and hurries away." Mrs. Phelter studied me as if to see if I comprehended the seriousness of the situation.

"I baked them lasagna," she continued, "but they wouldn't answer the door. I called, but they wouldn't answer the phone. And, as if all their tragedy isn't enough, I believe a man is stalking Leah. That is why I'm here. I want you to watch my guesthouse and catch this man the next time he comes around."

"Why do you think he's stalking Leah if she and her father won't talk to you?"

"I think he's a stalker because of his behavior. He's come by the guesthouse each of the last three evenings. He brings a red rose and talks to the closed door. That's how I know he wants to see Leah and not her father. I can see the guesthouse door from my window. It would appear that he is trying to be nice, with the rose and all. But something about him is off. I can't explain how I know it. I just know."

"He frightens you?"

"Yes. Why would he keep coming? If she wanted to talk to him, she would let him in. It doesn't feel right."

"You don't know who he is?" I said.

Mrs. Phelter shook her head. "I only know what he looks like. He's a big man with those large show muscles. He wears a black T-shirt even in the cold. And he has black hair, slicked back. He drives a black car. An older model."

"Did you call the police?"

"No. I was afraid that Dr. Kiyosawa would disapprove. I don't think he would want the intrusion of the authorities. And, besides, if he wanted the police involved, he would have called them himself, don't you agree?"

"What about friends of the doctor or of Leah's?" I asked.

"I'm afraid I can't help you there. As I said, Gary Kiyosawa is very private, and I think he passed that trait on to his daughter. I called the TV station that broadcasts Tahoe Live, but they wouldn't give me the names of any of Leah's friends."

"Was there a memorial service for Leah's husband? Her friends would have been there."

Mrs. Phelter shook her head. "As I said, Leah was in the hospital for a week or more after the accident. There was no service for the husband. The story in the paper said that memorials should go to charity."

"Surely Leah's had some friends come to call."

Mrs. Phelter was shaking her head again. "That's what you

would think. But other than the man that is bothering her, no one has come by that I know of. All I can imagine is that Leah told no one where she was going."

"So both father and daughter are hiding," I said.

"Yes, I think so. But from what, I don't know."

"Can you guess?" I asked.

"I've thought about it, but nothing seems clear. My guess is that the doctor has tried to, what's the expression, live under the radar." Mrs. Phelter looked down at her lap and picked at an invisible bit of lint. "I've met the doctor's sister, Amy Kiyosawa. She comes from Boston every year or so. We've had tea several times. She told me that she thinks Dr. Kiyosawa lost everything the year before he rented my guesthouse."

I waited.

"She didn't know why. He seems conservative to me. But maybe he got into some risky ventures? Doctors are smart, but they can get caught in the wrong investment vehicle just like everybody else. Whatever happened, now he is my poor, silent renter."

"What does he live on?"

"I don't know. He pays me cash for rent and utilities. I don't know where he gets it."

"Is the rent you charge inexpensive?"

Mrs. Phelter glared at me. "For the size and nature of my guesthouse, yes. Compared to a small house in town, no, of course not."

"Has Kiyosawa's daughter stayed with him before?"

"Not to my knowledge," she said.

"So other than the muscle man, there is nothing to make you worry."

"There is something else. It's a small thing, but it adds to my concern. When Leah was released from the hospital, Dr. Kiyosawa drove her to my guesthouse. I watched out the window. He was very caring, like a protective father would be. He ran around and opened her door, helped her out, and gave her a hug, rubbing her back to reassure her.

"As Kiyosawa held her, he looked around at the dark woods. Then, when he released his grip on her, she turned around and looked back toward the street. Like she was afraid. Before she went into the guesthouse, she again looked behind her. It was as if she thought someone was following her. It was the fear in their actions that makes me worry."

"Did you see anyone else?"

"No. But I thought they were in danger when I saw their fear. And now, three weeks later, she is being stalked, and they haven't come out of the house since the stalker showed up."

"Other than the stalker and the fear they showed that night, do you have any other reason to think they're in danger?" I asked.

"No. But my sense of dread is very strong. I'm rarely wrong about these things."

I thought about it. "She came to live with her father after the accident but three weeks before the stalker showed up. So it may be that their worried looks were not about the stalker."

"Precisely," Mrs. Phelter said.

"Is your guesthouse a safe place? Good locks? Drapes over the windows?"

"Yes. It is like the main house. My husband was security conscious. He had the builder use heavy solid oak doors, steel frames with dead bolts. The windows are a special type—I forget what Peter said—a particular kind of lamination and tempering or something. Anyway, they are supposed to be very difficult to break or force open. And of course, both houses have alarms. There are large windows without drapes on the ends of the great room, but they are up too high for anyone to look directly in. You'd have to climb up into the woods behind the house to see anyone inside. Even then, you'd need binoculars to get a good look. All the other windows in the house have drapes."

"If someone tries to break into the guesthouse," I said, "the alarm—assuming it's set—notifies the police, which, if Kiyosawa doesn't want his location known, he wouldn't like, correct?"

"No, I don't suppose he would. Which gets us back to your discretion. Would you go over there and check on them?"

"If they won't answer your knocks and calls, they certainly won't answer mine," I said.

"You could wait them out."

"When they do emerge, they still won't talk to me," I said.

"You could follow them. Make sure they're okay. I'm very worried.

I can pay you now, if you like." She reached into her purse.

I shook my head. "Let me look, first. What time has the man with the rose been coming by?"

"Six-thirty twice, seven the third time. A landlord has to pay attention to these things," she said defensively, aware that I might think her nosy.

I checked my calendar. "I've got a couple of errands to run this afternoon. But I can stop by this evening around six-thirty. Where do you live?"

She gave me an address up near the top of Kingsbury Grade, not far from the Boulder Lodge at Heavenly Ski Resort.

"You'll call me tomorrow and let me know what you think?"

"Yes."

Mrs. Phelter stood up and handed me a beige card with her name and number in dark brown script. I took it, then opened the door for her. She carefully stepped around Spot, who had flopped over onto his side nearby, taking up a third of the floor space in my office. He opened a sleepy eye at her, but didn't lift his head. Mrs. Phelter walked into the hallway, then turned and looked at me.

"You will be thoughtful about how you approach this?"

"Ever discreet," I said.

TWO

Street Casey had left that morning for an insect conference in Seattle, something she described as an excuse for a bunch of introverted entomologists to take the ferry across Puget Sound and go to a lodge on Whidbey Island for three days, where they would drink lots of vodka—the current libation of choice for such scientists—and talk the latest buzz on bugs. My friend Diamond Martinez had taken mercy on my loneliness and invited me to dinner down at his house in Carson Valley.

After my afternoon errands, Spot and I drove up Kingsbury Grade through swirling gray clouds and cold down-drafts. Although the beginning of May had been very warm, it had cooled off as June arrived. Winter was paying us another visit. A turbulent front was pushing in off the Pacific. Big, isolated raindrops pelted the windshield, stopped, then taunted us again. I turned off at the top of Daggett Pass and followed a winding road up higher. The rain was replaced with little white ice balls that hit the hood and windshield glass and bounced back into the air, something to be expected in early June at 7500 feet of elevation.

I found Lauren Phelter's house numbers displayed in brass on one of a pair of stone columns with brass light fixtures on the top. I parked on the street.

The drive was made of terra cotta-colored pavers, and it wound up past a large guesthouse near the street to a much larger house sprawling among giant boulders on the knoll above.

I got out and heard the distant thump of a boom car music system. I let Spot out of the Jeep, and we walked through cold gusty wind up the ice ball-coated drive toward the point where it curved around to the guesthouse entry, which was just out of sight. I heard a voice, put my finger across Spot's nose for silence, and stopped.

"C'mon, Leah. Open up and at least talk to me," a whiny male voice said. "I know your old man lives here. And I know you're in there. I saw the chimney smoke. I saw on TV where you talked about how wood fires make you calm."

I eased Spot forward behind two boulders that were artfully arranged at the base of a large Jeffrey pine. Leaning out, I could just see a man at the door of the guesthouse. His polished black '70s Firebird sat on a wide, kidney bean-shaped parking pad nearby, engine running, loud custom exhaust spoiling the neighborhood quiet, driver's door ajar, the door-open chime a tiny bird tweet against the bass-heavy rap song that competed with the rumble of the exhaust.

"Look, I know I got carried away when I came into the TV studio that time," he said to the closed door of the guesthouse. "I lose my temper sometimes. Everybody loses their temper sometimes, right? Anyway, it was my fault. Give me credit for admitting that, huh?"

The man was wearing a tight, black T-shirt, the short sleeves riding up over his thick biceps. On the back of the shirt was faded lettering in elaborate script. From my angle I couldn't see what it said. The shirt was tucked into tight black jeans, showing off his V-shaped chest and hard, narrow waist. His black hair was slicked back just as Mrs. Phelter had described, and it was greased to stay put. He looked maybe thirty, too old for the untied-Nikes affectation. I'd never met Leah, but I'd seen her show on Street's TV, and I knew she was a sophisticated woman around forty. In spite of the pink rose the bodybuilder held in his hand, I couldn't imagine her having anything to do with him. He represented the downside of TV celebrity.

"I didn't mean to come on so strong when I came to the station," he called out. "It wasn't my fault you got in that accident right after that. It was a coincidence. You know that, right? Open up. I've got something to show you. You'll forgive me, I promise. I can make you feel good. You can count on it. My word is good, Leah."

The man stepped to the side, spit onto the grass, then leaned up close to one of the dark windows, his hands cupping the sides of his face. In a moment, he went back to the front door. He pounded on it with his fist, six or seven times, the thuds clear above the booming bass of the rap song and car exhaust.

"I hear you moving around in there," he lied. "I know you're in there. Open up and talk to me!"

He stomped away like a frustrated child, slapping his shoes on the walk as if trying to smack the dust out of them. He threw the rose on the grass, did a fast one-eighty, and trotted back to the door, anger emanating from him like smoke.

"Listen, bitch! Open this door right now, or I'll hurt you worse than the accident did!"

Spot and I stepped out and walked toward him. "Time to leave," I said. I jerked my head toward his car, which was now spewing a screaming punk rock song.

"I'll leave when I want." He took a threatening step toward me. I sensed Spot tense at my side. Then the man stopped and suddenly gave me a big smile, revealing smooth white teeth so perfect that they were obviously crowns. The expensive teeth didn't go with the cheap car. "Because I'm so reasonable," he said, sneering, "I'll come back another time. Please tell Leah that I'll see her soon. My word is good as gold. Tell her I'm a big fan. She'll know what I mean."

He walked over to his car, carefully reached out to the car's roof, and, holding it with his right hand and the top of the car door with his left, he lowered himself into the driver's seat. His movements were slow and deliberate. Even though he'd turned, I still couldn't see what the shirt said. I'd expected something like "No Fear." But the faded script looked something like "Gretel."

He slammed the car door. Even with the door shut, I could still feel the throbbing bass of his sound system.

The man burned rubber as he backed up, then rocketed down the curving brick drive and shot out onto the street. The freshly-washed car had Nevada plates that were smeared with mud. I could only guess at one or two of the numbers.

I walked with Spot across to the guesthouse door. I knew from past experience that Spot's presence would increase the chances that someone would open the door. Something about him reassures.

I pressed the doorbell. Spot moseyed about. I pressed the doorbell again. Anyone inside would have heard us talking. They would have looked out the window and seen the man drive away.

"Dr. Kiyosawa?" I called out. "Leah Printner? My name is Owen McKenna." No one opened the door. I was confident that anyone in the house was on the other side, listening. Like the muscle man before me, I spoke to the closed door.

"I'm a private investigator, here at Mrs. Phelter's request. She's worried about you. I'd like to talk to you. I'm discreet and I'm capable. I'm also persistent. If Mrs. Phelter desires it, I will keep trying to be helpful. Eventually, I will succeed at being helpful. You can do us both a favor and shorten the wait."

There was no response.

"I'm putting my card into the weather stripping above the doorknob. My dog and I are going to leave. When you decide to let me help, give me a call and we'll talk."

I walked Spot back down the brick drive. The West Shore mountains were engulfed in heavy, low storm clouds that wrapped around the peaks. It was still a couple of hours before night, but already the gathering darkness felt oppressive.

Spot and I drove back down to the top of Daggett Pass, turned east and followed Kingsbury Grade down to Carson Valley, three thousand feet below.

THREE

Diamond Martinez was sitting on his front step in the twilight drinking a Pacifico as I pulled up to his perfect little house near the invisible border of Minden and Gardnerville, the twin farm towns a dozen miles south of Carson City.

"Sergeant," I said as I let Spot out of the back of the Jeep.

"You brought the hound," Diamond said in his noncommittal way that doesn't reveal anything of how he feels about it.

"He thinks Mexican cooking is the best," I said.

"Perspicacious canine," Diamond said. "He gonna drink my beer, too?"

"If you spill any, you won't need to wipe it up."

I sat on the front step next to him. Spot stuck his nose in Diamond's lap and pushed his hands around until Diamond gave his head a rough rub, then he lay down in the grass, a luxury valley carpet compared to the pine cone-dotted dirt at my cabin 3000 feet up on the mountain. Diamond popped the cap off a Pacifico and handed it to me.

"Any excitement in this metropolis?" I asked.

"Brought a thirteen-year-old kid in for stealing a six-pack at the gas station. Had those gang-banger pants with the waistband down below his butt. The guys and I couldn't figure out how they don't fall down. So we lifted up his sweatshirt and looked. Turns out the lowrider pants are stitched to the bottom of his boxer shorts. Now the kid's mother is threatening to sue for physical abuse."

"You looked at his clothes up close?" I said. "Civil liberties is a sacred thing in this country."

"Had to learn about ol' Tom Jefferson to pass the gringo citizenship exam," Diamond said. "White tights and wigs are even weirder than gang-banger pants hanging off boxers. Probably the civil liberties thing was so no one would yank the white wigs off the bald heads or check the varicose veins under the white leggings. You think?"

"No doubt." I drank beer.

"Kid had the word Grendel stitched on his T-shirt in fancy script."

"Name of a gang?"

"Maybe," Diamond said. "Name of the monster in Beowulf."

"Remind me."

"Beowulf was an epic poem, written back in the Dark Ages. It's about a monster named Grendel."

"I just rousted a dirtball up at the top of the grade. Wore a T-shirt that had a word on the back. Looked like Gretel to me. But maybe it was Grendel. What's with the monster?"

"Grendel is supposed to have descended from Cain, the bad son of Adam and Eve. Grendel lived with his mother in a cave out on the moors in, I think, Denmark. The Danish King was a guy named Hrothgar. If I remember correctly, Grendel resented that Hrothgar had a good life, so he decided to terrorize Hrothgar and his people in punishment for their good life."

"So he was the essence of evil, and all that."

"Yeah," Diamond said. "We're talking a real bad dude. He ate people."

"Why was the poem called Beowulf?"

"Beowulf was the fierce warrior who was the only guy tough enough to kill Grendel."

"Where do you get this stuff?" I asked. "Was that on the gringo exam?"

Diamond shook his head. "I like to read. Thought I'd try something from Old English."

"So Carson Valley gangs are more literate than most," I said. "But the guy I just saw didn't look like he'd be into Old English. Probably couldn't read the sports section without moving his lips."

"I'll ask some of the guys, see if there's some kind of Beowulf thing going around," Diamond said.

"You ask the kid about having Grendel on his T-shirt?"

"Sure. He said he found it. Not much we can do with that. So I asked him what it meant. He said he didn't know."

Diamond took us inside. We sat at the kitchen table. He pulled out the fixings for tacos and enchiladas as if he ran a restaurant, quick, smooth, efficient. I looked around while he cut up an onion, a couple of cloves of garlic, and put them in a fry pan. Then he chopped up a chicken breast and added it to the pan.

I noticed that Diamond had filled and sanded and painted the bullet holes from when Spot and I hid out at his house the previous summer, foolishly thinking we were safe from the killers of the pop star Glory.

I told Diamond about Lauren Phelter and her doctor renter and his talk show host daughter whose life had blown apart in the car accident.

"I was on that accident," Diamond said. "A peculiar sort-of-hit-and-run."

"What do you mean sort of?"

"Well, according to Leah Printner, a guy driving a dump truck pulled out from a side road on Highway Fifty just south of Cave Rock and hit them square on their driver's door, rolled them all the way over, killing her husband immediately. She said she was dazed but conscious, and she saw the dump truck driver get out and come over to the smashed car. He was wearing a mask. According to her, he reached in through the broken window and dropped a crawdaddy claw onto her husband's body."

"You mean, crawdaddy as in a crayfish? One of those pincer arms?"

"Yeah."

"What did he do after he dropped it in their car?" I asked.

"He got back in the dump truck and drove away."

"No sign of him since?"

Diamond shook his head as he worked over the fry pan. "Turned out the dump truck was stolen from a construction site. There were no fingerprints, no footprints, nothing."

"Something that deliberate, sounds like he caused the accident on purpose," I said.

Diamond nodded. "I've got a witness, and a dump truck that is a possible murder weapon, and even a chunk of dead crustacean as evidence. If I had a suspect with a motive and could prove he had a connection to the crawdad claw, I'd be on my way to court."

I gave Diamond the details of my encounter with the muscle

man stalker.

"Maybe he was the dump truck driver," I said. "And if the word on the guy's T-shirt was, in fact, Grendel," I said, "then that seems like too much of a coincidence after you found the kid with a Grendel shirt. They could be connected."

"Yeah. But it's a reach. It's rare to see a thirteen-year-old share anything with an adult unless the adult is a rap star. I'd guess the kid is telling the truth about finding the T-shirt."

"The stalker's car was a black, seventies Firebird. I could tell it had Nevada plates, but I couldn't get the number."

"I'll look into it," Diamond said. "I've seen Printner's show. She seems like an upscale woman. Kind of prim and proper, even. Seems like she'd call the cops with a stalker coming around."

"Yeah. Adds credence to the idea that father and daughter are hiding from someone and don't want to be found."

"Or hiding something from the world and don't want the world to find out." Diamond drank beer and set the bottle down. "The husband who died in the accident," Diamond said. "Wasn't he some kind of chef? I shoulda done that. Restaurant chef." Diamond put two plates on the table. Two enchiladas, two tacos and a pile of rice, each. Then he emptied a bag of ready-made salad into a bowl. We forked food into our mouths. "Chefs make good money, right?"

"Some do. But you pretty much gotta own your own restaurant, I think, and the restaurant has to be very successful. I heard he taught cooking. Adjunct professor at the Lake Tahoe Community College."

We ate in silence for a bit.

"Bummer if the beefcake gets to the TV lady," Diamond said. "Too often the stalker thing ends up bad. These guys laugh at restraining orders. Maybe Leah went to daddy for safety from the stalker as much as for recuperation from the accident. But by the sound of this jerk, maybe daddy can't provide enough safety."

"Maybe not." I ate. The food was excellent.

"You're pretty good protection," Diamond said, "but they gotta open the door to you if they want help."

"Too afraid," I said.

Diamond swigged beer. "A long time before Roosevelt uttered his line about fear, Thoreau said, 'Nothing is so much to be feared as fear.' If they won't even talk to you, they must be very scared of something."

I studied Diamond as I ate. It was still a surprise, this recent Mexican immigrant who knew more American and English history, spoke better English and understood American institutions better than most native-born Americans. That he could quote Thoreau or Emerson or Dickinson or Ben Franklin or Washington or Lincoln or Gertrude Stein or Fitzgerald or Hemingway or Twain or Edison or Einstein on and for any occasion was a role model for what made this country. I knew that the knee-jerk, xenophobic, anti-immigrant rants had been going on ever since we corralled the Indians and put them on the reservations, thereby deciding the country was for people of European descent only. But it seemed that it was getting worse. I wondered if Americans would ever appreciate the benefits that come from having the best and brightest and most ambitious from other countries trying to come here.

"You find this beef and want help sitting on him, my current schedule has me up at the lake most days," Diamond said. "If we can catch thirteen-year-old beer thieves, think what we could do with steroidal pea-brains who get their jollies stalking women. Put them in the county jail, they'd probably be afraid of the gang-banger kiddies."

Diamond had an extra enchilada that had cooled. He put it on a plate and set it outside on the back step, then shut the door. "You think your hound will eat TexMex?"

"Not sure. Hard to compete with sawdust chunks. I guess you could give it a try."

"Hey, largeness," Diamond said. "You like a chicken, cheese, salsa enchilada with Mama Martinez's secret seasoning?"

Spot scrambled up from where he'd been splayed across the living room carpet. I felt bad when I saw that his nails had torn out some carpet fibers.

Diamond did the little come-here finger motion and backed up, away from the kitchen door, toward the front door. Spot followed at a little distance, eyes and ears as focused as eyes and ears can get. He stared at Diamond, trying to figure it out.

Diamond backed out the front door and held it for Spot. Spot jumped past him into the darkness, landed on the grass, spun around to face Diamond. Spot's eyes sparkled in the porch light. His earring shot little light swords into the night.

"TexMex got a pretty good aroma, boy. If you're smart, you'd find it before the raccoons get there."

Spot studied him.

"Go on, boy." Diamond walked over to Spot and smacked him on his butt. "Go get your dinner."

Spot wagged, his tail high. He was confused but excited. He knew this was a search where the find was likely to be much more rewarding than a body under an avalanche slide, which he'd done the previous winter. His nostrils flexed. He jerked his head up, sniffing the air. He spun around, facing the street. He trotted toward the pavement, stopped, bounced up onto his rear legs for a moment, sniffing the air up high, then trotted in a widening spiral. At the apex of the curve he suddenly alerted, lowered his head and shot down the dark side drive and disappeared around the back of the house.

We heard a sucking, slurping schloop - schloop sound, then the clinking of the plate as it rattled, empty, on the back step. When Diamond and I came around the back corner of the house, Spot was carefully licking the ceramic.

Diamond turned on the hose and held it out. Spot lapped at the arc of water for a long minute.

Sated, Spot and I said our thanks and goodbye and headed back up Kingsbury Grade, climbing like a plane above the sparkling valley lights into the dark forests that surround Tahoe.

We were cresting the pass when my cell rang.

I dug the phone out of my pocket. "Hello?" I said.

The response was a woman's scream of terror, a gut-clenching, skin-rasping cry more frightening than anything I'd ever heard in my life.

FOUR

"Leah! Is that you?!" I shouted. Her scream rose, quaking, gasping, then shrunk. She sucked air, then screamed again.

I shouted. "Leah, I'm nearby. I'll be there in a minute. If there is an intruder, get out of the house. If you're on a portable, don't hang up. Take it with you. Run into the woods up behind Mrs. Phelter's house. I'll find you there. Go! Now!"

I set the phone on the seat without hanging up. Just after the top of the pass, I jerked the Jeep off the highway and onto the side street that wound its way through dark trees toward Lauren Phelter's house. I careened around the curves, the accelerator hard on the floor. Four turns later I skidded to a stop in front of the Phelter driveway, blocking anyone's exit.

I grabbed the phone, jumped out and let Spot out of the back. We ran through the dim glow of the gate lights, up the drive toward the guesthouse. All appeared quiet and serene except for a huge spider web of cracks in the big main-floor windows up above the street level. The fracture lines in the laminated glass sparkled like those in a windshield after a car accident. At the center of the web was a black hole.

The front door was closed and locked. The intruder would have gotten in another way. I ran past.

The other windows were shut. At the backside of the house was another large picture window. I could just make out a similar spider web and dark hole at the center. Looking in, I could see all the way through the house to the distant light of clouds. The two picture windows opposed each other across a large great room.

I'd screwed up. The intruder had never entered. He'd sat up in the woods and fired into the house. The same woods I'd told Leah to run to.

I lifted my cell, wondering if Leah had used a portable. I heard short, frantic breathing, whimpering, panicked cries.

"Leah? I'm outside the house. Are you there?"

"He was up in the woods," she said in choked, whispered words. "I'm in the garage. Help me!"

The emotion in her voice was wrenching.

"Stay there," I said. "Give me two minutes."

I sprinted up toward the dark forest, to the right of Lauren Phelter's house. A stick broke off in the woods. I stopped. I saw the vaguest of movement, a black shape in the black trees.

I grabbed Spot and jerked him over behind a large pine. "Police!" I shouted toward the forest. "Freeze or I'll send in the dog!"

The black shape moved, then disappeared.

"Spot!" I said, bending down. I put my right arm around him, my left hand on the front of his chest, vibrating him, getting him primed. Then I moved my forearm in a pointing motion. "Find the suspect, Spot! Take him down!" I gave him a pat, and he took off toward the trees.

Spot's black-on-white coloring was the opposite of camouflage, but a shooter would have a hard time hitting a moving target in the night. And as Spot shot into the shadows, he effectively disappeared.

A skidding sound like someone sliding on dirt and rocks came from where the knoll dropped off to the road behind the Phelter property. I sprinted in that direction. A car door slammed. An engine roared. I changed directions, trying to get within view of the road. Tires screeched, and the vehicle roared off. There was more screeching as the vehicle turned, then turned again.

Sirens rose in the distance. Somebody had already called the cops.

I spoke into my cell. "He's gone, Leah. Stay where you are. I'll be there in a minute. I'm going to hang up and dial the cops."

I pressed 911 and got the dispatcher, a woman I know.

"Sandra, it's Owen McKenna. I'm up at the Phelter residence."

"We got a nine-one-one call," she said, her voice tense. "The reporting party said there was a shooting. Several patrol units are responding."

"At least one suspect escaped," I said. "Tell the approaching cops to be on the lookout for a vehicle leaving the area at a high rate of speed, heading toward the grade." I hung up and ran to the garage.

"Leah," I called through the garage door. "It's Owen McKenna. The shooter is gone. How do I get inside?"

From within the garage came the sound of a motor grinding, and the garage door rose. The interior light came on. Spot appeared at my side. I ducked under the rising door. Spot followed me. The door reversed and started back down.

Leah stood over by an interior door. She shook violently. She looked thin and fragile. Her elbows were tucked in at her side, her face splotchy red, half covered by one hand. On one side of her face I could see an angry pink line where they'd stitched her up a month ago. The scar ran across her cheek to her ear, the top three quarters of which was gone. All that remained was a portion of the curved flesh behind her ear canal and the earlobe. Remnants of the old bruises from the accident still colored part of her face a mottled brownish purple.

There was a new wound on the edge of her jaw, a small cut where the skin had split open and bled. Blood was splattered on her clothes as well. Her hand pressed against her mouth. Above her hand, her eyes radiated terror. I told Spot to sit, and walked toward Leah, moving slowly, my hand out in a gesture of comfort.

She quaked as if she were standing on a vibration machine.

"It's okay, Leah," I said. "You're safe, now. My dog will stay with you. He won't let anything happen to you." I walked closer, wanting to reassure her, but not wanting to get so close that she felt trapped by a stranger. I stopped a few feet away. Her eyes showed white and darted from me to Spot to the closed door that went into the house. She looked about to explode with fear. I held my hand out as if to touch her shoulder, but stopped inches short. "I'm going to call my dog. He is very friendly. He will protect you." I turned to Spot.

"Spot, come here." He walked toward us. I pointed to a small bench near a blue '90s Chevy. "Sit, Spot." He sat with unusual obedience, perhaps sensing the seriousness of the situation. "Leah, I want you to sit on the bench next to Spot."

Her eyes darted around the garage with frantic intensity. I worried that she would implode in a psychotic breakdown. The sirens were getting louder.

I gestured, moving my arm in silent encouragement. She shifted, staring at Spot, then at the garage door. I'd never seen anyone so frightened.

"Spot will calm you. You will be safe with him."

She took a step. I shifted so my outstretched hand was behind her, as if I might pat her on the back. But I gave her space, didn't touch her.

Slowly, she moved to the bench. She lowered herself onto it, vibrating so hard she could end up with pulled muscles anywhere in her body.

I moved over to the other side of Spot and squatted down. "He likes it if you pet him," I said softly. I reached out and rubbed Spot between the ears. "Spot, stay with Leah. Guard her," I said. "You understand, Spot? Guard her."

I stood up and moved away. The sirens had stopped, and red light flashed in the crack under the bottom of the garage door. Spot leaned his head toward Leah. "Pet him, and he'll love you," I said. I stepped farther away. I pulled my cell out of my pocket and was punching up the menu for Diamond's number when it rang.

"Owen McKenna."

"We're surrounding the houses," Diamond said. "Where're you at?"

I turned from Leah and spoke softly. "I'm in the guesthouse garage with Leah. At least one suspect escaped in a vehicle on the other side of the knoll behind the houses. I'll open the garage door. You can send a team into the house from the garage while your other men watch the doors." I moved into a corner and whispered. "Leah is traumatized. If we minimize the noise..."

"Understood," Diamond said. "No shouting, no breaking down doors. Hit the garage button."

I turned. Spot had lowered his head into Leah's lap. She was bent over him, hugging his huge head. She still shivered, but less violently. "Leah, I'm going to open the garage door. The cops will come through the garage into the house. You can stay with Spot." I walked over and pressed the button.

The door rose, men rushed in, guns out. I stood on the other side of the bench so that I was between Leah and the cops.

One man stayed at the garage door entrance, gun out, watching out toward the drive. Diamond and the other men ran to the interior door and rushed through it. I stayed with Leah while they searched the house, distant thuds coming through the walls as the cops ran through the main floor rooms, then up the stairs to the second floor.

In time, Diamond reappeared at the interior door. He walked over to the cops outside as more sirens approached in the distance. "I want a large perimeter, both houses. Tell the medics to stage a block away until the area is cleared."

Diamond turned to me. "Owen," he said, gesturing toward the interior door.

I turned to Leah. "I'm going into the house, Leah. You stay here with Spot. I'll be back in a few minutes."

Diamond opened the interior door and took me up a half-flight of stairs, through the kitchen and out into the great room. They'd turned on the lights. It was like a lobby in a lodge, timber frame construction, two stories high. On the long side was a stone fireplace with the last remnants of hot embers on the grate. Above the mantle was a framed oil painting of a girl wearing what looked like an Easter dress, light blue, with a little matching hat, raked at a stylish angle. It was painted like a Vermeer portrait from centuries ago. The girl had her back to the viewer, but she was looking in an elaborately-framed round mirror on the wall. Her face was reflected in the mirror. By the amused look on her face, it looked like she was pleased with what she saw. I guessed the girl in the painting to be Leah when she was eight or ten.

In front of the fireplace were three leather couches arranged around a huge wooden footlocker. On the end walls of the room were the big opposing picture windows. The one toward the back of the house was starred where the bullet had shattered it about eight feet above the floor. On the window that faced the lake, the fracture was similar, but centered around a hole only three feet above the floor. It looked like the shooter had fired from the high ground above the house, and the round entered one window and exited the other.

Near the lakeside window was a long wooden dining table that looked dated and matched the footlocker in style. Around it were eight matching high-backed oak chairs. Six of them stood up undisturbed. The two near the lakeside window were knocked over. The top board on one of them had exploded into wood splinters.

A splatter of liquid covered the table. Two empty blue and white porcelain teacups waited to be poured. On the floor nearby was a heavy metal teapot. It lay on its side, splayed open into an unusual shape. The metal was bent inward where the round had penetrated and outward where the round exited. The explosive hydrostatic force had blown the teapot apart at its circumference.

Next to the old oak table, sprawled across one of the overturned chairs, was an elderly man, Asian ethnicity, no doubt Leah's father, Dr. Gary Kiyosawa. His chest was blown open at the base of his sternum. His glassy eyes stared at the ceiling, a kind of a peace in them as if he'd died in the instant before pouring his evening tea, died so fast that the trauma that caused his death never registered on his face.

FIVE

"Looks like the shooter was outside as Kiyosawa was about to sit down for his evening tea," Diamond said to me.

One of the deputies came through a door at the far side of the room. He carried binoculars. "Sarge, Fonseca and I climbed up the slope about thirty yards, out where that section of forest starts. There's a clearing at the edge of the woods that looks down on this house." He held the binoculars up. "You get down on the ground, the two bullet holes in these windows line up perfectly."

"Meaning," I said, "that there may be only one bullet, and it exited through the lake-side window."

Diamond said to the deputy, "You messed up the crime scene."

The man was biting his lip. "Sorry, sergeant. I didn't know that place was part of the crime scene until I saw how the bullet holes line up. Soon as we figured it out, we wanted to tell you."

"See a shell casing up there?"

"No." The deputy shook his head. "But we only had our flashlights."

"Okay. Davis and Johnson are setting up a perimeter," Diamond said. "Make sure they know to include those woods. I don't want anyone walking anywhere until the evidence guys get here."

The deputy nodded, then left.

Diamond spoke to me, "If the round still carried some speed, we may never find it. It would have gone past the drop-off on the other side of the street."

Two other deputies came in. "The area is cleared, Sarge," one of them said. "Johnson and I shined our lights under every bush and behind every tree. We're confident that no other suspects are on the property."

Diamond pulled his radio off his belt, held it to his face, and spoke to Dispatch. "The scene is secure. Have the medics roll in and meet Davis at the perimeter on the north side. The injured woman is in the garage. Don't let the medics walk anywhere else."

The deputies were young, but they radiated smarts. One of them reminded me of a high school football captain, the square-jawed darling of the girls, telegraphing cockiness. He stared at me, then back at Diamond.

"Yeah, Davis?" Diamond said.

The man looked at me again. He moved his big jaw back and forth. "No offense, sergeant, but this guy is a civilian. Should he even be here?"

Diamond looked at me. His dark eyes revealed nothing. He turned to the deputy. "Mr. McKenna is working this case. We are all cooperating with each other." Diamond's look was intense.

Davis swallowed. "No problem, sergeant. I don't have a problem with that." He wiggled his jaw a little.

Diamond kept his attention on the deputy. "Samantha and Drew will be our crime scene technicians on this. They'll be here in a minute. You and Johnson go help them. You know the routine. Collect, preserve, photograph. Start by getting some lights up to those woods where the shooter was. I'm worried that it will start raining again and destroy any footprints. Photograph everything, and make a diagram to show the relative positions of every mark. I want a close-up pic of every mark, and molds of every footprint. We can separate out which prints are cops and which are the shooter's, later. Make sure you don't miss anything. Same for any trails leading to and from that clearing. Then check the lake side of the house for the slug."

The deputy frowned and shook his head. "You can't even find a slug in the daylight. Not like they sparkle or anything. No way we're gonna see it at night."

Diamond continued as if the man hadn't spoken. "Check from just below the window to the street and down the slope below. Get more floods if you have to. And a metal detector. I want you to sift the dirt."

The men left as two more deputies arrived, one of them female. I assumed them to be Samantha and Drew. Half of the Douglas County Sheriff's Department must have gotten out of bed to help out. Diamond gave them instructions. The woman began taking meticulous and extensive photographs. After she had exhaustively recorded an area, the man began collecting evidence. They started with the body, then moved throughout the room.

"Tell me again what the relationship is between the deceased and the lady you talked to," Diamond said to me.

I reiterated that Mrs. Phelter had come to me because she was worried about her renter Dr. Gary Kiyosawa and his daughter Leah, who had come to stay with her father after the car accident that killed her husband.

"The stalker you told me about, maybe he's the shooter."

"Maybe," I said.

"Leah didn't open the door and talk to him," Diamond said.

"No," I said.

"So he's pissed off. But coming back with a gun is a hell of an overreaction."

Diamond turned to a deputy who was the size of an NFL player. "Hey, tackle. Can you go up to the main house and let Mrs. Phelter know what's going on? If she's home, she's probably scared to death. I'll get a statement from her later."

Tackle nodded and turned to leave.

"And remember what the community liaison consultant said."

Tackle turned just before he went out the door. "Right. Sensitivity. Make the people realize we're their friends."

"Good man." Diamond looked at me. "You got a guess on what weapon would have the punch to shatter a heavy window, explode a heavy-weight teapot, blow a cavern through a man, shatter an oak chair, then destroy the second window as if it had just left the rifle barrel?"

"High velocity, big bore, probably. Not much we can tell until we find some other evidence."

Diamond narrowed his eyes. "You guess the shooter was aiming for Leah and missed?"

"That might fit the stalker. But looking at this well-placed shot, I'd say probably not. It looks like he knew exactly what he was doing. Most guys with a gun that could do this would have had plenty of practice."

"If the old man was the target," Diamond muttered, "that makes it seem less like the stalker, huh?"

"Yeah. The stalker didn't seem to me like the type to use a precision weapon. Wrong personality for a sniper. Too impulsive. Snipers are calm and collected."

Diamond nodded.

A couple of deputies came through the door. "The paramedics are trying to help the woman in the garage," one of them said. "She's got a wound on her face. She needs treatment. But there's a huge dog with her and she won't leave it. When they reached for her, it growled at them."

"That's kind of an overstatement, Jason," the other man said. "Just a little rumble thing in its throat. Not like it bared its teeth or anything."

"You're the one jumped back when it rumbled."

"Anyway, we didn't want to upset the woman. She seems pretty freaked out."

"I'll take her to the ER," I said. "She can give you a statement later?"

Diamond nodded and picked up his radio. "I'll have Davis follow you to the hospital. Just in case. He's one of our two men who's a peace officer in both Nevada and California. Not like I expect any more trouble, but you never know."

I went back to the garage followed by Jason and his partner. Leah and Spot hadn't moved from their earlier position. The paramedics were standing back.

"I'll take her in," I said to them.

They made questioning looks toward the deputies.

"He's okay," Jason said. "Friend of the Sergeant. Ex-cop, too, right?" He turned to me.

"Yeah."

The paramedics nodded and moved away.

Leah had her arms around Spot's head. Her face was pressed into the back of his neck. She sobbed lightly, her body making slow moves up and down with labored breath. I sat on the bench next to her. She didn't lift her head.

"It's Owen," I said, so she wouldn't be alarmed. I touched her shoulder. "We should get your jaw looked at. You've got a cut that needs to get fixed."

"It's like he exploded." Her voice was strangely loud, but muffled by Spot's neck and her throat full of mucous. "I made some tea and daddy was going to pour it. He reached for it and then..." She choked as she gasped for air.

"I'm sorry," I said, the words ridiculously insufficient. I rubbed her shoulder.

In time her heavy breathing slowed. She pushed herself up off Spot a few inches. "What do I do? I don't know what to do." Her words were robotic.

"I'd like to take you to the hospital and have them look at your jaw," I repeated.

She lifted one hand off Spot's head and touched her face, then looked at her bloody fingers. "I don't remember. I must have hit something. I screamed at daddy not to die. But I knew it was too late. Then I was running. I don't know where. I remember turning off the lights. I dialed nine-one-one and told them. Then I found your card by the phone and I took it in here. It was dark, so I turned on the light for a second to read the number and dial. Then I waited in the dark."

She began sobbing again. "I don't want to go to the hospital. I don't want to leave daddy. I want to stay with your dog. What's his name again?"

"Spot. He will come with us. Let's go, Leah."

I lifted her elbow, and slowly she stood up. Spot stood, too, and Leah kept both hands on Spot's neck, leaning on him. Leah was probably five-eight and of medium heft, but she was dwarfed by Spot. We all walked together, my hand on Leah's elbow.

Davis was standing guard in the drive. "Sergeant said I should follow you."

I nodded and gestured toward the street where my Jeep still blocked the drive and the cruisers and ambulance blocked my Jeep.

"The Jeep is mine. Maybe someone can move a vehicle so we can get out."

Davis spoke into his radio, and soon another deputy appeared from the backside of the guesthouse and moved one of the squad cars.

I got Leah into the front of the Jeep, and put Spot in the backseat. Leah tried to reach for him, and he obliged by leaning his head over the seat and resting it on her shoulder. Leah hung onto him while I drove. Davis followed in one of the Douglas County Explorers, the flashers off.

Once I was past the emergency vehicles, the roads were dark and wet and quiet. I took it slow down the grade so that Leah wouldn't feel any excessive motion on the curves. Calm seemed more important than anything else. I tried to see everything, in front, to the sides, in the rearview mirror. Leah was quiet.

Davis stayed close.

When I got to the building where I rent office space, a vehicle pulled out of the lot and followed Davis. It was a dark pickup with a topper over the bed, but I couldn't see the make or exact color. It stayed well back.

I got on my cell, gave the dispatcher my number, and told her there was a cop named Davis behind me, and he needed to call me. She said she'd text it onto his Mobile Data Terminal. Davis called me a minute later.

"Pickup pulled out behind you," I said. "Be good if we could get the plate."

"I'll get someone to pull in behind him," Davis said.

I hung up and kept watch. Leah said nothing. She held onto Spot's head.

We drove over to the California side and most of the way across town to Third Street and still hadn't seen any backup. Budgets that were too tight combined with the random movements of too few officers on duty. The traffic was sparse. The cop following me stayed close. The pickup stayed behind the cop.

Then the pickup was gone. It must have made a quick turn onto a side street. In the distance behind, I saw two South Lake Tahoe black and whites pull up behind the Douglas County Explorer. I could imagine the radio conversation. One of the black and whites pulled a U-turn. The other turned off on a side street. I doubted they'd find the pickup.

I dialed the hospital. Doc Lee was on duty, and I gave him a brief explanation of the situation, keeping it dry so as not to intensify Leah's reaction.

Davis followed as I turned onto Third and drove to the hospital.

I parked, got out, and helped Leah out. Spot followed us. I

pushed in through the emergency room entrance doors, and we walked into the waiting room. The nurse recognized me and directed us to Doc Lee.

Lee had seen the worst of what went down in this relatively safe resort town. This situation had him very worried. "We heard about the shooting on the scanner. I didn't realize the talk show lady was involved. And coming so soon after the accident." He stopped and frowned, trying to comprehend it.

"I think she'll get very upset if we try to separate her from Spot," I said. "I'm going to bring him in with her, okay?"

"Against the rules," he said. "But he's such a small dog, maybe the nurses and I won't even notice him." He made the small joke with a voice as serious as his frown.

I appreciated his attempt at levity.

I brought Leah inside the ER. She blinked at the bright lights, her eyes worried. She held onto Spot's collar with both hands.

Doc Lee got her to lie down on a bed. Spot stood by her side, and she kept one hand clamped onto his collar. Doc Lee looked at the cut near the other scars. "I'm glad we sent you to that specialist in Reno after the car accident. It looks like he did a good job reconstructing. But I can take care of this little cut." Lee injected a local anesthetic, cleaned her up, and pulled a chip of glass from the gash on her jaw. He went to work with needle and thread. She continued to hold onto Spot.

"I'm sorry you had to come back and visit us again," Lee eventually said to her. He was as much at a loss for words as the rest of us. "I'm sorry about your father."

Leah didn't speak or move.

I left them and went outside to call Mrs. Phelter.

"Lauren Phelter," she answered in a shaky voice.

"Owen McKenna calling."

"Oh, my God, I've been calling your office number. A policeman told me that someone killed Dr. Kiyosawa. I heard the shot. It was so loud. Right outside my house. He said you were at the scene. But they won't let me leave my house. Not that I want to. What happened? There are a dozen police cars outside my window. It's frightening. When I talked to you this morning, I thought something bad would happen. But this is even worse than my worries. So much worse."

I explained the situation as gently as I could. "When they are done, they will let you know, and you will be free to leave your house. But don't try to go into the guesthouse. It will be sealed off."

"Did they catch the killer?" she asked.

"Not yet."

"Where are you? Will you come and talk to me?"

"Eventually. I'm at the hospital with Leah. She is quite traumatized."

"She can stay with me," Mrs. Phelter said.

"Thanks. I'll let her know. My guess is she will want to keep her distance from her father's house for a time. Does Leah have a mother or siblings or other relatives?"

"No siblings. She was an only child. Her mother went missing and was presumed dead years ago. Her only relative is her father's sister, the aunt in Boston who I told you about. Amy Kiyosawa."

"I remember."

"What should I do?" Mrs. Phelter asked. "This is very upsetting. I can't think."

"Stay put. It will sort out in time. I'll be in touch."

I said goodbye and went back into the ER. Doc Lee was just finishing. I thanked him. He took me aside, out of hearing range but within view of Leah.

"The woman is on the edge," he said. "A serious edge. I've tried to engage her. But she's non-responsive. Almost like she's going into shock, but her blood pressure is holding up. It's like some kind of catatonic reaction. Out of my league. It could be she comes out of it in a day or two. I'm afraid to give her any more sedatives. Some people have an adverse reaction in a situation like this. Their brain chemistry is screwed up by the trauma. I think she's on the verge of a collapse."

"Anyone would be after what she witnessed."

"We should keep her in the hospital for the next few days. Make sure she stabilizes."

"I'll stay with her. If I sense she's getting worse, I'll bring her in."

"Then you should at least get her to a shrink. In the meantime, I'd try very hard to keep her calm."

"I'll be careful," I said.

Leah was still agitated, still frightened, when I walked her out to the Jeep. She continued to hold onto Spot as we left. I drove slowly. Davis, the sheriff's deputy, followed.

I tried to concentrate on what I should do next. I was responsible for Leah's first tentative steps in surviving a life-shattering experience. But I had no clue what to do. My instincts told me to get Leah into Street's care, where Leah could have the thoughtful support of someone far smarter than I was at these things, but without the stress of white coats and official medical demeanor.

But Street was on an island up in the Pacific Northwest.

I felt numb as I drove. I couldn't concentrate. Deep down in the mental cellar was a nagging voice. I'd been hired to watch out for the father and daughter. The landlady had made it clear that she was very worried. She'd been emphatic about how her instincts regarding these things were always right. So she took care of her worries by hiring me. I was the professional, the ex-homicide inspector from the SFPD. I'd know what to do. I would keep the father and daughter safe.

And now the father was dead.

I felt despair and self-reproach pull me down, cloud my brain. It was like an acrid miasma swirling around me, interfering with my senses, my perception, my judgement. But the daughter was on the seat next to me. Her life had just blown apart, and she needed me to make the decisions about our next move.

I shook my head, tried to refocus on driving.

We were several blocks away from the hospital when both the front and rear windshields of the Jeep exploded simultaneously.

SIX

I shoved Leah down on the seat. Her screaming sounded like a cry of terror, not physical pain, so I hoped that she hadn't been hit. I jerked the wheel left and right to make us a difficult target, and stomped on the accelerator. Spot slid from side to side in the backseat. He hadn't made a noise, so I assumed that he, too, wasn't hit.

The front windshield was partly gone. The rest of the glass was a sagging mass of sparkling gems, held together by the lamination in the glass. I reached over the steering wheel with my fist and punched at the broken sheet. Over and over.

Some of the pieces fell inside the car, onto the dash, off onto Leah. Some slid off the hood as I jerked the Jeep left and right.

I made myself enough of an opening to see.

We were at a slight curve in the road. The shooter could have been in any of many dark places in the trees. There was no way to know if the round had come from behind us or in front of us. If the latter, we were about to deliver ourselves right to the shooter. I swerved to the left as we approached an intersection, an automotive feint, then jerked back to the right. We shot down a side street. I took a left, then another right.

Three blocks later we skidded onto Highway 50. Davis, the deputy who had been following me, was nowhere in sight. I shot up to 60 miles per hour through town, swerving around the traffic, looking for a cop and finding none. The wind roared through the open Jeep. My wind-burned eyes streamed tears. Leah was curled up, half on the floor, half on the seat. She sobbed. Even in the dark I could see her shaking.

I was in South Lake Tahoe. Diamond's jurisdiction is Douglas County, on the Nevada side of Stateline, so I dialed Mallory of the SLTPD.

"Commander," I said when Mallory answered. "McKenna here. I'm coming east down Fifty, approaching Al Tahoe Boulevard. We were just at the hospital getting Leah Printner fixed up. Took a sniper shot a few blocks from the hospital. Both front and back windshields were shattered."

"What's your next move?" Mallory said. He worked in an idyllic mountain resort town, yet he didn't let the violence change his demeanor.

"Can you set up a conference call with Diamond?"

"Yeah." Mallory was not one for extra talk. Even if a shooter was blowing out windshields in his jurisdiction.

I waited.

In a half minute, Diamond broke in. "I'm here. Davis told me the shooter took another shot. You all okay?"

"I think so," I said. "Took out my glass front and back."

"Scanner said you were investigating the sniper up on Kingsbury," Mallory said. "Same guy?"

I thought before answering. There didn't seem to be a good way to make it sound less harsh to Leah. "Probably," I said. "I assumed he made his mission. Apparently, he's got bigger plans."

"You're a few blocks away from us. You coming in to let us take over?" Mallory said. 'Or give her to Diamond?"

"Maybe later. Not much evidence in this Jeep. I'd like to give her some calm space, away from people. In the meantime, keep an eye out for a dark pickup that may have been following us."

"Roger that," Mallory said. "Watch your back, McKenna."

Diamond said to keep in touch, and we hung up.

I drove through town, wondering how the sniper knew where to find us near the hospital. Maybe it was a lucky guess. He'd naturally think that the private detective would take the woman to the hospital and, later, drive her away. The shooter could follow us, wait in the trees, and shoot us when we came back out of the hospital.

I looked in the mirror. A waving sheet of shattered glass. I checked the side mirror. Nothing.

Just before Stateline, I turned off Highway 50 and went through some twisty back streets I know well, streets that looped around and made it easy to see if someone was following at a distance.

I had no tail that I could see. Which meant that we were safe as long as we didn't go where the shooter might look. But we were very obvious in the damaged Jeep.

I pulled off the road into a shadowed stand of trees where no one would be able to see us. I shut off the lights and engine.

"Leah," I said, reaching over to where she was still bent down, huddled in as much of a fetal position as one can get in a Jeep. I touched her shoulder. "It's okay. No one knows where we are." I turned and spoke Spot's name. He stuck his big head over the seat back. I pointed to Leah. He bent down and sniffed her. She felt his presence. She slowly pushed herself up and held his head.

My phone rang, a startling intrusion. Leah jerked at the sound. I answered it quickly, before it could ring again.

"It's me," Mallory said, his rough voice recognizable in two words. "We picked up a guy. Could be him. Officer Lopez saw him moving in the forest not far from where your shooter might have been. He stopped and called out, and the guy ran. Lopez radioed for help. Several officers responded. They didn't catch him. But Jackson lives in that area. He had his scanner on."

I recognized the name. "He's got the canine unit."

"Yeah. Big Bones, the shepherd. He and Bones jumped in his cruiser as the other officers were saying they thought the guy escaped in the meadow that goes over to the Truckee River. Jackson glimpsed movement out in the brush, called the warning, and sent the canine after him. The dog took the suspect down. The guy didn't have his weapon. We'll do a thorough search for it come daylight."

"You have him in custody?"

"They're bringing him in as we speak. You want to come down?"

"We'll be there in a bit."

I hung up and turned to Leah. "They may have caught the killer."

She was sitting sideways on the seat, holding Spot, her rigid body a knot of tension. She didn't respond. Her rapid breathing made a terrible sound as it sucked back and forth through her clenched teeth.

"I'm going to drive to the police station. We'll see who this guy is."

Still no response.

"It could be the man who was pounding on your door earlier this evening. It could be someone you recognize."

I started the Jeep and took it slowly back through town, minimizing the wind blowing through the open vehicle. I turned left on Al Tahoe Blvd and eased down the long block toward Johnson and the police station. I'd just made the left turn at the signal when I heard sirens and saw flashing strobes over in the parking lot in front of the station. Two cop cars raced up from behind me, their sirens and light bars on. I didn't have time to pull over as they careened around the Jeep. More squads approached from down the road in front of me, sirens screaming.

Something was wrong.

The scene was chaos. I pulled off the road and waited. There were six or eight South Lake Tahoe police cars and another half-dozen El Dorado County Sheriff's SUVs. Two of the SUVs were bouncing through the rough forest across from the police station. Some squad cars were racing out of the parking lot as others raced in.

A voice yelled over a loudspeaker. Men ran into the woods across the street from the station, their flashlight beams shooting in all directions. A cop screeched to a stop behind us, its spotlights trained through the broken rear window.

I got out, my hands up. "Owen McKenna," I shouted. "Mallory's waiting for me."

The cop got out and came forward, his flashlight on my face. "McKenna. I recognize you. I'm Officer Spenner."

"What happened?"

He shook his head. "Guy busted out. I just heard it. I don't know the details. Pull into the lot. I'll follow you."

I drove down to the parking entrance and turned into the station lot. I parked at the far corner, as much away from the raucous noise and movement as possible. I left the engine on, heater blowing toward Leah, and got out.

Spenner stopped behind me and jumped out.

"You've got the woman," he said, pointing to the Jeep.

"Yeah. I'm going to go find Mallory. Will you stay here and watch her?"

"Maybe we should put her in the back of the patrol unit."

"No. She's pretty tense. I don't want to move her. Just stay right here. Keep an eye on the territory."

"Got it. I won't move."

I went to the Jeep and spoke through the windshield opening. "Leah, I'm going to go talk to Commander Mallory. Officer Spenner is standing just outside. He will stay here until I get back."

I didn't expect her to respond. I left and hurried toward a group of cops over by the courthouse, which stands next to the police station.

"McKenna here to see Mallory," I said.

"Do we know you?" one of them said.

"He's okay," another said. The man talked into his radio. "Mallory will be here in a minute," he said.

"Thanks."

I waited, and Mallory and another officer came hustling down the sidewalk from one of the other buildings. The frown on his forehead was like a map of canyons.

"You lost him," I said.

Mallory took a drag on a cigarette butt and threw it down on the sidewalk.

"Like a goddamn military operation. Jackson had the prisoner in the back of his cruiser. Big Bones was in the front seat. A guy with a scarf over his face came up just as Jackson was pulling into the secure garage. Guy pointed a pistol at Jackson's window. Jackson stopped, got out very slowly, and let the prisoner out of the back."

Mallory stomped on the ground. "Christ!" His breath was visible in the cold night air. "The man with the weapon held onto Jackson, his gun jammed into the back of Jackson's head. The crooks backed away with Jackson, went through the parking lot toward those trees across the street, shoved Jackson down and ran into the forest. We were all over that area in seconds. But it was like they vanished into the air. We hadn't even taken the guy's picture."

"Manny got a pic of him on his cell phone," a nearby officer said.

"What?" Mallory said. "Lemme see."

Another cop punched some buttons on his phone and handed it to Mallory.

"Crap," Mallory said. He passed the phone off to me.

The picture showed the cop Jackson, a man with a scarf over his face, and a blurred man with no recognizable facial features. All I could see was that the man had dark hair, combed close to his head. He was clean-shaven, and he wore a dark T-shirt. His arms, pulled behind his back and cuffed, were thick like his shoulders, and he had a flat stomach. Maybe he was Leah's stalker. Maybe not. The picture was no evidence.

"You get anything? A name? An ID?"

"Never said a word. Not a goddamn word." Mallory was practically hissing. "Jackson had searched him before putting him in the car. There was nothing in his pockets, either. Empty." Mallory looked out at the dark forest across the street. His jaw muscles clenched. "What does that sound like to you?" He said, more a statement than a question. "Neither one of them spoke a word, not to each other, or us. Totally fit. Disciplined."

"I hate to think it," I said. "It sounds like pros. Hired guns. No emotional outbursts. Like they do this for a living."

"What I thought," Mallory said, disgusted. "Just what we need here in a tourist town. Goddamn mercenaries."

The chief of police walked up along with several other men. "Mallory," the man said.

"One second, chief." Mallory turned to me. "Looks like I'm gonna be busy for awhile. You going to leave the woman with us?"

"Maybe not a good idea," I said, "now that we know that these guys aren't bashful about tracking her down."

"They can get to her easier with you than if she's with us. You take her, you're making a big mistake in judgment."

"Thanks for the advice, Mallory," I said. I turned and walked away.

SEVEN

I didn't know where to go.

I knew I could trust Diamond and Mallory without question. If I took either of them up on the offer to put Leah under their protection, they would do everything in their power to keep her safe. While Diamond and Mallory would be discreet, I couldn't know that about every person in their respective county and city departments. The business of law enforcement was predicated on teamwork. They had to delegate to get anything done. If I spoke to either of them about where I took Leah, information would inevitably flow toward their trusted colleagues. Cops use radios. Leah's whereabouts could be compromised.

Then again, maybe no one said anything. Maybe even Davis, behind me in the Douglas County SUV, said nothing on his radio.

The nearby forest was a logical place to wait for anyone leaving the hospital. While there were several other nearby routes, probably over half of all ER visitors would leave the same way we left, delivered directly to the sniper's cross hairs.

I walked back toward the Jeep. Officer Spenner was still standing nearby, his thumbs in the pockets of his pants. I stopped fifty feet away and dialed Street's cell. It was after midnight. I hoped she would have turned off her phone if she'd already gone to bed. She answered on the second ring.

"It's me," I said, trying not to sound stressed.

"Owen! Hold on. Let me move to a quiet place."

I heard people singing in the background. In a few seconds the noise softened. Street said, "I'm sorry. I'm at the conference kickoff party. They have this huge late-night campfire going out on a bluff over Puget Sound. These scientists, you wouldn't believe how raunchy they get after they fill their tanks with vodka. They're on their fourth rendition of Barnacle Bill The Sailor. What's happening in Tahoe?

It's late. Is everything okay?"

I tried to keep it brief. I spoke in a low voice to minimize any chance that Leah could hear from where she sat huddled in the Jeep.

Street went through the expected states of shock and fright. But after just a few oh-my-Gods she got very calm.

"Owen, what can I do? Should I get on a plane? But I don't even know the ferry schedule from this island!"

"No plane yet," I said. "I just need your brain power. This woman is a mess, and I'm not thinking clearly. I need to get her someplace safe. I can't take her to any of the obvious choices like my cabin or your condo because the shooter would figure it out."

"Okay," Street said. "Let me think a moment."

I waited in the dark, pacing a little this way, then that way. I could just make out the shape of the Jeep in the darkness. I visualized Street a thousand miles to the north, also outside in the dark. I knew she'd switched into problem-solving mode. I'd seen it before. Scientists are just as torn apart by trauma as the rest of us. But when the problem is identified, scientists are better at focusing on finding solutions. Street would be pacing just as I was, the big campfire and the rowdy entomologists singing in the distance. She'd take a few steps, turn, walk back, unaware of the ground beneath her hiking boots, oblivious to the newly invented exploits of Sailor Bill.

"I have an idea," she suddenly said in my ear. "I'll call you back. Give me four or five minutes."

"I'll be waiting," I said, and hung up.

I walked back to the Jeep. I was about to speak to Leah, but stopped when I realized she was not in the front seat where I left her. I felt the rush of adrenaline, then saw that she'd moved to the backseat. She'd slunk down next to Spot. Her arms held his head and neck in her lap. She had maybe 50 pounds of dog on her. It was too dark to see if her eyes were open. But she didn't react to my presence outside of the broken windshield. So I assumed she was chasing that elusive internal calm that can sometimes come if you are holding an animal who isn't judging you and simply loves your warmth and touch.

I nodded at Spenner in the dark, held up my phone so he'd understand my moves, then walked away, down several parking spaces. My phone chirped.

"Yeah?"

"I have a place for you," Street said. "I called my ex-professor Melba Rodriguez. She's retired. Lives in Burlingame. She has a house near Skyland. She doesn't use it as a vacation rental, but she lets friends stay there. I told her I had a friend who needs a place to stay and that my place won't work for a variety of reasons. That my friend has a dog that is neat and clean. I said I'd pay expenses, but Melba told me to give the money to Headstart, instead.

"Anyway, do you have a pen? I'll give you the number."

"No pen. I'll memorize it."

Street told me the address, and I repeated it three times.

"Near the garage door," Street said, "is a Welcome sign that is nailed onto the trunk of a pine tree. On the back of the sign is a little metal hide-a-key holder. Melba said the sign is up high, so you have to drag over one of the logs from the woodpile to stand on.

"The garage is empty. You can put your Jeep inside. If no one sees you go in, and you don't turn on the lights, no one will know you're there."

"No alarm?"

"No alarm. You and Leah should be safe. It'll give you some time to think of your next move. Does that help?"

"Street, my sweet, you have no idea. When do you get back?"

"The conference is Friday through Sunday. After that I was going to visit my friend in Tacoma and fly back next Wednesday night. Should I come back early? The conference will be okay, but Barnacle Bill wears poorly. I could help you in Tahoe."

"Please stay and party and sing the raunchy songs. We'll be in touch by phone. I love you."

She whispered her love in my ear, begged me to be safe, and clicked off.

I got back in the Jeep.

Leah appeared comatose in the backseat.

"I found a safe haven," I said as I shifted the open-air Jeep into Drive and drove away, raising my hand to the officer as I passed by.

EIGHT

I drove up the East Shore, attracting far too much attention with my missing windshield and rear window. Going through the casino area, nearly all of the late-night pedestrian gamblers stared at us. North of Zephyr Cove, just short of the Skyland neighborhood, I turned off to the right and let the sparse traffic behind me pass.

When no glow of headlights was visible in either direction, I raced up the road past Skyland, then turned off toward the lake. There was a group of houses that backed up to empty forest. I turned off my headlights as I approached, then stopped in the street.

"Stay here," I said. "I'll be right back."

In the glow from the neighbors' lights, I saw two floodlights above Melba's garage. I assumed that they were on a motion-sensitive switch. I walked around the perimeter of the dark yard and came in from the side to avoid the sensor. The Welcome sign was just visible up on the big pine. I didn't need a step up to reach the key. I fumbled it out of the little box.

Going back through the plantings, I got to the front door without setting off the light.

The door lock turned as if it had just been lubricated, and I stepped into an entry that smelled of spray cleaner. I shut the door behind me and navigated into the house by a dim blue glow that turned out to come from the kitchen microwave display.

The door to the garage went off the entrance hall. I stepped inside the garage and found the light switch. It lit two bright fluorescents. There were no windows in the garage. I was still safe.

On one wall were two other sets of switches. One was up. I turned it off. Nothing changed. I assumed it was the power for the motion light.

The garage door opener had a built-in light that would turn on as soon as the button was pushed. I popped off the plastic cover and loosened the bulb. I walked back to the wall, put my finger on the garage door button, took a mental snapshot of the garage, turned off the light, then pressed the button.

The motor ground up and the door made such a loud squeak as it rose that anyone in the neighborhood who wasn't rehearsing their rock band would know that Melba's garage door had just opened.

I walked out in a hurry so I could get the Jeep inside before anyone came out with a flashlight. The motion light above the garage came on, the floods blinding me. I trotted to the front door roof overhang, grabbed a large unsplit log that stood like a bookend at the edge of the woodpile and hustled it over to the middle of the garage opening. Standing on it, teetering because it had been cut at an angle, I unscrewed both floods just enough that they went out.

I got down off the log round, and returned it to the woodpile.

A few minutes later, I had the Jeep closed inside the garage, and I had maneuvered Leah and Spot onto a large couch in front of a gas fireplace. Spot sprawled on his side, his head gratefully ensconced on her lap. Leah held onto him like a drowning swimmer holding onto a life ring.

I found the thermostat for the fireplace and dialed it up. A lick of flame climbed up around the ceramic logs and cast the room in a soft yellow-blue light.

Leah was incommunicado, so I didn't inquire as to her wishes. I went into the kitchen and opened cupboards until I found decaf tea bags. Five minutes later, I brought her a steaming mug of something that claimed to calm and soothe, and I set it next to her on the wooden arm of the couch.

It didn't appear that Leah noticed.

I sat on a nearby chair and watched the gas flames while I drank my own tea. Self-recriminating thoughts crowded my own efforts at calm. The father was dead, the daughter was barely alive, and I was the guy who'd been hired to make sure none of this would happen.

Neither Leah nor Spot moved while I drank my tea. I had a thousand questions for Leah, but Doc Lee's warning about her potential breakdown echoed in my ears. He'd prescribed no stress, utter calm. I decided that included silence.

In time, I wandered the house, found the bedrooms. It was already three in the morning, and I needed Leah to get some sleep if she were to be functional in the morning. But she never moved from the couch. She never appeared to sleep, nor did she seem particularly conscious. It was as if she were in a semi-coma, able to move if prodded, but non-responsive to voices.

I opened the front door and stepped outside into the night. The well-to-do neighborhood was dark except for a few lights over front doors and a post light down the block. Like every neighborhood in Tahoe, the majority of houses were dark, empty most of the year except when the owners or vacation renters showed up at the holidays or on the weekends.

The night air of early summer smelled crisp and clean. The air was cold, probably in the mid 30s, a common summer occurrence in a mountain area with an average growing season of two months.

I decided that if I were going to break in, I'd come through the mud room door of the kitchen, because the backyard was fenced and dark and offered the most cover. So I dragged the recliner out of the living room and into the kitchen. I positioned it so that I could sit in it and be out of view from the windows.

I went through the kitchen looking for a weapon, once again questioning my decision not to carry a sidearm. There was a large selection of knives that would suffice. I slipped a serious knife down next to the seat cushion in the recliner. I found a small rack of wine and set a bottle on the floor next to the recliner.

There was a dimmer switch that worked the front hall wall sconces. The lights cast a low glow that filtered into the living room and the kitchen. Between the dim light from the sconces and the blue flicker from the gas fireplace, there was enough light for Leah to see if she wanted to find the bathroom. I turned on the outdoor lights at the front and back of the house, then stood in the relative darkness inside, considering my options should I hear the wrong kind of noises. In time, I sat down on the recliner.

All houses have a unique fingerprint of sounds, creaks, groans, and tickings as refrigerators and other appliances cycle, and air moves, and materials cool or warm, contracting and expanding in an endlessly repeating pattern. I sat in the dark, closed my eyes, and listened.

People are so accustomed to 24/7 TV and radio and music systems that they rarely stop long enough to discover the difference between a pine cone falling on the roof and the thunk of an unwanted visitor bumping the fence gate in the night.

Watch any dog in a new setting, and you will see how obsevant he is. I've seen it many times with Spot. When he is a visitor in a new house, he walks around, making an initial exploration, learning the shape and form of the new landscape. After that, he lies down in a place where he can watch the traffic flow, usually in the kitchen or living room or entry stair landing. Then he listens.

It looks like he is resting or even taking a nap. But his ears move one way, then the next, adjusting for reception from all directions. His nose twitches and continuously samples the air. If no people are moving, he stares at the walls, seeing nothing, but absorbing a complete landscape of sounds and smells.

While people are tuned into the TV as if it were the life-giving fire in the center of the cave, their dogs are tuned to the world outside of the cave. If another animal or someone from another tribe approaches in the dark, it is always the dog that sounds the alarm before the slow, media-dulled bipeds ever notice.

In the middle of the obnoxious sitcom laugh track that has overwhelmed our senses, we hear the dog bark. We're so dulled by our insatiable need for loud inputs that we have no idea what the dog is responding to. Our reaction is always, 'What are you barking at?' And the dog thinks we are so dense, always missing the obvious.

But even with our less sensitive hearing and sense of smell, we are trainable. People can learn from dogs. We can turn off the noise machines. We can listen and smell and feel the air currents across our hands and face. We can, as dogs do every day, spend an entire hour at a time just absorbing our environment. While we are handicapped with only a fraction of their sensitivity, we can nevertheless acquire a thorough awareness of the characteristics of the space around us.

I stayed aware, periodically felt for the knife, let my hand drop to the floor and wrap around the neck of the wine bottle. But an hour later I recognized that I'd had one of those weird thoughts, a surreal blend of dream and consciousness.

I looked up at the blue numbers on the microwave. 4:30 a.m. I finally let myself relax and drift off, relying on Spot and my own newfound awareness of the house to wake me if need be.

NINE

When I awoke from my nap in the recliner, the blue figures on the microwave said 8:15 a.m. The morning sun was flooding through the windows next to the front door, bouncing sunlight all the way back to the kitchen. I pried myself out of the chair and stood up. Spot came in from the living room and stuck his wet nose into my hand, his tail doing a loud percussive beat between the oven door and the center island. I opened the mud room door and let him out into the fenced backyard. If any of the neighbors were looking toward Melba's backyard, they would see him. As the only Harlequin Great Dane around, he was a billboard advertising my presence. If the shooter heard about Spot's presence, he'd know I was there. He'd assume there was a high likelihood that Leah was with me. But I didn't have much alternative.

I looked in the living room. Leah still sat where I'd left her a few hours before. The only change was that she'd taken off her shoes. Her stockinged feet were drawn up on the couch, her heels hooked on the edge of the seat cushion. The mug of tea I'd brought her the night before still sat on the couch arm, the cold tea untouched. Leah stared into space. The gas fireplace still burned, the blue flame nearly invisible against the light coming through cream-colored drapes.

"Morning," I said in a quiet voice. I walked over to the fireplace control and turned off the gas. The fireplace unit immediately began a light ticking as it cooled, accentuating the silence that pervaded the room.

Leah said nothing.

I picked up the cold mug of tea and carried it into the kitchen. I filled the coffee maker and went back in to Leah.

"Coffee? Cream or sugar?" I said, not having a clue if they were stocked in the kitchen.

Leah continued to stare at nothing except, presumably, the

nightmare visions in her head. Eventually, she spoke in a voice that was nearly a whisper, "Some milk." And after a pause, "In my coffee."

I went back and looked in the fridge. It was empty except for some Diet Coke, two kinds of mustard, mayonnaise, and a block of moldy cheese. I opened kitchen cupboards and looked in the drawers. One was a catchall stash of pens, coins, tourist brochures, fast-food Ketchup containers. I stirred the contents with my finger and found some non-dairy creamer packets. There was a half-full can of coffee in the cupboard above. Ten minutes later, I poured coffee into two mugs, put a creamer packet into one of them and brought the coffee out.

"Sorry, no milk. I put in powdered creamer. Will that do?"

Very slowly, she shifted her head and looked at me. "Okay," she said. It was like a robot talking at one-third normal speed.

I sat down in a nearby chair and drank my coffee. We didn't speak. Fifteen minutes later, I heard a muffled woof. It was the let-me-in version. I went and opened the mud room door. Spot walked past me and headed directly into the living room. I got there in time to see him sit before Leah. She still had her feet up on the couch, knees together in front of her. Sitting on his haunches, Spot was the right height to set his chin on her knees, a move that was not so much a trick as it was a handy way to take the large weight of his out-sized head and put the burden onto someone else. I'd seen it before, his Hallmark pose. They were nose to nose.

Leah reached up and caressed his ears, the diamond stud wiggling and sparkling. He shut his eyes, and I had no doubt that he was providing better therapy for her than any doctor or drug regimen could.

Over the next two hours I gently tried to get Leah to talk, to drink her coffee, to eat some of the food I'd found in the kitchen. But Leah just sat, her system numb and in shock. Even Spot eventually got bored, walked over, and lay in the sunshine that had moved around and was now shining through one of the dining room windows.

"I'm going to step out back for some fresh air," I said. "I'll be in the yard if you need anything." Anything, I thought. If only she wanted anything.

Spot followed me outside. I dialed Doc Lee's cell and caught him on his lunch break.

"I heard about the gunfire after you left the hospital," he said. "You and the patient okay?"

"Why I'm calling," I said. "She's severely traumatized. Kind of catatonic, like you said. I'm worried."

"Does she respond to anything?" Doc Lee asked.

"Only to Spot, and only just a little."

"She touches Spot? Talks to him?"

"Touches," I said.

"Well, that's something. I'm not a shrink, but it shows her emotions are not completely shut down. Is she eating?"

"No. Not drinking, either."

"That's bad. You gotta get food and liquid into her. Especially liquid. If she gets too dehydrated, her problems will be substantially exacerbated. You may have to bring her in for an IV."

"Any hints?"

"She's the same as you or me," Doc Lee said. "Like putting water on a sick cat's tongue. Get her to taste something she likes, it'll stimulate her appetite." He paused. "I'm assuming you've got her in a safe place?"

"Yeah."

"Good. She can't relax enough to ingest anything unless she feels safe from whomever is shooting at her."

I thanked him, and we hung up.

I found a phone book in a kitchen drawer and dialed a pizza shop and ordered a large pie, vegetarian on one half, pepperoni and the works on the other. By the time it was delivered, I had the kitchen table set with a cheery checkered cloth I'd found in a linen closet, silverware, and Diet Coke on ice in big glasses.

I paid the delivery girl at the door. I tried to block her view, but she stared past me at Spot and said, "Oh, my God, look at that huge dog. Is that an earring I see? Wow, your dog has an ear stud!" One more breach in the castle wall. I stuffed money in her hand and nearly had to push her out the door.

I carried the pizza to the kitchen table, Spot following me, his sniffing audible behind me. I took Spot by the collar so he wouldn't eat it, and went into the living room. I felt lousy, and I had my own dark cloud hanging over me, but I put on my best pleasant face and, still holding Spot by the collar, I reached my other hand out to Leah.

She slowly looked up from the couch.

"C'mon," I said. "I won't eat alone. You're a polite woman. So you gotta sit with me. Watch me eat." I kept my hand out.

Leah frowned. She obviously wanted me to go away.

"You're coming with me," I said. I wiggled my fingers on my out-stretched hand.

She shifted her hand on the couch, but didn't lift it.

I bent over and picked it up. I lifted slowly. Her arm was limp. I pulled.

"C'mon," I said again.

With obvious reluctance, she rose under my tug. I walked her into the kitchen and sat her down at the table. Spot sat next to the table, his head within easy striking distance of the pizza. I gave him a stern look. I picked up a piece, took a big bite and chewed noisily.

"Which do you usually like better," I asked, "veggie style, or Pepperoni Supreme?"

Her stare was vacant.

"Hmmm?" I mumbled, chewing, my eyebrows raised in question. I waited.

She pointed to the vegetarian half of the pizza.

"Good," I said, "'cause I like the decadent half. I can have it all for myself."

I cut a tiny slice of the vegetarian side and set it on her plate. "Taste it. Tell me what you think. You don't have to eat it. Just tell me if this outfit makes a good veggie pie. My girlfriend is very picky. Says you can't get a good vegetarian pizza anywhere. Have to make it yourself, she says. But I like to order out. I'd like your advice."

Leah gave me another vacant look. Then she surprised me by talking. "You're using psychology on me." Her voice was monotone. "I'm not a little kid."

I was glad for her protest. Any engagement was good.

I took another bite, shaking my head, chewing vigorously. "It's the truth," I mumbled. I swigged Diet Coke. "Her name is Street Casey. She's an entomologist. Not precisely a vegetarian. But she eats less meat every year. Probably her empathy for all creatures that crawl, walk, swim, or fly. Except she doesn't have much empathy for chickens. Something about their personality. So she's happy to eat them. Fish, if she didn't catch them. But she's got a thing for veggie pizza." I drank more Coke, took another slice of Pepperoni Supreme.

"I'm still waiting on your opinion," I mumbled through a full mouth.

Leah looked at the tiny slice of pizza. Looked at me. Back at the pizza. She picked it up and nibbled a tiny corner of the tiny slice. Like Street. She set the piece down. Chewed.

It's not like I inhale food the way Spot does, but I didn't know what there was for Leah to chew on for so long.

Spot watched her.

"Spot's watching you," I said. "If I gave him any indication that he was about to be graced with a piece, the drool would turn on. Two little faucets under his jowls, one on each side."

A small shadow of revulsion flickered across Leah's face. More engagement.

"Just like the water master at the Tahoe Dam in Tahoe City opening the gates to create the Truckee River," I said. "If I told him some of this was for him, the Great Dane saliva master would open the valve and twin streams would drop. It's actually quite a sight. The flow is robust and steady. Unless, natch, he shakes his head. Then watch out."

Leah's face changed a little. Not much. A touch of alarm mixed with disgust.

"Don't worry. You're safe because I haven't given him any indication that he gets a piece."

Leah looked at Spot.

"Oh, God, don't look at him!" I said. "I'll have to go check the levees."

Leah reached over and picked up the last piece from the Pepperoni Supreme half.

"Hey! That's from my side," I said.

She took a bite. It was a small bite, but it came from a large piece. There was promise in that, and it lifted my spirits. For the first time since she called in panic the night before, I felt like maybe she'd survive this ordeal.

I ate most of the veggie side while she worked through the one piece. There was still a veggie piece left when we both quit.

"You want to watch 'Feed the Hound?'" I said.

Leah looked at Spot again.

"No, don't look at him," I admonished. But it was too late. He had that laser look in his eyes.

There is little like it in nature. A wolf eyeing a fat bunny rabbit doesn't come close. A child staring at a candy bowl is nothing by comparison. No, a Great Dane is drawn to pizza at a primal, spiritual level.

I picked up the last veggie slice and went to the door before Spot could drool on the floor.

"Come watch," I said.

Leah didn't leave the table, but she turned toward the window.

I pulled open the door. Spot ran out, accelerating. I fired a pizza pass hard into the backyard.

Spot glanced sideways as he ran, sensing the speed and trajectory of the pizza. He went deep, then cut to the left and swiveled his head sideways as he leapt up and plucked it out of the air. Jerry Rice had nothing on him.

I looked back into the kitchen window. Leah wasn't smiling, but the shock and numbness had receded for the moment. As Spot and I came back in, she got up from the kitchen table, walked into the living room and lay down on the couch. I kept my distance. From the kitchen, I eventually heard deep breathing, perhaps her first sleep since the shot that killed her father.

Her nap was an opportunity to make some calls from the backyard.

TEN

I called Street, gave her an update on what had transpired, and thanked her for arranging our lodging.

"I miss you," I said. "I'm aware that during every minute since Dr. Kiyosawa's murder and every minute yet to come, you would have a better sense than I do of how to proceed with helping Leah."

"I can still leave early, if you like."

"No. Stay through your event. A question, though. If you were Leah, what do you think would help you get through this best, get you eating, get you talking?"

She repeated Doc Lee's words. "If she stays safe, she will recover. Make sure the killer can't find her."

I thought of the entire neighborhood hearing the garage door screech and groan in the middle of the night. The pizza delivery girl seeing Spot at the door. The next door neighbors seeing Spot run in the backyard.

"Got it," I said.

After we said goodbye, I called Diamond, then Mallory. I didn't tell either of them where I was.

They'd found no helpful evidence at either the forest above Mrs. Phelter's guesthouse or in the wooded areas near the hospital. There were no prints in the canine unit vehicle that carried the prisoner before he escaped. I was on my own. Local law enforcement would keep looking, but they had nothing to go on.

I explained to both Diamond and Mallory that Leah was not up to giving a statement regarding either shooting, and if they wanted the cover of doctor's orders to avoid any question of malfeasance, they could call Doc Lee. I added that I thought Leah might be up to talking in another day or so.

When I next checked in on Leah, she was awake, sitting on the couch, her legs folded to the side. She had her fist to her mouth and was biting down on a knuckle. Spot lay at her side. I sat on a nearby chair. I didn't speak.

We spent the day like that. Leah was indifferent to all of my attempts to draw her out.

Spot spent most of the day with her, sensing, I think, that she was broken in some critical way. I let him out into the backyard a couple of times, and when I let him back in, he always went straight to Leah.

Periodically, I made the rounds of the doors and windows, checking that they were still secure, and peeking out, looking for anything that seemed out of place. Of course, the killers may not have discovered our location, but they'd also demonstrated that they were determined. I had to operate on the assumption that they would have been to a local watering hole or two and acquired informants who would watch the main roads and ask around at businesses that would be in demand for people like us in hiding. Mobile windshield repair businesses. Or doctors who made house calls to wounded crime victims. Or pizza delivery businesses.

I considered how I'd proceed if I were one of the killers. I decided that given their demonstrated propensity to shoot from a distance, they would prefer to set up at a distance and pick Leah off as she walked outside the house. Or left in a vehicle.

But once they realized that she wasn't coming out anytime soon, they would probably come in at night, making a quick, quiet entry when we'd likely be asleep. Scientific studies had shown that, whether asleep or awake, people were the least alert between three and four in the morning. The shooters would think that even if the detective and his dog were trying to stay awake to guard the talk show woman, they'd both probably doze off around then.

I spent the day making preparations for that moment. Most were mental exercises.

Where would I station myself to best intercept an armed man at a door or window, their likely point of entry?

I dragged the recliner back into the living room and moved an uncomfortable chair to the point in the kitchen where I had good sight lines to the hall that went to the bedrooms, as well as to the front entry and into the dining/living area.

Off the kitchen was the mud room through which I'd taken Spot into the backyard. The door faced sideways to the back of the house. Which gave me an idea.

In the bathroom I found a handheld mirror. In the garage was a large cardboard box. I put a barstool in the center of the mud room. I set the box on the barstool and stuffed a pillow into the box. By punching the feather stuffing this way and that, I was able to prop the mirror on the pillow. After a few tries, I got the mirror adjusted so that when I was sitting in the chair in the kitchen, I could look at the mirror and see through the mini-blinds on the window in the mud room door. There were ten windows on the rear wall of the house. I could see six of them in the mirror. Because of the jog in the back of the house where the mud room projected out from the kitchen, four of the windows were out of my view. Those four were in the bedrooms behind the garage.

Of the windows that were in view in my mirror, two were in the kitchen not far from where I sat, two were in the dining room and two were in the living room. If anyone walked up to any of those six windows, I'd be able to see them.

The dining and living room windows were large. They would make a serious racket if broken. The kitchen windows were smaller, two feet wide by three feet high.

I thought the kitchen windows or mud room door were the most obvious places to break in.

While the bedroom windows were small, any tampering with them would be likely to wake a person or a dog sleeping in the bedroom. And a bedroom entry would cause a person to flee into the rest of the house, and thus be harder to find.

Entry in the kitchen would be the least likely to wake someone in the bedrooms or even someone sleeping on the living room couch. And kitchens had no place for people to take a nap. Once the intruder was in, the location of the kitchen made it easy to trap people in the bedrooms.

There were several more wine bottles in the rack. I stationed them at various points throughout the house. Unbroken, they made good clubs. Broken, they were a serious cut-and-thrust weapon. I did the same with several knives, and took care to conceal them from Leah's easy observation, in the event that she were to begin moving around. I didn't want to alarm her, but I wanted a knife ready to grab from under a seat cushion or a newspaper, or from behind an appliance or inside the refrigerator. They were all places about which I could concoct a story to tell an intruder, a story that would gain me proximity to the knife.

My last task addressed the most optimistic possible result of a late-night home invasion. If I were able to actually capture one or both of the killers, I would need to restrain them.

I made a thorough search of house and garage. There was no lightweight rope, but I found duct tape as well as two coiled, orange, electrical extension cords.

On a counter in the garage was a small tool box, which gave me another idea.

First, I let Spot out into the backyard for a last early-evening walk. Then I brought him inside for the night. I gave him only a small amount of food and water. I wanted him to stay with Leah until the following morning. He'd be hungry, but he'd survive.

When Spot came back in, I took a wire cutters from the tool box and went out into the backyard. Melba had a clothesline. I cut it off and used it to run some trip-lines from tree to tree a foot above the ground. I didn't have enough line to go all the way around the house. But I was able to cross the most likely approach paths. The lines would be unobtrusive come dark. They wouldn't disable anyone, but they would likely cause a stumble or maybe even a fall. The result would be a noise that Spot, and even I, might hear.

I knew my trip-line efforts may have been observed from a distance out in the forest, but I hoped that the backyard fence obscured the placement. Even if an intruder knew the lines were there, he would still be slowed by looking for their locations in the night.

I spent the rest of the evening looking out of the windows, trying to see into the forest beyond the fence. Then I went to the front of the house to peer past the neighboring houses to the street beyond, watching for anything out of place. I looked for a dark pickup in a neighborhood of minivans, SUVs, and all-wheel-drive luxury sedans.

Nothing seemed out of place.

Two or three times I tried to engage Leah, but with no success.

I made a light dinner of soup and crackers. Leah sipped a few spoonfuls, but lost interest. The time I spent worrying about her was exceeded only by the time I spent imagining a local kid trying to earn a cash incentive offered by a well-muscled mercenary he met at the local hangout. It's easy, dude. Just go around to every restaurant in town that makes food deliveries. You know. Pizza, Chinese, Thai, whatever. Look in the book. All you gotta do is ask if they brought food to a tall guy with a giant black-and-white dog. Get the address and you get the cash. Comprende?

When twilight began to dim the light coming in the windows, I told Leah that I wanted to keep the inside lights off for safety. Since it was cool, I could turn on the gas fireplace. She'd have that glow to look at, but nothing more.

She didn't react. I took that for acceptance.

I again switched on the outdoor lights over the front door and the mud room door.

We three sat in the dark, Leah in the living room, me in my observation chair in the kitchen near the mud room. Spot lay on the soft carpet near Leah. Periodically, he came into the hard-floor kitchen to see what craziness I was up to.

Every hour or so, I got up and made my rounds through the dark house. Then I returned to my chair, positioned so I could see the mirror and its view of the windows along the back of the house.

It was an exercise in no sleep in preparation for an event that would probably not happen. But I couldn't take that chance. I had to plan for what could happen, not for what would probably happen.

I believed that if an intruder did materialize, he would choose the back of the house. Except for the light above the mud room door, it was dark and out of view from the street, and it could be approached from the forest behind the fence.

Professional killers also might have thermal imaging equipment, able to look in dark windows and through thin drapes, and see the shapes of the relatively warm people and animals inside. But the living room windows had thick drapes with thin liner drapes behind them. As long as Spot and Leah stayed in the living room, I hoped they were effectively out of sight.

The flimsy little half-drapes on the kitchen windows covered only the bottom half of the glass. But my chair was over by the mud room and out of sight from someone peering in from back by the fence. If I stayed put, they would have a hard time picking up my glow in their night vision goggles.

I started making a pot of coffee, but realized that the coffee maker on the kitchen counter was in full view of the windows. Its warmth could easily be picked up by instruments. I set it on the floor near the mud room, accessible to me but out of sight. I made a pot of strong brew, determined to stay alert.

When my preparations were done, I settled into my observation post, determined to become like a dog, completely sentient, finding mental stimulation in the lightest of sounds, the tiniest glimmers of light, the faintest movements of air, the barest hints of smells.

The hours passed like I expected, with excruciating slowness. At first, my sentience did as I hoped, keeping me alert with the intense focus of monitoring all of my senses in the dark. It is amazing what you can pick up if you simply sit in the dark for an hour or five. I heard a growing cacophony of creaks and moans from the house itself, a discordant symphony that seemed to play from deep within the house's bones. I smelled soaps and detergents and scented candles and floor cleaners. From outside came hints of nightshade plants, a mix that reminded me of tobacco brush and sage. The night no longer seemed dark, so profuse were the interior glows that emanated from appliances and formerly unseen power strips, and the gentle wash of light that came from the bathroom night light, which was down a hallway and around two corners. The outside was brighter still with the outdoor lights flooding the yards and bouncing in through the windows.

The interior air was not calm at all, and was instead comprised of constant light breezes. Each time the refrigerator cycled on, a flow of warm air from its fan hit me 25 seconds later. Periodically, a gentle wave of cool air came down the wall behind me, a distant product, I finally guessed, from the current of heat coming out of the gas fireplace in the living room, rising up to the ceiling, and then pushing a circular flow of air into adjoining rooms. The air then cooled and coasted down the far walls and across the floors to reenter the living room and eventually be rewarmed by the fireplace.

In spite of my determined focus on my senses, my mind began to wander after a few hours. By 2:00 a.m., I realized I was thinking about Street, thinking about the events of the last day and a half as if

I were her, trying to decide how she would cope with Leah.

My foremost priority was to protect Leah. But that created a paradox. Baby-sitting Leah—guarding her from killers, from starvation and from mental collapse—meant that I couldn't work on her case. There were shooters out there that I could be tracking. But I was trapped with Leah. To do best by her, I had to stash her somewhere else. Someplace safe. Someplace where she would get the help and attention she needed without compromising anyone else's safety as well.

I had no clue where that would be. I couldn't place her at one of her friend's houses because a determined killer would figure out those possibilities. And I couldn't ship her to her aunt in Boston, the only family she had left, according to the landlord Lauren Phelter. That would be too obvious. Perhaps the best safe-house, one that no local would know of, would be for me to squirrel her off to an out-of-town hotel. But I needed to communicate with her in person. I had to probe her brain to figure out what was going on, why someone wanted her and her father dead. I couldn't do that if she were far away.

The need was clear. It would be best if I could find a safe place to put her locally, where I could visit her, monitor her situation and ask her a thousand questions when she was ready. And I had to be able to come and go without being seen.

A sudden, small sound jerked my attention back to my current job. It came from the direction of the garage. It was so small that Spot didn't make a sound, although I could picture his ears turning, monitoring, listening for a follow-up sound that would deserve a rumbling growl.

I didn't move, willing my mind to absorb every nano-component of every sound within and without the house. I stared into the dark. There was nothing more. Slowly, I turned my head, looked into the mirror to see the back of the house. Nothing. Again, slowly, I turned my head back toward the microwave to look at the time readout. 2:34 a.m. Too early. The optimum time for an assault was an hour or two off.

If they were out there.

I was desperately tired from almost no sleep the previous night. I looked again at the time. 2:40 a.m. The numbers wavered in my vision. They floated up, disappeared. My head started to loll to the side. I jerked myself awake. I thought of going into the living room and lying down. But the first rule of strategy is that you can only make it or alter it when you are alert and calm. I had to stay with the original plan.

I sipped coffee, my hands vibrating with the caffeine jitters. The time was 3:02 a.m. Either they would come in the next hour or two, or they wouldn't come at all. I was convinced of it. I believed it. I willed it to be true. The time ticked away without even the faintest sound. No accidental bump on a door. No tinking sound against glass. No deep bass plunk of one of the clothesline tripwires.

I began to fantasize about morning arriving. We were close to the summer solstice. It would begin to lighten before 5:00 a.m. Once it was daylight, I believed I could collapse in bed without repercussions.

I found myself watching the microwave clock. I studied the various LED segments that made up the numbers. I anticipated which segments would light up and which ones would go dark as each minute approached.

The blue letters had just flipped over to 3:19 when the light outside the mud room door went dark.

ELEVEN

I turned and stared into the mirror that I'd propped up in the mud room. I saw nothing in the sudden darkness where there'd previously been light. All I could see were the mini blinds on the window of the mud room door. I stared through the blinds, trying to focus on the blackness, willing my eyes to adjust to total night.

My heart beat loud and fast. My breath was short. I knew that someone had approached the mud room door from the side, reached up and quietly unscrewed the bulb.

After an agonizing minute, I had a vague sense of a dark object moving.

Gradually, the moving object in the mirror became the shape of a man dressed in black. He was at the kitchen window, bent over, doing something at the windowsill. He moved. I saw a bulge on his left side, up high. A shoulder holster. He was bold to wear his gun where all could see.

Except that no one other than me saw him.

The ambient light caught something shiny. He had a hunting knife. He was working the point into the wood at the side of the glass.

The window was a crank-out style. I wasn't sure what his plan was. Maybe he thought that if he could cut away enough wood, he could get the knife point up from below and pop the telescoping arm off the crank mechanism. The window would then swing out silently.

I reached down and picked up two wine bottles, holding them by the neck, one in each hand. I stood up very slowly, my knees creaking as I continued to stare at his image in the small mirror. The back of my right knee bumped the chair. It made a small sound. The man stopped moving. He shifted the knife into his left hand, reached up with his right and pulled his gun out of the holster.

I'd lost my chance at surprise. He would no longer think he could startle me with his presence. I had to get surprise back. The only way was to do something totally unexpected. There was no time to think. I had to move.

I quickly, silently stepped sideways along the kitchen wall. When I was next to the window I moved out from the wall just enough to see outside. He wasn't there.

I visualized him to the side of the window, his back up against the wall of the house, gun out, ready to fire.

My opportunity was gone. I had no choice but to wait.

He waited.

I had a couple of advantages. I absolutely knew he was there. But he didn't absolutely know I was there. He was merely fairly certain. If I waited long enough, he would begin to doubt what he'd heard. He would eventually resume his task. Further, it was almost certain that he had backup in the woods behind him. Backup often gives a person too much confidence.

But my main advantage was rage. Outside was a man—probably two men—who wanted to kill a helpless woman. That knowledge fueled a fire in me. It steeled me, created a tension that I knew would be explosive when released.

I stood frozen, facing the window at an angle. I could just barely see out. It would be hard for him to see me. My muscles quivered with anger.

Ten minutes passed before I saw movement. He waved his arm in front of the window, trying to provoke a reaction or even a shot from a gun he would assume I had.

Again he waved his arm. I didn't move. Gradually, he moved in front of the window and peered in, cupping his left hand, which still held the knife, to the side of his face, holding his gun with his right.

I stayed still. He tried to look sideways, but I was a dark figure off to the side in a dark room.

Seeing nothing, he pulled his hand away from the window, holstered his gun, and went back to work digging the knife point into the wood of the window frame.

I exploded like compressed springs being released.

I swung both wine bottles up and thrust them forward as if

they were cannonballs. They blasted through the window on either side of his head. The tempered glass shattered. The bottles rose on converging arcs, and I smashed them into the sides of his head. In one fluid movement, I released the bottles just after impact and grabbed onto his hair at his ears. I slammed his face down onto the windowsill, then smashed his head against the top of the window frame. He went limp and dropped his knife.

Spot came running, growling. He stopped next to me as he realized I wasn't the victim.

"Keep guard, Spot!" I yelled. The command combined with my tension kept him barking and snarling. I wanted his loud growls to give hesitation to the backup man.

I reached into the unconscious man's shoulder holster, pulled the gun out and tossed it across the kitchen floor. Then I took a good grip on the shoulders of his jacket, put a foot up on the windowsill and jerked his body through. He fell to the floor.

It took just a few seconds to use the duct tape to cuff his hands behind his back, a few more to tape his ankles. I unbuckled his pants, pulled them down below his knees, then taped his bare knees together.

I wondered if he could be a burglar with no relationship to the killers. But when I went through his pockets, I found nothing. No ID. No keys. No watch. No personal effects. Nothing that could be traced. It was enough to convince me that he was one of the killers.

I went back to taping.

When he started to resist, I bounced his head hard on the floor. I put tape over his mouth and over his eyes and ears, knowing that psychological deprivation is one of the fastest ways to destroy someone's resolve.

Spot stopped his growling.

"Spot!" I pointed to the dark broken window. "Guard the window!"

Again, my intensity encouraged him to growl and bark toward the outside.

Rolling the killer sideways, I ran tape under his legs just above and behind his knees. I brought the tape around and across his back and upper arms. I made several loops with the tape, gradually cinching him up so that his thighs were bound tightly against his chest. To prevent the tape on his back from slipping down, I ran a loop of tape from the main binding up and around his neck. If he struggled, the tape would tighten at his throat.

Once he was well-trussed, I turned back to the window. If the man's backup was beyond the fence, he'd either be waiting for a good shot with his big-bore rifle, or he'd be coming toward the house to try to save his partner.

I got down on the floor and felt around in the dark for his gun. It was over by the oven. I couldn't see it in the dark, but its shape and heft reminded me of a Beretta I'd once fired at the range.

With the gun in my hand and Spot still on guard at the window, I dialed Douglas County dispatch and reported the intruder. Then I called Diamond, woke him up and filled him in.

I knew Leah would be cowering in fear. I didn't dare walk to the living room because that would take my focus off of the broken window. It would also reveal her location to the backup man if he was watching with night vision equipment. So I spoke up enough that she could hear and talked to her from the kitchen.

"It's okay, Leah. I've caught one of the killers. Just stay put in the dark. Don't move, yet. The cops will be here very soon."

I waited in the dark kitchen, the trussed-up man on the floor at my feet. I remembered the man's knife. It had probably fallen outside of the window.

Navigating by feel, I lifted a large saucepan off of the hanging pan rack and filled it with ice-cold water from the fridge dispenser. The man hadn't moved. He was probably still unconscious. I took the ice water over to him, jerked the tape off his ears, then dumped half the water over his head and body, being careful to direct the ice water into his ears.

He jerked as if in a seizure, and tried to scream through his taped mouth. His inhalations wheezed around the edges of the tape.

Spot kept growling.

I ripped the tape off his mouth.

"What's your name?" I asked.

He said nothing.

I dumped more ice water into his ears and down the back of his neck. His gasp was less than before. Impressive control.

"How many men are outside?"

Silence.

"Why are you after the woman?"

His silence indicated adherence to a strict regimen, not the mark of a typical murderer.

I knew I wouldn't get any more out of him.

I calmed Spot, then stayed near the dark broken window, holding the man's gun, waiting.

It was frustrating. If he didn't confess his crimes, we probably wouldn't get far. Unless his prints were in the NCIC database, we might not be able to determine his identity. His vehicle would be stolen, with nothing linking him to it. He was wearing gloves. His gun would be stolen from somebody who stole it from somebody else. If we ever found the rifle used to shoot Kiyosawa, that too would be stolen. And unless he and his partner made stupid mistakes, we wouldn't find enough evidence to convict him of anything much more serious than burglary, possession of stolen property and an unregistered handgun.

Despite the indications of professionalism, this guy wasn't professional in several ways.

First, he had a partner, which was always the Achilles heel of any murder-for-hire operation. Second, no really good mercenary would ever let himself get into a situation where I could get my hands on him.

The evidence suggested that I was dealing with a guy who had pretensions to killers he'd seen on TV, but didn't know how to go about it.

I heard sirens rise in the distance. I told Spot to keep guarding, and ran to the front door as two vehicles pulled up. I opened the door and saw Diamond and two other deputies coming toward me, their guns out. I recognized the deputies as Jason and Davis from the night before. I called out to them.

"I've got the indoor lights turned off. We may still have a shooter outside."

I left the door open, and ran back to guard the broken kitchen window, staying against the wall to the side, my hand on Spot's collar.

Spot turned his head toward the men, and, recognizing their sounds and smells, stopped growling.

Diamond walked in, flashlight and gun held together, and saw me in the dark kitchen. He walked over and toed the trussed-up man on the floor.

"You didn't kill him?"

"No."

"Whole lotta tape on this guy. You catch Hannibal Lector?"

"Maybe."

Diamond spoke into his radio.

In the distance rose the sound of more sirens.

Diamond turned to me. "Surprised this guy's comrade didn't come forward."

"He still may. We should cover these windows before we turn on the lights."

The deputy named Jason came into the kitchen, saw Spot in the dark, and stopped. "That's the dog that growled in the garage last night."

Spot gave him a look.

"It's okay, Spot," I said.

Diamond walked over to where we stood to the side of the window and rubbed Spot's ears. "Doesn't seem so tough to me," Diamond said to Jason.

"Tell me that when he bares his teeth at you," Jason said. He bent down to the guy on the floor. "Hey, I think this guy is having trouble breathing."

"I used some tape to protect him from hurting himself," I said. "Probably should loosen the loop around his neck."

"He's all wet, too," Jason said.

Diamond looked at me. "The water was in case he tried self-immolation?"

"Sure."

Diamond shined his light at the gun in my hand. "That Beretta his sidearm?"

I nodded. "I got my prints on it, not that there will be any others." I set it on the kitchen counter.

"This the guy who was stalking Leah?" Diamond said.

"I thought so at first, but that guy was a whiner. I don't think he'd keep his mouth shut. Shine your light on his face." I walked over, grabbed his hair and lifted up his head. I tore the duct tape off his eyes. He screamed. His eyelids looked strange, the lids bagged out from the pull of the duct tape. The eyelashes were all gone, stuck to the tape.

"Hard to judge. His face is all red and puffy. Got some cuts where he tried to eat the windowsill. But I don't think it's him."

"Whose house is this?" Diamond asked.

"Friend of a friend," I said.

"And your charge?"

I jerked my head toward the living room.

Diamond looked toward the dark archway into the dark living room. "We'll get these windows covered so we can turn on the lights. Then we can stand this piece of shit up and let the victim take a look at him."

I nodded. "Remember, one of these guys busted the other one out of a clutch of cops in South Lake Tahoe," I said.

"Yeah, but neither you or me or your hound was there," Diamond said.

TWELVE

In the far distance, multiple sirens sounded like a flock of keening night birds. In a minute, the sirens grew to a loud wailing, and flashing lights pulsed ouside the front of the house. I glanced out the kitchen windows. Beyond the back fence, up by the highway, were more cruisers, their light bars flashing.

Diamond and the two deputies covered the kitchen windows with blankets from the bedrooms so that the suspect's partner couldn't see to shoot from the forest. I went into the dark living room. Leah was not on the couch. I felt the adrenaline surge, my heart thump. Could the killer's partner have come in the front door during the commotion in the kitchen?

I took a fast step toward a lamp and turned it on, jerking the switch so hard that the lamp teetered and almost fell to the floor.

Leah was sitting in the corner in the dark, her knees drawn up to her chest. She was squeezed in between an armchair and the armoire that held the TV. She had the quilt from the couch wrapped around her. Her eyes were frantic with fear.

I kneeled down in front of her.

"I keep screwing up, Leah. I try to get you someplace safe, and they find us. But this time we got one of them. Sergeant Martinez and his boys are going to take him away and lock him up. But first, we need you to look at him, see if you know him."

She stared at me, horrified, and shook her head.

"We need to know if you've seen this man somewhere before. It's a critical step in solving this."

Her head-shaking was vigorous. She tried to say something.

"What? I can't hear you." I bent my head down to her mouth.

"He'll see me," she said, her voice a whisper.

"I'll make it so he won't."

I stood up, turned off the lamp, walked toward the light coming in from the kitchen.

"Diamond, stand him up so we can see from the living room."

I turned back to Leah as I heard the sound of the cops tearing the duct tape off the prisoner, releasing his legs so he could stand up.

"Okay," Diamond called out.

"We're in the dark," I whispered to Leah. "The man can't see us in here. You can stand up and move so you can see him. But he won't be able to see you. C'mon." I reached for her hand, tugged her up to a standing position.

I walked her to the center of the dark living room. We could see the prisoner, but we were in the shadows. Diamond stood on one side of him, hanging onto his arms, which were still duct-taped behind his back. His pants were still down around his ankles. His knees and ankles were still taped. Jason stood on the other side. The third cop stayed over to the side of the broken, blanketed window. Spot was on the other side of the window.

"Do you recognize him?" I whispered to Leah.

She shook her head. She spoke the slow, soft robot-speak I'd heard over the last day. "I don't think so. But I can't see him well."

I called out to Diamond. "Move him forward a little so the kitchen lights shine on his face."

Diamond and Jason pushed him forward.

"His face has shadows on it," I said.

Diamond reached his hand up and grabbed the back of the man's hair. He pulled the man's head back with surprising gentleness, I thought, then turned the man's head back and forth.

Seeing him in the light for the first time, he didn't look like the stalker to me. He had delicate features. His eyebrows were thin and arched, although I realized it was partly because I'd ripped most of them off with the duct tape. The cut marks from the broken window obscured some of his features. But his eyes were large and dark. He had pronounced cheekbones, and his jaw, while large, had a thin, fragile quality to it, like the feminine warrior faces in the Japanese woodblock prints in one of my art books. His face didn't go with the heavy, muscled body.

"What do you think?" I whispered to Leah.

"I've never seen him," she said.

"He's not the stalker who came to your father's house?"

"No."

"You're sure?"

"I'm sure."

I maneuvered her over to the couch and sat her down. I went back to the kitchen.

"You can take him in," I said to Diamond.

I peeked around the blanket over one of the kitchen windows and looked out. There were cops with flashlights in the forest beyond the fence, more up by the highway. The trees flashed red and blue in the staccato strobes of the patrol units.

I stayed with Leah while Diamond and Jason took him out the front door. I knew they would lock him into the backseat of one of the Douglas County Sheriff's vehicles. Davis stayed on guard at the broken kitchen window.

"The man had a knife that fell just outside of the kitchen window," I said.

The man nodded.

"What's your plan?" Diamond said as he returned.

"You came in two vehicles, right?"

"Yeah."

"Then Leah and I could ride with you while Jason and Davis take the prisoner in."

I turned off the front light, and the cops provided cover while we rushed Leah through the dark into the back of one of the county SUVs. Spot got in back with her.

I rode shotgun while Diamond drove.

Jason and Davis drove the other vehicle with the prisoner. They led, we followed.

"You think the suspect's partner is still out there in the woods?" Diamond asked as he drove through the neighborhood up to the highway.

"A good assumption," I said. "He could have moved up to the highway to intercept us as we leave."

"If so, which way do you think we should go?"

"The obvious, direct way is south, then over Kingsbury Grade and down to the Douglas County Jail. So let's go the other way."

Diamond spoke into his radio. The vehicle in front us turned left at the highway. We stayed several car lengths behind.

"Leah," I said, "the back windows of this car are smoked. No one can see you. But it would be smart to lie down on the seat, just in case someone takes a potshot."

Diamond looked at me in the dark. The dashboard lights showed the alarm in his eyes.

I turned and saw Leah hunch down on top of Spot's body. His head stayed in her lap.

We drove north on 50, then up and over Spooner Summit. The lights of Carson City and Carson Valley still shimmered 3000 feet below, while the faint, distant dawn promised to push back the darkness.

THIRTEEN

At the bottom of the mountain, we turned south and made a fast trip down the valley to the county jail in Minden, a dozen miles south.

"You and Leah need a new place to stay," Diamond said.

"Yeah. And wheels with a windshield."

"You could take my pickup."

"That thing run better than the Green Flame?" I asked, referring to the Karmann Ghia that was a replacement for the venerable orange one, which was destroyed the previous summer.

"Yeah. Better cover, too," he said.

I looked in the side mirror at the few cars stretched out in the distance behind us. "Our suspect's partner could still be watching and following us. How do you recommend we switch vehicles?"

"Like that shell game you did last year in the parking ramp of the South Shore hotel. We take you into our maintenance garage, along with some other vehicles. We shut the door for a time. No one can see in. Then the door goes up and the vehicles drive out and all head in different directions. The vehicles all have dark windows. An observer can't tell which car you and Leah are in."

"The observer would know you are a friend. He might already know that you have a pickup."

Diamond thought about it. "Then I'll borrow my friend Maria's pickup. Different color."

"Maria isn't a cop?"

Diamond shot me a look. "You think a cop would give away your location?" He sounded defensive.

"No. But cops talk on radios. Easy to listen in on a scanner."

It was a minute before Diamond spoke. "No, Maria isn't a cop. She boards and raises horses over on the east side of the valley. She's got an old mobile home and a newish barn on five acres of scrub, fenced and cross-fenced, the payoff from twenty years of investing her waitressing income. She calls it the Ponderosa Pomposo. One of her prized possessions is an old Dodge rattletrap in worse shape than my pickup. It's camo-yellow, custom rusted. No chance of confusing it with mine."

"She won't mind lending it to me?"

Diamond made a little grin in the dashboard glow. "She likes to acquiesce to my desires."

"Acquiesce," I said.

He nodded in the dark. "You gringos got some good words in your language. You should try using them. Maria likes to adjudicate my culinary explorations. Assuage my wounds. Abrogate my tiresome habits. Attenuate my excessive impulses."

"Sounds like quite the woman," I said. I was aware that Leah could hear us from the backseat. It would be good for her to overhear small talk. It might help take her out of her current stress, if only momentarily. "How come I haven't heard of Maria before?"

"Just met her last week."

"You got to know her that well in a week?"

"She's a hot-blooded Latina," Diamond said as if that explained everything.

After our suspect was booked and locked away in the Douglas County jail in Minden, we played it as Diamond suggested, heading out of the maintenance garage with three other vehicles all driven by sheriff's deputies. Leah and Spot and I were in the backseat of a Chevy sedan. The four vehicles went in four different directions. Diamond wore a cowboy hat to obscure his features and drove fast.

He took us down through Gardnerville, then up the gentle slope to the east. We turned off on a dirt road and were at Maria's spread fifteen minutes later. The sun had risen. It was going to be a hot June day on the desert.

There was a narrow, blue, mobile box tucked into the slope. It had a spectacular view of Job's Peak rising 6000 feet above and across the valley. Just to the north of Job's were the curving white stripes of Heavenly's ski runs, still heavy with snow two months after they'd closed for the season.

Diamond parked near a pole barn with metal siding. There were several large window openings and big doors on the end, all open to let the cool night and morning breezes flow through. The barn was divided into stables on either side of a central breezeway. The stables were empty. On a slope below were a dozen or more horses, munching the sparse grasses that had already turned brown in the desert heat. The sweet smell of horse sweat rose up the slope.

Spot ran around, the excitements of a horse ranch obvious and enticing.

Diamond took us around the side of the barn where an old pickup was parked in the dirt. He got in, turned a key that was already in the ignition, and the pickup came to life, puffing out blue smoke. The exhaust shook and rumbled.

Diamond turned back to Leah. "My official opinion is we should put you up at the county facility, take care of you, keep you safe. Protective custody works. But this guy would probably disagree." Diamond looked at me.

"Hard to know what's safest," I said. "Staying in a secure facility where shooters can learn of your presence? Or hiding and staying on the run?"

I turned to Leah. "Do you have an opinion?"

Her eyes went past me, up and over my shoulder. I swiveled my head to see what she was looking at. A grouse-sized bird came in on a fast glide path. It made a couple of quick, small adjustments, like a plane tweaking its ailerons, rocking its wings, crabbing into the cross breeze to stay on track to the runway. Then the bird dropped into the sage brush just eight or nine yards away from where we were standing. It disappeared. I took a step sideways, moved my head around, trying to see the bird that I knew was standing right there. But it was effectively gone.

"The police had the man, and the other man still got to him," Leah said. "I think I should keep hiding."

Diamond nodded. "What I thought," he said. He went back to the Chevy and pulled a backpack out from the front seat, a bag I remembered seeing in the SUV that Diamond drove to Melba's house.

He handed it to me.

"I stopped at your cabin yesterday. I figured it would be awhile before it was safe for you to go there. I grabbed some of your clothes.

Found some of Street's, too. They might fit Leah. Been carrying them around." "There's some food and toiletry stuff in the backpack. Couple cans of dog food, too."

"Thanks," I said. "What about Maria? Should we be knocking on her door and explaining that we're not stealing her pickup?"

"No one would steal this pickup. Besides, she likes to sleep late. I'll tell her later." Diamond handed me a card. "Got a friend who owns this motel on the South Shore," he said. "It's just like any other dive, nice and inconspicuous. They're flexible when it comes to helping out people who don't have or don't want to pay with credit cards."

"This place part of the Mexican railroad?"

Diamond nodded. "Lot of us stayed there before we got our green cards. I told the owner I'd cover the fee and vouch for my friend Roger Jones and his niece Cynthia Jones. You can pay me back later. They're okay with dogs, too. You're booked for two nights. After that, I figure you're going to want to move on. We don't know if this shooter's comrade has more friends keeping watch around town. Best not to take chances."

"Thanks."

I took Leah's arm and steered her toward Maria's pickup. Spot came running. Leah opened her door. Spot jumped inside and squeezed up against me, his butt on the seat, his paws on the floor, his jaw on the dash. Leah got in, shoved him in farther, then shut the door. We headed off, waving at Diamond, trailing a dirt plume as we went down Maria's drive.

FOURTEEN

Leah and I didn't speak as we drove back across the desert floor of Carson Valley. In the un-irrigated areas, the scents of sage and dry dust wafted in the open windows, unchanged over the thousands of years that the Washoe Indians occupied the area, wintering in the valley and summering up at the lake.

Where there were water rights to let the Carson River flow through the fields, the sage was replaced with the verdant aroma of grass and alfalfa, which competed with the pungent tang of the grazing cattle.

Maria's pickup coughed and wheezed as I coaxed it up Kingsbury Grade. But it found the grit to make it to the summit, and from there it was an easy coast down to the south shore of the lake.

The motel was off Pioneer Trail not far from the Stateline area. It was in a neighborhood where many of the South Shore's Hispanic population lived. I didn't want to wake up the motel owner, so we waited until the "No" in the No Vacancy light switched off and the office blinds raised up at 7:00 a.m. The sun was already high, and people were walking toward their jobs at the hotels, hustling to stay warm in the cold, high-altitude morning air.

I left Leah and Spot in the pickup and went in. The smell of brewing coffee permeated the small space. A short dark-skinned man of about 60 looked up from a tiny desk piled high with papers. His face was so wrinkled that I knew he'd spent years doing hard farm labor in the fields.

"Roger Jones," I said. "My friend Diamond booked me a room for two nights."

The man nodded. He pulled a plastic key card out of a drawer, punched a number into the keypad on a magnetic coding machine, and swiped the card through the machine's slot.

"Room two-sixteen. Ice machine at the end of the building.

Closest food is at the Seven-Eleven down the block. Or the Border Fence Café just past the stop sign. Local phone calls are fifty cents each. Long distance is ten cents a minute. I'll keep track and collect from Diamond. Diamond said you'd like privacy. I know something about that. I recommend you don't use your cell phone because its GPS will give away your location."

He wagged his finger at me. "And no phone card, credit card, or cash card. Trust me when I say that you can never know if some computer is watching for you. Native-born Yankees think it takes a court order. They think only the FBI can pull the right strings. I know from experience, it is not true. It is very easy for someone to know someone. They make a call. The computer starts watching. You use a card anywhere, and the next thing you know, the person who wants you knows where you are."

He spoke with a plain voice, no emotion. It was a speech he'd given before, but it was no less effective for it. To have an immigrant explain the realities of our system to a jaded, cynical, American ex-cop was an eye-opener.

"If you need cash," he continued, "I'll give you some on Diamond's account." He raised his eyebrows in anticipation.

"Uh, yes, I guess that would be good," I said.

He reached under the counter, opened a hidden drawer, counted off fifteen twenties, and handed them to me. Then he shuffled over to the window and pointed out.

"Between those buildings is a path to the forest. Good place to walk your dog."

"Thanks," I said, realizing that he must have looked out at the pickup before he unlocked his office door.

I left, parked the truck down at the end of the building and took Leah and Spot up the stairs to our room. There was one double bed. A small TV on a stand. A tiny bathroom whose dripping faucet was audible from a good distance. A little desk with a pink, '60s Princess phone and a wooden chair tucked underneath. An upholstered chair in the corner.

The carpet was worn down to the jute backing near the door. There was a banana-shaped stain on the wall near the bathroom. But the place was vacuumed, the windows were clean, and the towels were neatly folded. To a couple and dog who were effectively homeless, it looked like the Fairmont Hotel in San Francisco.

Leah sat down in the corner chair as if it were a one-way trip.

"Do you want to walk with Spot? Get some fresh air?"

Leah's face was an unusual combination of frown and worry and slack. It seemed she'd lost the will to function, maybe even to live. The small part of her that was still reacting to the world showed only fear.

"It would do you good," I said.

She looked at the door, then at the window, then around toward the bathroom as if someone could come in that way. Her jaw muscles bulged, she swallowed, then she slowly shook her head.

I reached through the window drapes and checked that the window was shut and locked. "No one knows we're here. I won't go far, and I'll be back in twenty minutes. I have the key card. Don't go anywhere." I turned and shut the door behind me, testing it to make certain the lock had clicked shut.

Spot and I trotted down the stairs and headed into the woods. As before, I knew Spot would cause people to notice and talk, but the local Hispanic population is like any other immigrant community. They keep to themselves. I didn't think the news of our presence would easily find its way to the killer unless he was Hispanic.

FIFTEEN

Spot and I found the path the motel man had talked about. We went diagonally through a vacant lot back toward Heavenly Ski Resort, then into the forest. It was good to see Spot run around. Dogs get depressed more often than many people realize. But they bounce back fast. Take them outside, let them get away from the heavy atmosphere that people sometimes project, and they undergo an amazing transformation. They are rare among all creatures in that the simple act of being outside gives them joy, and they express it with exuberance.

We went a quarter mile into the forest, then angled back toward the Border Fence Café that the motel man had mentioned. I didn't want the attention that Spot would generate sitting out front, so I hooked on his leash, looped it to a tree behind the restaurant, and told him to be good.

Inside, I found an excessively-cheerful, white-guy owner who presided over a pretend Mexican restaurant with cutesy-sounding dishes that the real Mexican help must have found ridiculous. I ordered two Casa Coffees, Sombrero Salads and Oasis Omelets to go. They stuffed the Styrofoam containers, napkins and plastic forks into a Safeway bag while I stuffed my change through the narrow slot in the lid of the tip jar. Spot and I headed back to our room.

Leah hadn't moved from the chair.

I spread out the food on the little desk, then moved Leah's portion of egg and salad to her lap, put a fork into her hand and set her coffee and cream on the arm of her chair.

I sat on the bed while I ate my food. It wouldn't win awards, but it was a serviceable breakfast. Leah sat unmoving, the upright fork in her hand motionless and looking like the pitchfork in Grant Wood's American Gothic. When I was nearly done, Leah tried a tiny bite of egg. It was probably cold and rubbery, but she chewed and swallowed and then continued to nibble at her food.

Spot lay on the floor, patiently waiting for me to come to my senses and address the largest hunger in the room.

When I was through, I looked in the backpack and found that Diamond had included an opener along with several cans of dog food.

Canned food is very rich compared to Spot's normal fare, so I only opened one. I forked the cylinder of fat and meat onto my plastic takeout container, gave Spot the okay, and he sucked it down like a Shop-Vac on steroids.

I turned on the water in the sink and closed the drain plug. Spot knew it was for him, and he drank a long time. When he was done, I grabbed a towel and mopped his jowls before he could shake his head.

Spot turned and looked at Leah. She stared back without emotion. No patting her knee. No smile. No words.

At first, Spot had kept approaching her, pushing her hand around with his nose, waiting for the standard gush of affectionate stroking. Now, confused, he watched her from a distance. When he was once again ready for another installment of human vice-grip, he would walk over and put his head in her lap. By his current reserve, I could see that he wanted to wait a bit.

Leah finished eating a small portion of her food and set her plastic container on the floor. Spot immediately looked at me, his eyes on fire. He could have spoken English, so clear was his intent. This is the meaning of life, Owen. Here is a gift direct from the gods of food. This is my raison d'etre.

I picked up the tray, scraped off the salad onto mine and gave him Leah's remaining egg. It disappeared with a single swipe of the giant tongue.

I turned to Leah. "We should get you some fresh air."

She was holding her coffee in the air. She made the smallest of nods and lifted her coffee to take a sip when the room phone next to her rang at high volume.

Leah's entire body jerked at the loud sound. Her coffee cup seemed to explode, brown liquid flying through the air as if from a hose. The shock in Leah's eyes was profound. She sat stiff and quaking as I dove for the phone to prevent it ringing again. I picked it up, said, "Hold on," into the handpiece, and tossed it onto the bed.

I grabbed a big towel from the bathroom and worked on Leah, blotting her face first. I knew from my own coffee that it wasn't hot enough to burn her. But it seemed to sear through to her soul. At first, she was rigid with horror. Then she melted, collapsing into herself.

I picked up the phone and said, "Can I call you back?"

"Yeah. It's Diamond. Dial my cell." He hung up.

I turned to Leah. She was crying uncontrollably, her body jerking with spasms. I sat on the arm of her chair and reached my arms around her. I pulled the woman to me and held her as she imploded.

SIXTEEN

We sat there for fifteen minutes, me bent over holding Leah, rubbing her back, she clinging to me, her fingers gripping my shirt as if to tear the fabric. Her heaving, shrieking cries were heartbreaking. It was as if the horror of her father's murder was finally coming out.

Gradually, her wailing subsided to whimpers. Her spasms became less like a violent seizure and more like waves of pain.

In time, she began to shiver from the cold of wet clothing and the stress of nerves. I slowly separated myself from her and went into the bathroom. There was a red heat light in the ceiling. I switched it on, then turned on the hot water and pulled the shower button.

The bathroom began to fill with steam. When the little space was very warm, I pushed the shower button back in and drew a warm bath, adding some of the little shampoo bottle to the flow to make a thick layer of suds.

I went back to Leah, bent down and lifted her out of the chair and up to a standing position.

She was not present or self-aware in any normal sense. She stood bent and shivering violently, her elbows tucked at her sides, fists at her mouth, teeth cutting her knuckles. Her facial grimace pulled at the new stitches, each thread stretching and threatening to tear her skin. She didn't seem to breathe for a long time, then she gasped for air.

Over the years, I'd heard and read a little about breakdowns and disassociation from reality. I'd witnessed severe depression in a few people. And I'd seen a few examples of psychosis with drug overdoses in my work as a cop in San Francisco. But this was my first experience with someone coming completely unglued as a result of emotional trauma.

I knew the standard procedure was to call in the medical corps, begin the drug treatment, put the person in the hospital, tied to the bed if necessary. But it didn't feel right. Medical experts would no doubt disagree with me, but I couldn't see taking this fragile, broken person and submitting her to yet more trauma in the form of well-meaning people in white coats shining lights in her eyes, pumping chemicals into her veins, asking her questions, and taking away her physical freedoms.

And then there was the small issue of the remaining shooter who could easily find her in the hospital.

I decided to keep her with me, hidden from the world, untreated except for regular applications of Owen's standard medical routine: Quiet. Meals provided. More quiet. And most important of all, because it led to physical safety and possible future emotional calm, was the capture of her father's killers. So far, most of my efforts had failed.

"We need to get you warm," I said. "I've made a hot bath." I walked her into the steamy bathroom. She didn't come easily, but she didn't fight me, either. I sat her down on the toilet. Her fists were still at her mouth. She still shivered. I untied her shoes, pulled off her socks.

"Can you get the rest of your clothes?"

She made a little nod, her red face wet with tears.

"Take your time," I said. "I'll be just outside the door. Call if you need anything."

She didn't respond.

I left and shut the door.

I sat on the bed and used the motel phone to dial Diamond.

"Hello?"

"It's Owen."

"I called your cell," he said, "but it's off."

"Yeah." I didn't want to explain the motel man's warning about cell phone GPS. "But the motel phone ringer is so loud, it upset Leah. I'm turning it off. You can leave a message with the office and I'll get it."

"How's she doing?"

"As you would expect. She's in rough shape. Taking a bath as we speak. What's up?"

"I'm at Phelter's guesthouse, where her father was shot. The cleaning crew got here this morning to begin the mop-up. The place was burglarized last night."

"Any idea why? Was it vandals? Careless destruction?"

"No," Diamond said. "It was methodical, but thorough. The place was almost completely destroyed. The burglar was looking for something. He took apart everything. Cut open the cushions. Opened up every appliance. Took off switch plates. Tore the toilet paper holders off the walls. Dumped out spaghetti jars. Emptied the contents of the freezer and thawed it all in the microwave. Cut through the hamburger, shook out the peas, spread peanut butter and jam across newspaper. You get the idea. But he must have been interrupted because he only got through two-thirds of the place. The back two bedrooms upstairs were untouched."

"He must have been looking for something small, if it could be hidden inside peanut butter," I said.

"And he was motivated."

"Small and very valuable."

"So it seems." Diamond sounded weary. "You want to have a look?"

"Yeah. But I have some things I need to do with Leah, so it will be later today. Say, two o'clock."

"Meet you there," Diamond said.

SEVENTEEN

I waited twenty, then knocked on the bathroom door. "Are you okay?"

There was no response.

I knocked again, then cracked open the door. Leah was reclining in the tub, her head against the wall. She still wore her bra and underwear. The suds were gone. The water was probably cold.

"Are you okay?" I said again. "Do you want your water warmed up?"

She nodded. I walked in, shutting the door behind me. I bent down by the faucet and felt the water. It was tepid at best. Leah was once again shivering. It worried me that she hadn't had the willpower to turn on the warm water. I turned the knob and stirred it as hot water flowed in so it wouldn't burn her feet. I added more shampoo, creating another layer of insulating suds.

The excess water flowed down the overflow drain.

When the tub was hot, I turned it off.

"I'll give you a few minutes to warm up."

I left the bathroom and went through the backpack to see what of Street's clothes Diamond had found at my cabin. There were a couple of shirts, slacks, and pair of jeans, none of which would fit Leah. Leah wasn't heavy, but Street was very thin. Fortunately, there was also a set of sweats, which would stretch to fit Leah. I was glad to see that there was none of Street's underwear in the bag. I was happy that Diamond had a key to my place and could use it as he wanted, but I wanted to think that when he found Street's underthings in my drawers, he'd leave them be. And anyway, they'd be too small to be useful for Leah. My underwear would have to do. Diamond had grabbed several pair, obviously expecting that I shouldn't return to my cabin any time soon.

I knocked, then brought the clothes into the bathroom. "I have

Street's sweats along with one of my T-shirts and a pair of my jockey shorts. They'll be too big for you, but perhaps they're better than nothing. You can decide. Will you be okay draining the tub and getting dressed?"

Another nod.

I left the bathroom.

I heard sounds, and five long minutes later she emerged. Her long black hair was tousled, but otherwise she looked normal.

I handed her shoes to her. "We are leaving for a few hours."

She moved slowly and mechanically. In another five minutes, we were out the door and crammed into Maria's truck, Leah sitting next to me, Spot sitting on the right side, his head bent against the headliner. Leah reached her hands around his neck and head. Not to pet him. Just to hang on.

I drove across town and stopped at the supermarket.

"Requests for food?"

Leah shook her head.

I didn't like leaving her in the pickup, but Spot was with her. I'd only be a few minutes.

Back in the truck, we headed out 89, past Camp Rich and around Emerald Bay. It was a classic summer day in Tahoe, with hot sun in an azure cloudless sky. Although the weather had warmed back up to normal from the earlier cold spell, the air coming off the mountain snowpack was cool, a delicious contrast with the hot sun.

Emerald Bay was brilliant against the snow-covered slopes that rose up like walls on either side, living up to every bit of its postcard promise. As always until the 4th of July, the tourists and boats were few, and we had the world's most beautiful place mostly to ourselves.

I considered stopping and hiking down to the bay, but I wanted to go where there'd be fewer people. So I headed on past, and continued north several miles to D.L. Bliss State Park.

There were summer campers in their tents and 5th wheels, but the hiking crowd was minimal. And because it was a June weekday, we had the Rubicon Trail almost to ourselves.

Leah was silent as we went out the path that led all the way to Emerald Bay. The first part of the trail goes along a vertical wall of rock that extends from 100 feet above the water to 1200 feet below, one of the tallest fresh-water, under-water cliffs in the world. The color of the water is an artist's dream, a deep cerulean that quickly blends to dark ultramarine. On a lake known for superlative color, the Rubicon Trail is near the top of the list of viewpoints.

Leah didn't appear to notice the water. She hiked as if she were on a refugee march, keeping her head down as she followed Spot. I wondered if she were so familiar with the trail that it was an automatic hike. But when we came to the rocky overhang with the cliff railing and the duck-under boulders the size of apartment buildings, she looked at the trail as if she'd never been down this famous hike, a glaring omission for the host of Tahoe Live.

Spot stopped at one of the overlooks and gazed down at a yacht that was tucked in next to the cliff, ten stories below. Three girls in red, yellow, and green bikinis lay on its foredeck, while two men in tennis whites sat in captain's chairs on the high bridge. The white boat against the dark blue water looked like a tourist brochure photo that had been Photoshopped to make the colors pop unnaturally. On the slope above and behind us were the remains of the old West-Shore lighthouse, the highest-altitude lighthouse in the world.

As we caught up to Spot, he turned and trotted ahead.

I thought Leah would be hypoglycemic from hiking on so little fuel, but she didn't complain.

A couple of miles south, past the shore cliffs, where the trail leaves the lake and heads toward Emerald Bay, I called Spot. He returned from down the trail.

"We're leaving the trail, here," I said to Leah, and I turned into the forest.

We bushwhacked through the woods, walking around several old-growth Ponderosa pines that had escaped the 19th Century clear-cut of Tahoe's forests. Perfectly situated to Tahoe's climate of big-snow winters followed by very dry summers, the trees are monsters compared to their Rocky Mountain brothers. With some of them six or more feet in diameter, each stand of two or three form a temple of sorts, a sacred place that inspires awe.

I looked up at them, taking a deep breath as I considered what nature can produce if left alone by man.

Leah didn't notice. She paused where I paused, but she just looked at the ground.

Our destination was a secret beach, a crescent of sand and rock that rarely sees human footprints. I chose a sitting place in front of an old barkless log weathered smooth by the years. The sand made a soft seat and the log a comfortable backrest. The lake was a backdrop of unnaturally clear water.

Leah sat nearby. I handed her a sandwich and her own mini-bag of chips, hoping ownership of the bag would induce her to eat them all. I opened the small bag of dry dog food and propped it some distance away to minimize the danger that Spot might shake his slobber our way.

Leah ate slowly, but normally. She finished the sandwich, chips, apple and water.

I gave her time and space and let her relax in front of the gorgeous blue waves lapping at the shore.

After a half-hour of post-prandial silence punctuated by nothing other than watching Spot wade into the water to drink and stick his head under in pursuit of interesting objects on the sand below, I decided it was time for Leah to begin talking. Step two or three of Owen's medical arsenal. I suspected that she would be reticent. But I knew it was critical that she start processing what had happened to her. Talking about it was the best way.

"Leah?" I said.

She didn't respond.

"Why do you think someone wanted your father dead?"

"I don't know." The words were slow.

"What about you? Why would someone want you dead?"

She stared at the sand. "I don't know that, either."

"The man who pounded on your father's door when I showed up. Do you know who he is?"

Leah stared at the lake, her eyes slightly narrowed.

I waited.

"Not really," she said.

"What does that mean? Have you seen him before?"

"Yes."

"Where?"

It was a long half-minute before she spoke. "At a work party. It went late. We were in a back office. We... I don't know what to call it."

EIGHTEEN

Whatever answer I expected, it wasn't that.

"What is his name?"

Another pause. "I don't know."

"You had a relationship with a man whose name you don't know."

"It wasn't a relationship. It was just some kissing. And some touching. Too much touching. I'd drunk too much. I led him on. Then I said no before it went all the way. I never asked his name. It was, I don't know, a strange way of keeping things less intimate. A few days later he began stalking me. It was my fault. I never should have given him ideas."

"Stalking is never the victim's fault."

"I've heard people say that," Leah said, "but I was stupid." Leah looked down at the sand, picked up a twig, twirled it in her fingers, then snapped it in two.

She spoke in a deliberate, slow cadence.

"My husband Ruben was a good man. He was reliable, talented and worked very hard at his cooking even if he didn't make much money. My father adored him, and the few acquaintances we see thought he was a gem. Ruben had a real enthusiasm for life. It was that enthusiasm that kept me going through all six years of our marriage. Six years with no intimacy."

Leah stopped and drew in the sand with the broken twig. Spot was over in the trees, his mouth around what looked like a piece of wood, trying to jerk it free from some brush. As it came partway off the ground, I saw that it was a five-inch log about ten feet long.

"I never had much romance before I met Ruben," Leah said. "I wasn't what you'd call real experienced. I took a cooking class, and Ruben was the teacher. He was thirty-three. I was thirty-five. I'd just started my TV show. On our first date, he took me to Evan's for a champagne and steak dinner. He was a dream. I was even drawn to his seeming reluctance to have sex until we were married. Not that he made a big deal of it, he just said, 'let's wait' when I sort of pushed for it. I found it hopelessly romantic.

"But after we were married it never happened. There was always a reason why. He had a thousand reasons."

"Do you know the real reason?" I was surprised at Leah's sudden loquaciousness. Maybe she'd wanted to tell someone for a long time.

Leah shook her head. She was still looking down at the sand, drawing Xs with the broken twig. Spot had gotten the log separated from the brush. He held it up in the air like he was doing neck exercises with a very long, 80-pound barbell. He walked toward the beach, but the log hit a tree on the right. It curved his path in a clockwise direction until the log hit another tree on the left, stopping him. He backed up a few feet, tried again, was stopped again. Spot looked at me across the sand, the log held high.

"I still don't know why Ruben never wanted me," Leah said. "He said he wasn't gay. I never got any sense that he was gay. I don't think he had, you know, equipment problems. I don't think he secretly didn't find me attractive. It was more that he was asexual. I've read about it. Christ, in my stress and worry, I've read enough to become quite an expert about it. There are many men with low testosterone, and they have low libidos. We had Ruben tested, and his hormones were on the low side, but not too much. There are also men who have relationship issues, feelings that they aren't wanted or loved, and that can kill sex drive. So I pushed for counseling.

"Ruben finally agreed. We were in therapy for many months. The psychologist concluded that Ruben was one of those rare men who are otherwise healthy, but simply don't want sex. They don't know why it happens. Something wrong in part of the brain. Like those people who don't have a sense of smell. It is very rare, but I fell in love with one of them."

Her voice was still monotone, but it was the most she'd spoken since the shooting.

Spot dropped the log and stared at it, his head down, jowls drooping. Maybe if he looked at it long enough, it would solve the problem.

"Ruben tried to make me feel better. He insisted that it wasn't anything about me. He even said he thought I was beautiful. Imagine that."

"You are beautiful," I said.

"Don't do that, Owen. I can't stand it if you are going to lie or patronize me."

"I'm not. You have very pretty eyes, eyebrows like some kind of architectural wonder, and great cheekbones. I thought so the first time I saw your show."

Leah reached up and ran her finger along the scar from the car accident. The cord of pink tissue wrapped below the crest of her left cheekbone and back to the missing portion of her ear. Nearby was the new set of stitches where the fragment of broken glass from the shooting opened her cheek anew.

"Well, whatever I had is gone now," she said.

"After wounds have healed," I said, "plastic surgeons can often go back in and take out the scars, neaten things up a bit."

"Sure, neaten up my ear nub. I'll be an earring model when they're done." Her voice was caustic.

I didn't respond.

"Anyway," she continued, "maybe I wanted to test what Ruben said, prove whether or not anything about me was in fact desirable."

Leah looked out at the water. A sailboat moved slowly north in the far distance. Spot looked at the sailboat. He picked up a smaller stick, brought it out to the sand beach, lay down with it and chewed it into little chips in a few seconds. He stood up and walked back over to where he'd left the log, stared at it some more.

"The man was one of our regular delivery drivers at the TV station. He was quite attractive in a rough kind of way. He was unsophisticated in his manner. The opposite of Ruben. He would drop off packages, and while he waited for me to sign for them, I could tell that he looked at me. He even said suggestive things now and then. He'd say that I looked fit, and did I work out and did I have a boyfriend. Things like that. He was the opposite of my type. Ruben was my type. But look where that got me."

Leah stared at the lake. Once or twice, she'd begun to glance at me as she spoke, but then she quickly looked away, unable to face me.

"The truck driver sort of exuded a sexual magnetism. He was very fit and muscular, and he walked as if his every move was a challenge to women. It was if his body language said, I dare you to resist me.

"Well, we'd told him and our other regular delivery driver about a birthday party we were having for Cindy after work. They both stopped by. We played music, drank margaritas, and we all danced around like kids. Later, I was talking to this driver. We were in the back office. Things got suggestive. It was like a game. He was pushy, and I was tempting him to go further.

"After awhile, I stopped him. He was angry about it. He protested at first. But when I insisted that it would go no further, he got mad and left. He stomped out like a little boy. I was traumatized by the experience. And it happened just a few days before the accident. I haven't been on solid ground ever since."

"And you never learned his name," I said.

"No. He started stalking me the next day. Following me to my car after work. Saying lewd things. Parking in the street outside of my house. Watching me. And after the car accident, he somehow found out that I'd gone to live with my father after I got out of the hospital. No one knew where my father lived. But the man showed up there. How he found out, I don't know. I thought I'd die when he came to the house. I never opened the door. I haven't spoken to him since before the car accident. He frightens me."

"Did you get a restraining order?"

"No. I thought about it before the accident, but I was too embarrassed. I knew my behavior would come out and be the talk of the town. Since the accident, I haven't had the mental wherewithal to deal with it. And now my father is dead. And someone wants me dead."

"Do you think the stalker killed your father?"

Leah shook her head. "No. I think he is a natural thug. I think he may have sociopathic tendencies, but cold-blooded murder? I don't think he's capable of that. Do you? My God, do you think I started something that resulted in my father's death?" She looked at me in horror. She began shaking her head, over and over. "I couldn't live with that. I couldn't possibly carry on..."

"No, I don't think so," I said. "My guess is that this is about something more than a jilted would-be lover. But I have to ask the questions. We have to consider the possibility that the stalker was going to shoot you and missed and got your father instead."

Leah still looked horrified.

"Do you know where he lives?" I asked.

"No."

"Can you find out his name?"

"Yes, I suppose... But I'd have to call the women at the station. I don't think that I could make that phone call. They don't know that he and I..."

"What else do you know about this man?"

"Very little."

Leah leaned over sideways until she was lying on the beach. She curled up in a fetal position, her black hair mixing with the sand.

Tired from his logging activities, Spot walked over and lay down next to her.

"One month," Leah said. "That's all it took for my life to be destroyed. And maybe it was my stupid actions that started this nightmare."

"You can rebuild your life," I said.

"No, Owen, I can't!" she yelled without moving. I saw the sand near her mouth jump from the violent air movement of her words. "I can never get my old life back!"

NINETEEN

We sat on the sand in silence for a few minutes, getting some distance on Leah's outburst. I had many questions I needed answers to, but I waited. She'd gone from being nearly mute over the previous day and a half to talking, her pent-up thoughts finally coming out. I didn't want to prod too much and get an adverse reaction. Better to wait and see.

Eventually, she spoke.

"When my husband died in the accident last month, I thought it was the end of the world." Her words came slowly, and her voice exuded depression. "I don't think I loved him very much or very well, and obviously we had serious problems, but he was very important to me." She pushed herself up, knees to her chest, then straightened one leg out across the sand. She had on Street's lavender socks, which came two inches short of the black sweatpants. Pale, dry skin showed between. "Now my father is dead. In some ways, he was a cranky old man, but I adored him. He did everything for me."

Leah turned her head and looked at me. Her eyes brimmed with tears. "I don't know what to do," she said, her voice a whisper. She grimaced with emotional pain, her left cheek folding in an unusual way because of the puckering of the fresh scar.

She took a deep breath. "I've been questioning everything, including Ruben's death in the car accident. Maybe someone wants to kill me. In the first attempt, Ruben died. In the second attempt, my father died."

"That could be," I said. "But it could also be that Ruben's death was about Ruben, and your father's death was about him."

"I can't imagine why anyone would want to kill either of them," she said. "They were both good men. Sure, my father was gruff, but if you got to know him you'd agree that he was as honorable as a person can be. And he could be a sweetheart."

Leah looked up at the blue sky. "Once when I was very young he was showing me the stars. I asked him if I could ever go to the stars and he said, 'Always dream big, my little Leah. Dream big, and you could go to the stars.'"

I wondered if she routinely reached back to this single old memory in order to believe that her father was sweet. I waited before I spoke.

"Try to think of any friction in his life," I said. "Business relationships gone bad. Someone he upset. Did your father have any recent disagreements with anyone?"

Leah shook her head. "Not that I know of. He didn't see anyone. There wasn't anyone to have a disagreement with. He was a loner."

"Did he have any old feuds from the past?"

Another head shake.

"Did he ever get in trouble with the law?"

"No trouble ever, that I know of."

"Was he a drinker? Did he go to bars?"

"He drank wine and brandy. Never very much. But he didn't go to bars. He always drank alone. A glass of wine with dinner and a little brandy after."

I kept throwing out ideas, hoping that something would trigger a memory. "There are several motives that could have applied. For example, he might have angered someone to an explosive degree, or double-crossed them on a business deal."

"I don't think he had any business deals. And he wouldn't double-cross someone if he did."

"He might have represented a threat to someone."

Leah frowned. "How?"

"He could have witnessed a crime and threatened to turn someone in."

"I don't think so," she said. "It wasn't like he was involved in the kind of things where crime is a factor. He went for long walks. He read the New York Times. He read books. He occasionally watched movies on late-night TV. He listened to NPR on the radio."

"Did he have any relationships with women?" I asked. "Could he have had an affair with another man's wife or girlfriend?"

Leah didn't reply for a time. I couldn't tell if she was pondering my question or if she was thinking of her own life. Eventually, she said, "I think he'd recently been seeing a woman. But I don't think he would see a married woman, or someone who was involved with another man."

"He mentioned a woman?"

Leah shook her head. "No. But he acted different in the last couple of weeks. One night he was quite nervous when he came home. He couldn't sit still. He kept watching the clock. I couldn't place the pattern at the time.

"Then, the next morning, he dressed in very nice clothes and left early. Finally, I realized that it was as if he'd gone out on a date. As soon as I thought of it, his behavior fit. He would be like that. He would get nervous."

"You have no idea who it could be?"

"No. None at all.

"He's never introduced you to a woman?"

"No. In fact, since my mother left, I've never seen him with a woman in my entire life. He's always been a loner. His only social interaction is when he's running errands, going to the store, places like that."

"He was a retired doctor, right?"

She nodded.

"What did he practice?"

"He was a dermatologist."

"Any holdover problems from his career? Patients who felt he harmed them by misjudging their situation?"

Leah shook her head.

"Most doctors own their own homes," I said. "Your father rented. Any reason?"

"He was conservative. He thought housing prices were going to fall. He sold his house at a good time. Renting suited him. He liked knowing he didn't have to keep track of the maintenance."

"So he had no financial problems?"

"No. None that I'm aware of."

"Was he wealthy?"

Leah paused. "No. He gave all his money away. He believed in charity for children." She sounded resentful. Maybe she thought she'd been ignored.

"I talked to Lauren Phelter, his landlord. She said that your father's sister in Boston told her that your father lost everything."

Leah shook her head. "My father didn't share his personal life or his financial decisions with Aunt Amy. She has no clue about us."

"Did he ever work a part-time job?"

"No."

I picked up my water bottle and drank the rest of it. Leah saw me and, apparently unaware of her actions, did the same.

"What happened to your mother?" I asked.

"She left when I was four. I have only a foggy memory of her."

"Why did she leave?"

"I never knew. Dad never spoke of it."

"Did you ask?"

Leah thought about it. "Somehow I knew not to ask. Like I said, dad is fiercely private. Fiercely proud." She stopped. Her eyes filled. "Was," she said. She reached up with both arms, put the fingers of one hand inside the sleeve of the other arm and used the fabric to blot her tears. "Maybe it's his Japanese heritage. He never spoke about why she left. Maybe he couldn't stand to think about why she left us." Leah reached over and gave Spot a single pet between his ears. He opened his eyes halfway, then shut them.

"What do you know about her?"

"Not much. I believe she had some kind of mental illness. Dad said she was an amazing artist, a watercolor painter. He said that her paintings were more real to her than the real world was. Like she was disconnected from the here and now and lived in a fictional world that she created on watercolor paper."

Leah gazed off toward the distant sky. "He often spoke of her in an idealistic way. She was pure. Unfettered by the tedium of reality. He said she lived in a dream-state where there was justice, and good triumphed over evil, and moral ambiguity didn't exist. She worshipped color. She didn't care about material possessions except those that had value as tools or symbols."

"What do you mean?" I asked.

"Well, her brushes, for example. Dad said that mom's paintbrushes were not just her tools, but extensions of herself.

"Let me explain. Dad met her at Berkeley, where he was an associate professor at the Medical School. The first time he saw her, she was sitting on the grass on campus doing a watercolor painting.

He stopped to talk to her, and she went off on some long-winded talk about brushes and how they were the most important tools in life. He said that her strangeness and her enthusiasm was captivating. So he began to stop by the same place where she often painted.

"He later found out that she was a nursing student and that she'd enlisted in the army. So when she was sent overseas, he sent her a set of expensive brushes, wrapped in a special type of brush holder. She still had it when they married a few years later. It's one of the few things I remember from when I was a little girl. It had a flower pattern, and little green beads on the edges of it, and when it was rolled up, the beads came together at the end of the roll. They sparkled like a hundred tiny emeralds. It was quite beautiful. Like a little baton with glowing green ends."

Leah pushed her hands down into the sand, lifting herself a little so she could scoot back and lean against the big fallen log.

"Long after I grew up, I came to understand that the military gave her an early discharge because of medical problems. Mental problems. Dad once said that there was mention about her disassociation from reality. I think he maybe agreed with them in principle, but he clearly thought they were wrong in many ways. I forget what the psychological terms were, but he said that they made some point about how she projected an unhealthy significance onto her brushes. That she treated them like pets, as if they were alive. Dad was very disdainful of the military doctor's judgements. He said it was true that her brushes were important to her, but that it wasn't to a detrimental degree. Dad said that she never thought they were actually alive, just that she thought they were important tools. So when she talked to them, it was like a carpenter naming his tools, or saying to his hammer, 'C'mon, hit that nail.'

"I'm a painter, too," Leah continued. "Although nowhere near as skillful as my father, or, based on what he's said about her, my mother. But I understand the importance of paintbrushes. And if she were trapped in a rigid military hierarchy, she would have seen her brushes as tools for her independence, mechanisms for escape. I've only seen a few of her paintings, some landscapes and a picture of the brushes he gave her, painted by those very brushes. She mailed it to him from overseas as a thank-you for his gift. It still sits on his dresser. It is quite spectacular. The brushes look absolutely real and alive."

"Like a photo?" I said. "I'm always amazed at how painters can do that."

"No, it's not photo-real," Leah said. "Some painters feel that hyper-realism is too literal and less artistic than other approaches. My mother's watercolor is done in a painterly style. Yet, even with the somewhat soft focus of the marks, those brushes still look like they actually exist.

"Dad said she could paint anything," Leah continued. "If so, her brushes gave her a doorway into a new world. And for an artist like my mother, which world would be more attractive? Where would she want to spend her time? In the strict world of military command, or the freeing world of her imagination?"

"People have always imbued tokens with great significance," I said. "Lucky coins, special lockets, trinkets and charms. But those are inanimate objects. Whereas brushes provide practical value. I can see that they could take on much more meaning."

"Right. Dad said that she talked to her brushes as if they were imaginary friends. I've heard the story many times about how my mother would say out loud, 'if you guys are safe, then I'm safe.'

"Then she'd kiss the brush holder before she'd put it into her paint box."

"Have you ever heard from her since she left?"

Leah shook her head. "No. It has always been painful. When I was young, I spent some time with a counselor, trying to come to terms with it, trying to believe that it wasn't my fault, that I hadn't so disappointed her that she left her only child. The psychologist tried very hard to convince me that my mother leaving was about her and not about me. Most of the time I think that's true. But it still bothers me."

"Is she still alive?"

"I have no idea. She'd only be in her sixties, so it's certainly possible."

I scooped up sand and let it sift through my fingers, the small grains falling through, the bigger bits catching and staying behind. I opened my hand to look at those larger pieces, broken pine needles, a part of some kind of shell, a shiny pebble fractured down the middle.

"You mentioned your father acting nervous one night when he came home. It sounded as if it was a regular thing, him coming home in the evening. Was he often gone during the day?"

"Usually, yes. He would walk. Nearly every day."

"For how long?" I asked.

"Hours. Although, now that I say that, I realize it wasn't strictly true. When those storms came in last week, he didn't go. I think he didn't want to go out driving in the snow."

"Where did he walk?"

"I don't know. It was one of those things that would be prying if I asked."

"Like asking about your mother."

"Yes." Leah turned so that she was leaning sideways against the log, her arm lifted over it. She had long fingernails, and she used one to trace the hieroglyphic patterns the bark beetles had chewed in the wood under the bark, patterns revealed now that the bark had sloughed off the dead tree.

"Please don't judge me," she said.

"I'm not. I'm just trying to understand. In the last few weeks, when you were living at your father's house, did he ever say anything unusual?"

"As I've explained, much about him was different. He often said things that others would think were unusual."

"I don't mean in contrast to others. I mean, did he do or say anything that was unusual for him?"

Leah shook her head. "Aside from the time he had what I think was a date, no. He was always..." She stopped. Her eyes searched the air, seeing internally. "Well, there was one thing he said that was sort of unusual."

I waited.

She thought about it. "After the car accident that killed my husband..." Leah stopped mid-sentence and stared at the lake. It was obvious she was seeing the carnage from a month before. "The hit-and-run driver was in an old dump truck. It was big and heavy, with a huge bumper. It caved in Ruben's door with an astonishing impact. It bounced our car off the road, and we rolled over. I could tell that Ruben was dead. His body was..." She stopped, swallowed, continued.

"What wasn't in the paper was that the truck driver got out and walked over to our crushed car. It was dark, and I couldn't see him well, but I could tell that he had some kind of mask on. He reached in through the broken window and dropped a claw onto Ruben's body. It was like he didn't care if I saw him. Maybe he even wanted me to see him. Or maybe he thought I was dead. Then he got back in the dump truck and left. Just then, two other drivers stopped, and they saw the dump truck drive away. They later identified it to the cops, but it turned out to be stolen. It was abandoned a few miles away." Leah stopped.

"Sergeant Martinez told me about it," I said. "Can you describe the claw?"

"It was small, maybe an inch long, like from a crayfish or something. It was gross. It still had some dried flesh on it."

"You were saying your father did something unusual."

"Yes. Later, in the hospital, my father visited every day. I told him about the truck driver and how he put the claw in our car. Dad got very pale. Almost white. It looked like he was going to be sick. Then he took my hand and said he was so sorry. He said he could never tell me how sorry he was."

"Why?"

"He said the accident was all his fault."

TWENTY

"Do you think your father meant that the accident was purpously caused because of something he did? Or that it was murder?"

"I've thought about it. But it doesn't seem possible. So I wondered if he just thought he'd gone wrong in being so supportive of Ruben. Like if I hadn't married him, then I never would have been in the car that night with Ruben driving."

"You said his face went pale when he heard about the crayfish claw. Why would that bother him so much?"

"I don't know. I think it's just so creepy. Dropping dead animal parts into our car after causing an accident is like something out of a horror movie. It's pretty sick."

Leah touched her wedding ring, rotated it a few times. "Maybe dad thought that Ruben was involved in something bad."

"Do you think that?"

"No. I think Ruben was one of those really innocent guys. He just wanted to teach and practice his cooking. He was a quiet man most of the time. His outlet was inventing new dishes. His idea of a good time was to work in the kitchen all alone and cook for eight hours. He was similar to my father in that he didn't go out and engage much with other people. So I can't imagine him getting involved in something where he could do something bad enough that someone would want to kill him."

"Yet it sounds like your father thought Ruben's death was murder?"

"I suppose it's possible."

"The point when he said it was his fault was when you told him about the claw?"

"Right. He didn't say why. But I was foggy from shock and drugs, so it didn't make much sense to me."

"Did you ask him about the claw later?"

"Yes, after I got out of the hospital and came to stay with him, I tried to ask him about it. He did this thing he's always done to shush me up. He holds up his finger, closes his eyes, and shakes his head. He would say, 'Not now.' And that was it. That meant I wasn't to bring it up again."

"He sounds very controlling."

"Yes, he was in many ways. But it wasn't because he was a natural dictator. It was more because he was afraid to have me confront reality. It was his idea of how to protect me from the world."

I stood up to stretch my legs and back. Spot lifted his head to see what I was doing, decided I wasn't going anywhere, and lowered it back to the sand. I took a few steps away, deciding how to phrase my next question.

"Leah, the man who shot your father tried to shoot you in my Jeep."

Leah's face looked numb, as if she shut down at the thought.

"Somebody wants to kill you. You've already asked yourself if the car accident was an attempt on your life. In retrospect, it certainly looks like it. Can you think of a reason why someone would want you dead?"

She moved her head side-to-side in a slow shake. "I've tried to think about it, but it doesn't make sense to me. What have I ever done to anyone?" She was emphatic.

"All those questions I asked about your dad," I said. "Do any of them apply to you? Any altercations with anyone, any deals gone bad, someone who feels you've crossed them? Anything that would make someone very angry at you?"

"No." Again her voice was firm. Too firm, I thought.

I pressed on. "What about your show? Did you ever do anything like an exposé on Tahoe Live? Did your show ever make anyone mad?"

Leah was still shaking her head. "I already told you, no." She was insistent. Frustrated. "I did segments on having fun in Tahoe. Skiing, boating, hiking, stuff like that. No one's going to kill me for that."

She stood up, flush-faced. Spot got up and walked toward her. But Leah turned away from him and walked off the beach, back into the forest.

Spot turned and looked at me, confused, his forehead wrinkled with worry.

I gathered our things, stuffed them in the backpack, and followed. It wasn't clear to me why she'd suddenly left. I'd kept asking questions of a traumatized woman. I'd been focused on the task, ignoring the person. Maybe I'd pushed her too far, handled it wrong.

Her abrupt change in mood felt as if the sun had been partially eclipsed. The world darkened a shade.

It was hard not to beat myself up over my misreading of the cues. When I bumped into the stalker, I witnessed the threat that Lauren Phelter had clearly articulated and hired me to stop. So how did I respond?

By eating TexMex with Diamond while a killer was setting up shop in the woods behind the Phelter guesthouse.

Never mind whether or not the stalker was the killer. His presence still made it clear to anyone with half a brain that things were going very badly in the world of Kiyosawa. The only way the stalker's anger and innuendo could have been more threatening would have been if he'd said he was going to come back shooting.

The fact that Leah and her father were so afraid that they stayed hidden and did not call the police was as specific an indication of life under assault as I've ever seen.

So the proprietor of McKenna Investigations made a crack about being persistent, put his card in the door, and was swigging Diamond's beer twenty-five minutes later.

Old man Kiyosawa got dead, and the lovely talk-show lady got almost-dead two or three times.

TWENTY-ONE

I called Diamond on my cell phone while I walked. It was a potential breach of privacy, and a safety risk, broadcasting my location to the cell phone network computers, but I needed to get him the information. I kept my voice low. Leah was so far ahead of me that I was confident she couldn't hear my words.

Spot came trotting down the trail toward me as Diamond's phone rang. He tagged me with his nose, then turned and trotted back to catch up to Leah.

"The stalker," I said when Diamond answered, "was a regular delivery driver at the TV station that aired Leah's show. They got semi-intimate at a work party. But she stopped him. He started stalking her after that night. Leah doesn't know how he found out that she went to live with her father after the accident, nor how he learned where her father lived. The man scared her, and she never opened the door. It shouldn't be too hard to track him down."

"Name?" Diamond asked.

"She doesn't know."

"But you said..."

"Yeah, but she didn't want to know his name."

"That's a new one," he said. "Okay, let me see what I can find out. You still coming to Lady Phelter's guesthouse?"

"We're about an hour away."

"Will you bring Leah? She should see what I've found. She may have a comment."

"Will do."

I hung up. We continued to hike, separated by a hundred yards and a lot of discomfort, to Maria's truck. Leah let Spot in the passenger door first, so she wouldn't have to sit close to me. I had to shove Spot's body back toward Leah and into a proper sitting position so that I could fit behind the wheel. He sat with his butt over against Leah, his front feet on the floor next to mine and his jaw resting on the dash, nose up against the windshield glass. His ears were tickled by the windshield and he flicked them sideways, the little rhinestone stud making a tiny tick-tick noise as it struck the glass.

We'd driven a good distance before I spoke. "Do you think you're ready to go back to your father's house? The cleaning crew came to take care of the earlier mess, but the place was burglarized last night. It's a risk taking this truck there, but Sergeant Martinez wants you to see the place, see if you can help."

Leah didn't seem shocked, which didn't surprise me. What could shock a person after what she'd been through?

"Why would someone break in? You don't murder someone so you can break in a few nights later."

"You'd think," I said.

We drove back around Emerald Bay and on into town, then headed up Kingsbury Grade. I parked Maria's truck next to Diamond's Douglas County cruiser.

"Are you okay with coming inside?" I asked.

She thought about it. "Is the blood gone?"

"I don't know. The shattered windows are still there. It will remind you of what happened."

She stared out the windshield, not looking up at the house, not seeing anything. Her eyes looked dead. She didn't move. "I don't think I can take any more of this," she said.

"Sargeant Martinez and I need your help. Think of what your father would want. He'd want you to do what you can to help us find the killer, and then get on with your life."

I worried about her, about the impact that seeing the house would have. I felt like I was in a cave-dark maze, feeling my way on all fours, looking for a route to sunshine. But her life was nearly destroyed. Maybe there was no way out of the cave, no route to the light. And maybe the deep, whispered, labored exertion noises in my head were Grendel, the evil monster, just on the other side of the maze partition, coming to enjoy his next feast.

I realized I was gripping the wheel of Maria's old truck as if I were driving through a blizzard instead of sitting parked in the street in front of Lauren Phelter's guesthouse.

"You are a strong woman, Leah. You have the kind of constitution that can take an idea and start a business, tackle the thousand problems that need to be solved, build a following, handle all the complications that come with it, create something significant out of thin air. This thing in your life is the biggest problem you've ever had. The ultimate test. You lose your loved ones, you lose your center.

"So you have a choice to make, two options to choose from. The first option is, you can give up. That's the easiest thing to do. Just stop struggling and let the monster take you down.

"Or you can fight back," I continued. "I think people should fight. I know that many of them won't be any good at it. They don't have the mental or physical resources. They don't have anyone to help. They will lose.

"But some of them, the ones who have the extra courage, the extra determination, the ones whose inner fire burns a little hotter than the rest, they will eventually win the battle. It won't be easy. And they will suffer emotional terror and physical torment. But they are the ones who will slay the beast. They will grab Grendel by his hairy throat, sear him with one final burning look into his evil, rheumy eyes, and choke the life out of him."

My voice had risen, and I found myself taking heavy breaths.

Leah spoke in a slow, low voice. "What is Grendel? Some kind of monster?"

"Yes. Sergeant Martinez told me about him. Grendel is from an old epic poem. He is the worst that life can throw at you. But I believe that if you have enough desire, then you have the power to crush him."

Leah sat at the side of the pickup's seat, Spot pushing against her from her left side. Her breathing was fast and shallow. She pinched her lower lip under her front teeth, let it go, pinched it again. She forced a few deep breaths, shut her eyes, went to that deep place where you close the doors and shut out the inputs. Where you take a count of your emotional inventories, gauge your stock, make the ultimate measure of your situation. Come to a difficult decision.

Eventually, she spoke, her words slow. "I don't know if I can do it, face down this... this Grendel. It's so difficult." She stopped, took a single deep breath and let it out.

"Can you try?"

She fingered a series of sun-dried stress cracks in the old plastic of the dashboard, cracks that gathered together until they met at a large hole in the dash that looked like it had been caused by an explosion.

She nodded.

I got out, went around and opened her door. Leah got out, holding onto Spot like before, and we headed to the guesthouse.

TWENTY-TWO

The front door was unlocked. We let ourselves in. The deputy named Jackson was there. "Sergeant's in the kitchen," he said, gesturing with his head, but keeping his eyes on Spot. Spot went to sniff him. Jackson widened his eyes, didn't move.

We found Diamond standing by the center island in the kitchen. The place was trashed. The debris from the burglar's efforts to find whatever he was looking for covered every surface.

Leah stared, but she didn't react. I noticed that she'd shifted her hair so it hung down over her scarred cheek and ear.

Spot left Deputy Jackson, walked around, sniffed the kitchen surfaces. I knew that a professional search dog could pick up hints of a person days later, and, under the right conditions, alert if they encountered that person. Like any other dog, Spot could pick up every odor in the house including whatever smells were left by the intruder. But there were too many human scents unaccounted for to make it useful information for all but the best trained dogs. It was equivalent to a human investigator looking at many footprints in the dirt around a house. If there are enough different kinds, it is an ineffective way of identifying a burglar.

Diamond came over. "Guy made a mess, but was careful. Wore gloves, maybe even a hair net. We haven't found so much as fiber from his clothing. Come with me." He was all business. No questions to Leah about how she was doing. Probably a good thing.

We followed him.

"Anything interesting?" I said as we went up the stairs.

"Mostly, it was interesting what we didn't find. The burglar managed to rip apart most of the house before he quit. It looks like he got interrupted and scared off by something. His progress through the upstairs was obvious." Diamond got to the top of the stairs and stopped.

"He started in the first bedroom," Diamond said, pointing through one of the doors, "then moved into the bathroom. Tore both all to hell. In the second bedroom, he quit halfway through. Take a look at where he stopped." Diamond walked into the second bedroom. "He was taking off switch-plate covers." Diamond pointed to three covers removed. "Now look at this one. One of the screws is out. The other was only half unscrewed. It's pretty clear he was still searching when he stopped abruptly."

Diamond gestured around the room. "So the boys and I have been continuing his search. Only money we've found is a quarter under the bed. Only drugs are several bottles of aspirin. That was it. No secret stash of stamps, no treasure maps, no rare wine collection, nothing I can see that deserved a search mission."

"What about surprises?" I asked. "Things you wouldn't expect to find."

"Just one item," Diamond said. He walked into the master bedroom and over to a small wooden desk. On it was a small framed watercolor painting depicting Leah's mother's brush holder with the brushes lined up in order of size.

Diamond reached an object out of a little wooden box on top of the desk, and handed it to me.

"A crawdad claw," he said, dropping it into my outstretched palm.

Leah saw it, gasped and jerked back.

"Just like the one the dump truck driver put into your car after the accident," Diamond said.

I turned to Leah. "So that's why your father reacted when you told him about the claw. He'd already had a connection with someone who gave him a claw. It indicated to your father that the accident was both intentional and connected to him."

"That's sick," Leah said, her voice a whisper.

"I finally realized the significance," Diamond said. "I feel stupid that I didn't see it before."

We both looked at him.

"The monster in the Beowulf poem," he said.

"Grendel," I said.

"Right. Instead of arms, Grendel had claws."

TWENTY-THREE

I turned to Leah. She was shaky, but she was holding together. Maybe the process of connecting the dots, no matter how painful, was reassuring. It meant progress.

"The man stalking you," I said, "wore a T-shirt with writing on it. I'm not positive, but I think it said Grendel."

"Yes," she said. "I remember now. I saw it through the window blinds. I didn't pay attention to it. But now that you say it said Grendel, I agree."

"Can you think of any time he referred to Grendel? Or Beowulf?"

Leah shook her head.

"Or mentioned crayfish claws? Or crayfish fishing?"

She shook her head again.

"Did he study old English poems? Did he have an interest in history? In literature?"

"No. He wasn't literate to speak of. Nothing about him would suggest he would even know who Grendel was."

Diamond said, "We caught a valley kid shoplifting. He wore a Grendel T-shirt. Did the stalker ever mention a kid or say anything that would suggest he was spending time with kids?"

"No."

"What about your father?" I said. "Did he ever mention Grendel or Beowulf?"

Leah shook her head.

"Did he ever fish for crayfish?"

"No."

"Come into his art studio room," Diamond said. "I have a question."

Leah gave him a puzzled look. "What do you mean, art studio?"

Diamond walked over to a door that led to a large walk-in closet on the left and a dressing room on the right.

The room was filled with artist supplies. Leah stopped at the door, her face showing amazement and surprise.

"My God! This door was always closed. I never knew..."

"You've been living here for three weeks," Diamond said, "and you didn't know he had an art studio?"

"My father was very private. Whenever I came to his bedroom, this door was closed."

Diamond made a small nod.

Leah walked through the door and carefully stepped onto a large drop cloth that covered the carpet. I watched as Leah explored the small room. Spot came next to me, looked at Leah, and walked in on the drop cloth, sniffing every surface and every object.

"Two or three times I thought I smelled oil paint," Leah said. "But I assumed I was adjusting to the strange smells of a new place to live."

Leah paused at a painter's mixing palette, a horizontal piece of plate glass that comprised the top of a rolling cart. On the glass were dozens of dabs of paint, in muted colors, tan and brown, and a range of greens and blues. Along one edge of the palette was an egg carton. Eight of the compartments held powdered pigments, all earth tone colors. Nearby was a wooden box with dozens of tubes of paint, twisted and squeezed into crushed shapes. One new tube of yellow paint stood out in the mix, plump and smooth, its label already sullied by paint from the painter's fingers. Next to the wooden box was a cardboard dispenser box of blue latex surgical gloves. A crumpled, used pair, covered with paint, sat nearby, three fingers of one glove pointing improbably straight out.

There was a large wooden easel and on it a canvas about 24 inches high and 30 inches wide. Leah picked it up. It had the beginnings of a painting, a horizontal line across it, with paint below and the white canvas above. On the lower edge was some bright green and on the side were some mottled areas of darker greens and browns. A few detailed marks in the dark greens looked like trees. It looked like the beginnings of a landscape. Leah set the painting down. In one corner was a cabinet with vertical dividers. One slot held another canvas. Leah pulled it out.

It was an old painting, the paint cracked and dirty. The image was a flat farm landscape, with cultivated rows of small plants. The fields were large and rectangular and interrupted by rows of raised earth. They reminded me of the levees on the floodplain just east of Sacramento.

Leah turned it over. The stretcher bars that held the canvas were dark brown with age. The back of the canvas was also brown and looked more like a tight-weave burlap sack material than an artist's canvas.

She carried the old canvas over and held it up next to the new, painting-in-progress. They weren't the same composition, but the similarity was obvious.

"Your father was an accomplished artist?" Diamond asked.

"Yeah. Dad taught me to paint when I was a child," Leah said as she set the old canvas down. "He showed me how to paint people, not landscapes. He was an excellent artist, but he always said that my mother was an even better artist than he was." She pointed through the door at the watercolor painting of paintbrushes that sat on the bedroom desk. "She did that. And you've seen the portrait of me as a kid, hanging over the mantle in the living room. Dad did that one. They were both amazing painters. It was always my dream to paint like them. I even majored in art for awhile.

"I spoke to him about my struggles with painting at the time. But I never knew that he was still interested in painting. And I never knew that he'd taken it up again. It doesn't make sense. Why would he hide his painting from me? Why wouldn't he talk to me about it?" Leah's surprise seemed genuine. "Painting is a fascinating and difficult pursuit. Talking about it is natural."

"He must have said something over the years," Diamond said, disbelief on his face.

Leah shook her head.

"You never saw any of his work?"

"Not since I was a little girl. I thought the last painting he did was the one hanging over the mantel."

"I looked at it," Diamond said, raising his eyebrows. "He was obviously very talented. It looks like something done by a master."

"He was very *skillful*," Leah corrected him in a stern tone. "He detested the use of the word talent. He often said that what people call talent is really years and years of hard work. You may be born with good vision and coordination, but you still have to study countless hours to learn to paint. Saying someone is talented, as if they were born with it, diminishes their efforts and accomplishments."

Diamond kept his face blank, perhaps thinking like me that it was good that Leah abraded him for his statement because it momentarily drew her out of her pain.

"Sorry, you're right," Diamond said. "Now that I realize you didn't know he was painting, this takes on more significance." He gestured toward the studio room. "It seems he was being so secretive. What do you think this was about?"

"His motivation for painting?" Leah said.

"Yeah. Think back over the years. Can you think of any reference he made to art? Or something he said that in retrospect makes more sense now that you know he's kept an art studio in his home, kept it secret from you?"

Leah shook her head. "No. I don't get it. Why would he do that? Keep it secret? What is the point?"

"Was he secretive about other things?" I asked.

"Beyond his privacy, no. He was taciturn. He saw no need to talk for social interaction. He spoke if he had a request or if he wanted to tell you something important. He didn't talk just to trade social niceties. But being private and taciturn is very different from being secretive. Maybe he was like me. I always wanted to go back to painting," Leah said. "Two years ago, I started painting again. Maybe it's just because it's in my blood. I would dream of it. Mixing up luscious colors. Making those brushstrokes on a clean white canvas. Maybe dad felt that pull, too. Perhaps he did it in this room as a way of experimenting with painting without having to explain to onlookers."

"But the fact that you didn't know about it even though you lived here means he must have been very careful to avoid the subject." Diamond walked into the room and picked up a scrunched paint tube from the box. "There's a lot of equipment and supplies in this room. A lot of thought and decision-making went into it. It's hard to imagine that he wouldn't talk about it. Especially considering that you are a painter, too. There must have been some awkward explanations here and there when you maybe asked him where he'd been and he would have had to make up something to avoid telling you he'd been painting in his art studio."

"Obviously, he was hiding something. As if he were painting a present for me. Or maybe he was just hiding his ambition at an age when all of his colleagues are golfing their way through retirement."

Diamond stepped backward over the wrinkled dropcloth and leaned against the wall. He seemed to be studying Leah as much as the room and its contents.

"And here's another funny thing," Leah said. She picked up the partially-painted landscape again. "This canvas is only lightly stretched. Just four staples on each side. It would be normal to have three times that many staples. It would hold the canvas tighter. Less bounce when you paint."

"Why would he do that?" Diamond asked.

"The only reason would be that he intended to take the canvas off the stretcher when he was done."

"To roll it up for shipping?" I said.

"Maybe."

As she held the painting at an angle to the light, I saw a faint grid drawn on the unpainted white areas. Each grid square was about three inches across.

"What's with the grid lines?" I asked.

"That's a simple way to transfer a sketch in your sketchbook onto the canvas. You draw a grid with pencil over the drawing that you want to paint, one line every inch or so.

"Then, on the canvas, you take charcoal and draw a similar grid, the same number of squares. But because the canvas is so much bigger than your sketch, your lines are that much farther apart, maybe four inches apart instead of one inch like in your sketchbook. Now, each square in your sketchbook corresponds to each square on the canvas. So the grid becomes your guide as you redraw your sketch, making it four times bigger. Painters have used that technique for centuries."

Leah looked around the room. She moved supplies on the shelf under the palette, lifted up some loose pieces of canvas, scanned the walls of the room. Over on a shelf, she found several pieces of paper. She lifted them up, put all but the top one back.

She held it up near the canvas. On it was a colored pencil sketch of a landscape. Superimposed over the sketch was another grid of lines, each square maybe a half inch across. She held it up next to the canvas. They matched.

"Why not just scan the sketch into your computer and then use one of those projectors to blow up the image and project it onto the canvas? Then you could just trace the outlines." Diamond said.

Leah frowned at him. "Well, I suppose you could do that. It would probably speed up the process. But then you might lose some of the painterly qualities." She pointed at the grid. "Obviously, my father was of the old school. He would feel that the ancient ways were more authentic."

"The paint goes over the canvas and covers up the charcoal?" I said, more of a statement than a question.

"Yes. Some paint and some colors are more opaque than others," Leah said. "There are some famous paintings where you can still see hints of previous paintings under the paint."

"Is that painting oil paint, or acrylic?" I asked.

"Oil," she said, without even looking at the tubes. "You can smell it in the air as soon as you walk into the room."

I sniffed the air, not sure I could tell the difference between one kind of paint and another.

"Let's sit down in the bedroom," Diamond said. He gestured toward two upholstered chairs in the corner. Leah and Diamond each took one. I sat on the bed. Spot gave me a look of anticipation.

"No, Spot. The floor has thick carpet." I pointed. His eyes drooped a little. He looked down at the floor, turned around once and lay down.

"When a person keeps something secret," Diamond said, "it is because that thing is special and something about it would be compromised if others found out. Or, something about other people would be compromised if others found out. There are lots of categories of things or concepts that can fit that perception. I want you to consider how painting could fit into it."

"I think you've lost me," Leah said.

"Let me say it this way. Maybe your father was killed because he knew something incriminating about the killer. He was putting that incriminating information into a painting. If you'd seen the painting when it was done, you would have come under threat from the killer. So your father didn't want you, or anyone else, to know about it."

Leah slowly shook her head. "It doesn't seem likely."

Diamond continued. "How about this. Your father knew the location of something valuable. A treasure of sorts. He was painting a picture that would reveal its location to whomever knew how to read the painting, someone close to him who would know how he thinks and how he might encode the painting. The painting was going to be a confessional in case he got killed when he went to try to retrieve the treasure."

Leah shook her head. "That doesn't feel right, either."

"Okay," Diamond said. "Your father had a secret art career. He made paintings that sold for good money in art galleries. Maybe he had some debts, so he kept the entire enterprise secret to avoid having to pay them. Or he was cheating the IRS."

Leah was silent.

"What do you think?" Diamond said. "Could he have had an ongoing art career? He had the gallery pay him in cash and he kept it under the table?"

Leah thought about it. "You need to know something about dad. He was rigorously ethical. He always paid his bills, paid his taxes. Whatever the reason he kept his painting to himself, it wouldn't be about trying to evade paying his debts."

"Do you have health insurance?" Diamond asked.

"What does that have to do with my father?"

"Do you?" Diamond repeated.

"No. I was self-employed as the producer and host of my TV show. My show was going well. But it was not the money-maker that people probably thought. They'd see me on TV every day and think I was rich like some big-city anchorperson. I had decent ad revenue, but I poured everything back into show promotion. I checked into my trade group to see what their group insurance coverage would cost, but it was prohibitive. And of course you can't just go out and buy health insurance as an individual unless you are quite well-to-do. My husband didn't have insurance either. He was a chef and taught as an adjunct faculty, which, basically, is the way schools get teachers without having to pay benefits. Mind you, I'm not complaining. My husband and I chose to go the self-employed route. But the reality is that health insurance is designed for groups of people. If you decide to go through life without being part of a corporate team, then you forego the support of the team."

"How did you plan to pay for your surgery after the car accident?"

"I don't know."

Diamond didn't respond.

"I have some savings. Not much. But I've lost the show." Leah reached up under her hair and unconsciously fingered her scars. She ran her finger up to the nub of her ear, then pulled her hand away as if she'd burned her finger. "If I go back on TV, the audience won't be listening to my guests or what they say. They'll be staring at my face, my crooked eye, my missing ear." She swallowed, gritted her teeth, kept her emotions under control. "I'll figure out something. Some way to earn a living. Then I can make payments to the doctor and the hospital."

"Do you know how much your surgery cost?" Diamond said.

Leah shook her head. "No. I got the bill from the local hospital. But all the major expense was at the Reno hospital. They tried to go over it with me before I left. But I couldn't face it. I said I'd call. I still intend to call them. But I haven't. I'm too... I guess I'm a bad person."

"It came to almost two hundred thousand dollars," Diamond said. "Intensive care, multiple surgeries, numerous other expenses."

"Two hundred! Oh my God. I never realized... I'm ruined. I don't even have that much equity in my house. I'll have to get three jobs." Leah looked horrified. She started to quake.

"Your father paid it," Diamond said. "Four days after you left the hospital. He drove down to Reno, walked in, and paid the bill in cash."

TWENTY-FOUR

"What?" Leah's face showed fear more than shock. "But my father didn't have that kind of money. How could he pay it? I don't understand."

"He went in with a large bubble mailer full of hundred dollar bills. One thousand, eight hundred and ninety-two hundred dollar bills."

Leah looked terrified. "That's why he was murdered, wasn't it? Someone wanted that money."

"We don't know, Leah," Diamond said. "You say your father didn't have that kind of money. Why not? He was a retired doctor."

Leah seemed distracted, worried. "He bought some annuities years ago. They provided his living expenses. His other money he gave to charity. I don't see how he could pay my medical bill."

"Your father kept both the money and the art secret. It's logical to assume that they are connected. Anything come to mind? Anything he's said recently that takes on new meaning in light of it?"

Leah, stunned by the revelations, shook her head.

I stood up, looked at Diamond. "Maybe now would be a good time to get Leah's statement."

"Does that work for you?" Diamond said to Leah.

She nodded.

He pulled a small recorder out of his pocket and began his routine with her as I walked across the bedroom and went back into the studio.

I looked around at the various materials. None of it meant much to me. In addition to several dozen tubes of paint, there were two vases full of brushes in different shapes and sizes. I could see a slight darkening in the bristles of most of them, staining from repeated use. Under the palette were shelves with jars and cans. I looked at some of the labels. Linseed oil. Stand oil. Turpentine. All of the containers were stained with paint from repeated openings.

Against one wall was another shelf with a small stereo and stacks of CDs, all classical selections. There were three books on portraiture lying on their sides. The CDs and the books also had paint stains on them.

It seemed obvious that the studio was well-used, that Dr. Kiyosawa spent many hours working on his craft. To use so many paint tubes and brushes, he must have painted several paintings at the minimum.

But where were the paintings?

There was the cabinet with vertical dividers. But other than the old landscape that Leah had pulled from it, it was empty. The only other canvas in the room was the newer, partially-painted landscape.

I squatted down to see if anything had been lost under the easel or cabinets. Nothing but dust balls. I lowered my head to the floor and looked under the rolling palette. A piece of paper caught the light.

The palette was heavy and difficult to roll on the dropcloth-covered carpet. I moved it to the side and picked up the paper.

It was heavy weight with significant texture, similar to the paper in a sketchbook. It had a drawing in colored pencil, a background of browns and umbers and olive greens. In the center, was an oval of blank white paper with no marks.

I set it on the easel and stepped back to take a look. It looked vaguely like the beginning of a portrait. The background had been roughed in, but the subject had yet to be sketched.

I left it on the easel and walked back through the bedroom and into the hallway. Diamond and Leah glanced at me as I passed. Spot jumped up from his nap and joined me.

Down in the kitchen I found a small desk with a phone book in one of the drawers. I flipped to the yellow pages and looked up art galleries. There were many scattered around the lake. Spot inspected the stovetop on the center island as I used the desk phone and started calling galleries.

When the first woman answered, I made my explanation as brief as possible.

"Hi, I wonder if you sell or know anything about paintings by a

Tahoe artist named Dr. Gary Kiyosawa?"

"No, I'm sorry," the woman said. "That name doesn't ring a bell. But we have many works by other Tahoe painters, if you're looking for work by local artists."

"It's possible he works under a pseudonym," I said. "He's in his seventies, about five-six, a small moustache, Japanese American."

The woman told me that she didn't know an artist of that description.

I thanked her and dialed the next gallery on the list. I spoke to another woman who had the same reaction.

I continued down the page, speaking to a wide variety of people, none of whom knew an artist matching Kiyosawa's description, but all of whom were certain they could help me find the perfect works of art that would enhance my home. Throughout their phone pitches were subliminal indications that the art they could sell would bring me stature in the community, impress my friends, and possibly increase my cultural intelligence as well.

I spoke to sales people at venues in South Lake Tahoe, Incline Village, Crystal Bay, Kings Beach, Carnelian Bay. In Tahoe City, I finally got a positive reaction.

"Twin Peaks Art," a man answered, his voice excessively cheery. "My name's Paul, and I'll be your art consultant today, tomorrow, or for the rest of your life." He said it with the flair of performance.

I gave him the same description of Dr. Gary Kiyosawa.

"He sounds a wee bit familiar," Paul told me, his flamboyance discernible over the phone. "A ghost from my past. A faint bird song in the dark of night... Wait, I do remember! He came in some weeks ago. Or months. Time is a rushing river, don't you agree? Anyway, the man was short. A little older. Moustache. Japanese American, you said?"

"Yeah."

"Well, we don't sell his work. I didn't even know he was an artist. He was on the frame side."

"What does that mean?"

"We're a two-store operation joined at the hip. Art gallery on one side, picture framing on the other. That's where the Twin Peaks name comes from. Your man was asking questions about framing. He was here for hours. My gosh, doesn't your poor friend have a life?

Imagine spending that much time talking about framing. Anyway, he wanted to know all about old frames. And we have walls covered in new frames. What was he thinking? That we make money just by talking?"

"Right," I said. "Thank you for your time."

"And when you need art, remember..."

"Paul, the art consultant," I interrupted.

"Oh, you are good," he said before we hung up.

I went back upstairs and looked in the master bedroom. Diamond was still going through his questions with Leah. I left and went outside. Spot came along as I walked up the drive to the main house. The weather had turned warmer, the sun was hot, and the breeze was redolent of the scents of sun-baked pine needles. Twelve hundred feet below, the giant lake showed complex wind patterns, dark blue against lighter blue.

I found the bell as Spot wandered off. Lauren Phelter came to the door. She wore an apron and had on leather work gloves and held a small pruning shears in one hand.

"Mr. McKenna, I'm so glad you stopped by. I've been working in the greenhouse, trying to keep my mind occupied. But this frightful thing at my guesthouse..." She looked down the drive and shook her head in dismay. "First the policeman said that the cleaning crew had come, and I was going to be able to get going on the repairs. Then they said that someone had broken in and that I still was to stay away. I'm beside myself. What is happening? First, poor Dr. Kiyosawa is killed. Then, someone shoots at Leah and you in your car. Next, my guesthouse is burglarized. Are the criminals just taking over? Have you learned anything of who perpetrated this terrible business? And here I go, talking away, and you're standing outside. Please come in."

She was turning as Spot came around the corner of the house.

"Oh, there is your dog. I didn't know you brought him. Is he okay being outside? Or maybe we should talk outside. He does shed, right? I don't think it would be best if, you know... My house is very clean, and I'd hate to have... Anyway, how is the doctor's daughter?"

"I think she'll be okay, Mrs. Phelter. And your guesthouse has no permanent damage."

"But the murderer is still running loose." Her voice was stern, as if I weren't doing my job.

"We haven't caught him yet, no. I need to know if you'd like me to continue."

Mrs. Phelter looked shocked. "Well, the killer needs to be caught, right?"

"Yes. But you don't need to privately finance society's obligations. Your concerns as a neighbor don't extend to finding criminals. I can give you a final bill."

"Absolutely not. An assault on my tenant is an assault on me. You will track down this killer. I insist."

"I would continue to have expenses in addition to my fee."

"Of course! Whatever it takes."

Diamond was through with Leah when I went back to the guesthouse bedroom. I walked through into the studio, retrieved the colored pencil sketch from the easel, and showed it to Diamond and Leah.

"I found this under the palette. What do you think, Leah?"

She took it from me. "Well, it's not like the landscapes. More like the beginnings of a portrait, like what he used to paint years ago. I don't think he planned on painting anything like this because the colors he'd mixed up on the palette are different."

"Oil paint doesn't dry fast like acrylic, right?"

"Right," Leah said.

"Can you tell from the paint on the palette how long ago he was using it?"

She raised her eyebrows. "Let me see." She stood up and walked into the studio room. She touched the dabs of paint. "They're skinned over, but still soft underneath. I don't see any driers on his palette, and the colors are thick and intense, so I'm guessing he used them straight and didn't mix in any turpentine. In that case, with normal air circulation and temperature, I'd guess he was painting with these as recently as a day or two before he..."

Diamond came to the studio door.

"Leah thought of something," he said to me. "Something about her father that may seem more significant now that we know of his art studio." He looked at Leah.

She looked at me. "It may not be anything. But who knows? For some time, he's periodically sent me postcards. Just one-line notes of encouragement. Things like, 'Saw your TV show today about parasailing. Well done. Love, dad.' Or, 'Congrats on the award. It was a good idea to put the plaque on your desk where it shows on camera.' Things like that."

"What does that have to do with his studio?" I asked.

"Oh, sorry. They are always art cards. You know, a picture of a famous painting. Like what they sell in museum stores. I asked him once where he got them all, and he just shrugged his shoulders. He said he'd had them for years."

"Do you still have any of the cards?"

"Most of them, I think. I put them on my fridge. It's practically covered. I call it the art fridge. Anyway, maybe those cards would reveal something about his art."

"I'd like to look." I stood up. I turned to Diamond. "No escort this time, thanks. I'll keep you informed, but I'm going to be extra careful."

Diamond nodded. "I've been thinking the same thing. Never know who talks to whom. But someone could be watching Leah's house."

Leah looked from me to Diamond and back to me, worry creasing her forehead.

"I won't put you in danger," I said, wondering how I would pull that off.

TWENTY-FIVE

L eah and I left the guesthouse. Remembering when we last left after her father had been shot, I asked her to once again lie down, leaning her upper body over Spot so that they were not easily visible as I drove down the grade. Maria's rusted pickup was good cover, and I had a baseball cap, but I didn't want to take any chances. Leah did her best and Spot didn't complain. No matter how much human weight is upon him, he thinks it's love and affection.

I watched to see if someone was following us, but no vehicle in my mirror remained there for long.

The problem with finding anonymity on the roads of Tahoe is that there are many choke points where all traffic has to pass along Highway 50 or one of the grades because there are no other routes from one area to the next. All someone need do to find you is to wait at one of those points and watch the traffic to see you come through. And if they don't know your likely driving routes, they can hire a few sentries to watch several choke points, effectively making it impossible for you to move about unobserved. The only way to remain hidden is to periodically change your clothes, your hat, and your vehicle.

I could easily switch to Street's VW bug, which she'd left in her condo garage. But it would be easy for someone to watch me if I borrowed it. I didn't have any other options except calling friends and asking to borrow their vehicles. Unfortunately, that would alert even more people to my activities. Better to limit my contacts with the world.

Near the bottom of Kingsbury Grade, I drove off into a neighborhood where there was a tangle of curving roads. By making several loops and coming back to the grade in a different spot I assured myself that no one was following us.

But the bottom of the Grade was another choke point. I had no choice.

"Where is your house?" I asked Leah.

"Out in Meyers," she called up from her bent position, leaning over Spot. "Not far from where Highway Fifty comes down from Echo Summit."

"Are you okay about going there? People may see us."

"Yeah."

I turned toward South Lake Tahoe. Just past the Heavenly gondola, I turned left onto Pioneer Trail, drove past the turn-off to our motel, and headed out toward the little community that serves as the southwestern entrance to South Lake Tahoe.

Leah stayed down and out of sight as she gave me instructions to her house. I thought she and Spot must both be cramping up, but neither of them complained.

"Turn right just after the Bug Station," she said, referring to the Agricultural Inspection building where, in deference to California's pursuit of bad insects, all drivers coming in from out of state have to stop and confess their stash of produce purchased from points east.

I went through the locals lane, then turned. Leah explained how to get to her house.

I pulled up in front of a small rambler. The front door was shut, but I could see from a distance that the lock had been broken by a crow bar or tire iron.

"We're here," I said. "Although I'm sorry to report that your house has been broken into as well."

Leah pushed herself up off of Spot. She looked at the front door, inhaled, but otherwise didn't react.

"Whatever the burglar was looking for at dad's house, he also looked for it here," she said.

"Stay here and stay down while I take Spot and check the house."

I got out of Maria's pickup, locked the door, opened the passenger door, let Spot out, and locked that door. Holding his collar, I walked to the side of the living room window and looked in. There was enough light coming in other windows to see that the place had been ripped apart just the same as Leah's father's place had.

I moved to the front door, aware that while the house was easy to see from two neighbors' houses, the door itself was out of view, blocked by a stand of fir trees on one side and the garage on the other.

"Are you ready, Spot?" I said in a low voice. "I want you to find the suspect. Do you understand?"

Again, I stayed to the side of the door, turned the knob and pushed it in.

The door swung open. I listened. Nothing. I gave Spot a shake. "Find the suspect, Spot!"

I smacked him on his rear and he ran into the house. As always, he had enthusiasm for the search game, but I could tell from his manner that there was no fresh human scent in the house.

Just to be sure, I waited a moment, then went in.

Spot was ambling, sniffing around without much focus.

I glanced through the rooms. They were predictably torn up, but I wanted to make certain that there was nothing sick or frightening that would threaten Leah's mental state further. Every room was the same, drawers emptied, cushions cut apart, containers opened. It looked awful, but it was clearly a professional search and in some ways less upsetting than the kind of burglary where a neighbor kid breaks in and spray paints graffiti or leaves other insults.

The garage was Leah's painting studio, though much less fancy than her father's. She had an easel and brushes and paints, but everything was smaller and less organized. Attached to large sheets of fiber board were many beautiful landscapes of California's coastal mountains, grass-covered humps with trees climbing up the ravines.

I went back outside, opened Leah's door, and explained the situation.

"You don't have to come inside," I said. "It is very upsetting to have someone go through all of your personal belongings."

She frowned. "I better see what's missing."

I walked with her inside. "Don't touch anything, just look," I said. "The cops will want to dust for prints." If the burglary was connected to the one at Lauren Phelter's guesthouse, there wouldn't be any prints. But we didn't know that yet.

She handled it well, tensing before looking into every room, but resigned to the destruction.

The house was a giant mess. It would take days to clean up and weeks to replace the furniture and other items that were destroyed. Leah looked in some drawers and cupboards, looked into a shoebox that sat open on a pile of clothes in front of a bedroom closet, peered into a coffee can on the floor in front of the kitchen sink, looked at some papers on a desk in the dining area.

"Did you have any valuables in the house?"

"Not to any degree worth mentioning. Some jewelry in my dresser drawer. But my important things are still here. Thrown about, but okay. My checkbook is still on the desk. My laptop is out of its carry case, but it looks okay."

"Any idea what this guy was looking for?"

Leah shook her head. We were standing in the living room. She held her head strangely still, while her eyes went back and forth, taking in the destruction. "He thought that both my father and I had something valuable hidden in our houses. Something small. I can't imagine what it would be. Maybe he thinks my father had something important, and instead of hiding it at his house, he hid it in my house."

"Has your father been over here recently?"

"No. The last time he was here was a month before the accident. No, wait, he came here after I got out of the hospital. He picked up some of my clothes and personal things."

"So he could have hidden something here at that time."

"Yes."

I turned to the fridge, the top third of which was wallpapered with art cards. "Your father sent a lot of these," I said.

"Yeah. He started about a year ago. Probably averaged one a week."

They each hung from a small piece of Scotch tape. I used a pen from my pocket to flip some of them up to peer at the backside, turning my head to read the sweet upside-down one-liners on the backs.

The pictures spanned a wide range of genres. It seemed that Dr. Kiyosawa was a little like me in that he appreciated paintings and sculpture from all major periods.

I saw many images I recognized from my art books. I read some more of his notes. They didn't reveal anything of his secret life.

In addition to the reproductions of famous paintings, there were a dozen or more cards with a single calligraphic character. I pointed to one.

"What do you think?" Leah said.

"I like these. What do they mean?"

"They are kanji characters. Drawn with sumi brushes and sumi ink. Kanji is the Japanese writing that was originally developed from Chinese characters. The evolution of Japanese writing is very complex. There are so many characters that the government has been trying to limit the teaching of kanji to less than two thousand characters. And they've introduced some Roman components into the language. Part of integrating with the rest of the world. I can't speak Japanese, but I love kanji as an art form. I've only learned a hundred characters or so, but I love to look at them. Each character has a different meaning."

"Where did your father get these kanji cards?"

"I don't know. Probably Japantown in San Francisco. Can I make you some coffee?" Leah asked. "Oh, I shouldn't touch that, either, right?"

I nodded. I tore off a paper towel, used it to gently hold Leah's house phone and used my pen to dial Diamond. I filled him in on the burglary at Leah's house. He muttered something about what he'd do with the bastard when he caught him. He mixed Spanish words with English. I couldn't make out the details. Because Leah's house was outside of the city limits of South Lake Tahoe, Diamond said he'd call the El Dorado County Sheriff's Department and inform them of the burglary. We hung up.

"Do you have any photos of your father? I'd like to take one with me."

"Only some old ones." I went with her into one of the bedrooms. She pointed to a box on the dresser. It was overflowing with a jumbled mass of photographs. "God, the burglar even went through these! What was he looking for?"

I handed Leah my pen and the paper towel so she could flip through them without touching them. She eventually sorted out three. "He was very shy. Later in life, he would never allow a picture to be taken. These are the only ones I have."

They showed the doctor at a Christmas gathering, standing in front of the old DeYoung Museum before it was rebuilt, and in his doctor whites in what looked like a hospital lobby.

"These all show him with darker hair. And none of them shows his moustache."

"I know." Leah frowned, then raised her eyebrows. "I have an idea. I'll draw you one."

"You can draw like that? And do it from memory?"

Leah smiled. "I said I could never paint as well as my father or mother. I didn't say I wasn't a pretty good artist." She walked toward her desk. "Can I touch any paper?"

I took my pen and used it to pull a piece of copy paper from the middle of the stack in her printer. I handed it and the pen to her. "Draw on this?"

She sat down at the kitchen table. "How big shall I make it?"

"Doesn't matter."

She made some rough sketch lines, some positioning marks, and then quickly made a thorough drawing of her father. Although I'd only seen him in death, I could tell the drawing was very accurate.

Five minutes later, she handed it to me. "Will that work?"

"Perfect. Thanks."

I folded it and slipped it into my shirt pocket.

"I saw some paintings when I glanced in the garage earlier."

"Yeah. Come, I'll show you my studio."

Spot followed us into the garage.

"Can I turn on my lights?"

I handed her the paper towel.

She turned on lights above her paintings by using the towel to just graze the edge of the switch. The fluorescent tubes had blueish daylight coloring.

"Nice work, Leah," I said.

"Don't just say that," she said.

"I'm not. They glow. Do you show them?"

"No. I've contacted a few galleries. But I don't have an art name. They don't care as much about the actual art as about how many dollars they can count on selling."

"You're a local celebrity. Tahoe people would buy your work."

"Tahoe is relatively small. The galleries want a national platform. If my show went out on national cable, that would be different. If I still had my show..." Leah stopped and hugged herself. "Anyway, they want serious sales history. One gallery director told me that his walls were like priceless real estate, so valuable that only famous artists will ever hang on them."

"Then you should ignore him and contact more galleries. Someone will eventually recognize how good this stuff is."

"Eventually can be a very long time," she said. "I could be sixty or seventy before it happens."

"You're going to turn seventy someday anyway. May as well pursue it."

There was an easel and near it a small table with 15 or 20 brushes spread out across it. There were a variety of shapes and sizes, and had I not just seen her father's huge collection, I would have considered Leah's grouping a large number.

I pointed to her brushes. "These are your tools."

"Yeah. But I've never thought they were special. My mother's were sacred, her tools for ordering life into manageable components. According to dad, her art was her life. For me, it's just been a hobby. Also, my mother painted watercolors. Those brushes are like a jeweler's tools. Sable hairs. Exquisitely shaped. Soft and very delicate. Because watercolor is so liquid, you need a precise brush to control it. And expensive." She pointed to a brush on her easel.

"A Kolinsky sable watercolor brush in this size can cost two hundred dollars. Whereas us oil painters, we use relatively cheap bristle brushes. The stiff bristles allow us to push around heavy oil paint. We usually don't need the precision that watercolorists need."

"You ever thought of making art your life? Paint full time?"

"I'd love to do that. So would a million other artists. But try paying the bills."

I looked at the various paintings, then realized I was indulging a luxury of time that we didn't have.

"We shouldn't stay here," I said. "Too much risk."

Leah flashed me a look of worry, and I regretted saying it.

We walked back into the kitchen and left.

Leah once again lay down on Spot to minimize her profile. I pulled my cap down low, and we drove back into town.

We were approaching our motel hideout, when I saw police cars from a distance.

I drove right on by without stopping. There were four South

Lake Tahoe cruisers in the motel parking lot. I turned to look as we went by and saw that the door to our room had been kicked in.

The killer might be near, watching, so I repeated my trip around the blocks of the congested neighborhood nearby. I didn't see any tail, but obviously, he was tracking us somehow.

I took back roads over to the casino hotels and parked in the Harvey's Hotel ramp. A dark corner where I could think.

"What's wrong?" Leah said when the darkness of the ramp swept over the pickup. She pushed herself up.

"Cops at our motel," I said, worrying that the news would set Leah back. But I decided it was best to tell her the truth. "Our room had been broken into."

Leah didn't speak. She went back into her quiet mode, staring at the wall in front of us. Eventually, she said, "What do we do now?"

"We need to get you someplace safe. You have an aunt in Boston, right? Your father's sister?"

Leah shook her head. "No, I won't go there. The man who killed my father, and probably my husband, is obviously determined. It would be easy for him to find out I have an aunt in Boston. Not only would he find me there, but I'd be putting her at risk. Am I right about that?"

I thought about it. "Probably."

"He thinks I have something that is his. Or whatever. In his mind, I will always have that information regardless of where I run. If he ever catches up with me, he will still want to kill me. If we don't catch him, then my life isn't worth living. I'll always know that he's out there. And if it is my stalker... Well, I know him enough to know he is very persistent in his own way. He won't stop looking for me."

"We don't know that he is the killer."

"True. But we don't know that he isn't, either. So I want to stay in Tahoe. If I'm in the area, maybe the killer will sense that from yours or the cops' actions. If he thinks I'm around, it'll be like I'm bait. He'll keep trying to come find me. Then you can catch him."

"You're brave," I said.

"No," she shook her head. "I'm desperate. I can't live knowing that this monster is out there, just waiting to kill me. Unless you catch him, that's what my life would be. Hiding and worrying. I'd rather we entice this guy, draw him out and catch this Grendel.

TWENTY-SIX

Leah and Spot and I sat in the dark ramp for some time. I felt helpless. I couldn't track the killer, but the killer was doing a good job of tracking us.

"I have some leads I can pursue," I finally said to Leah, "but it's hard to know the best way to keep you safe."

"I'm a dead weight around your neck. You can't function. You can't do your job because you're stuck baby-sitting me."

"That's not quite the way I would put it, but yes. What about your friends? Could any of them put you up safely? In a vacant rental home or vacation home that one of them owns?"

"I don't really have any close friends. I've tried to think through all my acquaintances. None of them seems like a good choice. They don't have rentals. Most of them have kids, and I wouldn't want to bring risk into their lives. I know a couple of guys who are dealers at the casinos. I could stay with them, but, frankly, they are not very responsible. They mean well, but I don't think they would be careful enough with what they said or who they talked to.

"There's one woman who would let me stay with her, and she is very discreet. But the problem is she lives in one of those new condos at Heavenly Village. Even if I came and went in the middle of the night, there would be so many people who would see me. Everyone in town would recognize me, even if I'm all scarred up.

"If only I knew someone who has a big boat I could live on. I could disappear onto the water when needed, come back to show my face when you want bait for the killer."

"That's a good idea," I said. "I know someone with a boat."

"Really? Who?"

"A young woman named Jennifer Salazar. She's still in college at Harvard, but she might be back for summer vacation. She used to have a powerboat, but it overturned after an accident last summer.

They hoisted it out, but Jennifer decided it was quite damaged. So she sold it and bought another."

"Was this when the other boat blew up? The one with the call girl on it? And you were on the powerboat when it overturned?"

I nodded in the dark. "Yes."

"I did a show on boating safety after that. It was back-story for the dangers of boating in cold water like Tahoe. You and Spot almost succumbed to hypothermia, didn't you?"

"Yeah. Anyway, Jennifer wanted to get a boat that could be lent out to the UC Davis scientists who are studying the decline of lake clarity. They have their own research vessel. But like lots of non-profit organizations, they have to work within strict budgets, and Jennifer wanted to alleviate those budget issues. So she replaced her damaged powerboat with a larger boat that she could loan to the scientists whenever they need it. It is big enough to live aboard. And it has some nice features that the scientists like."

"Scientific equipment?"

"No. Their research vessel has plenty of that. Her boat offers the more basic amenities that makes their lives easier. Like hot showers."

"Hot showers," Leah repeated. "Showers as in plural?"

"Yes. It's a big boat. She said the scientists love having some comfort when they're out on the water. That way they don't have to put in every night and stay at a hotel."

"This girl has some money."

"Yeah. She inherited the world's fourth largest clothing company and a big house on the lake."

"But she goes to Harvard, so you're going to tell me that she's not an airhead rich girl."

"Correct. Heavy-hitter brainpower. I think when she graduates college in a couple of years she'll be eighteen."

Leah didn't speak while that sunk in.

"She has no parents?"

"Her father is dead. Her mother is ill with schizophrenia."

"If she's only sixteen, who controls her money? Who's her legal guardian?"

"She is. I don't know how it worked. She has some company lawyers who gave her advice, but as I understand it, she pursued it through the courts by herself. She wrote her own legal papers, made her own oral arguments. It went up a couple of levels, and eventually they found a way to circumvent the laws regarding minors and give her full control of her money."

"How can they make a special case for a rich girl?"

"I think there was some good old-fashioned financial arm-twisting involved. She let it be known that she had to make a decision on where to build her next plant, which is going to employ almost a thousand people. The Bay Area's superior business infrastructure, and its larger skilled workforce was compelling. But in return for a favorable outcome on her wishes with the State of Nevada, she let them know that she would be willing to go to the extra effort involved in bringing that investment to Nevada instead."

"So they gave her exactly what she wanted," Leah said.

"Anybody would," I said.

"Even though she's a minor child."

"Even though," I said.

"And you think this girl will be willing to help me?"

I nodded. "Yeah, I think so. As long as UC Davis isn't currently using the boat."

"But Jennifer doesn't even know me."

"She likes to help me. She believes my word and opinion have value."

"Why?"

"Because I saved her life."

"I suppose that would give someone a bit of a bias. I still find it hard to believe that a stranger would help me like this."

"When you meet her, you'll understand."

TWENTY-SEVEN

I had to walk around the parking ramp to find good cell reception, once again advertising my location to the phone company computers. I had Jennifer's private number in my phone menu.

"Owen, I'm so excited to hear from you!" she gushed.

"Are you in town?"

"Yes, I just got back from a trip to India. We're building a fabric plant there that is totally green."

"You mean, one of those buildings that makes its own power?"

"That and more. It has a huge solar installation on the roof and the grounds, and we've purchased a stake in a large wind farm that is going up nearby. Between the wind turbines and the sun, we'll be energy independent. But we're also using building materials with the least embodied energy. So instead of concrete, which is hugely energy-intensive to produce, we're going with... Oh, what am I doing rattling on and on? It's just that you are such a good listener. What's up? Can you and Street and Spot get together while I'm in town?"

"I hope so. But Street's out of town for several days. I'm calling on a different matter." I gave her a quick rundown of Leah's situation.

"Is this Leah Printner as in the Tahoe Live talk show?"

"Yeah."

"Oh, I love her. I think she's the greatest."

"Well, we need to find her a place to stay that would be safe and a good cover, but also be mobile. I'm wondering if she could park on your boat for a few days. I would go with her at first, anchor somewhere out of sight. Unless, it's being used by the university."

"Actually, UC Davis isn't using it until a few days from now. But I have a better idea. I recently got a sailboat that would be better for her. It's much cozier than the big boat. Tell Leah it's hers to use as she needs. How soon will she come over? I'll get my new man Randall to check and make sure the towels are fresh and the fridge is stocked."

"I'm also wondering if you can spare a few clothes. I think she's a little bigger than you, but if you had something a little baggy for you, it would fit her well."

"Of course. This old mausoleum has so many closets you'd need a map to find them all. I'm sure we've got lots of clothes that would work."

"One more thing. Any chance you have a cell phone we could borrow? I'd like to leave one with Leah, but I not mine. The GPS would give away her location to anyone watching me."

"I have a couple that are registered to the company. San Francisco address and all that. You could each have one."

"Perfect. We're actually nearby. How about if we come over in about twenty minutes?"

"I'll be waiting. What are you driving? I'll tell Randall to be at the gate."

"An old pickup, yellow in the few places that aren't rusted out."

I hung up and went back to Maria's truck.

"Jennifer is excited to be able to help. She says her sailboat will be much better for you than the big cruiser. She's going to send her houseman down to the boat right now to make sure the towels are fresh and the fridge is stocked. She's waiting for us to come."

Leah's eyes immediately overflowed. Her breathing caught and she seemed to melt, slouching down next to Spot, leaning on him.

We drove up the East Shore and were at the grand gate to the Salazar estate fifteen minutes later. A large, hard-looking man was waiting. He waved, gave us a little smile, pressed a button on a remote, and the fancy wrought iron gate opened. We drove through, and it shut behind us. As I drove down the winding drive, I could see Randall in the mirror, following us on his golf cart.

As we came around the last curve and saw the French Renaissance mansion, Leah gasped.

"My God, it's huge."

"Yeah. But Jennifer doesn't like it. She calls it the mausoleum."

Jennifer ran out, bouncing like the sweet sixteen-year-old girl that she was as we pulled around the circular drive. She opened Leah's door.

"Hi Leah, I'm Jennifer. I'm so glad to meet you. You've been a role model to me with your TV show, showing girls like myself that a woman can take charge and do anything she puts her mind to." Jennifer took Leah's hand in both of hers, gave no reaction to Leah's stitches and scars, then hugged her hard as Leah stepped out of the truck. Leah's tears flowed again.

Spot pranced around Jennifer, puzzled that he wasn't the center of attention. But Jennifer focused on Leah, walked her inside, her arm around Leah's shoulder.

Randall opened the garage, and I put the pickup in one of the seven spaces. Spot and I followed Jennifer and Leah through the entrance hall and down to a small cozy study with a view of the lawn leading down to the pier. On one side was the boathouse. On the other side was a large cruiser, brilliant white against the blue of Tahoe. Farther out, attached to a buoy, was a sleek sailboat, looking like the ultimate water toy.

The late-afternoon sun sparkled through the beveled panes of the study windows, filling the room with little prisms of shooting light. When Jennifer and Leah were seated, Spot finally got Jennifer's attention, and she gave him a long head rub.

A middle-aged woman I recognized came in with a tray of baked treats, a pitcher of iced tea and glasses with ice in them.

"Hello, Marjorie. Good to see you again," I said.

She grinned at me. "The pleasure is all mine, Mr. McKenna."

When Marjorie left, Jennifer spoke in a low voice. "I already spoke to both Marjorie and Randall. I explained that it is paramount that they not breathe a word of your presence to anyone. We have a gentle relationship around here, all soft sell when it comes to explaining our position on anything. But they also know that I'm not to be trifled with. They need their employment, and I pay them well. I think your presence won't be compromised."

"Thank you," Leah said, obviously relieved and grateful. "I'm so touched by your kindness to a stranger."

"It's nothing," Jennifer said. "The world is a chaotic place. I find that even small bits of grace here and there are what make life worth living. Owen and Street and Spot bring grace into my life, as does any friend of theirs. If I can return some of that, great. And besides, you are not a stranger. You are Leah Printner of Tahoe Live. I've watched you ever since you went on the air—what was it—four years ago? One of your special abilities is that you make your listeners feel like you are their friend. So this is my chance to repay you some of what I've gotten from you."

Leah looked at me, shaking her head. "You were right, Owen."

"What?" Jennifer said. She beamed at me. "Were you telling stories behind my back?"

"Not really. I didn't even get to the elephants."

"Oh!" Jennifer said. She turned to Leah. "Wait 'til you hear about my elephant study. But we can talk about that later. Let me show you your new home."

"Your boat." Leah said.

"Yes, it's very comfortable and seaworthy. You can take it wherever you want on the lake. Drop anchor over at Secret Harbor north of here or anywhere you like."

"I've driven powerboats," Leah said. "But I don't know how to sail."

"No problem," Jennifer said. "It has an engine. You can drive it like any other powerboat. It's just a lot slower. I don't know how to sail, either. But I've always wanted to learn. I've got Norm Washburn teaching me. Do you know him, Owen?"

"No."

"Well, he's an old salt from back east. Knew Grampa Abe. Now he teaches sailing out of a couple of the marinas on the North Shore. He'll be coming over here when I'm in town later this summer to put me through the ropes. Or I guess I should say, to put me through the lines, shouldn't I! Boating lingo is so different. The kitchen is a galley, the bathroom is a head, the bedrooms are cabins, beds are berths, the couch is a settee, the dining area is the saloon, a hallway is a companionway, closets are lockers, left is port and right is starboard, you don't put anything away, you stow it, windows are portholes, skylights that open are hatches, a wall is a bulkhead, and you don't steer from the driver's seat, you steer from the helm! Who dreamed up all this stuff? It was easier to learn French!"

"You speak French?" Leah said.

"And German and Spanish," I said.

"Shall we go down to the boat?" Jennifer was excited to show us.

We followed a winding path down the lawn to the pier where the cabin cruiser was docked across from the boathouse, which was too small to contain it. Spot trotted around the lawn and spied a tiny Douglas squirrel stripping a big Jeffrey pinecone. Spot lowered his body down a bit so that he would be hidden in his imagined world of tall grass on the Serengeti, then stalked the squirrel, moving toward it an inch at a time. The squirrel ignored him.

"The company vice presidents made me buy this cruiser," Jennifer said, pointing at the huge, glossy boat that was more yacht than cruiser. "I said we could save money by doing our business meetings at our offices in San Francisco. Do you know what they told me? They said that the offices were for business meetings and the boat was for dignitaries from other countries. Can you believe it?"

"So you cruise Tahoe with government bigshots to buy their favors," I said.

"Yes, exactly. That is so counter to my sense of how things should be. But you know what? That's how we got this new fabric plant in India to be so green. The Indian officials in charge wanted us to use the contractors who were in their pockets, the ones who build in all the standard, inefficient ways. So we flew some of those officials to Reno and brought them up to spend two days on the boat, fishing and eating fancy meals prepared by a gourmet chef. At the end of their stay, they were happy to do it our way, totally green, better for the workers because they have no toxic chemicals in the new factory. Better for the environment in every way, and something those officials could brag about."

"The old quid pro quo worked for the common good."

"Yes. Jeremy—he's the vice president who really pushed me hard on getting the cruiser—he was so excited when our green factory finally got green-lighted. He sent me a huge bouquet of flowers for congratulations."

"And then you gave him a raise," I said, winking.

"How did you guess?"

"Quid pro quo."

Randall was standing at the end of the pier near the runabout, which was tied to the pier. Tied to the runabout was a dinghy, a heavy-duty inflatable with two wooden seats and a five-horse outboard.

Jennifer pointed at the sailboat floating serenely about 25 yards from the shore. "The sailboat has to be moored out at the buoy because its draft is six feet. It's got that deep, lead keel design.

Whereas the cruiser only has four feet of draft. It can be moored at the pier."

Jennifer walked down some stairs, stepped into the runabout and sat down, Leah went next.

"You're bringing Spot, right?" Jennifer said.

I turned and looked for Spot. He was twelve feet from the squirrel. He suddenly shot forward. The squirrel jumped up on the nearby tree and looked down on Spot from ten feet up. Spot leaped up, front paws on the tree bark. The squirrel screamed at him.

I called Spot. He turned his head to look at me, then looked back up at the squirrel. The squirrel was gone. Spot dropped his front legs back down to the ground. He looked around for the squirrel. It had disappeared. Spot had witnessed this magic trick before. He turned and loped toward us.

Spot came down the steps and jumped into the boat. It leaned precariously, the gunwale dipping down toward the water's surface. Leah inhaled.

Randall, unperturbed, followed Spot and tossed the line into the back of the boat. He sat at the little driver's seat amidships, and pushed the starter button. The Mercury outboard came to life. Randall shifted into forward without raising the throttle, and we gently idled our way, towing the dinghy, out to the anchored sailboat. Spot stood in the prow, his head out like the carved busts on the forward spar of the old Square Riggers.

The sailboat was gorgeous, with long, low lines, painted navy blue with white accents, trimmed with teak moulding.

"What kind is this?" I asked.

"It's a French make," Jennifer said. "A Ciel Forty."

"Meaning forty feet long?"

"Yes. And twelve feet at beam. Norm explained that beam means width."

"Jennifer, you keep buying toys like these, even your bank account will start to feel the pinch."

"Oh, the cruiser is a company asset. I didn't have to pay for it out of my personal funds. Yes, this Ciel is a personal indulgence. But I'm pretty sure I still have enough left to pay the electric bill."

Randall shifted into neutral and we coasted up to the rear of the boat. The name was in script across the stern.

Beaufort's Beauty

Jennifer leaped onto the sailboat, then tipped the helmsman seat to open the transom and expose the boarding platform. She held Leah's hand as Leah stepped out of the runabout onto the boarding platform. Spot was next. I followed. Randall stayed in the runabout, lightly running the bow line around a cleat on the Ciel. He untied the dinghy from the runabout and retied it to the sailboat.

Jennifer showed us around topside, then spoke in the best manner of a marine tour guide, "Shall we go down the companionway?" She walked down the stairs. "First stop below decks is the galley, portside." It was a perfect little kitchen, far better outfitted than the kitchen nook in my cabin. The only thing lacking was headroom. Unless I opened the various hatches and stood with my head poking up through the deck above, the six-foot ceiling height would be tough. I leaned on the galley counter as Jennifer continued her tour.

"Over here on the starboard side is the head." She opened the door. The little room was illuminated with a port-light and a translucent hatch to the deck. "Just in front of the head on the starboard side is the chart table with hinged desktop."

She looked back up the companionway and saw Spot staring down at us, hanging his head.

"Your largeness, do you want to come down?" Jennifer turned to me. "Do you think he can get down those steps?"

"Sure. But his nails might rip the carpet."

"I'm not worried." She tapped her foot on the thick pile. "Spot, c'mon down."

He wagged, lowered his head farther.

"C'mon, you can do it."

Spot reached his right front paw down to the first step, then lowered his left. Repeated the motion. And again. Eventually, his front legs were most of the way down the narrow steps, while his rear paws were still topside.

He looked over at me for approval.

"Ahoy, Cap'n. Join us in the hold."

He made a little jump, landed well and made a one-two congratulatory wag before he began serious inspections with his nose.

Jennifer continued. "The saloon has two comfy settees." She gestured to the fore of the galley where there was a U-shaped arrangement of cushioned benches that wrapped around a dining table. Opposite, on the starboard side, was another settee. The saloon was well-lit by multiple port-lights and another deck hatch.

"Behind and below the settee cushions you will find ample stowage for all your live-aboard accoutrements."

Jennifer moved through the saloon to another doorway. "Leah, I think you will enjoy the forward cabin. It features a large berth with stowage lockers under and a sea-fiddle over."

"What's a sea-fiddle?" Leah asked, staring into the beautiful bedroom with a plush feather bed, and leather and mahogany appointments.

"I don't know. I picked up that nomenclature from the brochure. Maybe that was an option I didn't get. But it could be something here in front of us."

Jennifer turned and came back through the saloon. "Owen, I think you'll like the aft cabin on the port side. Of course, you're seriously long-of-body for sea-going accommodations, but maybe you can curl up at an angle or something."

"I'll be fine."

"On the starboard side of the companionway steps, is the shower." She opened the door. It was larger than the shower in my cabin. Spot wedged his head in next to Jennifer and looked up at the skylight above.

"And finally," Jennifer said, "the starboard aft cabin is called the wet locker. It is basically a walk-in closet for sail stowage, but you'll find you can use it for any extra stuff you want to put out of sight."

We all went back topside.

"Will you show us how to drive?" Leah asked.

"Yes. We won't worry about sailing for now because I haven't learned that part yet. But the driving part is easy."

She showed us all of the steps from running the bilge pump to clearing the engine compartment with the ventilation blower, to starting the engine, to the basics of piloting the craft. She also explained how the engine battery is separate from the service battery, and what the charging sequence was.

"The main thing they stressed during the training session is to remember your depth. The keel on this is six feet deep. You can check the depth finder, here, but mostly you just use common sense. Tahoe is so clear that you can pretty much see where it is deeper than six feet and where it is not. They told me to think in terms of twelve feet, not six. Because you never know when a wave will bounce you deeper than you think. Of course, if you run aground, you have the cell phone." She winked at Leah, who looked alarmed. "Just kidding," Jennifer said. "Don't worry, you'll be fine.

"Randall stocked all the provisions you'll need in the logical places. The company cell phones have their numbers written on the back. They're in one of the galley cupboards. We included the twelve-volt cell phone charger because Beaufort's Beauty has a twelve-volt electrical system. It's just like charging your phone from your car.

"Marjorie put some clothes for you in your cabin locker, Leah. And she collected an assortment of foods. Meat and produce and everything in between. Randall put those items in the galley and the fridge. Marjorie also raided the mausoleum's wine cellar. You will find the wine rack in one of the stowage lockers below the settee."

Jennifer handed me a remote and key ring. "Owen, this remote will open the boathouse garage door, the auto garage door and the driveway gate. Press two-seven for the boathouse garage door, because B for boathouse is the second letter of the alphabet, and G for garage door is the seventh letter of the alphabet. The auto garage is one-seven for AG. And the driveway gate is four-seven for DG. Make sense?"

"Yes."

"There is a Toyota Rav Four in the garage, key in the ignition. I never knew you had a pickup," she segued. "It's so old! A classic."

"It's Diamond's friend's."

"Oh. Anyway, in case someone saw you in the truck, you can drive the Toyota. That will give you some additional privacy. The way I figure it, you can stay on Beaufort's Beauty anywhere on the lake. No one will be able to find you without knowing exactly what to look for and where to look. Then, if you want to be able to move around, you can anchor nearby, and come ashore on the dinghy."

She turned to Leah. "Owen can come and go in the runabout, take it back to the boathouse and use the Toyota to get around, and you'll still have the dinghy to get to shore."

"You have another car?" I said. "This won't compromise you in any way?"

Jennifer smiled. "I thought detectives were more observant than that. There is a BMW in the garage. Randall mostly drives the Toyota, but he can use the Beamer if he needs to. I don't even have my driver's license yet, which is a situation that is about to change. But as you can see, I'm a big believer in backup. I have backup for everything important, computers, cars, boats. I even have an extra bicycle. If the mausoleum were to burn down, I can stay at the condo in San Francisco. So, no, having you take the Toyota won't matter."

Leah reached out and took Jennifer's hand. "Jennifer, you are so kind. Thank you."

"It's nothing."

"I have one more question," I said, gesturing with my head. I went below decks. Jennifer followed. I spoke in a soft voice.

"I've met Marjorie in the past. But not Randall. How well do you know him?"

"He's been here for three months. He came with good references. His last job was four years at the Merriwell family in the Oakland Hills. You may have heard of them. They funded that new arts center in the East Bay. Their business was Merriwell Finance. Picked up by Bank Of America a few years ago?"

I shook my head.

"Well, anyway, I talked to Sheila, and she said he'd been very good, and the only reason they let him go was that he desperately wanted to try life in ski country before he turned forty and his knees gave out. He's big into snowboarding. So I pulled a credit report on him and other than some old school loans that are still unpaid, he's pretty clean. Of course, I've been gone at school, but Marjorie says he's been very..."

My cell phone rang, interrupting our talk. I'd forgotten to turn it off. It had been broadcasting my location ever since I used it to call Jennifer from the hotel parking ramp.

I looked at the number. "Diamond," I answered.

"The stalker. Leah's ex-lover. We found out who he is."

"Hold on," I said. I turned to Jennifer. "I need to take this call."

"Got it," she said. "I'll go topside and keep Leah company."

TWENTY-EIGHT

"Leah's boyfriend," Diamond said, "is Thomson Snowberry. Goes by Tommy Snow. His car matches your description. A black seventy-six Firebird. Nevada plates like you said. He lives in a small rental house he shares with two other guys. They didn't want to talk, but fortunately, one of them is on probation. We used that to squeeze him pretty good, and he decided ratting out Tommy boy was the best way to avoid another trip back to the chicken house.

"He confirmed Snowberry's physical description, his job as a delivery driver, his fixation on guns, pumping iron and, of course, Leah Printner. Snow repeatedly bragged about getting skin-to-skin with her. Whenever he and his housemates had their intellectual repartee, he would reportedly punch his thumb into his chest and say, "Don't forget, this tomcat will soon be screwing a TV star."

"You haven't found him," I said.

"No. He apparently disappeared the night Dr. Kiyosawa was shot. The guys said he left early that evening—probably on his way to knock on Leah's door where you spoke to him—and as far as they know, he didn't come home after that. But they also admitted that their normal routine at night is to pretty much drink beer and smoke weed until they pass out while watching TV. The tomcat could have come home later, and maybe they wouldn't have heard him. So you, Owen, may be the last person who talked to him before he split town. The timing of his disappearing act certainly is suspicious."

"Yeah," I said. "Then again, he might have heard that Leah and her father were shot at, realized he would be suspected, and ran."

"That would fit, too," Diamond said. "His roommates also said that Tom is into the sniper subculture. He reads the magazines, spends hours in the internet chatrooms that these guys frequent, drives to an informal gun club in the desert mountains where these guys shoot. He spends most weekends out there."

I thought about my previous guess that the stalker was too hotheaded and impulsive to fit a sniper personality. Never place too much stock in first impressions.

"Are the gun club guys into big bore rifles?" I said.

"Sí. Specifically, fifty caliber, according to Tommy's house buddies. You familiar with those weapons?"

"By some measures, the most powerful rifles made," I said. "I've heard that a round from a fifty caliber will penetrate a concrete block or the kind of armor plating they use to protect government limousines from sniper fire."

"Hate to think of that kind of hardware in our cozy mountain hamlet," Diamond said. "But it fits with the damage we saw at the Phelter guesthouse."

"The tomcat owns one?" I asked.

"Not according to his roommates. But he was planning to buy one as soon as he'd saved enough money. When he wasn't talking about his sexual exploits, he talked about the rifle that one of the guys brings to the shooting range. The other guys who show up lust after this gun. It's quite a little business. The owner charges fifteen bucks a shot to fire it. But that includes the ten dollar round, so, in the words of the idiot on probation, 'it's like a really good deal, dude.'"

"Right," I said. "Good to know that the most powerful rifle on earth is in such responsible hands. They know who the owner of the rifle is?"

"No. Just some guy that Tommy Snow meets in the desert." Diamond gave me a sad, defeated sigh over the phone, a sound that betrayed the sour taste of helplessness that all cops periodically experience when they think of the ease with which stupid thugs can obtain such weapons.

"So many men use their spare time to pursue productive activities," Diamond said, ruminating, "it's easy to forget about those who think that the most fun to be had in life is to shoot guns that were designed to kill other humans from a mile away."

"The other notable thing," Diamond continued, "is that this guy was recently showing strain over being rejected by Leah. He started saying—and I quote the roommate quoting Tom—'she better put out, soon, or I'm gonna teach the bitch about consequences.'"

"If this dirtball spends much time out in his little black car, a cop will eventually see him. We'll be able to talk to him soon."

Diamond grunted, and we hung up.

This time I turned off my phone, took one of Jennifer's company phones from the galley cupboard, and put it in my pocket.

I rejoined Leah, Jennifer, Raymond and Spot topside.

TWENTY-NINE

"**A**re you coming back to the house or leaving from here?" Jennifer asked when I climbed back up the companionway.

"It's late afternoon. We were up all night. I'm thinking we should head out and find a place to drop anchor. Leah will finally be safe, and she can get some rest." Leah and I looked at each other. We both knew that I was speaking for myself as much as for her.

"Then you should drop Raymond and me on the dock," Jennifer said. "You can come right back and tow the runabout behind the Ciel. It handles well if it isn't too wavy. The dinghy will bounce along beside it. After you find a place to anchor, you can leave on the runabout and Leah can still get to shore on the dinghy if she wants. Okay?" Jennifer looked at Leah. Leah nodded.

Spot stayed with Leah as I ferried Jennifer and Raymond back to the pier. Jennifer gave me a kiss on the cheek as they got out of the boat.

"She'll be fine, now," Jennifer said, her preternatural maturity hard to reconcile with a sixteen-year-old kid. "And if you ever need to get across the lake faster, you can use my neighbor's speedboat, the rocket. It's in the boathouse next to the runabout. He lets us use it in exchange for storing it there."

"Thanks, Jennifer. We won't go far."

"I don't want to know," she said with a grin. "That way they can't even torture it out of me."

It was a joke, but I had a hard time putting it away, and it haunted me as I idled back to the Ciel.

Spot acted all excited when I got back into the sailboat. I pet him and told him how brave he was to be 75 feet away from me for five whole minutes. He wagged agreement.

I tied the line from the bow of the runabout to a stern cleat, then went about turning on the Ciel's system, first the bilge pump, then the engine compartment ventilation blower, then the engine. I left the running lights off. If another boat came near, I could turn them on. While the engine warmed up, I went below and found a detailed map of Tahoe at the chart table. I took it topside and spread it out in the cockpit to show Leah.

"The most deserted shoreline on the lake is the East Shore north of Glenbrook," I said. "I propose we head up there and anchor near one of these coves. Secret Beach, Hidden Beach, Skunk Harbor."

"Why not just stay out in the lake?" she said. "We'd be farther from campers and such after the sun goes down."

"It's too deep to anchor. We need to stay put for the night if we are to get any rest."

"Right," she said.

I hoisted anchor, shifted into forward at idle, and the Ciel moved ahead. The runabout and the dinghy had drifted around to the starboard side, but soon fell into line behind the sailboat. We motored slowly out into the lake and then angled north.

"Aren't those coves on the northeast shore popular? That's where the nude beaches are. Lots of boaters and hikers will be on those beaches."

"True, during the day. But all the rest of the beaches around the lake are more popular. We could anchor on a stretch of private homes and estates, but we wouldn't be able to bring Spot ashore for a run. The northeast shore is good because it is forty thousand acres of state park. And camping isn't allowed at night. Except for the odd group that ignores the rules, those areas should clear out at night. The park rangers make regular rounds during the summer. My guess is we'll have relative privacy. If I leave Spot with you, you will have to take him ashore in the dinghy at least three times a day. The northeast shore is the best place for that."

Leah looked alarmed. "Of course you will leave Spot with me. Won't you? I don't think I could stay on this boat alone." Spot sensed her worry. Or he responded to his name. He stuck his nose into Leah's stomach. She grabbed his head. "Am I wrong about that? Were you thinking of leaving me alone?" Her voice raised in pitch and volume.

"No, don't worry. Spot will stay with you. But you will need to remember that he is an advertisement for your presence. Harlequin

Great Danes attract a lot of attention. Boaters will see him when he's topside, and they will stop to talk to you about him."

"I'll put my hair up and wear those sunglasses and that huge sombrero that Jennifer put on board. And I'll keep Spot below if anyone is near."

"Good idea. Or try to get him to lie down in the cockpit and then take him below decks when you see a boat approaching."

I spread out the map and pointed. "We're here. Eight or nine miles to the north is Glenbrook. This land that projects out north of Glenbrook Bay is Deadman Point. I'm thinking that we go just past that to where the shore is more sheltered at Skunk Harbor."

"I did a show on that once," Leah said. "George Newhall was a playboy who inherited a fortune from his father in the nineteen-twenties. So he built a fabulous stone house as his beach cottage at Skunk Harbor, across the lake from his huge estate on the West Shore. The beach cottage had its own dam for a water system and a cookhouse for the family chef. You could only get there by boat, so Newhall's family and friends would boat across the lake and they would swim and picnic and make roaring fires in the giant stone fireplace in the big living room. Now the house is run-down, but what's left is preserved by the Park system."

"The Newhall family ghosts will keep us company," I said, hoping for some levity, but immediately worrying that it was the wrong thing to say.

"Right," Leah said, easing my concern.

I eased the throttle forward and Beaufort's Beauty pulled ahead at a strong five or six knots, the perfect lines of its hull slicing through the small chop of the lake. With its deep heavy keel, it was much more stable than a similar-sized cruiser. Ninety minutes later, we came even with Deadman Point, turned northeast around the rocks, and headed toward Skunk Harbor.

In the distance was a boat at anchor and another beached on the sand. I slowed as we approached and finally stopped well out from the beach. The water was so clear that we could see the rocks on the sandy bottom. I estimated it to be about 25 feet deep, which would leave us with plenty of anchor chain to spare. Just to be sure, I checked the depth finder. It said we were in 70 feet of water, too deep for our anchor chain.

Not wanting to be any closer to the people on the beach, I shifted back into forward and eased toward the rocks on Deadman Point, watching the depth finder. When it said 35 feet, I stopped.

I dropped anchor, watching it fall and dig into the sandy bottom. Satisfied that we weren't going to drift away, I cut the engine.

Leah fidgeted as if she didn't know what to do with herself. So I went below decks, pulled out one of Jennifer's wines, a Mount Aukum zin from the Fair Play appellation just down the mountain from Tahoe. I pulled the cork, found some nice large wine glasses, poured a couple of inches into them, and brought them topside.

Leah was standing at the stern, looking into the water. Spot stood next to her. Leah turned.

I pointed at the portside chair. "Sit," I said.

She came over and sat.

I handed her one of the glasses. "Your medicine," I said. "Drink."

She took a sip. I sat in the other chair.

I pointed at the setting sun across the lake. "Now look at the view."

She looked, took another sip, and for the first time in the 45 hours since her father was shot, I believed that she felt safe.

THIRTY

We sat and drank wine and watched the sky grow hot pink as the sun went behind a cloud just above the mountains on the distant shore.

The boat on the beach left first, three kids pushing it off the sand while the fourth worked the controls. They backed away slowly, then turned and roared out into the lake, eventually vanishing into its vastness.

Twenty minutes later, the boat at anchor hoisted its mooring, and it too took off at high speed as soon as its occupants thought they had cleared any nearby rocks.

We were alone. We clambered into the dinghy, Spot making it roll side to side. The little boat had two bench seats, each comprised of a slab of wood about four feet across. I sat on the front one, Leah on the rear where she could reach the twist-grip handle on the outboard to drive and steer. Spot stood across the front seat with his rear legs just behind the board and his front legs up on the big, bouncy, buoyant tube that comprised the perimeter of the inflatable boat.

I asked Leah if she knew how to start the little outboard. She made a blanket claim of ignorance about all things that floated, a claim that I didn't believe. But I talked her through starting the engine. She drove us toward the beach, slowing very little as she deliberately drove us up onto the sand.

Spot jumped out and ran around, making quick reversals in the soft sand and then disappearing into the forest. Leah and I walked the perfect crescent of beach that glowed in the setting sun. We stopped to look at the stone house that Newhall built. The roof and walls were intact. But the windows were gone. The empty rectangular openings were dark in the approaching twilight. They stared at us like eyes of history, having seen much of the story of Tahoe after all but a few of the native Washoe had left.

The sun dropped toward the peaks over by Squaw Valley across the lake. We stood on the shore and watched as it touched the mountains and then dimmed for a slow two minutes. I was aware of a calm in Leah that I hadn't yet seen. The sun flickered, then disappeared. As if by turning a thermostat, the air temperature began to plummet. With miles of 50 degree water and the cold high altitude sky, there was no lingering warmth in the air.

I called Spot and he appeared from the trees out by Deadman Point. He ran up and did a quick stop in front of the dinghy, spraying sand everywhere. Leah and Spot got back into the inflatable boat. I pushed it off the sand and jumped in as it floated away. Leah started the engine on her own and drove it with assurance back to the sailboat. She handled it well enough that I knew she'd be okay when I left her in the morning.

Back on the Ciel, we went below decks. Leah lit a couple of votive candles, and I made a spaghetti dinner. The galley was designed for maximum efficiency in a small space, and while I had to stand spread-eagled and still bow my head to accommodate the six-foot ceiling, I wished I had a galley just like it in place of the kitchen nook in my cabin.

Marjorie had even included a baguette among the food stores, so our feast was complete. I kept the conversation focused on the beach and the sunset, and the combination of that and the food and wine conspired to give Leah an appetite. She ate well.

After dinner, we sat at the table. I poured more wine into our glasses. Spot lay on the carpeted floor. He was curved in an arc, positioned with his head up and resting on the cushion next to Leah. The white areas on his head matched the white leather of the cushion. If I blurred my eyes a little, all I saw in the dim candlelight were irregular black spots on the cushion. Floating above the optical illusion was Leah's hand as she pet him between his ears. His eyes were shut. A half-snore rumbled through his nose, which meant he was half-asleep and half-high on the narcotic of her touch.

I'd gone over the rules with Leah. No cabin lights. Be very careful not to bump the wrong switch and accidentally turn on the running lights or the cockpit lights. Drapes were to stay pulled tight. A maximum of three votive candles for ambient light. For any brighter needs, stick with the penlight and make certain it didn't ever shine on the drapes. Leah had asked if the glowing red clock numbers on the stereo would be too bright. I assured her that they wouldn't be a problem as long as the drapes were closed.

I was sitting on the opposite settee, under the shelves with electronics. The votive candles on the table where Leah sat suddenly flickered under a phantom breeze. Shadows leaped around the boat, then went still as the candle flames calmed.

As the temperature outside cooled further, I shut the one hatch I'd left cracked open. The air went still, and the temperature, maintained by our body heat and the candles, held steady.

I reached up and turned on the stereo, hoping to put on calming music. Jennifer had told us that her onboard library covered every category of music. She'd jokingly explained that she'd assembled a collection of CDs just in case she ever had boat guests like me, who weren't familiar with iPod navigation.

I picked a CD and put it in. Hidden speakers groaned out a weird song sung by an androgynous duo and accompanied by discordant guitar. I replaced the CD and on came another piece of work that could claim neither harmony, melody, nor intelligible lyrics. A third and fourth try brought the same result. Where were The Beatles when you needed them? Or Clapton, or Aaron Copeland, or Oscar Peterson, or Simon and Garfunkle, or Brubeck and Desmond, or Crosby, Stills and Nash, or Samuel Barber, or Gershwin, or Joni Mitchell or Bonnie Raitt?

I continued to run through a selection of Jennifer's music, playing ten or fifteen seconds of each until either Leah or myself broke into a grimace at the strange sounds from bands whose names we'd never heard of.

After my seventh or eighth attempt, Leah couldn't contain herself anymore, and she said, "What is it with this music?"

"I don't know. Maybe this is what they study at Harvard."

Finally, we found both relief and generational intersection with a Norah Jones CD. We drank our wine.

In the spirit of a good work ethic, I poured the rest of the bottle. I thought about mentioning Diamond's call, the name of the TV station delivery driver and his fixation on guns, but decided not to.

Instead, I sipped the rich, elegant liquid, chewed on it like they taught at wine tours, swallowed, and thought that not everything was bleak out on the dark cold giant lake.

In time, Leah said, "I never wanted to be a TV personality."

"You said you majored in art for awhile. Did you always want to be a painter?" I asked.

"Yeah. My dad was supposed to have been a good doctor. I guess I don't know for sure. I assume so. But he probably could have made it as a painter. He was amazing. When I was little, I thought it was magic. Start with some paint and canvas and end up with an image of a person. I know that influenced me."

"Would he have been happier as a painter? It's much harder to make a living in art than it is in medicine."

"I don't know about happiness. But I think it would have been worth it for him to try. When a person gets old and looks back at their life, how do they score comfort and standard-of-living compared to the pursuit of something much more challenging, something they were more likely to fail at, something that would almost preclude them from having comfort and an easy standard-of-living?"

I didn't have an answer for that. "That portrait above the fireplace," I said. "You said it was you as a little girl?"

Leah nodded.

"It looked like a Vermeer," I said. "Very impressive. Do you ever paint like that?"

"No. I could never paint like that. I'm not that accomplished. Landscapes are easier than portraits," she said. "At least for me, anyway."

"The painting your dad had started, the one in his studio, that was a landscape."

"Yeah. I don't ever remember him painting landscapes when I was young."

"If he never painted landscapes, how did you end up focusing on them?

"I've never thought about it. We lived in Berkeley, so mostly I was exposed to an urban landscape. But when we'd head out of the Bay Area, I was always taken with those big rounded hills, green in the winter and spring and golden by early summer. And the trees climbing up the slopes made those fantastic patterns. I guess the shapes drew me to paint them."

"After majoring in art, why didn't you pursue it full time?"

"I knew it wasn't practical. I got a job working at a TV station right out of college. I was able to pay the bills from day one. Even the best painters take years of building a career before they can pay the bills."

Leah held her glass by the stem and moved it around one of the candles, watching how the wine refracted the light.

"I always liked a lot of those Nineteenth Century landscapes," I said. "Cole and Church and Bierstadt."

Leah raised her eyebrows. "You know about art?"

"Not much. I have some art books I like to look at."

"I love those romantic painters, but I could never paint like them. I don't have that ability. My paintings are more about color. A sort of romance with the land. Grasses shimmering in the sunshine, and Black oak trees almost as dark as their name. I'm kind of fixated on the patterns of the trees on the hills. It's like calligraphy. But just saying those descriptions makes me sound so naïve," she said. "I should have a better description."

"No, that description is fine." I wanted to keep her talking. "Did you learn how to paint from watching your father?"

"Not much. He never taught me directly. In some ways I learned more from my mother, even though she left when I was very young. As I grew older, I studied the few paintings she left behind. Dad often said she was a better painter than he was. Several years after she left, he gave me a set of her paintings. They were watercolors on paper, very small, four-by-six inches. Landscapes. Their detail was exquisite. I studied them for hours when I was young. I still do. In the beginning I tried to copy them, but that was futile. So I made up my own style, a little looser."

"Do you think you will ever show your paintings?"

She shook her head. "I'd love to, if anyone liked them. But I won't. When those galleries said no to me, that was hard. It took the fun out of painting. You put so much effort into a pursuit like this, you want to think that someone else might like them. It was my first experience with that kind of rejection. Very painful." Leah touched the tip of her finger to the liquid wax in one of the candles. She held her finger up and watched as the wax congealed. "I've told myself that it isn't personal, that the burning pain will go away with time. And I suppose it has. But I'm not eager to face that again. And now with my..." She started to raise her hand toward what was left of her ear, then stopped and consciously lowered her hand back to the table. "I could never go before the public."

"Sure, you could," I said. "People look past scars. They see the person behind the face."

"No," Leah said, looking at me hard. "They don't. I *know* TV. For years, I heard all the comments about my flawless skin, my eyebrows, my teeth. I never once heard anybody comment on my trenchant interviewing style. Not one time did anyone at a party ever say that I was good at being a talk show host. No one ever sent me an email saying I should be nominated for any of the awards. Instead, they would always say things like I looked so good on TV. Or my face was so photogenic."

Leah raised her hand again, this time unaware of her movements. She traced the scar that pulled at her eyebrow, ran her fingertip along the raised pink welt below her cheekbone, and stopped at the bandage where Doc Lee had put in the new stitches two nights ago.

"I could never face the public again. I would be petrified and humiliated."

"I know it's hard, Leah, but you will get over it."

"You don't understand, Owen! I never was a beauty queen, but I've made my living from how I look! My very identity is wrapped up in that. Now it's gone! It would be like if you got in an accident and were injured, and when you woke up you no longer had what makes you Owen McKenna. No one would call you and ask for your help. They would know that their previous concept of you was no longer there."

I disagreed with her, but everything I was inclined to say would only reinforce her notion that I didn't get it. "I believe that your core group of viewers would still tune in if you went back on the air."

"Sure. For awhile." Leah's voice was a sneer. "They'd want to see if the newspaper stories were true. Was I an ugly witch? It would be like gawkers at an accident. And the people who never liked me or resented my success, they would tune in to gloat. There's a great reason to go back on the air."

"I didn't mean it that way, Leah. I meant that the people who cared about you, the strangers out there in TV land who thought of you as their friend, they would still find a connection to you. Viewers like Jennifer. You would be a role model for coping with adversity."

"Wow, that's what we all want," she said with sarcasm, "not to be appreciated for our abilities alone, but for our abilities in spite of our handicaps. I could be the poster child for accident victims."

She reached over to one of the candles and bent in the edges of the aluminum tin, misshaping it into a crooked form. Her small movements were imbued with anger.

"Yeah," I said. "I get it. Maybe it will still burn, but who will want it?"

"Well, it's a moot point, anyway. Last week, before dad... before all this, I called the station. Just to, you know, kind of see what was happening. I talked to Cindy, the office manager. I asked if anyone had called. You know what she said? She said that three of my show sponsors had called. Do you know why? They were worried that their contracts would require them to continue to pay their fees even though I'd been in an accident. They wanted Cindy to know that no way would they pay, that they were backing out no matter what the contract said."

"It was just an awkward way of saying that they would accept no substitutes, that the station couldn't get by with putting in someone else."

"Right." Leah's hands were on the table in front of her, tightened into fists, her knuckles white from clenching. "Not one of them even asked how I was doing. They didn't care about my injuries. They didn't call to say that they were staying on until I could go back on the air. I thought I had accumulated some goodwill, that they were on board with me for more than just my weekly ratings." Tears ran down her cheeks making shiny tracks that reflected the candlelight.

"I can never face them again." She made a small head shake. Tears dropped onto the table. "I don't even know how I will ever be able to go to the grocery store again. I'll have to move away."

"It's a fear you can get over," I said.

"No." She sounded adamant. "It's worse than my fear of this psycho or whoever's trying to kill me. Fine, let him kill me. At least I won't have to face my old life again. I won't have to see the looks on people's faces when they stare at my scars."

THIRTY-ONE

I tried to steer our conversation around to a better subject, but my attempts were awkward and forced. Leah's mind was in a rough place, and I'm not one of those people who believe that you can just think happy thoughts and snap out of it. Depression and grief are as serious as any physical wounds, and they take a long time to heal. If Leah could ever get past the psychic trauma and broken heart, she had more surgery and physical stress to look forward to.

Without saying another word, Leah picked up one of the candles, went into the forward cabin and shut the door. I took the one remaining candle and went into the port-side, aft cabin, leaving the door open. Spot came in, sniffed around, then walked back to the forward cabin and sniffed at Leah's door. He eventually lay down on the saloon floor, the half-way-point between us.

I wanted to call Street, but I was afraid that I'd pass on my dark thoughts. Even more, I worried that Leah would overhear me talking to Street and feel additional despair as she was reminded that the two closest people in her life were gone.

So I kept my phone off and hoped that if Street called and got my voice mail, she'd phone Jennifer. I knew that Jennifer would do a good job of explaining where I was and reassuring Street that Leah and I were safe.

The bed in my cabin was big for a boat. Which meant that when I angled myself diagonally on the bed, my cold toes only hung a half-foot off the end. I blew out the candle and lay there, struggling with my recent missteps.

In spite of having been up for nearly two days, sleep came with reluctance and visited in bits and pieces. Somewhere in the middle of the night I jerked awake after having a dream about a monster with stinking fur and brown teeth and claw arms. I couldn't shake the image.

With dawn, I got up and made coffee.

When Leah emerged from the forward cabin, she didn't look any more rested than I felt. We were polite if perfunctory in our short conversations, and we focused on the basics of how Leah could spend the day, taking Spot to the shore, minimizing the time he would attract attention. I finished with the admonition that she always keep Jennifer's company's cell phone on her.

I said goodbye, left on the runabout, and piloted it at its maximum speed of fifteen or sixteen miles per hour back to Jennifer's mansion. The remote worked as advertised, and the boathouse door raised up. I tied the runabout to the indoor dock, opposite the rocket speedboat, lowered the door, and walked up toward the house. I thought of stopping to say hello, but saw Jennifer on the phone through the windows in the study. We waved, and I continued around to the garage, where I passed over Maria's rusted pickup for Jennifer's new Toyota.

I let myself out of the big gate at the end of the drive, drove up the East Shore and around to Tahoe City on the northwest shore. The day was stunning in its blue sky, blue water elegance. I tried to spend my time in productive thought, but it was hard to reconcile such beauty with Grendel and company.

Twin Peaks Art was on the lake-side of Tahoe City's main street. I parked a block down. The art side and the frame side each had their own door. I went in the frame side.

The space was narrow and deep and was divided half way back by a counter that bisected the store from left to right. The front half of the store had carpeted walls on which were stuck what seemed like thousands of corner samples of picture frame moulding. They ran from skinny half-inch-wide pieces all the way up to heavy six-inch-wide chunks. The styles and finishes were too numerous to count, from clean modern designs to grandiose, ornate mouldings in metallic golds, silvers and pewters.

The front door opened behind me and in came a large, muscular man about 30 years old. He walked bent forward from the shoulders and carried a plastic grocery bag.

"Hi," he said to me. "I'm Jeter. I'll get Vienna to help you. Or Paul. Paul could help you. I know they're around here someplace." He didn't enunciate very well, and he spoke with lots of lip and jaw movement. But he put a smile in every word. "Just let me put down this bag. This is my lunch. I get my lunch at the grocery store. That way I can choose from all of the different foods. And I save money, too. Today I got a tuna salad sandwich. Do you like tuna salad?"

"Yes, I do."

"Me too." He grinned. "Okay, I'll get Vienna."

He took large syncopated steps as he walked, making a thud each time his left foot hit the floor. He went through the opening into the gallery and disappeared.

I walked over and looked at a large machine that was on the other side of the central counter. It had a narrow, horizontal metal platform, maybe ten feet long, with ruler marks on it. In the middle of the platform, poised six inches above it, were two giant blades, 8" X 8" slabs of metal, polished and shiny as knives in a Hitchcock movie. The blades were set at an angle to the platform.

"Helluva piece of framing equipment, huh?"

I turned to see a man about my age wearing a navy-blue, pinstriped business suit with a pink handkerchief tucked in the breast pocket, a rare sight in the land of jeans and sweatshirts.

I gestured at the machine. "For cutting moulding?"

"Yeah. My favorite framing tool." He pointed toward the back wall of the shop. "The big saw over there works better on most of the mouldings, but this is a real beauty on soft woods. It's called a chopper. Put the moulding on the rail, hit the compressed-air switch, and bam. One chop. Cuts the moulding at a perfect forty-five degree angle. Or, as the case may be, you can chop off your body parts at a perfect forty-five degree angle. One chop." He came over to me and held out his hand. "I'm Paul."

"And you'll be my art consultant today, tomorrow, or for the rest of my life." I shook his hand.

"You called," he said. "I remember you. But I forget what we talked about."

"A man named Dr. Kiyosawa," I said. "An artist I know. You said you didn't sell his work but that he'd been in asking questions about framing."

"Yes, of course."

The young man came back through, lurching with every step of his left foot. He spoke in a loud voice as if announcing to a large group. "Vienna's in her office talking on the phone to her boyfriend. She said to tell you that she's busy. But she said you can talk to Paul. That's Paul." He pointed.

Paul rolled his eyes the way teenaged girls do. "In case you didn't notice, he's already talking to me, Jeets."

"Oh. I didn't know. Okay." Jeter left.

"Do you remember what Dr. Kiyosawa wanted to know about framing?" I asked.

Paul frowned and turned his head a bit to the side, judging me.

"Sorry if that seems like an invasion of privacy," I said. "But if I'm able to buy one of his paintings, I'd like to put it in a frame that I know he'd approve of."

"Actually, he was interested in the classic old frames. He wondered if there were new mouldings that look old."

"Are there?"

Paul walked over to one of the display walls, started removing corner samples from their Velcro mounts and set them on the counter. Jeter came out of the back area carrying a large plastic trash can. He set it down near the front door, then went into the gallery side, thumping on his left foot. He returned with a smaller wastebasket and dumped its trash into the larger can. Some papers missed and fluttered across the floor.

"Damnit, Jeetsie!" Paul shouted. "I told you not to do garbage when a customer is in the store!"

"But the trash was full." Jeter's face turned tomato red.

"You can wait until the customer leaves!"

"I'm sorry. I'm sorry." Jeter quickly scrambled to scoop up the loose papers and put them in the trash can. But instead of taking it out the front door, he took the longer route and hauled the can back past us and into the back of the frame shop. He looked confused and afraid as he went by.

After he got the trash in back, he came back out without the can, his face heavy with contrition. "I'm sorry, Paul. I won't do it again."

Paul waved him away with a disgusted swipe of his hand.

"Just a minute," I said to Paul. I went in back and walked over to Jeter who stood facing the wall.

"Hey, Jeter," I said. I put my hand on his shoulder. "Paul's concern is a good one, about not irritating customers with garbage chores, but I want you to know that it didn't bother me. So don't sweat it this time, okay?"

Jeter turned and looked at me. His eyes were moist. He made a solemn nod.

I went back to Paul.

"So, before we were rudely interrupted," Paul said with melodramatic inflection, "I was going to show you these mouldings. All old looking. Italian Renaissance, mostly. But I should explain that when we build frames, you will have a mitered corner. We putty the gilded compo areas so the seams look good, but they're still mitered."

"And that's not the way they were originally done," I said.

"No. The Renaissance craftsmen built the sub-frame first. Then they layered on plaster to create the elaborate hand-carved look. The plaster covered all the corner joints. After they gilded the plaster and put a patina on it, the entire front of the frame was seamless. We can actually order that type of frame in any size for you, but instead of paying, say, six hundred bucks for a mitered frame about this size," he held his arms out in front of him, "you'd pay ten or fifteen times as much for a closed-corner, custom-gilded frame."

"Out of my league," I said.

"Me, too," he said.

"I'm guessing that Dr. Kiyosawa would probably like one of those, what did you call it, closed-corner frames?"

"Yes. That's what he said. He said he'd think about it, and he left."

"I've called all the galleries I found in the book," I said. "Any idea where else I might look to find out who sells his paintings?"

Paul shook is head. "I suppose you might try Olympia. She has connections all over the country."

"Who's Olympia?" I asked.

"Atelier Olympia? On the West Shore? Down by Tahoma? They are one of the major ateliers west of the Hudson River."

"You mean the Hudson River as in New York."

"Is there another Hudson River?"

"Just checking," I said. "Atelier Olympia is named for the woman who owns it?"

"Oh, yes." Paul did the eye-roll again. "She is the big cheese, the chief of chiefs. Do you have a favorite Latin American dictator? An African tyrant you're particularly fond of? If so, Olympia—pardon my French—could whip his ass. I believe the order is, meet her, genuflect before her, then watch your backside. She's chewed up more artists and collectors than your average T-Rex ate Bambi's ancestors."

"You have a way with description."

Paul flipped his hand like he was batting at a fly. "It's the actor in me. Years and years of dinner theater. Just between you and me, you can make more money in one good week of selling art than you can make in a year of performing on stage.

"Anyway, if you want art info, start at the top is my motto. Even if the top is a killer lizard with a little Grendel in its DNA."

"Grendel?" I said, amazed that the word could come up again in so short a time.

"Oh, yes, Grendel. It's a word for the meanest dude around, I guess. I heard it used the other day. Something about evil. I love new words, don't you? So I'm using it every chance I get. That's how I learn new words. I use them over and over. So when the subject of the monstrous Olympia came up, well, I just had to throw that in."

"Curious," I said. "What was this thing you heard about Grendel?"

"Just that. I was somewhere, in a store or at my hairdresser, or someplace. Someone said, 'Grendel is the baddest gang going.' As an ex-actor, I have an ear for unusual words. When I heard the word Grendel, it stuck in my brain like a poppy seed in my teeth."

"Do you remember who said it?"

"No. It was, like, someone on the other side of the aisle in the supermarket. I didn't care about the person. I just liked the word. Grendel. It even sounds evil, doesn't it?

"Now," he continued, holding up his index finger, "if Olympia darling is not in, try Gracie. A wee thing, frail as a feather, but she knows her stuff. Don't talk too loud, though, or she'll blow over. It's not that she's so tiny—although she is small—it's that she's so meek. How she teaches with that shy manner and miniature voice, is beyond me. It must be that her expertise comes through."

"She teaches painting?"

"She owns painting. She is painting. The entire breadth and

depth of the subject belongs to her. Why she teaches when she could be turning out masterpieces is beyond me. I swear, that woman could paint a Vermeer if she wanted to, and no one could tell the difference."

"Why do you say Vermeer?" I asked.

"A figure of speech. Because she can paint anything. So why doesn't she? Instead, she teaches others to paint. Sure, some of her students are very good—I've seen some of the work—but wouldn't it be more fun to paint a Vermeer? Hell, you could sell it on the black market. Think of the change even a fake Vermeer would bring. Of course, if *she* did it, no one could tell it was fake. Anyway, Gracie is Madam Olympia's secret weapon.

"So go crash the soiree over at Atelier Olympia. That's another new word. For me, anyway. Soiree. Isn't it fun? Then, when you're ready to buy some art, you know who to talk to." He grinned and took a grand bow, sweeping his hand down in a big arc.

A woman appeared in the gallery opening. "Your young client couple from the other day is back, Paul," she said.

Paul turned toward the woman.

"They're looking at the large Emerald Bay." Her eyes sparkled, and she made a big, obvious wink.

Paul turned back to me. "Do you mind if I..."

"You've got a live wire, go for it," I said.

He leaned toward me and spoke in a conspiratorial whisper. "When young couples are exposed to the world of art according to Paul, they are helpless against my expertise."

"You could be their art consultant today, tomorrow..."

"And for the rest of their lives!" Paul said as he rushed into the gallery.

I followed him into the gallery, then turned to leave. I changed my mind and walked back toward the frame shop, wondering if I could get Jeter alone and pick his brain for information on all the people who come and go through Twin Peaks Art. He might be slow, but that didn't mean he wasn't observant.

I paused at the opening between the two stores and looked in.

Jeter didn't see me. He was bent over the chopper, sliding a long piece of fancy moulding along the rail. He moved slowly and methodically. When he got the piece to the correct place on the ruled scales, he snapped heavy-duty clamps down on the moulding to hold it in place. Then he swung an articulated lamp around and shined it where the end of the moulding rested against the ruler. Jeter leaned in even closer, aligned his fingernail at the exact point on the scale, scrunched up his face, squinted his eyes in concentration. He methodically released the clamps, made a micro adjustment, reset the clamps. Checked again. Released the clamps a second time. Made an even tinier micro-micro adjustment. Set the clamps a third time, checked yet again. Stood back and took in the big picture. The moulding faced the correct way. The setting was NASA-engineer-accurate. He held his hands up and looked at them. All fingers accounted for. He flipped a switch in a hard-to-reach location on the machine. Probably turning the safety off. Hands went into his pockets, just to be sure. Moved to the side. Carefully, very carefully, reached the toe of his shoe out to the foot-activated compressed-air switch. Toe made contact.

BAM! Flash of Hitchcock blades. Blast of compressed air. One chop. Two ends cut. Center cutoff piece dropped into catch bucket. Perfect 45-degree angles. All fingers still safe in pockets.

I decided I'd talk to him later.

I pushed out the front door and headed down the sidewalk having absorbed the first lesson of making picture frames with very expensive moulding. Measure sixty-nine times, cut once.

THIRTY-TWO

I got the atelier's number from Information and called them.

"You've reached Atelier Olympia," answered a computerized female voice with a BBC accent. "If you know your party's extension, dial it now. For the class schedule, press one. For directions to our atelier, press two. For..."

I pressed two. The computer gave me confusing instructions on how to get to the school. It was south of the Homewood Ski Area, south of the Tahoma Market. On the lake side. I found some paper and made some notes.

I drove down the West Shore, passed Sunnyside and continued several more miles. Address numbers were sparse. The old residences had wooden signs tacked to trees at the entrances to long, narrow driveways, the numbers long since faded to near-invisibility. The new mansions had addresses cast in what looked like gold and embedded in ostentatious gates set into over-arching gatehouses made of stone and heavy timbers. I tried to concentrate on the numbers as I drove, but I couldn't stop wondering about Paul's mention of Grendel. From my first day as a rookie cop twenty-some years ago, I learned not to believe in coincidences with crime.

I went through Tahoma, then realized I'd missed my turnoff. Doubling back, I slowed when I thought I was close, then spotted a tiny sign, mottled black letters on a peeling gray background. ATELIER OLYMPIA.

The road was pebbles covered with pine needles and interspersed with tufts of grass and a few weeds. The natural debris was ground fine where the wheel tracks were, with a thicker mat of duff in the center. I drove at walking speed down the bumping drive, winding through heavy stands of fir. A tenth of a mile in, the trees opened up, and there was a lawn, the green grass thin under the thick canopy of towering California Red fir above. There was a parking area, unpaved but marked by a perimeter line of cobbles. I parked on grassy dirt alongside eight or ten cars, most of them older models as would fit those of typical art students.

The building was an old Tahoe-style lodge with sheets of bark for siding and large logs that made over-hanging roof trusses on each end. It was probably built as a summer lodge 80 years ago. It had since been remodeled with large skylights and new, large picture windows. But the bark siding, having weathered the elements well for all these years, had been left untouched.

I walked up onto the wide porch. The deck boards were worn smooth from decades of use. One of the double front doors was propped open. I stepped into an entry room that had sheetrock walls and showed no trace of the original construction. Lit by fluorescent ceiling fixtures, it had a library table with six chairs, racks with art brochures, a pad of pre-printed Atelier Olympia registration forms, a computer with an art slide show as a screen saver. One side of the entry room was nearly covered by a large bulletin board with show notices, postcards for gallery openings, roommate-wanted ads with tear-off phone numbers, help-wanted ads, studio space opportunities, art supply discount coupons for stores in Reno and Sacramento, calls for models, notices of critique groups offered and critique groups wanted, comic strips with art themes, canvas stretching workshops offered, and a number of 3 X 5 cards with art jokes on them, one of which caught my attention. "Corot painted 2000 paintings during his life, 5000 of which are in collections in the United States."

Nearby was another, smaller bulletin board with just enough room for a sheet that had the class schedule. There were only three classes offered for the summer, spanning from the middle of June to the middle of August.

Portraiture: Lessons from the Masters
Light: Creating Drama with Natural Light
Landscape: Effective Compositions

The portrait class was taught by Olympia. One word. No last name needed for someone of her stature.

The other two classes were taught by Gracie Crumpton, the woman that Paul from Twin Peaks Art told me about.

According to the schedule, the landscape class would be under way at that moment.

I pushed open one of the interior double doors just enough to look in and see that the room was empty. I walked in.

It was a large, lofty space, with a cathedral ceiling 30 feet high, white walls, a white vinyl tile floor. Many skylights were installed on the north side of the roof.

A dozen large wooden easels were arranged in a semi-circle. Each had a canvas on it with a landscape painting in progress. None of the paintings was the same, but they all had water in them. Every one was beautifully painted in a style that seemed hundreds of years old. Clearly, you didn't get to be a student at the atelier unless you were already very good. Equally clear was that no grunge, punk, or in-your-face modern artists need apply.

I studied a few of the paintings, then walked out through the doors on the lake side of the building.

Like the front side of the lodge, the back side had a large covered porch. Steps led down to a lawn, which stretched to the lake. In the distance above Incline Village on the far shore, the ski runs of Diamond Peak had lost most of their snow to the June sun. Above and to the north, Mt. Rose was still white with a snowpack that would last another month or two.

On the lawn in front of me was a group down by the water. A tiny woman was talking to them. I didn't want to interrupt, so I sat on one of the Adirondack deck chairs and waited.

Listening very carefully, I could just make out what she was saying in her very soft voice.

She was talking about painting water.

"One of our missions in painting like the Renaissance masters is painting stunning detail. Not everywhere on your canvas, of course. But where the focus of the painting is, the detail should often be dazzling. I don't mean photo-real. I mean soft-focus dazzling.

"But here's the problem. Let's say you've got a boat on the water, and the boat is the focus of the painting. You will be tempted to paint the nearby water with detail appropriate to the detail of the boat. But you can't do it, because no one from those past eras had ever seen the detail in moving water. Even after the invention of photography, it wasn't until well into the Twentieth Century before they developed the high-speed shutters necessary to freeze the image of moving water. We've all studied those patterns that photographs reveal in water. It is very hard to get rid of that influence. But to paint like the masters from centuries ago, you have to remove your modern-day knowledge of how water looks frozen in time."

She waved her hand out at the lake, which had a gentle chop under a soft breeze. "You have to look at water and paint only what you see, not what you know. That is your challenge. Paint the color, the movement, the shape, the reflected light. But none of those detailed patterns from photographs.

"Okay, back to your painting. We've got another hour."

The students turned and ambled back up the lawn. Some glanced at me as they walked up the steps to the back porch. Others were busy talking and didn't notice my presence.

The ten or twelve students comprised a remarkable age range, from a boy who could not have been more than fourteen or fifteen, to a woman who was in her eighties. None of them looked much like a typical student at a typical art school, festooned with ragged clothes, multiple body piercings and purple hair. These were the conservatives of the art world, intensely focused and dedicated, less concerned with making a splash and starting a new look, and more concerned with learning to paint extremely well.

Eventually, the last student separated from the teacher, and the teacher came up the lawn alone. I went down the steps to meet her on the grass.

She was as wee and frail as Paul had said, barely five feet tall, her drab bulky clothes unable to conceal a thin body that swayed as if it had no bones. She was maybe fifty years old, and her gray-brown hair looked as if it hadn't been combed for half of those years. It was a thick, ratty, scraggly nest that was pulled behind her head and wrestled into submission by one of those clamps that secretaries use when they have too many sheets of paper for a simple paperclip. The woman looked clean, but otherwise reminded me of a peasant woman from the past centuries that she talked about.

"Hello, my name's Owen McKenna, and I'm looking for Gracie."

She held out a tiny hand. "That would be me," she said. "How can I help you?"

We shook. Her tiny, soft hand felt like that of a five-year-old.

"I'm hoping you know of an artist named Dr. Gary Kiyosawa."

"No. I've never heard of him."

"Japanese-American. About five-six. Short gray hair. Mid-seventies. A little moustache. Smart, quiet, very private." I remembered Leah's complaint about Diamond confusing skill with talent. "He was a very skilled painter. I had his daughter make a little drawing of him." I pulled it out of my pocket and showed her.

"This is John Saki. At least, that is the name he gave me. He's taken my class on natural light, and he also just took the portrait class, which I teach in the winter when Olympia is in Mexico. Nice drawing, by the way. His daughter has some of his talent. Is something wrong? How strange that he would use a different name."

"I'm very sorry to say that he died three days ago."

"Oh, God. Oh, my. What happened? Was he ill? He seemed healthy as can be."

"He was murdered."

She put her hand to her mouth in that universal look of horror.

"I'm a private investigator working with the Douglas County Sheriff's Office." I handed her a card. "We believe that the motive of the killer may have had some connection with the doctor's painting."

Gracie's eyes showed nothing but shock. "You think he was killed because of his painting? I've never heard of anything so ridiculous."

"He went to great lengths to keep his painting a secret. Not even his daughter who recently lived with him knew about it. He had an art studio in his house, but he never showed it to her. And now you've just told me that he used a pseudonym when he took your class."

"Well, you just described him as private. Many painters pursue painting for personal growth or private joy. They aren't interested in selling or answering questions about why they are painting."

"What did Kiyosawa, or Saki, as you knew him, paint?"

Gracie looked at me. "You want me to violate that privacy that we were just discussing."

"He's dead. The killer is now after his daughter. Her name is Leah Printner. You maybe know of her. She was the host of the TV talk show, Tahoe Live."

Gracie raised her eyebrows. "She is his daughter? Maybe that's why he was so private. Because she was so public."

"Not anymore. The killer caused a car accident that killed her husband and gave her serious injuries. She's lost her show and her livelihood. She may be the next victim if we can't catch her father's murderer."

Gracie looked at her watch. "I'm sorry, I have many things I have to finish before I can close up the school."

"Can I talk to you later?"

"I have to leave here after I close up. This afternoon is studio time. I'm very rigorous about making time for my own painting."

"The murderer shot at Kiyosawa's daughter. We hid her at a house, then at a motel, and the killer found out, broke in both places. She is now in a new hiding place. If the killer can find her, she is dead. Is your studio time worth more than her life?"

Gracie made a big sigh. "Okay. Come to my studio at four? Here is the address." She handed me a card. "I'm just west of here, in the little neighborhood across the main street."

THIRTY-THREE

Gracie's studio was in a small neighborhood within walking distance of the Tahoma Market. I turned off the highway onto a side street with a few new, huge houses mixed in with older homes and some old log cabins.

I found Gracie's number on the side of one of those cabins. From the outside, it looked to be a two-room design, almost as small as mine. The log walls were darkened with age and varnished to a high sheen. Several large California Red fir towered above while a small white fir stood near the door. It was bent from too much winter snow and looked as frail as the woman inside the cabin. An old Subaru was parked on the sand in front. I pulled Jennifer's Toyota to a stop on the side of the road and got out.

Despite the bright summer afternoon sun, little light came through the heavy tree canopy. Gracie's corner of the neighborhood was in almost permanent twilight.

I tapped on the door, and she opened it in a few seconds.

"Come on in," she said in her soft voice. "My studio is also my house, so there is very little room."

I stepped into a living room that was about the same size as the dressing room that Dr. Kiyosawa used for his studio. Gracie had an easel that held a partially completed landscape of vineyards and mountains. Nearby was a small rolling cart with what looked like hundreds of paint tubes in the lower bins and hundreds of brushes in coffee cans on the top. She also had a rocking chair, a foot locker, two file cabinets, a small table and single chair. All of the room's contents were situated to give large berth to an old wood-burning stove, which, when hot, would cook anything near it. In stark contrast to Kiyosawa's neat studio with its clean white walls and the unmarred drop cloth protecting the floor, Gracie's space was a cluttered mess of stacked canvases, cardboard boxes with miscellaneous jars and other supplies. In front of the easel was a wooden barstool.

"Please sit on the rocker," she said as she hitched a leg up and perched on the stool. "What can I tell you about my poor, departed art student?"

I stepped through the clutter, careful not to knock over any of her stuff, and sat on the rocker.

"How long have you known Dr. Kiyosawa?"

"Let me think. The man I knew as John Saki took his first class at the atelier a year ago this last spring. So about fifteen months."

"Were you his teacher?"

"Yes. Normally, Olympia—she's the founder of the atelier—she teaches portraiture. But not during the winter when John took it. So I taught both of John's, I mean, Dr. Kiyosawa's classes."

"Pardon me for this question, but why do people take classes at an atelier? What do you teach that is different from, say, art classes at a university?"

"We teach similar subjects. The difference is intensity. We only work with students who have a serious level of skill and focus. Often, they already have MFAs from good art schools. But they want to go to the next level."

"So they have to apply? They can't just pay the money and sign up?"

"Correct. First, they show us their portfolio. If we feel they are of sufficient caliber, then we interview them extensively. We look for a proper attitude about art, confidence but with appropriate humility. We cannot deal with prima donnas or those who are arrogant and self-centered. We are in service to the making of art, not to the aggrandizement of the artists."

"Are most of your students like Kiyosawa? Serious hobbyists?"

"Oh, no. Most of our students are professional painters who are represented in the finest galleries. We currently have only two who are not actively pursuing a professional career. One is a young boy, a prodigy who is still in high school. The other is, was, John. Dr. Kiyosawa. All of our other students have come in from across the country to study with Olympia."

"And you."

Gracie made a little self-conscious nod. "And me."

"Olympia must be a very accomplished painter."

"Yes, but even more, she is an amazing teacher. It is like any field. The really excellent science professor or music teacher or football coach, they all have or had great skill. But even more, they know how to teach and inspire to a great level. Olympia's students are at the top of their field. Their work is in demand around the world."

I pointed at the painting on the easel. "You obviously do landscapes. Is that your specialty? Or are you equally adept at portraits?"

"Landscape is my specialty as a painter. But I have a good ability to see. I understand portraiture. I'm good at teaching it. I'm like a string player whose performing strength is on the cello, but who has an equal ear for the violin. I can watch as someone is developing a portrait and see what often escapes them. I have mid-wifed some amazing portraits from my students over the years."

"I'm curious," I said. "Why the teaching? Why not just be a painter?" I gestured at the landscape. "This is amazing work. Couldn't you sell your work in galleries? Maybe make more money?"

"It's hard to explain. I like teaching. Helping a good artist develop into a great artist is very rewarding. But I also recognize that I don't have the right personality to market myself. The business of art is ninety percent business. You have to do lots of openings, work the crowd, meet hundreds of people, have dinner with collectors, give talks to groups. Successful artists are natural promoters. Sure, it takes art ability to make it. But if you look at Turner or Picasso or Dali or any of a hundred contemporary art stars, you see artists who spend most of their time promoting their work. That's not me. I'm just a shy woman who likes to stay home with my cat. The first time I taught, I threw up from the nausea of nervousness. When they say that people are more afraid of public speaking than anything else, that is me a hundred times over. I could no more attend my own opening than I could run for president."

"So you don't sell your work in galleries?"

"I do. I have a gallery in New York that puts my work in their back room. They sell three or four pieces a year. They've said that I could raise my prices, sell many more, and do very well if I came to New York and did the opening routine, pressed the flesh and such, but I can't imagine it. I'd rather have this life, small as it is."

"Let me ask you about Dr. Kiyosawa."

"Please. I'd like to help you catch this person who killed him. Do you have any idea who did it, or why?"

"Not much. The motive for his death is a mystery. But what stands out is that he went to some lengths to keep his art secret. He also recently spent nearly two hundred thousand dollars on his daughter's medical expenses. Until recently, he didn't appear to have that kind of money. I suspect that he obtained the money with his paintings."

Gracie looked astonished. She shook her head as if in denial. "I don't think that's possible unless you are famous."

"His daughter said that he painted many years ago," I continued, "but she never knew he'd taken it up again. The situation suggests that he took it up as a business proposition. Perhaps he saw an opportunity to make some money. What I'd like from you are any thoughts you might have on how Kiyosawa could have earned a great deal of money from his art."

"I thought he was a skillful hobbyist," Gracie said. "I assumed he was a well-to-do retired man who was focusing on art as a love, not a business. I can't imagine how he could make that kind of money with paintings. I certainly couldn't."

Gracie shifted on the barstool so that her other hip was perched on the seat.

"What did he paint in your classes?"

"He painted portraits. He was especially good at Vermeer's style. He did some copies of Vermeer's portraits. I swear even I would've thought they were the originals, had I seen them in a museum."

"Is that normal, to do copies of famous portraits? Isn't that, in a sense, a forgery?"

"Nonsense. Painters have copied long-gone painters for centuries. They're called studies. It's how you learn. It's not a forgery unless you try to pass it off as an original. John Saki or..."

"Dr. Kiyosawa," I said.

"Dr. Kiyosawa would never do that."

"Let's forget, for the moment, what he would do. If, as you stated, you would have been fooled by his Vermeer studies, then others could have thought they were originals, too. He could make money selling forgeries, right?"

"Yes, I suppose. But I just can't see it. I have a good sense of character, and he was a man of fine character."

"His daughter had large medical expenses. He was up against a financial wall." But as I said it, I realized that it made no sense. Leah's accident, and the resulting expense, was recent. Kiyosawa had obviously been hiding his painting for some time.

"Anyway," Gracie continued, ignoring what I'd said, "how can you sell a painting as an original if the original is hanging in a museum, right there for all the world to see?"

"It would have to be a painting that was out of circulation, hanging in some private collector's house," I said.

Gracie shook her head. "But that would only work if the collector was intensely private and secretive. Think about it. Say I had a valuable, important painting. If people started saying that mine was a fake and that another one that showed up on the market was real, then I would be worried. I'd invite curators and other experts into my house to verify that my painting was, in fact, the original."

"Good point," I said. "So the forgery would have to be of a stolen painting. Then anyone who was interested in buying it, whether the original or the fake, would not bring in the experts because it would expose them as being interested in a stolen painting. They would have to rely on their own judgement and maybe the opinion of a close confidant. It might be relatively easy to sell them a good fake. In fact, it's possible that if a forger had the right contacts, he could sell several copies of a stolen painting. A collector in Japan or China or South Africa might not find out that several other people around the world all thought they bought the original stolen painting."

Gracie shook her head. "I just can't see the doctor that way." She stood up, picked up the painting on the easel and turned it upside down. She walked back toward her front door and looked at it from a distance. "And anyway, the Vermeer studies he did were of paintings that are in the Metropolitan Museum."

"In New York."

"Right. He did two paintings. They were a couple of the famous ones."

"Have you heard of any Vermeers that have been stolen?" I asked.

"Maybe. My memory is not clear. Certainly there are lots of famous paintings that have been stolen over the years. I don't pay attention to international art news. But I remember Munch's The Scream was taken out of the Munch Museum in Oslo. And just last year, Van Gogh's Marketplace at Arles was stolen from a train car when it was on tour with that Impressionist show. And that famous sketch that Michelangelo did for one of his Madonna sculptures was stolen from a Swiss banker's private collection during a party he had. I'm sure there are lots more."

"Maybe Kiyosawa was painting like some of those other artists?"

Gracie shook her head. "I doubt it. Becoming an accomplished painter in Vermeer's style is one thing. Doing it with a completely different style would be extremely difficult. It would be like a virtuoso violinist switching to the bassoon. Sure, they would have the advantage of their deep understanding of music. But they'd still have to learn an entirely new technique, a very difficult technique."

"What about other Dutch painters with similar styles? Frans Hals or Rembrandt?"

She raised her eyebrows. "You know something of painting?"

"I've just been to a few museums, read a few books. Do you think that would be possible, Kiyosawa painting in a similar style?"

"I suppose that would be a little easier. I still don't believe it, though. And besides, Hals and Rembrandt and Vermeer had quite different styles."

"I meant they were similar in a broad sense. One can compare them to each other., It wouldn't be like comparing a Vermeer to a Chuck Close."

"No, of course not."

"Let's say you painted a forgery and you wanted to sell it. Do you have any idea where you would go? Who you would talk to?"

"Mr. McKenna, I'm sure you are joking. I'm an art teacher. I live in Tahoe. Sure, it's a fabulous place where the rich and famous come to play, and maybe even some serious art collectors vacation. But it's an artistic backwater. I would no more know the answer to that than I would know how to sell a forged manuscript or pirated movies."

THIRTY-FOUR

Special Agent Ramos was out when I stopped by the FBI Office in South Lake Tahoe. The secretary thought he'd be back soon. I walked down to the nearest coffee shop, reloaded my caffeine supplies and came back. Ramos was in.

"McKenna," he said when he saw me.

Ramos and I had a mutually disagreeable relationship similar to that of some cops and FBI agents. Cops sometimes feel that they do the hard work of fighting crime in the streets, and FBI agents often come in with the arrogance that comes with law degrees and higher authority and take over—and often mess up—the cops' cases. Agents sometimes feel that cops are excessively protective of their territory and that cops don't appreciate the responsibility that agents carry in dealing with the serious scope of the crimes they are charged with solving.

"Agent Ramos," I said. "Good to see you."

"Yes, I'm sure we both agree on that."

"I'm working on the Kiyosawa murder."

"I heard. You think this is going to come under FBI purview?"

"Maybe. Maybe not. I think Kiyosawa was involved in painting art forgeries."

"You have any evidence?"

"No. Suggestive circumstances. Enough to bring me here." I gave him the basics.

Ramos breathed out heavily, his natural hubris filling the small office. He was an important man, had important things to do, and I was a small-town PI taking up his valuable time with nothing but supposition.

"And you want what from me?" he said.

"A call to your Art Crimes Team. A question about anything going down regarding stolen Vermeers or any paintings by other

Seventeenth Century Dutch artists."

"You think that was what Kiyosawa was doing in his little secret art studio? Painting Vermeers?" Ramos made what looked like a genuine smile while he put a sneer into his words.

"Yeah. That's what I think."

"And then our retired doctor found his way into the international art wing of the mob in New York City and sold these forgeries, which were so masterful that the mob believed his song and dance—whatever it was—about how he came by these Vermeers."

"No," I said.

"Then what do you think?"

"I think someone approached him some time back to create a painting to order. Maybe he did it. But then he had second thoughts and resisted the deal. So the killer forced him to follow through by purposely causing the accident that wounded his daughter and killed his son-in-law. The daughter did not have health insurance, so that became the way to both pressure the doctor financially and scare him about what could happen to his daughter if he didn't comply."

"You think he forged a painting that was stolen?"

"Yeah."

"And the money they paid him is what he used to pay off the daughter's hospital bill?"

"Yeah."

"Two hundred large is a big fee," Ramos said.

"True," I said, noticing that Ramos knew the amount of the hospital bill.

"Then why was Kiyosawa killed?"

"I don't know," I said. "Maybe the two hundred thou was a down payment and they killed him so that they didn't have to pay him the balance they owed. Maybe he did several paintings and they paid for the first batch but wanted to get out of the last batch."

"Or," Ramos said, "they wanted to silence him after they got what they wanted."

"Yeah."

"Then how do you explain the burglary of Lauren Phelter's guesthouse after they killed him?"

"Could be unrelated. Or maybe they paid him more money than what Kiyosawa used to pay off the hospital bill, and they wanted it back. He couldn't have put a large amount of cash in the bank. So they would have assumed he hid it someplace. That would explain why they tore the place apart."

Ramos leaned back in his chair. He twitched the perfect little moustache, sniffled as if the inside of his nose itched.

"You paint a very elaborate picture of how Kiyosawa got himself iced," he said.

"You got a less elaborate picture?" I asked.

"I don't need to. Not my crime. Yet." He flipped through a stack of papers on his desk. Opened his Blackberry and punched some buttons. He sighed. He was so busy. Had so many responsibilities. "Okay, maybe I can squeeze in time for a call." He looked at me and waited. I understood he wanted me to leave. Didn't want me to overhear secret FBI talk.

"Thanks," I said. I took a pencil and Post-it note out of the dispenser on his desk. I wrote down the number for the Salazar company cell phone. "Call me at this number?"

He nodded.

I left.

I went out and got in Jennifer's Toyota, trying to figure my next move. Ramos knew that I knew that he didn't have to help me. But we both also knew that I'd been useful to him over the years. And it had been less than two years since Ramos's rep was on the line when the firestarter was torching Tahoe, burning people along with trees. Ramos got it wrong, and he didn't like that I'd solved the case. But he was probably inside making that phone call now because I had stopped the carnage before his reputation went up in flames.

I didn't know if Ramos would get back to me in five minutes, five days, or never. I drove across South Lake Tahoe, then north to Jennifer's, and was out on Beaufort's Beauty by late afternoon.

Leah was quiet. She stayed below while Spot and I sat topside. I didn't know if I should attempt to engage her or let her be introspective in private.

Eventually, I went below and Frankensteined up a batch of Owen's Chili, substituting eight of the nine essential ingredients to accommodate the fixings that Jennifer's housekeeper had put onboard.

Leah was silent through it all.

I set the bowls on the little table, tried to talk while we ate, told her about my day, tried to draw her out, but didn't have much success.

We went to bed soon after we ate.

That night I got up at 3:00 a.m. to use the head on Beaufort's Beauty. I saw a light as I opened my cabin door.

There was a single candle burning on the galley counter. Leah was sitting on the settee, elbows on the table, face in her hands. She looked up at me. She'd been crying.

"Would you like to talk?" I said.

She shook her head.

"Would you like me to sit with you?"

Another shake.

"If I can help, knock on my door."

She nodded.

Leah was cutting up cantaloupe when I emerged from my cabin early in the morning. She looked better.

She handed me a mug of coffee, and I went topside to another perfect Tahoe day. I dialed the phone at my cabin and punched in my voicemail code to retrieve my messages.

The first one was from Street, saying she'd try Jennifer. The second one was from Diamond.

"Got a lead on our mute prisoner. Gimme a call."

I dialed Diamond.

"The kid I told you about who stole the six-pack of beer?" Diamond said after I identified myself. "One of the guys brought him in again on another shoplifting charge. What is it with these kids? You let them go, and they immediately go for an encore? Anyway, this time Jim and I took the kid in and showed him the adult jail. We thought maybe we could scare him with the consequences of choosing the wrong path in life."

"Did it work?"

"Don't know. But we got a payoff, anyway. The kid recognized our mute prisoner."

"Did he say his name?"

"No. In fact, he pretended that he didn't recognize him. But the pretending was so obvious that both Jim and I could tell. So we waited until the kid's lawyer showed up and we made him a deal."

"He talks, you let him go," I said.

"Yeah."

"It work?"

"Maybe. We have a meet scheduled for eight this morning. Us, the kid, his mom, his lawyer, and you, if you want."

"I'll be there."

We met in a conference room at the Douglas County Sheriff's Office. The kid sat on one side of a long table. The lawyer was on his left, his mother on his right. The kid looked about 12 years old. He wore a large T-shirt with the name Grendel printed in large script. I couldn't see his gang-banger pants under the table, but I remembered that Diamond said they hung down off his ass. The kid was small and had soft skin, but he didn't look afraid. He radiated sullen like a roadkill skunk radiates stink.

Diamond and I sat on the other side of the table. Diamond spoke first.

"You recognized the prisoner in our jail."

The kid nodded.

"What is his name?"

"I dunno."

"How do you know him?"

The kid shook his head. "I don't know him. I just seen him."

"Where?"

"Up at Miner's Gulch."

Diamond looked at me. "You know where that is?"

I shook my head.

"Where's Miner's Gulch?" Diamond asked the kid.

"I dunno how to say. You go up the grade toward Tahoe. There's a place where the road makes a big curve, and you take this trail up above the highway. Up in there. You walk way up, and there's, like, a narrow valley. Like a canyon with walls. You can't see it from the highway. You can't see the highway from in the canyon, either."

"You ride bicycles there? Up the grade?" Diamond said.

The kid shook his head. "My friend drives. His mom's car."

"What do you do there?"

"We shoot. The canyon keeps the noise from going to the cars on the highway."

"Shoot what?" Diamond said.

"My friend's gun."

"What kind of gun?"

"I dunno. A hand gun. But not like in cowboy movies. A city gun."

"Not a revolver," Diamond said. "A pistol. A semi-automatic."

"Yeah. Like that."

"Where do you get your ammo?"

"My friend's brother."

The lawyer broke in. "Sergeant, let's stay on track, here."

Diamond stared at the man.

"You target shoot?" Diamond said to the kid.

"Yeah. Cans 'n stuff."

"And you saw our prisoner there?"

"Yeah."

"He see you see him?"

"No. We heard these shots. Real loud. We snuck up the rim of the canyon and peeked in. They was there. Him and some other guys."

"And they were shooting," Diamond said.

"Yeah. A big rifle. Like in the army. The Marines. I seen it on TV."

"You've seen the rifle on TV?"

"Yeah. Or just like it."

"They were target shooting?"

"I guess. We couldn't see their target. It musta been a long ways off. Out of our sight."

"What did it sound like?" Diamond asked.

"Y'mean, the shot?"

"Yeah."

"I dunno. Like a rifle, I guess."

Diamond unbuckled his leather belt and slid it out of his pants. He folded it in two and held it out in front of him, the double ends in each hand. He moved his hands together so that the two strips of leather moved apart. Then he snapped his hands apart. The two halves of the belt smacked together and made a loud cracking noise.

The kid flinched.

"Like that?" Diamond asked.

The kid shook his head. "No. That's, like, a little snapping sound. This was a big sound. A big boom that made a ripping sound. Like the sky got tore open."

"Describe what the rifle looked like," Diamond said.

"I dunno. It was real long. Big scope. Like what our science teacher showed us for looking at the moon. And it had, like, these little supports that came down under the barrel."

"Did the rifle hold itself up?" Diamond asked.

"Wha'd'ya mean?"

"When the men let go and stood up and walked away, did the rifle remain propped exactly like when they were shooting it?"

"Yeah. It didn't move."

Diamond turned to me. "A bipod or a tripod. Big bore sniper rifle."

I looked at the kid.

"How many men were there?" I asked.

"I dunno. Three." The kid looked into space. He moved his index finger back and forth. "Four. There were four."

"And one of them was the prisoner."

"Yeah."

Diamond handed the kid a photo of Leah's stalker, Thomson Snowberry. "Was this guy one of the men you saw there?"

The kid frowned and scrunched up his face as he studied the photograph.

"Maybe. I think so. They all wore black clothes. Black T-shirts and stuff. This guy in the photo has a black T-shirt. It coulda been him."

"What did the other men look like?" I asked.

"I dunno. Like the prisoner guy. Tall. Big muscles. One of them was a Indian."

"What do you mean?" Diamond asked.

"Brown skin. Not like me 'n you. But not white, either. Long black hair."

"He look Washoe?"

"I dunno. Like a TV Indian."

"What else did the men do?" Diamond asked.

"Nothin'. They each shot the rifle a bunch. Sometimes they would whoop 'n yell and high-five each other. Then, after awhile they left. We stayed up behind the ridge so they didn't see us."

I was thinking about the big bore rifle round that killed Kiyosawa and caused the destruction we saw at his house. Those rifles are designed for penetrating armor and killing people at ridiculous distances. No ordinary shooting range or even any ordinary Miner's Gulch has enough space to give exercise to such a weapon. Even out on the open desert, testing those weapons would involve shooting at a target a mile or more away, then getting in a vehicle and driving some minutes to inspect the target.

"What else did they do?" Diamond asked.

"Nothin'."

"They shot the rifle and high-fived each other. Nothing else? They eat sandwiches? They play a boom box? They shout?"

The kid shook his head. "Just shoot. And spit a lot."

"You hear anything they say?" I asked.

The kid shook his head. "We could hear they was talkin'. But we couldn't hear the words."

"Where'd you get the T-shirt?" I asked.

"Found it."

"Where?"

"There, at Miner's Gulch. It was hot that day. One of those men took it off and hung it on this tree. He forgot to take it when he left. Finders keepers."

"It says Grendel on it," I said. "What's that mean?"

"I dunno."

"You have no idea?"

The kid shook his head. "Maybe like a name or sumpin. Like Nike shoes. Grendel shirts."

THIRTY-FIVE

I drove back up to Tahoe, over to the West Shore and was at Gracie's cabin by 10:00 a.m. She was gone. I had no cell number for her, so I waited.

She drove up fifteen minutes later, her car full of groceries. I helped her carry them in. She seemed frustrated that I was interrupting her work, but she offered me tea. I accepted, and she went over to her corner kitchen, put a teakettle of water on the stovetop, and pulled out cups and teapot and tea while I looked around.

Her cabin was as messy as before, filled with every kind of art-related item. Stacks of art books teetered precariously on the floor. Folding metal easels filled the corner behind the door. Art postcards, not unlike Leah's, were taped up on the wall that separated the living area from the bedroom. The most interesting items were a series of skulls on the mantel. They were arranged by size, a tiny bird skull on the left, then a small rodent skull, perhaps that of a chipmunk, a slightly bigger skull the size of an oblong ping pong ball, which by its fangs, must have been a carnivore. I guessed a mink or something similar. The next one I recognized by its huge front teeth as a beaver. Then came a larger carnivore, with a long pointed snout. I guessed it to be a coyote. There was a similar-sized carnivore skull that wasn't pointed, a bobcat maybe. The next was a deer, followed by some kind of cow or steer's skull complete with large horns.

"Are the skulls for drawing?" I asked.

"Yeah," Gracie said from the kitchen. "Drawing the basics is always good. You can never do that too much."

At the end of the mantle, to the side of the large steer's skull, was a woven Washoe basket. In the basket were other animal-related trinkets. There were multiple seashells, a rattle from a rattlesnake, a tiny gray-brown bird's nest, which, except for its small size, looked similar to Gracie's hair when she had it clipped up above her head. I lifted the nest out of the basket to give it a closer look. I stopped.

Underneath the nest was a large crayfish claw.

I waited until Gracie came with the tea. As she handed me a cup, I held out the claw.

"I'm curious where you got this?" I said.

She instantly blushed. "What do you mean?" Her voice wavered. Her hand holding her mug of tea must have been vibrating very fast because the surface of her tea was covered in tiny violent waves.

"Dr. Kiyosawa had a crayfish claw. Quite a coincidence."

"I... I don't remember. Where it came from, I mean."

"An unusual item to forget," I said.

She glanced at me, then looked away, busying herself with the brushes on the palette. "Someone gave it to me," she finally said. "A guy I know."

"Because you might like to draw it?"

"Yes. I like to draw all things in nature."

"Who's the guy?"

A pause. "I'd prefer that you don't mention it to him. I'm, well, fond of him. If he thought..." She looked down, drank some tea.

"I'm investigating a murder. If I give your name to the D.A., you'll wish you had told me."

Gracie looked at me, shook her head. "I haven't had a date in twenty years. I'm hoping he will call again. If I tell you, you'll talk to him. Then he'll never call."

"You're willing to risk engaging the court system to preserve the possibility of a phone call from a man who may be connected to a murder?"

"There could never be a connection between this man and a murder. That is obvious." She shook her head.

"Then he won't go to jail, but you might for contempt of court."

"No, I won't. If the court demands it, I will tell them. But I won't tell you. Not now."

I thought about ways of intimidating her. But the tiny, meek woman could be tough, too. I'd have to push hard. I decided to wait.

Gracie picked up a razor holder and began scraping dried paint off of her palette. "So," she said, "what brought you over here?" Her voice was cheerful. Standing up to me was a mood brightener.

"Gracie, I'm wondering if there is a particular kind of paint that you and Olympia use in your classes."

"We use oil, not acrylic or watercolor, if that's what you mean. Or are you wondering about a certain brand?"

"I don't think the brand would matter. But maybe. I'm trying to find out if your students' paintings would smell different from paintings by other artists."

There was a long pause. No guffaws or giggles, just silence.

"I'm not sure I understand," Gracie said, her voice was quiet. She went from sounding scared of me to sounding suspicious of me.

"I'm specifically thinking about Dr. Kiyosawa's paintings. I saw his studio. He has many tubes of paints. Powdered pigments. Jars of stuff I know nothing about. If he were to paint a forgery of an old master's painting, are there ingredients that he might have used that would smell distinctly different from other paintings?"

It seemed that Gracie needed some time to process such a ridiculous idea.

"I've never thought of that before," she said. "I think that all oil paintings pretty much just smell the same. I suppose that different pigments might have different odors. But I don't think you could ever detect the difference between colors even if the individual ingredients smell a little different. The subtle differences would be overwhelmed by the strong smells of oil and turpentine."

"But a trained dog might be able to detect the difference?"

Gracie frowned. "This is new territory for me, Mr. McKenna."

"Owen, please. A dog can detect odors at one ten-thousandth of the concentration that it takes for us to smell them. So let's say that Dr. Kiyosawa painted a forgery of an old masterwork, and that painting is hanging in a room with a bunch of other paintings. I'm wondering if I could send a dog into the room and have him be able to find the painting that Dr. Kiyosawa painted based on the smell of ingredients that Kiyosawa used, ingredients that most other painters and long-dead painters would not have used."

I couldn't read Gracie's face, skepticism wrestling with worry, maybe. Like she no longer thought I was benign. I was a threat to her in some way.

"If you taught Kiyosawa to use any ingredients that are different from typical oil paintings, I could get some samples of those and use them to train a dog. I would have a way to detect a Kiyosawa painting without touching it."

Gracie made a single, thoughtful nod. "I once saw a special on TV that showed these super smart German Shepherd police dogs that can find suspects," Gracie said. "Is that what you mean, only with paintings instead of suspects?"

"Sort of."

Gracie screwed up her face, thinking. "Before you go any further with this line of thinking, I should remind you that forging a painting like a Vermeer is almost impossible. Almost no one can do it successfully. In fact, most rumors of forgery are just rumors. The idea is exciting enough that they put it in movies, but the reality is highly doubtful."

"You said yourself that Kiyosawa's painting was so good, that you wouldn't even be able to tell."

"But Mr. Mc... Owen. I was just saying that as praise for how well he painted. I didn't literally mean that no one could detect it. The image is only part of a forgery. You have to have the exact old canvas and stretcher, and you have to have records and history of ownership, the provenance, it's called. And that provenance also has to be forged. If it were a Vermeer, that stuff would have to go way back, and it would have to be written on the right kind of paper in the right kind of ink. There are a thousand things to figure out beyond just the ability to paint like a master."

"Right." It seemed to me that she was reversing herself from the day before when she'd sounded like she thought Kiyosawa painting a forgery was a possibility. "Then just think of it as a hypothetical question," I said.

I heard Gracie breathing.

I said, "Investigators spend a lot of time saying, 'What if...' Comes with the trade. So indulge me. What do you think?"

"About paint smells?"

"Yes."

"Well, I don't know that the various brands of paints would smell that much different from each other. But mediums have unique smells."

"What are mediums?"

"Mediums are what artists mix in with the paint."

"Like thinner?"

"Not necessarily. A medium doesn't thin paint a great deal, but it can change the consistency and workability of paint. It also changes the look after the painting dries. There's linseed oil and stand oil and many others, mixtures of different chemicals. You can mix powdered pigments directly into an oil and make your own paint. There are also varnishes and dryers."

"Which are..."

"A dryer is a mix of ingredients that you add to your paint to make it dry faster. Otherwise, some colors of oil can take a year or more to fully dry." She reached for a small jar of amber liquid and held it up.

I said, "So the faster it dries, the easier you can paint without smearing what you did the day before?"

"True, but if you use too much dryer, the paint will crack."

"Is that something an artist could use to artificially cause cracking?"

"You mean, to make the paint look old? Like in a forgery?"

"Yeah."

She nodded. "Mediums are just one of the tools to make a young painting look very old. The old look can also be painted directly."

"Like painting cracks on your painting?"

"Not so much cracks, but other aspects of age. You look at every aspect of an old painting and try to paint that look. Easy to say. Hard to do."

She put the jar down and pointed to a large plastic container. "This is gesso, a canvas primer. Some people use rabbit skin glue. Especially in the old days. Dr. Kiyosawa experimented with that. It might smell distinct to a dog."

I raised my eyebrows.

"It was a good primer to seal the canvas and keep the impurities in the canvas from staining the paint."

She picked up another jar. "As for varnishes, they have strong odors. Damar varnish smells a little different from retouch. Probably being non-permeable makes a big difference. There's also..."

"Non-permeable?"

"Many artists like to put a protective layer of varnish on their paintings before the paint is dry. If you use a non-permeable varnish, it will never dry. So they first use a permeable varnish called retouch varnish, which is somewhat protective and allows the paint to continue to dry through the varnish layer. After the painting is completely dry, we put a Damar varnish on to give it the maximum protection."

"Sounds like marine varnish for boats."

"Probably is similar. Damar varnish is also special in that it can be removed without damaging the paint. A painting can have its dirty varnish stripped every few hundred years, restoring the painting's luster and color. Then it is revarnished."

"Artists think a long time into the future."

Gracie shook her head. "Most don't care, actually. But they should. Of all the important treasures that people have saved from past civilizations, paintings are at the top of the list. They give a window into the past unlike anything else man produces."

Gracie turned toward the mantel, then looked at the landscape painting on her easel. I couldn't tell if she was thinking about the potential life of her painting, or if she was grappling with my discovery of the crayfish claw.

"If most artists use these oils and varnishes, then their paintings would all smell alike."

Gracie nodded. "That's what I think."

"So I'm looking for something that Atelier Olympia does differently. Can you think of anything you teach that would be unlike what most art schools teach? An approach that makes the Atelier Olympia brand unique?"

Gracie pushed her lips up against her nose, thinking. "Other than our painting techniques, which wouldn't alter the smell of the painting in any way, there is just the mixture of mediums that we show students to help them get the right kind of depth in their paint."

"Is it just like what other schools teach, what other artists use?"

"It's probably similar. Although I suppose we use more wax. Wax extends a paint, makes it more translucent."

"You referred to it as a mixture. Is this like a recipe? Two parts of this, to three parts of that?"

"Pretty much."

"So your students use the same various ingredients as artists anywhere, but the Atelier Olympia's recipe might be a little different than the recipes at other art schools?"

"I suppose. Here, I'll show you what we show our students."

Gracie pulled up a sheet of heavy plastic that covered one side of her palette. Under the plastic were sheets of thin plastic food wrap, pressed down over rows of paint mixtures.

"I've mixed tints of different colors by stirring titanium white into the concentrated paint out of the tube. These tints are my starting point. When I want to paint, I add in my mediums. I start with wax."

As I watched I thought about how all of these items would have distinct odors to a dog, and I got a little more hopeful about my idea.

Gracie unscrewed the top off of a jug the size of a gallon paint can. She picked up a heavy knife, scooped out some wax, and put it on her palette. She switched to another small knife and mixed some of the wax in with each of several dabs of green paint.

"I'm going to use an impasto technique on part of my painting, so I need the paint stiffer than normal, but not too stiff. So, as I add in some wax, I'll also stir in some of Olympia's glazing medium."

"Which is?"

"It makes the paint less viscous and more workable," she said as she opened another, much smaller jar filled with amber-colored fluid not unlike a light whiskey. It was much runnier than the paint. She dipped her palette knife into it and slurped out a bunch of it onto the palette.

"This is a glazing recipe that Olympia developed. At first I was skeptical. But she insisted I try it. It allowed me to add the wax for translucency, but keep the paint from becoming too viscous. And the medium makes the wax less brittle. I ended up loving the result, and I've been using it ever since." Gracie added a few drops of the glazing medium to each of the green colors that she'd mixed up. She stirred vigorously until the green paint had exactly the consistency that she wanted.

"The glazing medium is Olympia's secret recipe?"

"So to speak, yes," Gracie said.

"What's in it?"

"Linseed oil, stand oil, and safflower oil. Then she adds a little pure gum turp, the real turpentine made from pine trees. Lots of artists prefer odorless mineral spirits because it's less toxic and doesn't smell so much, but Olympia is a purist."

"Is this recipe written down?" I asked.

"Oh, yes. We give it to all of the students and expect them to mix up their own batch."

"And the recipe wouldn't be exactly the same as what other schools use?"

"I can't imagine that, no. I suppose we might have former students who teach at different schools across the country, and they might still use Olympia's formula, but there couldn't be a lot of them."

"Can you do me a big favor and write down the ingredients of Olympia's glazing formula?"

"We have a preprinted sheet." She went over to her desk, pulled out a piece of paper and handed it to me. "This is what we give our students. This sheet has our recommended supplies list, paints, canvas, brushes etc. It also has the glazing components and the glazing medium recipe."

"Where do you recommend I get the materials?"

"There's a good art supplies store in Reno. The address is on the sheet."

"What about if someone wants to mix their own pigments like painters from centuries ago?"

"Oh, we always give students an introduction to that. We want students to have a grounding in the basics. We explain where the pigments originally come from and then provide them with ground pigment samples."

"Did Dr. Kiyosawa show much interest in hand-mixing his paints?"

"Yes. On several occasions I saw him stirring powdered pigments into Linseed oil. Once he came to class with an egg carton with a wide range of what looked like colored dirt, from yellow to orange to red to red brown to brown to deep umber. I asked him where he got them. You won't believe what he said."

"Hmm?"

"He said he got them all on the side of the road driving from

Carson City up to Virginia City. Every time he saw a new strong color, he stopped and dug up some of the dirt. Then he turned them into paint in our class. It's probably similar to the way some of the Renaissance painters got their pigments."

"I've seen those colors heading up through Gold Hill."

Gracie paused, looking into the air. "Now that I think of it, those colors are very much like Vermeer's palette."

I thanked Gracie for her time and information.

As I turned to leave I looked at the fireplace mantel where I'd left the crayfish claw next to the Washoe basket. Even from a distance, it looked sharp.

THIRTY-SIX

I drove north from Gracie's cabin to Tahoe City, and turned in again at Twin Peaks Art. Paul was walking out the front door as I approached.

"Mr..." he said, trying to remember my name. Big grin. Firm handshake. Left hand on my forearm. I was his best friend.

"Hi Paul. Owen McKenna."

"Yes, of course. Owen McKenna. You were here the other day. Yesterday." He pointed to his head. "Nothing escapes this brain." Bigger grin. "What were we talking about?"

"My artist friend Dr. Kiyosawa. You referred me to Atelier Olympia, which was helpful, thanks. I had another question."

Paul hiked up the sleeve of his tailored sport coat, checked a large gold watch with multiple dials over an image of an old square-rigger. "Tell you what, I have an early lunch appointment. Could we talk later?" He moved to head down the sidewalk.

"Just a quick question, then." I stepped in front of him.

Paul frowned, irritated or worried. Then the smile was back as if a small fast cloud had obscured the sun for just two seconds. "Of course, a quick question."

"Yesterday you mentioned Grendel. You said you heard the word somewhere. Do you recall where?"

"Oh, that. That was just, I don't know, just something some stranger said. I have no idea."

"Then you made a joke about forging a Vermeer. Where did that come from?"

"I don't know what you mean."

"What gave you the thought? Was that also something some stranger said?"

More big grin. "Hey, I'm an art consultant. We always hear talk about famous works being forged. Even the new artists who have a name are finding their works pirated. Illegal prints made in China. Stuff like that."

"Nothing specific came up to make you think about forging Vermeers?"

"No, I don't think so." He frowned and shook his head, all serious now. "No, I'm certain of that. It was just a silly thought that popped into my mind."

"One more question."

Paul looked down the street, flashed another glance at the fancy watch.

"Let's say I acquired a forgery of a Vermeer, and I wanted to sell it on the black market. Where would I go? How would I do it?"

"I don't understand." Paul looked confused by my question, but his confusion seemed too obvious. Like acting.

"Pretend I'm a crook. I've got a fake painting I'm trying to pass off as the real thing. What's my next move."

Paul was suddenly affronted. "And you're asking me? How would I know? I'm a legitimate art consultant. I work for Vienna Montrose, legitimate art broker and owner of Twin Peaks Art. I would never come up against the people you're talking about." He hurried past me and down the sidewalk.

I watched him go. I was about to go inside the gallery when I saw Jeter driving a van down the street. The lettering on the side of the van said Twin Peaks Gallery. He turned into an alley driveway a few doors down and headed toward the back of the buildings.

I walked over and followed on foot, somewhat surprised that he would have a driver's license. But I realized that if he could figure out frame measurements and work framing machinery, he could probably pass the driver's license test. Slow did not mean incompetent.

When I came around the corner, Jeter was at the back of the van, which he'd parked behind the gallery and frameshop. He had the rear doors open and was sliding out a couple of sheets of plywood.

"Hey, Jeter," I said. "Can I help you with that?"

He looked at me and grinned. "I remember you."

"I was in yesterday just as you came back with your tuna salad sandwich."

He smiled. "That was a good sandwich. But I spilled the garbage and Paul got mad."

"Paul is like that, huh?"

"Yeah."

I reached for one side of the plywood. "This stuff is heavy. I'll help you slide it out."

"Wait, I forgot my gloves," Jeter said. He walked around to the driver's door, came back with leather gloves, held them up for me to see. "These keep you from getting splinters. Plywood has splinters." He pointed at the edge.

"You're right. I'll be careful."

Together we slid the plywood out and leaned it against the side of the building. Then we pulled out some 2 X 4s.

"What're you building?"

"I'm building a crate for a big painting. That's because tourists can't take them on the plane. Vienna showed me how. First, I measure the painting. Then Vienna helps me figure out how much to add for the padding. Then I cut all the pieces. I use screws to make it extra strong. Plus, you can unscrew it to get the painting out." When we'd leaned all the wood against the back of the building, Jeter stopped, pulled up his sleeve, looked at his watch.

"It's noon. Time for my lunch break. You want to eat lunch with me by the water? I like to sit by the water. The waves sound nice."

"Sure."

He got his lunch bag from inside the store. We walked down to the end of the parking lot, went down some broken steps. I followed as Jeter walked over to a fallen tree.

"I sit on the tree trunk," he said. "Today I have peanut butter. Do you like peanut butter?"

"I like tuna salad better," I said.

Jeter smiled. "Me too." He took a bite of his sandwich. "Where's your lunch?"

"I'll have mine later."

He reached out his sandwich. "You can have some of mine. I bit to right there." He pointed. "That's half way. You could have this side."

"Thanks, Jeter, but I'll be fine."

He ate and we looked at the water. Twenty-five miles away, at the south end of the lake, was Heavenly Resort. The ski runs were brilliant white in the sun and they arced down the mountain from individual points at the top like the white smoke trails from fireworks.

"How long have you worked at Twin Peaks Art?" I asked.

"I work at Twin Peaks Frame. I don't work in the gallery. That's where Vienna and Paul work. And Mandy and... I can't remember the other girl. Mandy's real pretty." Jeter made an embarrassed giggle. "I work for Gerald, the framer. He's my boss. And Paul is his boss. I like Gerald more than Paul. I kind of like Vienna, but she's the big boss. So I don't like her too much."

"How long have you worked there?" I asked again.

"Oh, I forgot you asked that. A year and... I can't remember. More than a year."

"Do you like it?"

Jeter grinned. His teeth were thick with peanut butter.

"I like it more than working at MacDonald's. But I like their food. Twin Peaks doesn't have food." He laughed at his joke. "Do you like MacDonald's?"

I nodded. "How long has Paul worked at Twin Peaks?"

"A long time. Even longer than me. But I bet I end up working longer."

"What do you mean?"

"'Cause of what he said. He said he had itchy feet. He said he wants to make real money. I told him I make real money. And he said that real money means working someplace else. I wasn't sure what that meant."

We talked throughout his lunch. I asked him about the business, the customers, the employees. I asked him if he'd ever heard of Grendel or Vermeer. He hadn't heard of Grendel, but he had a friend when he was a little boy, and the friend had a cat named Vermeer.

When Jeter was done with his lunch, he said, "I like you. Do you want to be my friend?"

"Sure, I'll be your friend."

"Then I have a surprise for you."

"What's that?"

Jeter pulled out his wallet, lifted up a flap and carefully removed a business card. He handed it to me.

It said 'I'M JETER SALLE'S FRIEND.'

"Thank you, Jeter."

Jeter grinned at me. "You write in the boxes on the order form and mail it in with a check. Vienna wrote a check for me. The company mailed the cards back to me in a box. I've given out thirty-nine cards."

"You keep track?"

He nodded. "I put twenty in my wallet. I gave them all away. Then I put in twenty more. And now I have one left. So that is twenty plus nineteen. Thirty-nine."

"That's a lot of friends," I said.

He nodded. Grinned some more.

I put his card in my shirt pocket, thanked him again, and walked with him back to the store. I said goodbye. Jeter had already turned and was carefully putting on his leather gloves.

THIRTY-SEVEN

I drove out 89 along the Truckee River, turned onto Interstate 80 in Truckee, and headed east down toward Reno. I felt pressed for time, so despite not having a hands-free phone, I used Jennifer's company phone to call Ellie Ibsen at her search-dog training ranch down in the foothills by the American River, just north of Placerville.

"Owen!" she said, her almost-ninety-year-old-voice sounding gleeful. "How are you? And how is that boy doing?"

"His largeness is well, although he is delinquent with his obedience-training homework. He still won't bring me the newspaper without pulping it first. I'm calling with a question."

"About dogs, I hope. At my age I've forgotten most everything else except what I learned before the age of twelve."

"About dogs," I said. "I want to teach Spot how to distinguish between different kinds of paint."

There was a short silence. "It sounded like you said paint."

"Yes. Paint. As in that which an artist puts on canvas."

Another pause. "Well, I'm not sure I understand," Ellie said.

"I'm entertaining an idea. I've learned of an artist who uses a certain mixture. Artist's oils, wax, glazing medium. The components are all standard stuff that lots of artists may use from time to time. But this artist has a special combination that is consistent from one painting to the next. My goal is to be able to train Spot to recognize the smell of that particular combination of ingredients."

"I'm sorry," Ellie muttered, "I think I'm missing something."

"I'm just not being clear. What I mean is that I want to be able to let Spot smell a bunch of paintings and tell if any of them were painted by this particular painter."

"It sounds interesting. But I don't know anything about paint," Ellie said. "Or art, for that matter."

"But you are one of the world's premier dog trainers."

"My," Ellie said. "Premier. I don't usually associate that word with me. What do I have to do to earn that distinction?"

"How would you go about it? Teaching a dog to alert on paintings that were done with a special mixture of paint?"

I waited while Ellie thought.

"Do you have those kinds of art supplies?" she said.

"I'm on my way to get them."

"And you know the mixture the artist uses?"

"Another artist wrote it down. Like a recipe. A dab of this, several drops of that, and so forth. I can replicate it."

"You said these are oils. There must be a strong solvent."

"Turpentine," I said. "It is also on the recipe."

"I remember years ago when I was first learning about accelerants," Ellie said. "I drove down to UC Davis to take a course on arson. When the fire marshal was going over accelerants, he said that the most common were gas and kerosene, which is what most lighter fluid is. But he mentioned turpentine, too. Some accelerants originate from crude oil, some are made from plants, and some are synthetic. But they're all called Volatile Organic Compounds. VOCs. Fancy words for chemicals that burn very well. They also evaporate readily, and they are very intense for dogs to smell."

I was thinking back to when her dog Natasha helped me trace an arsonist. "I remember how Natasha can smell the tiniest trace of gasoline."

"Yes!" Ellie brightened at the mention of her star German Shepherd. "A dog smelling a micro-drop of VOCs would be like us smelling the spray of a hundred skunks."

"That bad, huh?"

"That strong, anyway. But you wanted to know about paint. I think the trick for Spot—or for any dog, even one trained in accelerants—is going to be differentiation among the different VOCs. You could train Spot to be very good at searching a building for artist paint. But to smell lots of paintings and pick out one painted with a particular mixture is not going to be easy."

She paused. "I was listening to National Public Radio the other day and I heard something that applies. There was an astronomer who was focusing his instruments on radio waves, and he talked about the signal-to-noise ratio."

"And this applies to paint?" I said.

"Let me explain it this way," Ellie said. "Suppose I train you to smell a skunk, and we practice so that you alert to even the tiniest trace of skunk."

"And..."

"You would probably get very accomplished at it. Especially during those times when we focused you on the task."

"Like when you gave Natasha a sniff of gas and then told her, 'Find the gasoline.'"

"Yes. If I said, 'Owen, I think there might be skunk in the air,' you'd be very likely to notice if there were any skunk odor whatsoever. But here's where I see a problem."

"I'm talking about a particular kind of skunk," I said.

"Right. For example, let's say I want you to alert on a sub-species of skunk that is found in New Jersey. While New Jersey skunks smell very similar to other skunks, there is a tiny difference. So I send you out to look for the odor of the New Jersey skunk, but the problem is that New Jersey skunks are often found where lots of other skunks are found."

"I see. The other skunks are the noise that drown out the Jersey skunk signal."

"Exactly." Ellie took a breath. "I'm afraid that the odors of artist paints and solvents would smell so strong to a dog that the dog would face the same problem in trying to search out a particular combination of volatile organic compounds."

"Point taken," I said. "But suppose I test it? If you were to make the attempt to train Natasha to differentiate one person's paintings from others based on a unique combination of ingredients, how would you go about it?"

Another pause.

"I'd set up a group of paintings, six or eight, with only one using the ingredients you are talking about. I'd make everything else about the paintings appear the same. I'd even make the paintings be of the same subject with the same colors. Try to make them appear as exact duplicates of each other." She paused, thinking. "Of course, you'll have to have some tiny difference so that you can tell which one is the special one.

"It won't be easy," she continued. "Never forget how smart

dogs are. The only thing they don't do is speak English. But they understand much of it, and they understand most of what you're doing even when you're trying to fool them."

Ellie paused again. "Then you set up the basic puzzle. Line the paintings up in a room. Do it with Spot outside so he can't get a sense of you paying more attention to one painting than the others. Then you go out and have Spot sniff a piece of canvas on which you've used the same special ingredients. Maybe you call it the special paint. You say, 'Spot, sniff the special paint. Do you smell the special paint? Okay, Spot, find the special paint!' Then you let him into the room and see if he can find the one with the special ingredients." It sounded like Ellie inhaled sharply.

"Are you okay, Ellie?"

"Yes! I'm just excited! This sounds fun!"

"I hope Spot thinks so."

"Oh, he will! And when he succeeds in finding the correct one, you give him lots of love and hugs and praise. Then take him back outside to get fresh air while you go in and rearrange the paintings. Tell him to find the special paint again and see if he can do it. Remember to throw in the occasional treat just to keep him motivated when he's had his fill of hugs. And I'm not talking about micro-waved Danishes!"

"That was Diamond's dirty work. I've been focusing on renewing Spot's love of chunked sawdust ever since."

"Good. You will let me know how Spot performs as a painting detective?"

"Yeah. Let's hope he has a nose for it."

"He may. Don't sell him short. Do the training and see what you end up with. I'm not confident it would work even with Natasha. But Spot may surprise you."

"Can I call you with more questions?"

"Of course. After Spot, you're my favorite guy out there."

"Thanks. By the way, where did you learn about the New Jersey skunks that smell different than other skunks?"

Ellie laughed, her small voice as lovely and musical as a songbird. "Owen, I'm amazed! You fell for that?"

It took me a second to process that I'd been had. "I amaze a lot of women that way, Ellie," I said.

THIRTY-EIGHT

I found the art store just off Virginia Street south of downtown Reno. They were pleased to have a new artist to load up with materials, although it was obvious that they thought I was excessive in my ambition regarding mediums and other ingredients for Olympia's secret recipe.

I hauled the paints and brushes and canvases and easel out to the Toyota and completed the circle loop south to Carson City and back up over Spooner Summit. I considered asking Jennifer if I could convert one of the mausoleum's forty rooms into an art studio, but decided I didn't want to make my art performance debut under the watchful eyes of housekeeper Marjorie or the new houseman Raymond.

I couldn't go home without advertising Jennifer's Toyota as my new wheels.

So I called Glenda Gorman at the paper. We made a little small talk before she began to hit me with questions about the case.

"That's what I'm calling about," I said. "I wondered if you're still obsessively neat and have the only garage in Tahoe that isn't filled with kayaks, skis, and snowblowers."

"And this connects to Dr. Kiyosawa's murder how?"

"It connects because if I could borrow your garage for an art experiment this afternoon, I would show my appreciation by giving you dibs on all the details of the case when it's over."

"But Owen," she said with dramatic flair, "you would do that anyway."

"True. But after borrowing your garage, I would do it with feeling and enthusiasm."

"What is this art experiment?"

I told her my plan.

She said she thought I was nuts, but to 'have at it.' She gave me the key code for the garage door. "Don't drink all my Sierra Nevada Pale Ale," she said.

I was coming into South Lake Tahoe when I saw a big black four-door pickup off to the side of the road. I'd gone past Kingsbury Grade and was at the chokepoint where all traffic must flow along Edgewood Golf Course. The pickup was at the first intersection, positioned so its occupants could easily watch the traffic going by.

I made all the wrong moves. When it caught my eye, I turned and looked directly at it. I saw nothing but a vague dark shape in a dark interior with smoked windows. But in Jennifer's Toyota with the clear windows, my movements were easy to see, advertising my identity. I didn't even have my cap on.

I cruised through the intersection. The pickup pulled out and followed, two cars back. I knew he wouldn't shoot me unless I came after him. He only wanted to follow me to Leah. I also knew that he didn't want to take a chance on getting caught. The only reason he pulled out was the hope that I had just been rubbernecking at surrounding vehicles and hadn't realized who he was.

My goal was to trap him.

There were a couple of ways I could play it. Call Dispatch and get some patrol units to scramble in behind him. But I didn't have a hands-free phone. My movements to use the phone would be obvious. He'd see them and drive away.

Another approach was to play dumb and let him follow me, as I looked for a way to get behind him. As I came up to Harvey's Hotel, I remembered a quirk of the entrance layout that I could use to my advantage. I turned on my signal well in advance. I shifted to the right in my lane so he could see the turn signal around the car between us. I slowed to a stop for a group of passersby, then turned in. Just past the first visual barrier, I stomped on the accelerator and jerked Jennifer's Toyota off the pavement, onto a patch of landscaping and in between dense fir trees. If he turned in, I'd be on his tail before he knew he'd been tricked.

I strained to watch through the foliage.

He didn't turn in, just cruised on past, happy, no doubt, to learn what kind of vehicle I was driving.

I raced out of the landscaping, squealed rubber as I went around the turn-around, and shot back against the one-way traffic. I almost hit a limo as I bounced and screeched back onto the main street. I raced past cars, looking down cross streets and into turnoffs, but he was gone.

Ten minutes later, still breathing hard, I pulled up to Glennie's house in the Tahoe Keys. The houses on either side were vacation rentals, and they appeared vacant. I got my art supplies into her garage without any obvious observers.

I put the easel in a rear corner near the door that opened on the backyard and the canal that led to the lake. I put the palette on a counter where Glennie had a worklight and a paper towel dispenser. The counter's Formica surface looked as if it had never been used. I took out the oil tubes and squeezed gobs of paint onto the palette. Ten big dabs of color arranged in a circle. They glistened, each hue thick and rich and succulent. The smell of oil was immediate and full.

I propped a canvas on the easel.

The number five Filbert brush looked like a useful tool, so I dipped it into the scarlet vermilion and painted a healthy streak across the canvas. I was delighted to discover that it became orange when spread out on white material. I wasn't sure of proper artist behavior, but I felt compelled to step back and study the result.

"Clearly impetuous," I said to no one. "Breathtaking, actually. Art lovers, look out. McKenna has come to town."

I realized that neither of the women in the art store had explained to me how or if I needed to clean the brushes before switching colors, so I set the Filbert down, picked up a number three Round and dipped it into the permanent green light. Multiple little arcs of springtime seemed to appear under my flicking wrist. My largest round worked well to turn a touch of yellow and a big gob of brown into a vague splotch. I kept up the brushwork for awhile. Then I switched to a palette knife and assaulted the canvas with diox purple. The knife was easy to wipe off, so I added some cobalt blue, some carbon black, some alizarin crimson.

Another observation from six feet away confirmed my genius.

The Salazar company cell phone rang.

"McKenna here."

"I dialed your cabin, but then remembered," Street said. "How are you? How is Leah?"

"Leah's still ensconced in Beaufort's Beauty. I'm putting together a lesson plan for Spot." I described my activities in Glennie's garage.

"You're painting? For Spot? Six canvases? Wow, this I'd like to see. Are you wearing an apron? I bet you look cute."

"No apron. But cute as one of your bugs."

"What is your subject?" she asked.

I thought about it. "They're purely expressive."

"Expressing what?" she asked.

I thought about that, too. I'd avoided artistic humiliation at Jennifer's house only to flirt with it over the phone.

I decided to be bold in my description. "I'm painting thrills," I said. "The thrill of dropping into Mott Canyon on a fresh powder day. The thrill of entering Emerald Bay by boat for the first time. The thrill of signing the closing documents and getting the key to your Tahoe vacation property. The thrill of hiking to the top of Mt. Tallac. Abstract Expressionism is great. You can make any kind of brush strokes, say it's about anything you want, and call it art."

I traded the Round brush for my largest Flat and stabbed it into the ultramarine blue on my palette, then smeared it onto the canvas as I spoke.

"It sounds like you're pleased with the result," Street said.

"Yes. I'm now expressing a sky across the bottom of the canvas. Tell me. Would you concur that I should continue this artistic inquiry before calling the curators at the Museum of Modern Art? Or is an emergency alert to them in order?"

Street thought about it. "I think it's a great idea, Owen. But you might want to let the paintings dry a bit, maybe finish your current murder project, first."

"Ever practical," I said. "Unrecognized genius is one of the constants that we artists have to put up with. You will understand the urgency when you behold these in person. I may have rendered the last century's artists moot." I looked at the clock. "One hour and fifteen minutes from start to finish. If I sell them for thirty thousand each, I'll never again regret not becoming a cardiac surgeon."

"Owen, sweetie, I love it when you're in a good mood. I'm just wondering if anyone has slipped something into your beer."

"I had milk for lunch. Imagine my creative output come cocktail hour."

"Yes, I'll imagine," she said.

We spoke for another ten minutes. Street told me that the entomology conference was boring, but that anything involving bugs can't be all bad. I told her that I agreed but that she would probably switch careers when she saw my paintings.

After we hung up, I unwrapped my other five canvases and proceeded to make duplicates of the first one.

When they were nearing completion, I got out Olympia's secret recipe and mixed up the magic potion. Multiple kinds of oils and turpentine all in the right proportions. A tablespoon of this, a teaspoon of that, then stir it into a quarter cup of this. I scooped some of the special mixture out onto my palette and mixed it into two of the paint colors. When done, I smeared those special paints onto one of the canvases, taking care to make it look as close to the others as possible. Other than being a little shinier, the painting was indistinguishable from the others. I made a tiny mark in one corner so that I could identify it after I'd mixed them up.

I was once again admiring my paintings from across the floor of Glennie's garage, when the phone rang again. It was Diamond. Wondering what was new. I told him about Spot's imminent intro into the world of art.

"I'm at Stateline. Shall I cross town to check on you?"

"Sure."

THIRTY-NINE

By the time Diamond arrived ten minutes later, my paintings seemed less cheeky and had lost some luster.

I heard his vehicle, and I opened the garage door.

"Where's Maria's truck?" he asked.

"In Jennifer Salazar's garage. This Toyota is additional disguise. Although, I think the shooter saw me in it." I told Diamond about the man in the black pickup.

"Maybe go back to using Maria's truck, huh?" He walked in and stopped abruptly, staring at the paintings.

"What do you think?" I said.

"Interesting," he said.

"The universal euphemism. Tell me the truth, please. Be a harsh critic."

Diamond shrugged. "Dip Spot's tail in paint and he could do better than that," Diamond said.

"Hey, go easy," I said. "Besides, this is Abstract Expressionism. It's about movement and color and emotion."

"Still looks like crap. I thought the whole point of being an artist was you got to look at girls and then paint them."

"That's the beauty of Abstract Expressionism. It can be anything you want." I gestured at some of my lines. "There's some pretty nice curves here."

"Don't look like no Senorita to me. Why're you doing this?"

"I'm going to train Spot to sniff different paintings and tell if any of them are painted with a certain combination of paints and mediums."

"That's a joke, right?"

"No. Dr. Kiyosawa took art lessons from a woman named Gracie at the Atelier Olympia on the West Shore. All of the students mix up the same painting medium. Olympia's secret recipe. If Spot could learn to alert on that combination, he might be able to sniff out a painting done by Kiyosawa."

"And where will Spot look for this painting?"

"I haven't figured out that part, yet. It just seemed like a good skill for Spot to have."

"You think he's going to want to smell paint? Most dogs would turn away from those stinky smells, wouldn't they?"

"You ever paid attention to the stuff dogs like to smell?"

"Good point."

"You on duty?"

"Yeah. Off at four." Diamond looked at his watch. "Ten minutes."

"Do me a favor?"

"Huh?"

"Spot is staying with Leah for protection. I need to borrow him back to try this special-paint training. Technically, you could call it work. Interviewing and protecting a witness and crime victim."

"You want me to baby-sit," Diamond said, shaking his head. "I don't do baby-sitting."

"Only for two hours. Three, max."

"You're serious."

"Of course, I'm serious," I said.

"Where is she?"

"On a boat."

"You want me to baby-sit on a boat?" Diamond was incredulous. "Tell her to anchor out on the lake someplace. That'll make her safe."

"She is anchored out on the lake. She's still afraid to be alone. Probably with good reason."

Diamond looked at his watch again.

"I'll shuttle you out to the boat," I said, "come back here with Spot, then pick you up when I'm done. She's got wine on the boat, if that helps."

"You ever see a former lettuce picker drink wine? Even the grape jockeys in Napa drink beer. Mexican beer."

"We'll stop on the way," I said.

Diamond turned, disgusted, walked out the door and got into his cruiser.

FORTY

We put Jennifer's Toyota and Diamond's cruiser next to Maria's pickup in the big garage.

As we walked across the circular drive, Diamond glanced at the mausoleum like he was looking at a Safeway. "Kid's got a nice spread."

"You ever met Jennifer?" I asked.

"Can't remember. Lotta rich white girls around this lake."

I let the comment stand. Jennifer was not a typical rich white girl, but I didn't need to make a point out of it.

"Where's this boat we have to ride on?"

I took Diamond around the mansion, down the lawn to the lake, and into the boathouse. We were in the runabout a few minutes later, heading north up the shore.

"The talk show lady holding up?" Diamond said.

"More or less. Be good to go easy on her."

Diamond looked at me. "She's a crime victim, sure, but I think she's holding back something. You're too soft or you'd see it."

"Didn't you learn the innocent-until-proven-guilty thing at the same time you learned about civil liberties?"

"You're a hopeless romantic," Diamond said. "You see a damaged woman and you imagine saving her. But your illusion requires that she be emotionally and morally pure. I'm a realist. I find a bird with a broken wing, it's sad, sure. But it doesn't mean that the bird wasn't a flawed character before she fell from the sky."

"More rewarding to save them, the purer they are," I said.

"Like I said. You're hopeless."

We got out to Beaufort's Beauty a half-hour later. Diamond acted like the boat was no big deal, even though I saw him taking in every detail. He stepped over the transom and pet Spot who bounded up the companionway to meet us.

Leah followed, said hello to Diamond, and looked at me with a question on her face.

"I need to borrow Spot for a bit. Diamond is going to hang out while I'm gone, if that's all right with you."

Leah looked at the gun on Diamond's belt, and nodded slowly. "Sure, I don't see why not."

"C'mon," I said to Diamond. "Let us show you this little tub."

We took him below decks, gave him an abridged tour. Then we all parked on the settee for a bit.

"Owen told me about Tom Snow," Diamond said, diving right in.

Leah looked at Diamond.

"You know who I mean," he said.

"No. I don't. Well, maybe I do." Leah turned to me.

"That's your stalker's name," I said.

"Oh. Another driver came into the station once when he was there. I was in the back room. I heard the other driver say his first name. His voice was muffled. It sounded a little like Tom. I couldn't tell for sure. And I never heard his last name."

"His full name is actually Thomson Snowberry."

Leah looked down at the floor. "I'm so ashamed," she said.

"I'm not concerned with those aspects of your life," Diamond said. "But I am concerned that this guy has harassed you."

Leah nodded again.

"Turns out he disappeared four nights ago."

"When my father was killed?" Leah looked confused.

"And," Diamond continued, "Snow was into guns. Did you know that?"

"He mentioned guns a couple of times. I didn't pay much attention. I figured he was probably a hunter."

"Tom was not into typical hunting guns. He was fixated on sniper guns, the kind of rifles that are designed to kill people from long distances." Diamond watched Leah carefully. "His roommates said he planned to buy one."

Leah's confusion turned to horror. "You think he killed my father? Why?"

"We don't know enough to think that," Diamond said. "But it is suspicious that he disappeared at the same time. You should know that his roommates said that Tom made threats about you. Said he would hurt you if you didn't come across for him."

"You think he meant to kill me that night, but missed and hit my father instead? I can't bear to think that. That would mean I'm at fault for my father's death. That would be more than I..."

Diamond put his hand up. "I don't think that is the case. Snipers don't usually miss their targets when their targets are stationary. A moving vehicle is different. I think the person who shot your father meant to. Maybe he meant to kill you next, but you moved too fast. So he tried to catch you in Owen's car after you left the hospital. My question is whether there is some kind of connection between your father and Snow. Could they have known each other?"

Leah thought about it. "I don't think so. The first time he was pounding on our door wanting to talk to me, my father looked out. He said, 'who's that?' I don't think that would have been his response if he'd known the man. My father wasn't naturally that quick to be devious."

Diamond looked like he doubted her.

I pushed myself up from the little settee. "I'll let you two talk. I'll buzz back to Glennie's with Spot. We've got some nose work to do. I'm guessing a couple of hours. I'll be back after that."

Diamond nodded.

Spot and I climbed back topside and left in the runabout. This time we took Maria's truck. When we got back to the Keys, Spot ran around excited.

I opened the garage door. I'd left a mess from earlier, so I did a little neatening, putting my brushes and palette on the small work counter so that Spot wouldn't knock them over with his tail. I pushed the easel up against the wall and set the jars of medium back into the art store bag on the floor so they wouldn't fall and break.

Then I took the six paintings and lined them up, leaning them against the wall of the garage. They looked nearly identical. Only I was aware of the secret of painting number four.

I was eager to do a test drive of my experiment. I called Spot in and lowered the garage door. He sniffed around, investigating all the new strong smells. I gave him some time, then called him over to me.

"Spot," I said with enthusiasm. "Come here."

He looked at me but didn't move.

"I've got something for you to smell. This is the Special Paint."
I held out a rag onto which I'd rubbed a tiny quantity of the special mixture. "Do you have the scent, Spot? Do you have the scent?"

We'd done this type of game many times in the past. But it was usually associated with search and rescue. It is a game that dogs love because finding a missing person is always exciting. Although Spot had a little experience with non-human search, most notably when he accompanied Ellie's dog Natasha on the accelerant searches during the arson-set forest fires, I didn't have much confidence that my painting experiment was going to work.

"Spot, do you smell the Special Paint?" I said again.

Spot looked at me and wagged.

Okay, Spot. Find the Special Paint!" I folded the rag and put it in my pocket. "Find the Special Paint!" I pointed toward the six paintings lined up against the wall, looking like a proud little First Grade art show, and gave him a smack on his rear end.

Spot turned, took two steps toward the work counter, reached out toward my palette, which, I saw too late, was hanging off the edge of the counter. He picked it up in his teeth, his jowls dragging through the colors.

I jumped up and ran to intercept, imagining that oil paint was probably high on the list of inappropriate doggie nutrition. But I stopped myself from scolding him. He'd done exactly what I wanted, finding the scent where I'd originally mixed it up. I took the palette out of his mouth, grabbed the roll of paper towels from the dispenser, and praised him while I tried to wipe six or seven colors from his teeth and tongue and lips.

"Good job, boy! But don't ever do that again!"

He pulled away from my hands and wiped his muzzle on his foreleg getting oil color everywhere. The black and white dog was now multi-colored.

I couldn't use turpentine as solvent to remove the paint because it was probably more poisonous than the paint. So I took him into Glennie's kitchen and used lots of detergent and water, repeated at length.

When I'd removed all but a few lingering stains from his mouth and fur, I wrapped the palette in a garbage bag and put it inside the cupboard beneath the Formica counter.

I came back out, praised Spot again, then showed him the paintings lined up at the base of the wall. The technique is simple. When you want Spot to notice a bird or a particular person or a painting, you put your hands next to his head, palms against his cheekbones, and turn his head in the appropriate direction. I directed him at the paintings, panning his head from left to right like a movie camera. "See the paintings, Spot? One of those has the Special Paint."

He paid no attention. When I let go of his head, he immediately turned and walked away as if repulsed by the images. I picked up the Special Paint rag and tried again. I held it near his snout and said, "Smell the Special Paint, Spot! Do you have the scent? Do you? Okay, find the Special Painting!"

Spot stared at me.

"Come on, Spot. I'm serious. Do you have the scent? Find the Special Painting!"

Spot turned and looked out the side door window as if checking the weather. Then he slowly walked past the six canvases, turned and pawed just once at the cupboard where I'd hidden the palette.

Instead of disappointment, I should have been elated. If Dr. Kiyosawa's palette went missing, we'd be in luck.

"Good boy! What a sniffer you've got!" I pet him and hugged him and was as effusive as if he'd found a long-lost Da Vinci. "You're going to be a champion art detective."

I tried yet again, certain that Spot was wishing he could be once again trapped on the Ciel 40. "Spot, smell the Special Paint." I held the rag with the mixture in front of his nose. "Do you have the scent? Do you? Find the Special Paint, Spot. Find the Special Paint!"

Spot sniffed at the stinky rag, turned and went over to the row of paintings. He pawed at the first one, the wrong one, and tore it with his claws as it fell to the floor.

"No, Spot. No. Find the Special Paint!"

Spot pawed at the next one, and it bounced sideways under the assault and knocked down three other paintings.

I realized that this was what Ellie meant when she talked about the signal-to-noise ratio. All the paintings had such strong oil smells that a slight difference in the components was nothing against the larger impact of oil odors.

The project had been a failure. I was gathering up my various supplies to give to Gracie when my phone rang.

"Special Agent Ramos," the voice said after I answered, "calling with some information."

"What you got?" I said.

"An agent on the Art Crimes Team called me. Only stolen paintings on our docket that fit your description are some paintings that were taken from the Isabella Stewart Gardner Museum in Boston twenty years ago."

"You know what paintings?"

"Yes. Three Rembrandts, a Vermeer, a Manet and some others."

"Dr. Kiyosawa could have painted the Vermeer. For that matter, he could probably paint a Rembrandt, too. Or three Rembrandts."

"I never understood his popularity," Ramos said. "I'm more of a Diego Rivera fan myself. Anyway, I reiterated your particulars. The guy said he'd call you if he thought you could add to their investigation."

"Don't tell me that's all."

"They didn't want to be forthcoming. So just because I'm such a good bud of yours, McKenna, I pushed. He mentioned the name of an informant they use. I don't think he wanted that to slip. But you can't unring the bell. A Jimmy Jamaica in the Big Apple. Into art stuff."

"Name like that doesn't inspire confidence," I said.

"Informants never do," Ramos said. "This agent also talked about the Chelsea district. Maybe Jamaica and Chelsea go together some way."

"But no contact info," I said.

"No, senor."

"Thanks, Ramos," I said.

Spot and I drove back to the mausoleum, and motored out to Beaufort's Beauty.

"I've learned something that may help," I told Diamond and Leah. "Agent Ramos called with a lead. I've got to go see Mrs. Phelter. Then I'll be back out to the boat. The sun's getting low. I'll probably be back well after dark."

"Really?" Leah sounded worried.

"Spot's with you. You'll be fine. I'll call before I come so you'll know it's me when I approach on the boat."

It took several seconds for her to respond. "Okay," she said in a shaky voice. "Please don't decide it's too late or something and not come at all."

"I won't."

Diamond and I left Leah and Spot on the sailboat and headed back to Jennifer's. I explained what Ramos had said.

"You going to New York?"

"If Mrs. Phelter is willing to pay the bill, yes."

We got to shore and hustled around to Jennifer's garage. Diamond left in his cruiser. Again, I took Maria's pickup and drove up Kingsbury Grade to Lauren Phelter's house.

FORTY-ONE

We sat in Mrs. Phelter's living room, a tiny space that probably couldn't hold much more than two of my cabins. I followed her while she wandered through the various seating areas before choosing to sit down in a corner where two big leather chairs faced out the windows toward the lake and the mountains beyond. The sun was setting. Spectacular as it was, it couldn't brighten the dark mood. We sat side-by-side while we looked at the view and talked.

"I have a lead on what Kiyosawa may have been doing that got him killed. It means I have to go to New York City."

She nodded.

"I wanted to check and see if you want me to continue my investigation."

"Yes. My comfortable world is gone. First the murder, then the attempted murder on Leah, then the burglary. A killer is out there someplace. The police came and asked me a hundred questions. It frightens me so. And then there is this talk of some monster named Grendel. What is happening that the police are talking about a monster? I don't know what to do with myself."

"Grendel is a character in fiction. From a thousand years ago. Don't worry about that."

"Yes, that's what they said. But they also said there is some gang called Grendel. So it's not just an ancient concept, correct? There's something else going on."

"There are some guys who wear Grendel T-shirts, but I think that's all it is."

Lauren Phelter had her hands clasped in front of her. They exuded tension. "I want you to continue. I want you to catch whoever did this. My life will be a constant upset until I have some closure on this. I haven't begun to think about getting the guesthouse repaired. I can't bring myself to go over there. Every hour of the day and night,

I just worry."

"Going to New York will add to the expense," I said.

"I don't care."

"I'm going to try to find an FBI informant. It could easily add a thousand dollars or more to the expense."

Mrs. Phelter didn't hesitate. "When we built this house, my husband had a safe installed. He said you never know when you might need some emergency cash. An informant probably would not take a check. Isn't that true?"

"That's true."

She left the room and was gone five minutes. She came back and handed me a bundle of hundred dollar bills bound with several rubber bands. "I counted out fifty of those. Will that be enough?"

"Five thousand? Yes."

Lauren Phelter reached over and put her hand on my forearm, squeezing it with surprising strength. "Do what you can to solve this. Please." Her hand shook.

"I will, Mrs. Phelter."

I drove down to Street's lab at the bottom of Kingsbury Grade. If the killer had lots of helpers, then maybe it was being watched. But I hoped any spotters were focused on my cabin and my office. My office was close to Street's lab, but you couldn't see one from the other.

I kept the blinds of the lab windows closed. I turned on the bathroom light and shut the door to a crack to let a little light spill out. It gave me just enough illumination while I used Street's computer. I found a seat on the early plane out of Reno. A departure at 6:30 a.m. meant I'd have to drive out of Tahoe a little after 4:00 a.m. It wasn't my week for sleep.

I called Street first, and gave her an update. Then I called Jennifer, explained where I was and where I was going. She said that she'd talked to Leah within the last couple of hours and that Leah seemed to be holding up. Jennifer also assured me that if Leah needed help, all she had to do was call.

"She told me she's just up at Skunk Harbor," Jennifer said. "So I could use the runabout to get to her in a short while. Or I could use the rocket to get there in a few minutes."

That concerned me. "You didn't pass on her whereabouts to

anyone else, did you?"

"No. I would never do that. And I was talking from my bedroom, so I'm pretty sure Randall and Marjorie couldn't hear me."

"Pretty sure."

"Oh, that sounded bad, didn't it? Well, let me think. Marjorie was in the kitchen, and Randall was... he came in from the garage not long after that, so he must have been outside. So I'm sure her location is still secure."

I paused. Jennifer had gotten the message. No point in hammering it in.

"Thanks, Jennifer. I'll be coming by in another hour to grab the runabout and go back to Beaufort's Beauty to spend a few hours with Leah before I head to the airport. I'll call you from New York in a day or so."

Next, I called Leah.

"You taking good care of his largeness?" I said when she answered. "He kind of ate some paint earlier. Probably not good for him."

"That explains the yellow and blue stains on his jowls. Anyway, he's taking care of me. I'm sitting in the cockpit chair. I opened a bottle of wine. Spot's lying next to me."

"You've got the lights off?"

"Yes. It's very dark. I suppose that's best. But I'm scared. I hear noises."

"What kind of noises?"

"I don't know. From over on the shore. In the forest."

"You are safe. Spot will see to that. I'm on my way back. I'll be there in an hour. So don't be alarmed when I pull up to the boat. Although maybe you'll be asleep by then."

"Oh, no, no, Mr. McKenna. You have no idea where my brain is at. No way in hell am I going to sleep until you're on this boat."

"Got it. See you in a few."

The better part of an hour later, I slowed the runabout to idle and coasted toward the dark sailboat on dark water in the darkest bay on Tahoe. I'd long before turned off my running lights and didn't use any beam to locate Beaufort's Beauty.

As I drew nearer to where I knew she was anchored, the sleek, dark shape gradually materialized in the light of the stars.

I heard the deep rumble of Spot's growl followed in an instant by Leah's whispered voice.

"Spot, quiet!"

I tied up the runabout, climbed aboard the Ciel, opened the companionway hatch and let myself down the steps into the candlelit saloon.

Spot was eager in his greeting, and Leah had only an instant to move the candles before Spot swept them off the table with his tail. I did a little stationary rough-housing with him, gripping him hard and pushing and pulling as he tried to move in opposite directions. Then I got him to lie back down.

Leah fetched another glass and poured me some wine.

I told her about going to the Tahoe City art gallery, then down the west shore to the Atelier Olympia, over to instructor Gracie's cabin and art studio and her comments about her student John Saki who was really Leah's father. I explained how she mentioned his ability to paint like Vermeer and how Agent Ramos spoke with the FBI's Art Crime Team and learned that three priceless Rembrandts stolen in Boston two decades ago are still missing and are on their Top Ten Art Crimes List.

"I'm leaving on the early plane to New York."

"You're kidding." Leah didn't sound happy.

"I've got a lead from the FBI on an informant who can tell me about the market for stolen Rembrandts." I didn't mention that I had no idea of how to contact him, or that he went by the name Jimmy Jamaica, no doubt a street name designed specifically to make him impossible to find.

"So you won't be back until when?"

"Not sure. A few days, maybe. I'll call you and let you know how it goes. If you want some company, you can always go back to Jennifer's. But I think you're safer out here. You have lots of food. There's plenty of water in the tanks for hot showers. You've got the radio and stereo. But play it at very low volume."

"Mostly, I've got Spot."

"He won't leave your side."

"Can he sleep with me?"

"Sure, but there are caveats. Don't let him roll over on you. Human knees are especially vulnerable in bed with a hundred-seventy-pound canine. And once you let him into your bed, it's hard to get him out of it unless you're offering steak. I don't let him in my bed. But I've camped with him in a tent. I should let you know that he does this thing where he pushes out with his legs in his sleep. He'll push you right off the bed, if you're not careful. And his nails are sharp."

"I'll be wearing Street's sweats."

"Not enough protection."

"Okay, I've been warned."

"How has the dinghy shuttle been going?" I asked.

"Fine. I took Spot to shore early in the morning for a long run, then a short visit at noon, then another long run just before sunset. Each time, I went when there were no people around. But then people came down the trail. Two different times. They kind of shrieked a little when they saw him. Not like they were scared. Like they were excited. Then they wanted to hug him. Is that normal? I've always seen people want to pet dogs, but not hugs like that."

"It's normal."

"So the only problem was when Spot pretty much tipped the dinghy over when he saw a Merganser, and he leaned out toward it. But then the bird disappeared under water. Spot sort of fell into the water, but we were near shore. And I realized why that little ice cream bucket is tied to the seat in the dinghy. I used it to bail out the water that got in. After that, Spot stopped leaning so much. We made it okay. I've figured out how to get him to lie down before I climb in. What I did was put a blanket between the seats. I don't think it gives him much padding. It's more like the message of where he should lie. When we get to the shore, he jumps out before we hit the sand, and then he runs all through the forest like he's a little crazy. But I figured out that if I throw a stick in the water and he sees me, he runs out of the woods and swims out and gets it. He's not real good at bringing it back to me, though. He mostly just chews them up into little pieces. One thing I learned when he gets wet, you have to be careful when he shakes off! That tail is wicked."

"It sounds like you've got him figured out. He won't want to move back in with me."

Leah finished her wine. "Okay, maybe I'll try sharing the bed with Spot now, while you're still here."

FORTY-TWO

I woke up a few hours later, said goodbye to a sleepy Leah and a sleepier Spot, and took the runabout back to Jennifer's boathouse. This time I switched back to Jennifer's Toyota. Maybe I could lead the killer to New York. I was heading up Spooner Summit as the first light of dawn began to pink the eastern sky. The June snowpack was still heavy and white on the mountain peaks, and it shimmered pink in the predawn alpenglow. Still before dawn, I drove down out of the mountains and caught the early bird out of dry, red-sky Reno.

We rose up to meet the sun's first rays, then climbed high into the deep sun-scoured blue over central Nevada. I changed planes at the monster concrete network in the middle of the prairie outside of Denver. Eight hours and three time zones later, we dropped down to LaGuardia through heavy turbulence between skinny thunderstorms that looked like mushroom stalks in a misty gray jungle. The pilot banked over the dark water of Long Island Sound and descended fast toward the East River. Two seconds before the gear would have hit the messy water, the flotsam was replaced with tarmac, and the wheels bumped and skidded along a rain-wet runway so rough with cracks, the jet would need a chiropractic adjustment before it would feel up to more exercise.

By the time I got to my hotel, my best guess was that the taxi driver was Iranian, the cop rerouting traffic around construction at the Queens Midtown tunnel was Irish, the bellhop at the boutique 5th Avenue hotel was Russian, the desk clerk was Kenyan, the concierge Mexican, and the man who bagged my beer, bagel, and cream cheese at the corner takeout was Korean. I knew that Los Angeles County, with 160-plus languages in its school system, was in fact the world's greatest melting pot, but nowhere was the cultural deck-shuffling more concentrated than in the service industries of Manhattan.

Adding the three hours I lost traveling east, my day was largely over. When I was done with my bagel dinner, I turned in early.

The hotel bed was firm but two inches shorter in both directions than the bed on Beaufort's Beauty, so my feet were numb after spending the night out in the gale off the window air-conditioning unit. To warm them up, I decided to hoof it over to Chelsea, which is on the west side and down in the 20s.

The thunderstorms of the previous day had blown through, and the weather was as fine as it gets in a city that is often either too hot or too cold. I went by the Empire State and Madison Square Garden and was across town in fifteen minutes.

A mix of old rundown warehouses and fancy retrofitted warehouses, Chelsea is a hotspot for art, especially big contemporary paintings and sculptural installations. The galleries are large open cubes tended by well-dressed, mostly young, salespeople. There is some art by big names and more by a wide range of unknowns hoping to become the next Jean-Michel Basquiat. Some of the art is obviously superlative in quality, and more is junk masquerading as hip punkish stuff that will stamp your loft with next-generation cool.

There were two ways I could take my search for Jimmy Jamaica. I could make discreet inquiries here and there, talk to the concierges at the nearby hotels, leave small hints and large tips for waiters at the local restaurants, and quietly pump the gallery art consultants, hoping to eventually pry loose a reference to the dives or parties or street corners where Jimmy Jamaica hangs out. The other way to conduct a search was to abandon discretion in favor of loud and obnoxious, hoping to get a lot of attention and bring Jamaica running to shut me up before his cover was completely blown.

I chose the latter.

I stuck my head into the first gallery I came to. There were three groups of people looking at a pile of twisted, rusted, welded metal on the floor. Bernini, look out. A haughty young saleswoman was talking to them.

"Sorry to interrupt," I called out in my loudest voice. They all turned and stared. "Looking for Jimmy Jamaica. Guy who's supposed to know about all the stolen paintings. He been around?"

The saleswoman frowned and shook her head. "I have no idea who you're talking about."

"Okay, later, sister."

I left and went to the next gallery. "Yo, dude!" I called over the heads of some shoppers, getting the attention of a man in a suit who was standing with a customer in front of a giant white canvas that looked to be coated with shiny polyurethane and consisted of a single eyeball, Cyclops-style, in the middle of the field of white. "Seen a guy named Jimmy Jamaica? The go-to guy for stolen art? Ring a bell?"

He looked horrified, shook his head, and turned away from me.

I repeated my technique at several more galleries and got the cold shoulder at all of them. But I knew that someone, somewhere, would place a frantic phone call after I left, talk to someone who knew someone who knew Jimmy Jamaica. If I kept making enough noise, they'd find me.

On the next block south, I got bolder.

"Hey man," I called out to an art consultant in front of a roomful of people looking at inscrutable junk—shredded doormats, maybe—hanging from ropes attached to the ceiling. "You know those stolen paintings y'all been sellin'? Tell Jimmy Jamaica I've got news for him. He got the provenance wrong on that last series. I just heard that the FBI is on it. In fact, if I were you, I'd lock up fast and head for Bermuda."

I left, and shortly afterward, several of the gallery's customers came out behind me and hurried down the street. I went around the block.

The first squad car arrived fifteen minutes later. I trotted up to them and spoke into the window.

"Hello, officers, I'm Tony Ivory from Gallery Alpha. Are you looking for that drunk who's disturbing the peace?"

"Yeah. Talking 'bout stolen paintings?" the cop in the passenger seat said.

"Right. Well, after he left my gallery, he headed up toward twenty-third. He's a tall guy, almost as tall as me. Stoned out of his mind."

"Got it." The cops nodded at me and pulled away.

I headed down to 21st.

I kept up the ruckus and single-handedly ruined the artsy

ambience of the neighborhood. I was crossing an intersection when an old Ford van pulled over. Two guys jumped out and ran toward me.

There was an alley on the next street. I sprinted over and turned in at a full run, obviously trying to make distance. The moment I was out of their sight, I skidded to a stop and ran back to the edge of the building where the alley started. I flattened myself against the wall.

They came around fast, their shoes sliding as they took the corner. I waited while the first one went by, then timed it so that when I jumped out, the second man didn't have time to react. He tripped over my out-stretched leg and went down hard. By the time the first man realized what had happened and had turned to come back, I was there with a hard gut punch. He didn't fall, but staggered back, bent, hands to his stomach, his diaphragm seized, unable to breathe.

The other man pushed himself up off the pavement, his hands and knees and face skinned in several places. He held his hands up, palms out.

"Hey, man," he said. "We was just tryin' to talk to you. Nothin' more, man. Now you banged us up good."

He backed up as I approached.

"One of you Jimmy Jamaica?"

"No way, man. We work for Jimmy, but we ain't even seen what he looks like."

"How do I reach him?"

"You don't. We do. That's the rules."

"Rules have changed," I said.

"There," he said, pointing at the ground behind me. "I dropped my note from him."

I knew it was a setup. So I pretended to fall for it, looking just enough to entice his attack.

He came at me fast. I sidestepped, grabbed him from behind and used his own momentum to keep him running. I held his back, pushed hard, and steered him across the alley into a nearby dumpster.

The collision was loud, and he collapsed to the ground. I walked over to the man I'd punched. He had one hand at his belly, his other arm out in front of him like a Zombie. He concentrated on sucking air, his head bobbing with each tiny breath.

I got out Jennifer's cell phone. "Jimmy Jamaica's number," I said.

He didn't acknowledge me and just stared ahead, concentrating, gasping for breath.

"Jimmy's number or we start round two."

I saw worry peeking through his panic over not being able to breathe. Very slowly he rasped out the numbers, one at a time. I dialed as he said them.

The phone on the other end rang, and was answered on the second ring.

"Howdy do," said a big, deep voice with a reggae accent, James Earl Jones meets Bob Marley.

"Your boys are lying on the ground in an alley in Chelsea. They are desperately hoping that you are going to be agreeable with me."

"I agree with whatever you want, mon," he said.

"Then you will meet me at the Metropolitan Museum this afternoon. Let's say two o'clock. Give you plenty of time to get your dreads washed and waxed and find some new boys to watch your back. Find the Rembrandt self-portraits. I'll be the tall white guy in a Mets cap. I'm authorized to pay you a thousand in cash just to shoot the breeze for a little bit, assuming you don't hold back."

"Okay, mon, I'll be there."

"One more thing, Jimmy. If you don't show, I call the G-men who put me onto you. After we find you, you'll wish you'd never left Kingston."

I hung up.

It was one of those silly conversations full of bravado and bluster straight out of a '40s noir movie. But I'd learned over the years that idiots are sucked in by that stuff like gambling addicts are sucked in by the racetrack.

Either Jimmy would show, or he'd be thinking about heading out of the state, if not the country.

FORTY-THREE

The Metropolitan Museum of Art is on the east side of Central Park, so I zig-zagged east across the island as I hoofed it uptown. For lunch, I found a Chinese takeout counter near Times Square, then walked over to Fifth Avenue and turned north.

Manhattan has one of the world's great subway systems. It's old and noisy, but it goes everywhere. However, walking Manhattan on a beautiful summer day is the best. I went up Fifth Avenue among the shoppers and strollers and business people all looking rich and beautiful, past the Rockefeller Center, past the Museum of Modern Art, past the Trump Tower where Sinatra was singing "New York, New York" through unseen speakers, and on up to the Plaza Hotel, which hosted Brazilian princesses and English dukes and Chinese emperors and Greek shipping magnates and the odd software billionaire from Silicon Valley.

When I got to Central Park, the horse-drawn carriages were out en masse, taking farmers from Iowa and wedding parties from Long Island and retirees from Arizona through the park. Ten thousand tourists recorded everything with their video recorders, and mounted police pranced on their steeds.

I stayed on Fifth for another mile or so and came to the Metropolitan Museum with time to spare.

I studied the guide and found the Rembrandt section on the museum map. My destination was the Evelyn Borchard Metzger Gallery in the European Paintings section on the second floor.

The Met probably has a third of all the great art in the world, so the building ain't petite. After I paid the New York-sized toll, I hiked for 15 minutes before I arrived at the appointed place.

The masterful paintings in the Metzger Galley were shocking in the magnitude of their quantity, as well as their quality. Using the conservative figure of $15 million per painting and multiplying by the number of Rembrandts, Vermeers and other 17th Century masterpieces that adorned its walls, I figured the collection in Evelyn's boudoir was worth $200 million. And that didn't count the uncountable other rooms in all directions.

I walked over and looked at one of the famous self-portraits. Rembrandt rendered himself with a curious mix of sophistication-meets-peasant-farmer, his rough skin and reddened pores as obvious as his distinguished flair and intelligence.

"You realize it is a fake," a small voice said, the accent possibly Southeast Asian.

I turned. The tiny man next to me was over a foot shorter and a hundred pounds lighter than I am. He wore a plain black, collarless shirt that hung over black pants. His clothes had no folds, no cuffs, no pleats and no pockets that I could see. If he'd had a straw hat, he would fit the cliché of a well-dressed worker from a rice paddy.

"You are interested in Rembrandt?" he asked.

I nodded.

"Jimmy Jamaica," he said.

"Owen McKenna." We shook, his hand as small in mine as a doll's.

"You were very rude to my men," Jamaica said.

"They chased me."

"You sullied my name. They are loyal. I do not deal in stolen art, as you suggested to the galleries. I inform people about art opportunities, some of which arise from art thefts. There is a difference. Why are you asking about art?"

"I'm a private investigator looking into an art forgery. The Jimmy Jamaica on the phone made me think island boy goes NBA," I said.

"Part of my security. I have several friends. They receive my calls when necessary. Set up appointments. My friends come with many accents. Sometimes, I am Jean Francois from Marseilles. Sometimes, Ricardo Verdi from Milano. Or Jose Rodriguez from Mexico City. But Jimmy is my favorite. The voice is the chef at a restaurant in the Village. And, yes, tall enough to be an NBA center. Taller than you."

"What is your real name?" I asked.

"All real and all fake. Like this painting. What is the difference? Maybe Rembrandt van Rijn put his brush to this canvas. Maybe not. But it displays in the Metropolitan. Millions of people admire it. If I am Alberto or Ling or Hyuntai or Jimmy, I am still as real as myself."

I nodded my head at the Rembrandt. "You really believe this is fake?"

"What matters if I believe it? But look around. This museum has hundreds of guards. Where are they? Not in this room with Rembrandt and Vermeer. Not in the room with Van Gogh. They are in the rooms with the less expensive paintings. Bonnard. Cezanne. Manet. Not only do the less expensive paintings have the guards, they also have museum glass over them. The glass has a special coating, like a camera lens. With the special museum lighting, the glass is almost impossible to see. But it is good protection for the art."

"If the museum glass is protective, why isn't it on the Rembrandts?" I asked.

"That's my point," Jimmy said.

"You said yourself it is nearly invisible. Maybe it's there and we just can't see it."

Jamaica motioned for me to follow. "Come." He walked into a neighboring room and bent down in front of a painting I didn't recognize. "If you get to your knee under the painting and look up, you can see the reflection of the light on the ceiling. It is the only way to tell if the painting has the special glass. Now go back and look at the Rembrandts from your knee. No glass."

We went back into Evelyn's room and looked at all the masterpieces with no glass and no guards.

"If you're right," I said, "where are the originals?"

"Who is to say? In the vault? In the Wall Street offices of the big-dollar donors? In their mansions up and down the Hudson River? It doesn't matter as long as the originals hanging in their homes and offices are explained to be fake. Explained to be the work of the talented art student perfecting his technique."

Like an actor in a play, Jamaica switched his speech to a heavy Brooklyn accent. "I know a guy, put me onto this girl. I went to her loft in Soho. She does copies of the masters. Calls them studies, if you can believe that. Freakin' amazing, huh? Now I got me a couple hanging above my fireplace."

"The Hudson River rich talk like wiseguys?" I said.

Jamaica shrugged his shoulders. The Southeast Asian accent was back. "Maybe not just talk. Maybe they *are* the wiseguys."

I pointed at the self-portrait. "If this is fake, how do they make it look so old? You can see the cracks in the paint."

Jamaica sighed. "I can put wet paint in the sun and have cracks by tomorrow. Experienced painters say the look of age is the easiest part of forgery."

"Obviously, this painting's good enough to fool the experts," I said.

When Jamaica grinned he looked like a frog. "Many professors come through with their students. They lecture about the paint marks, the brush strokes, the texture built up. They use big words. Stylistic fluency. Compositional formalism. Makes you want to drink a bottle of turpentine. They don't have a clue that this painting was actually done by a twenty-eight-year-old student at the Atelier Bourdeaux, pride of Montreal."

"Is that a fact or hyperbole?"

"I don't know hyperbole. But in the art world, the only reality that matters is final product. If it is good, if it is made with the proper ancient canvas and the old hand-cut weathered stretcher stock and the canvas is stretched with hand-forged tacks, and it has the correct provenance attached to it, you can take a big check to the bank."

"You don't know hyperbole, but you know provenance," I said.

"Provenance produces money. I'm not so sure about hyperbole."

"When a famous painting is stolen," I said, "how does the media reporting the theft know that it was the original that was stolen and not a copy that the thief thought was an original?"

"Good question. The media ask a curator, of course. They ask art professors. They ask art historians. They ask restoration experts and picture framers and artists who paint similar work. But do any of them really know? Does the curator tell the truth? Even if the painting is real, the curator maybe wants to say it was a fake, hung in place of the original just in case somebody might steal it. The museum patrons and benefactors are less upset if they think the real painting is safe in a bank vault."

"When a collector wants to buy a stolen painting, how does the collector verify that he or she is getting the real thing?"

Jamaica did the frog grin again. "The same way, asking experts. The problem is, you want your expert to be very discreet about the stolen painting. So you pay him extra."

"A bribe to be quiet."

"Yes. It can be expensive. And it's hard to find experts willing to provide advice on paintings and keep quiet about it."

"Which, in some ways, might make it easier to sell a stolen painting than one that isn't stolen," I said.

"Now you are beginning to think like a true art entrepreneur. Which, I think, is a bigger word than your hyperbole. And I know entrepreneur very well."

I walked over to the Rembrandt and looked at it up close. It was surprising how uneven the surface was. The canvas underneath the paint was tighter in some places, looser in others. The paint was uneven in its thickness. It had cracks and chips in the surface. The varnish was shiny over some colors, duller over others. To my uneducated eye, the quality of the image was spectacular, while the overall quality of the painted surface was lousy.

"When experts look at a painting to decide if it is real, what are their techniques?"

Jamaica glanced around at the room, which still had no guards in it. "Tell me, you are very expert about something you spend a lot of time with?"

"No, I wouldn't say I'm an expert in any area of significance."

"No, no," Jamaica said. "I'm not talking about some area that you think is significant. I'm talking about your things. Items you have that you know better than anyone."

"I have some art books I've spent many hours with," I said. "A couple of them are old and out of print. It would be hard to produce a forgery of those books that would fool me."

"The perfect example." Jamaica nodded with vigor. "So you wonder if your book has been switched. You use your senses. You look, you feel, you smell, you listen, maybe you taste. And the sixth sense, too."

"What is that?"

Jamaica put his hands on his flat abdomen and moved them like he was shaking an imaginary belly. "In here. What you feel in here. It is the best way to tell if your old book is a forgery. Of course, the pride of Atelier Bordeaux is very smart. He knows to make the paper look smudged and make it smell like your other books. He knows to make the paper bent and crinkled to feel like it is old and worn."

Jamaica took a step to his right and held his right index finger up. "But you are smart, and you have a microscope and an X-ray machine and a light machine to analyze marks you cannot see."

Jamaica stepped to his left, held up his left index finger. "But the pride of the Atelier is equally smart. And he has the money to buy many things."

"Maybe even buy some art experts who will give their opinion," I said.

Jimmy Jamaica was a grinning frog again. "Say you are asked to judge whether someone else's old art book is real or not. You make a careful observation. It looks quite genuine. Of course, you can never be absolutely certain. To help you make your decision, an anonymous communication tells you that a large, untraceable deposit will be made in a Cayman Island bank account with your name on it."

"So I decide the book is real. And if it is later shown that I'm wrong, people will forgive me because it was a reasonable call."

"Yes."

"The problem I'm working on is about a painter who was very good at painting Vermeers. He was murdered just after he acquired a large sum of cash. I believe that before he was killed, he painted a Vermeer, or maybe one of the three Rembrandts that were stolen in Boston a couple of decades ago. I want to know where I would go and who I would talk to to find out what, if anything, has been sold recently on the black market."

"You would ask me."

"You claim to know everything that happens around the world when it comes to art?"

"As with finance and fashion and publishing, New York is the center of the art world. Sure, we'll always have Paris." Jimmy did the frog grin again. "But New York is at the center. And I'm at the center of New York. You would ask me."

"Okay. Have you heard of a Rembrandt being sold recently on the black market?"

"No. And there's a big problem with your scenario."

I waited.

"Those three Rembrandts that were stolen from the Isabella Stewart Gardner Museum in Boston are the only significant Rembrandts that have gone missing in a century or more. Your clever painter would have to paint one of those three, right? The location of all the other famous Rembrandt paintings is common knowledge. Your painter, or his customer, would have to present the forgeries of the Boston paintings for sale. Those paintings are very well known. The attention and examination would be intense. I've seen a lot of impressive feats in the art world. But selling forgeries of those Rembrandts is—how do you put it in English—almost beyond belief."

Jamaica shook his head. "There is only one other possibility that I can think of. It is perhaps too bold to consider. But in some ways it would be easier. I was at an opening at a gallery in The Village two weeks ago, and I heard something interesting."

"What about?

"The Night Portraits," he said.

FORTY-FOUR

"The Night Portraits? What are those?"

"You've never heard of The Night Portraits?" Jamaica was incredulous. I was a philistine. An art illiterate. An embarrassment to the art world. The museum should screen people like me at the door.

He ignored my question. "The gallery is owned by a big-shot. Has gallery openings the fourth Friday of every month. A preview party the second Wednesday every month at his brownstone on the Upper East Side.

"A man was talking to another man. Back in a corner of the gallery. By the bathroom. I was nearby with my friend. In my business, I've gotten very good at hearing at a distance. One man said to the other man, 'I've got a great idea for a movie or a book or something. A guy who's a really good painter wants to make some big bucks. He wants to try a forgery, but he's not connected enough to the world of art experts to get the proper info on paintings that get stolen.' The other guy says, 'Yeah, you gotta know the paint chemistry, the right kind of canvas from the period, the history, the chain of ownership, all that shit.' Then the first guy says, 'The way he gets around it is to make up a painting that supposedly exists but no one's ever seen.' And the second guy says, 'Like what?' And the first guy makes this crazy grin. I saw it because by then I was interested and I'd turned to face him. So he grins and says, 'Well, maybe these paintings are the Night Portraits or something.'"

Jamaica waited for me to respond.

"I told you, I've never heard of the Night Portraits."

Jamaica sighed. "I suppose you're not the only one. And many of the people who know about them doubt their existence. I read an essay an art historian wrote in ARTnews about the Night Portraits. A very smart essay. Lots of words I don't know. Some of the words in Dutch, too. Why do writers do that? It's hard enough for me to follow one foreign language. This writer examined all the written evidence and decided that he doesn't think these portraits exist. But others believe them to exist just as surely as these paintings in this museum exist."

"What are the Night Portraits?"

"Some background information will help me explain. In the sixteen-thirties, Rembrandt painted many group portraits. They were a great way for artists at that time to earn money. Each person in the portrait would only pay a small fee. But there were lots of people in the painting. For a few guilders, or whatever they used back then, each person got to see themselves looking good. The total amount of money added up to a large fee for the artist. At least sixty-five of Rembrandt's group portraits survive. But historians agree that several other group portraits were lost.

"One remarkable painting from that period is called, 'The Anatomy Lesson of Dr. Tulp,' which hangs in the Mauritshuis Museum of The Hague. It was painted in sixteen thirty-two, and shows a corpse that is the central focus of the painting. Dr. Tulp has dissected the arm of the corpse and is holding out the various muscles. Standing around the corpse is a bunch of men, all watching with much interest. The painting cemented Rembrandt's reputation as a great portrait artist. The men in the painting all got their money's worth. For a low fee, they are close to immortal.

"The story goes that in the same year, Rembrandt did similar paintings of the van Gelden family standing around a tiny corpse. Father, mother, son and daughter were all staring at the body of their recently deceased baby. As in 'The Anatomy Lesson of Dr. Tulp,' the corpse is the central focus of the painting. But unlike the curious faces of the students around the corpse in 'Dr. Tulp,' the faces of the van Gelden family members look as if the life force of the family was in the baby. Their faces are painted in very dark tones, and the background is almost black. The overall feel is as if an emotional night has descended on the family. It is a painting of death both in terms of the baby and in terms of its effect on the family.

"Over the next few months, Rembrandt revisited the family and did more portraits of them, each one showing how the family unraveled over time. There are supposed to be five Night Portraits in

all. One with the entire family and the dead baby in the center, and
four more, one of each family member."

"What is the evidence for their existence?"

"Several references in journals from the time. Rembrandt himself
made notes about the Night Portraits. The mother of the van Gelden
family mentioned in her diary each time one of the family members
sat for Rembrandt. And just before Rembrandt's first wife, Saskia,
died in sixteen forty-two, she wrote of the Night Portraits in a letter
to a cousin. Rembrandt had taken her to see the portraits after he
and Saskia were married. As Saskia was dying, she said that she felt
the way the baby in the painting looked."

"Why do some art historians think they don't exist?"

"Mostly because no one knows where they are. So the—what
is the English word—presumption? So the presumption is that if
you can't produce a painting, you have a hard time proving it ever
existed. Another reason some historians think they don't exist is that
based on the written accounts, the Night Portraits weren't done in
the portrait format of the era."

"You mean, the painting technique?"

"No, more like the way they looked. The presentation. Portraits
of that time usually showed bright faces against darker backgrounds.
The artists would arrange their subjects so that light always shined
on the people. But these paintings reputedly show darkened faces
that reveal their dark moods. That is why they are called the Night
Portraits, because they are about emotional darkness. What also
makes the Night Portraits even more significant is that they are
thought to be the first documentary of its type, showing a family's
destruction over time."

"You know a lot about art," I said. "Why aren't you a teacher?"

"No credentials. This society doesn't value knowledge as much as
it values credentials. You can have a prestigious job if you have letters
after your name, never mind what you know. I came from Viet Nam
thirty years ago. I was too poor to go to university. But I learned on
my own. Now I make my living around the edges of the art world.
I provide information to people who value knowledge whether it
comes with credentials or not."

I turned a slow circle, looking at the various Rembrandts. "Any
idea what size the Night Portraits were supposed to be?" I was

thinking of Kiyosawa's small studio. It would be difficult for him to work with canvases as large as the Rembrandts before us, which looked to be in the 3 X 5-foot or 4 X 6-foot range.

"That's another problem the historians have. The Night Portraits are supposed to be small. Maybe two feet by three. Maybe smaller still. Unlike Rembrandt's most significant paintings, which are much larger. So there are several reasons to think they don't exist."

"Did Rembrandt make any sketches of these paintings?"

"Not that anyone has found."

"So," I said, "if no one knows where they are, and no one knows what they look like, then that might make it relatively easy to paint forgeries of them and sell them."

"Like I said," Jamaica grinned, "it would be very bold. One day I heard a professor talk to his students about the Night Portraits, talk about this very thing. He said that if no one had seen them for centuries, they would be ripe for forgeries. He used a word to describe to his students what painting the forgeries would be. It started with an A. Awe-day something."

"Audacious," I said.

Jamaica nodded. "It would be very audacious."

FORTY-FIVE

We'd left the Metropolitan and were sitting at an outdoor table at one of the restaurants in Central Park. I had a beer. Jamaica had tea and a huge chocolate-covered muffin. People cruised by on roller blades. A cardinal serenaded us from a nearby tree. On a grassy slope, two girls tossed a pink Frisbee. In the distance, a man on stilts and wearing a clown costume juggled for a group of little kids having a birthday party.

"Have I earned my talking fee, yet?" Jamaica said.

"Almost. Any other buzz on the Night Portraits recently?"

"Buzz? What is a buzz?"

"News. Chatter. Gossip. Other than the man at the gallery opening, have you heard anyone talk about these paintings?"

Jamaica shook his head.

"Let's say I'm a broker," I said. "I sell art here and there. I have big news to tell the art world."

"That you have found the Night Portraits?" Jamaica said.

"Yes. How would I go about it?"

"Well, you could go directly to the media, make your announcement and begin meetings with museum officials and collectors so that they could view them, bring in their experts and begin purchase negotiations. But there would be a risk."

I was sipping beer. I raised my eyebrows.

"If the Night Portraits really do exist," Jamaica said, "then the owner has kept them secret all this time. Maybe they've been handed down through a family over the centuries. They've been content to keep the portraits secret because if their existence became known, the family would no longer be able to enjoy them in their home."

"Because it would present too much of a risk?"

"Yes. The paintings would be worth many millions. Once the word got out, they would be very attractive to thieves. And insurance companies would never cover them unless they were hanging in a secure museum with guards and alarms."

"But," I said, thinking, "if I come along and proclaim that I have the portraits, that might motivate the family to come forward. Their sense of personal history would be wrapped up in the authenticity of the paintings. It would be an insult to their honor to think that someone else was claiming to have the paintings."

"Yes, you said that well. I like the part about the insult to their honor. That is what I find hard about English. To get the flavor right."

"So if there is much chance of the paintings still existing, then I might want to sell them on the black market, instead."

Jamaica was eating his muffin. He nodded. He had chocolate on his lip. "You could make up a good story. You bought a group of paintings at an estate sale. No one had really looked at them. You alone knew that these are the Night Portraits. You don't want the information made public because there are other valuable paintings still available for purchase at a good price. If the word got out about where you got the Night Portraits, the heirs selling the estate will be alerted to take a closer look at their remaining paintings. You want to buy the remaining paintings, but you don't have enough funds. To get the funds, you are willing to sell the Night Portraits cheap as long as the purchaser agrees to keep the transaction secret for a year."

"How cheap?" I said.

"Hard to say. A private collector might not blink at a million each for the five paintings. With good provenance and multiple experts agreeing on their authenticity, Sotheby's or Christie's could probably fetch ten million each for them. A private collector would understand that the reason you are selling them for only a million each is that you cannot produce many experts because of your need to keep it quiet so you can go back and purchase more paintings from the estate. The private collector would be very tempted by your cheap price."

"Devious," I said. "But I can see that it might work."

"Especially if you tell the collector that he will get first option on the additional paintings you are going to buy. There are many rich collectors out there who are scratching around, looking for a good deal. Sometimes, they will buy a painting without asking anyone else to verify its authenticity. Such collectors are quite, what's the word? They think they are better than others."

"Arrogant?"

"Yes, these collectors are sometimes so arrogant that they think they are expert enough to recognize a real Rembrandt. But mostly, they are gamblers. They cannot resist what looks like a good bet."

"Do you know who the man was at the opening, the man who mentioned the Night Portraits?"

Jamaica shook his head. "No. Maybe he has come to other Fourth Friday gallery openings, or to the gallery owner's Second Wednesday preview parties. But I haven't seen him." Jamaica looked at his watch, a gold Rolex. "Today is the second Wednesday of the month. The next preview party is tonight. Unfortunately, I can't go to it."

"What is the gallery owner's name?"

"Vladimir Petruschka. 'With a C,' he always says, as if anyone could spell his name anyway. They call him Vlad The Launcher because whenever Vladimir chooses to represent a new artist, it is said that the artist's career is launched into space."

"Do you think Vladimir knows about the Night Portraits and whether they've been recently sold?"

"Vlad is the only man who knows more about the New York art scene than me. If I had the Night Portraits, I would call Vlad first. If they are really out there, he would probably know of them. Maybe he was the broker. Maybe he sold them to one of his rich, secretive clients."

"How do I talk to him?"

Jamaica shook his head. "Not possible unless you are very connected."

"How do I get connected?"

"It will cost you another thousand."

"Are you tough enough to call my bluff?" I asked.

"Are you rich enough to pay if I succeed?"

I drank the rest of my beer. Lauren Phelter had a lot of money. She would want to pay it.

"Okay," I said.

I pulled out my money clip and counted out 20 hundred dollar bills and set them on the table.

Jamaica's hand moved like a flash of light, and the money disappeared into his pocket the way a tossed beef tenderloin disappears into Spot's jaws.

He reached into an invisible pocket in his pants and pulled out a torn piece of buff-colored paper. It was the size of a large postage stamp, with a lot of texture and what looked like printed marks on it.

"Vladimir Petruschka has one of the best marketing techniques ever invented. Better than viral marketing on the internet. For every Second Wednesday preview party at his house, he has one of his artists complete a work on paper. Then he tears it up into pieces. The pieces are the tickets to the party. This one comes from an intaglio print done by a young woman whose career is on the next rocket launch. Vlad hands out the torn pieces to influential people in the collector community, and he gives a few of them to people in the media. Each person is allowed to re-tear their piece into two or three or four smaller pieces and hand them out to other people. The rule is only that each piece must still be recognizable as having come from the original work of art."

"Got it," I said. "You can't tear them too small, or the origin of the piece won't be clear and you won't get in the door. But the gimmick gives you motivation to tear your piece a few ways and give them away to your special friends who are interested in art. Clever, and very exclusive."

Jamaica studied his piece of intaglio print, turned it just so, then tore it in half and held one of the pieces out to me.

"You said the party's on the Upper East Side?" I said.

"You have a pen?" Jamaica asked.

I pulled one out and handed it to him. He reached for my $2,000 scrap of intaglio print, turned it over and wrote an address on the back side.

"Time?"

"Eight o'clock tonight," he said.

FORTY-SIX

I walked east a couple of blocks from Central Park and caught the southbound Lexington Ave subway. It was crowded with Wednesday afternoon commuters. In just a few minutes of shake, rattle, and roll, I climbed back out of the tunnels at the 33rd Street Station, picked up a sandwich at a deli, and was back in my hotel room a few minutes later.

I called Street on her cell and caught her waiting for the ferry to take her across the Sound to Seattle, where she'd catch the shuttle to Sea-Tac Airport and a plane back to Reno.

I gave her the blow-by-blow of my day and said that I was going to lie down for a bit before I headed out for the Second-Wednesday preview party at Vlad-The-Launcher's pad on the Upper East Side.

Street said she was exhausted and hoped to grab a few Zs on the plane. So we agreed to share naptime, albeit 3000 miles apart.

I ate, snoozed, showered, traded my jeans and running shoes for the dockers and leather shoes that Diamond had fetched from my cabin. I took a cab to Vladimir Petruschka's place, arriving a fashionable twenty minutes late.

I went up the broad steps of the brownstone, which was actually made of dark gray stone blocks, and showed my scrap of intaglio print to the man at the entrance. He nodded and opened the door.

"Elevator is on your left. Take it to the fifth floor."

"Thank you."

There was a couple inside, waiting at the elevator. They were in their thirties, dressed in what I thought of as New York Cocktail Party, much fancier than what I expected for an art party. She had on a sleek black dress and red heels. His trendy-cut suit and bow tie were one notch below Best Man at a hip wedding. The elevator opened, and we three got into a box that would, at most, fit six people if they were thin and very friendly.

"Friends of the Launcher?" the man said.

"Here to meet him," I said.

"Good timing," the man said. "He'll be in fine form tonight. These things he puts on are great people watching, too. The young artists will be trying to out-weird each other. And the Collectorati will be inspecting them like judges inspecting a state fair cattle show."

"The artist is more important than the art they make?" I said.

Both the man and the woman chuckled. "Hell, their tattoos and clothes are more important than the art they make," the man said. "It's all about what personality they project and how it strikes clients at an opening. If they can schmooze, better. If they are willing to sleep with the patrons, better still."

I nodded. "Nothing changes, huh? You two are collectors?"

They smiled and nodded.

We heard loud music as the elevator slowed and stopped. The door opened on a scene that was, in fact, reminiscent of a livestock show mixed with masquerade ball.

There was a mass of people in a large, open, attic loft. Above our heads, round, silvery corrugated duct work wove through old wooden roof trusses like huge metallic snakes. Far above was the steep-pitched roof.

In the far corner was what looked like a band of sorts with three young men and one young woman, all playing guitars and standing in front of microphones. There were no bass, drums, or keyboards. Fifteen seconds of listening suggested that it wasn't a band after all, but an art performance group whose mission was to use banshee screeching to loosen the building's mortar joints and the partygoers' fillings alike.

Spotting the artists among the collectors was like spotting a few thistles in a flower garden. The artists affected a look that was discordant and dissonant, with black clothes, some torn and ragged, others intact but with strangeness as the guiding design principle. The artists were all young. Their hair looked like it would draw blood if you bumped it. Some appeared to have spent their life savings on tattoos. Others decided to invest in precious metals and have their stockpile attached to their faces so that they wouldn't have to rent a safe-deposit box. All but one of the artists were skinny, some almost waif-like. Their naturally gaunt faces were enhanced with dark makeup to give them a vampire edginess.

The collectors comprised an equally conformist herd, although more pleasant to look at. The women all wore elegant suits or dresses, most in black or muted tones. Each had an accessory that provided a splash of color. The most popular outfit for the men was a black jacket and black tie over a dark gray shirt. The second most popular was the same but with the gray and black reversed. The Collectorati's footgear came in a range of styles, but not one showed a scuff or any sign of wear. By their shoes alone, the collectors radiated wealth, privilege, education, and style.

Moving through the crowd was a man who didn't fit either group. I took him for Vladimir. He was huge in breadth and depth, and, like a larger-than-life opera star, was preceded by a belly suitable for a Sumo wrestler. Mercifully, his flesh was covered by a purple satin suit with a black cummerbund. In his lapel was a large orange-pink orchid.

Unlike the meticulously kempt hair of the artists and collectors, his shiny, olive brown hair appeared to have been unattended for years, and it splayed across his head like a wide mat of still-wet kelp that had been hoisted from the ocean, complete with bits and pieces of deep-sea detritus.

As he flowed through the room, the crowds opened up like grips parting for Orson Welles on a movie set. If outrageousness were the prerequisite for art-god status, it was easy to see why Vladimir had been anointed.

Around the perimeter of the loft was a variety of paintings. Most were large. They were hung in groups of three, each group easily identified by the similar style. There appeared to be five groups.

"Five new artists," a man standing next to me said, as he noticed my perusal of the art. He twirled the wine in his glass. "He's expanding from his usual introduction of three. What do you think?"

"Not sure I'm qualified to have an opinion," I said.

"Oh? I assumed you were an expert. You're the only one here who is looking at the art instead of at the people."

"A newbie's naivete," I said. "I figured we're supposed to check out Vlad first, then the Collectorati, then the artists, then the art."

"Good rule."

"How does this work?" I said.

"It's pretty straightforward. These are Vladimir's choices for Best New Artists. He hypes them in his art paper, and in his magazine column. Of course, his influence is largely local to New York. But for the artists who are chosen, Vlad's endorsement is probably the singular most important event that will ever happen in their art careers. After judging the response tonight, Vlad will decide which of the five will be given a solo show for his Fourth Friday opening."

"Ah," I said.

"Well, cheerio," the man said as he moved off.

I found the bar, picked up a glass of Meursault Burgundy, and milled around, listening to actual oohs and ahs from the Collectorati as they circulated past each other and remarked on every outfit. I saw just one of them stop and stare at one of the inscrutable canvases that shared with paintings everywhere the fact that paint had been applied to canvas, but nothing else. That these wall coverings could elicit any positive reaction suggested that either the art business was a bleak game in which the contestants vied to outdo one another in how far they could take a cynical remove, or that this particular assemblage of artists was comprised of people who would score lower on the Picasso/Matisse Differentiation Test than your average armadillo.

The man looking at the canvas made a little head shake as if he were coming out of a petit mal seizure and went back to scrutinizing the clothing on his colleagues.

The Collectorati weren't constrained by age. They ranged from late twenties on up. From the idle chatter that floated around me as I milled about, it appeared that they came from a variety of backgrounds, their only common ground—in addition to their uniform fixation on sharp clothes and their lack of mental acuity in art appreciation—being a large bank account. I couldn't imagine sustaining an interest in any of their lives unless one of them should choose to become a patron of the arts of private investigation and award me a merit-based grant so that I could retire to write my memoir.

Career Launcher Vlad kept up a frenetic pace of making the rounds of his castle. It wasn't until I'd returned to the bar for another glass of wine that I sensed an opening.

He'd been stopped by an elderly woman who'd grabbed his sleeve and hung on while she explained her reaction to the paintings by the youngest and skinniest of the girl-artists. Vlad looked seriously annoyed but stayed to hear the diatribe. The woman's past patronage must have run to many figures.

I saw my opportunity.

After the woman had talked at him for a minute, I approached. I took Vlad's arm as I bent down to the woman and said, "Excuse me madam, but I need a quick comment from Vladimir for the New York Times Art Section. He'll be right back."

She turned to see who was talking, but I was already steering Vladimir away.

"Thank you, thank you," Vladimir said in a heavy Russian accent. He was my height, so his garlic breath was hot on my face as he turned to me. "Her artistic ignorance is breathtaking."

"Unlike the rest of the Collectorati?"

"Collectorati," he said with a dismissive huff. "I don't remember meeting you before. Tell me, are we off the record?"

"Yes."

He nodded as we threaded our way through the crowd. "You have been talking to the heretics. Your implication is accurate. They are all imbeciles. They fall for any paintings I hang on my gallery walls. It doesn't matter that I have a vision, that I can see the future of art. They don't understand it. They don't even look at them before they buy them. They are like a herd of cattle. They just follow the leader. So tell me, Mr..."

"McKenna."

"Mr. McKenna. You are a journalist. But are you really interested in the future of art? The vanguard of the next movement?"

"I'm more interested in the past."

"Worse than a heretic. And what past would this be? I've worked with many famous artists over the last four decades. Rauschenberg to Johns to Diebenkorn."

"Much earlier. Seventeenth Century. Rembrandt."

Vladimir jerked, looked at me, tried to seem puzzled. "I am, of course, an expert on the Dutchman, but why ask me? I create the next wave. I don't live in the past."

"I'm talking about the Night Portraits."

Vladimir exhaled like a startled bull.

FORTY-SEVEN

Vladimir's rough face gained enough color to resemble a giant yam. He looked around at the crowd, his eyes searching.

"Noisy in here," he said, fumbling for words. "Come." He turned and walked over toward the short hallway with the elevator. We continued past the elevator and went through a door to a narrow stairway that was the original route down from the attic loft. He trundled slowly down the steps, as if careful not to fall, turning his big feet sideways on each shallow stair tread, breathing hard. We went down to another door, which opened onto the upper floor of bedrooms. The hallway carpet was like that in a hotel, with thick, smooth nap and an ornate pattern of navy blue swirls with tiny gold highlights against a maroon background.

Vladimir walked over to a grand, winding, central stairway that was the core of the house. The stairs were wooden with a heavy carpet runner that matched that in the hallway. The varnished railing was supported by turned balustrades. It went down in a graceful spiral. Vladimir put his hand on the railing, and, reassured by its support, went down the stairs at twice the speed he'd used on the narrow attic stairway.

Vladimir led me down two flights to the second floor, then went over to a pair of French doors that were made of small panes of leaded glass. I followed him into a large office, lit only by picture lights that shined on a dozen old paintings, mostly traditional still lifes, almost a direct opposite from the modern stuff on display in the attic loft. Vladimir shut the door behind us. His breath was fast and shallow from the labors of our descent, but the time interval had given him a chance to regain his composure.

"What did you say about Rembrandt?" he asked, his voice straining to be casual.

"The Night Portraits. I want to know who you bought them

from."

"You are referring to a fable. Rumors. Supposition. Speculation. The idea of the Night Portraits was conjured up by a creative historian who was looking for a trump card to play against his colleagues. It didn't work. The concept of the missing portraits has lingered through the centuries, but the historian was forgotten."

"You are saying the paintings don't exist, that you didn't sell them?"

"I'm a respected art dealer and broker. I don't deal in anything that isn't..." he stopped.

"I'm not interested in undermining your business. But I have a credible witness who will testify that you bought and sold the paintings." It was a lie, but I knew it would have an impact. "I can prove that the Night Portraits were painted by a contemporary painter who was murdered a few nights ago. I don't care about the portraits or who bought them. All I want is the person who sold them to you."

Vladimir walked over to a wall with two sets of matching bookshelves. On a small table between them was a silver tray, and on it a bottle of Remy Martin and four snifters. He poured himself some cognac, took a sip, made a popping noise with his lips. He held up his glass. "You want some?"

"No thanks."

"This is for a story in the Times?" he said.

"No. I'm a former Homicide Inspector from the San Francisco PD, now a private investigator." I handed him my card. "I'm after the murderer of Gary Kiyosawa, a retired doctor and a painter of astonishing skill. He studied at the Atelier Olympia in Tahoe and specialized in Rembrandt-style portraits. He painted the Night Portraits."

"I'm going to call the police. The last thug who tried to shake me down spent two nights in jail. Unfortunately, for him, he'd spread several bad rumors about me. Two clients of mine backed out of purchase agreements on paintings that I was acquiring from Russia. I sued the man for slander, and the jury awarded me five hundred and fifty thousand dollars, the amount of my lost sales. Last I heard, the man is now mowing lawns for a living."

I pulled out Jennifer's phone, fished FBI Agent Ramos's business card out of my wallet and began pressing the numbers of my home phone line.

"Who are you calling?" Vladimir said.

I walked over and showed him Ramos's card. He could hear my home phone ringing in the background. "One of his colleagues put me onto a man who helps the FBI's Art Crimes Team. The man works hard for their expense-account scraps. I met him at the Metropolitan Museum. He knew several details about how you acquired the Night..." I stopped when my answering machine picked up. I pressed my phone against my ear so Vladimir couldn't hear my own words on the other end of the line. "Yes, Ramos. McKenna here. You were right. The Art Crimes boys are good. What? Oh, right. The team is headed by a woman. Anyway, I'm standing in the office of..." Vladimir raised his hand. His eyes were aflame. "Hold on," I said into the phone.

Vladimir whispered the words, "Hang up. Maybe I can be of help."

"Ramos, something came up. Let me get back to you?"

I waited a second, then clicked off.

Vladimir gritted his teeth and stared at me.

I held his eyes. Eventually, he looked down at his glass.

"The paintings have complete provenance," he said, a reversal of his earlier denial.

"Provenance is much easier to forge than the paintings themselves."

Vladimir was shaking his head in denial. "Even the frames are from Rembrandt's era. The backs of the frames have a removable protective cover. I've taken them off. It is one of the ways to consider the authenticity. These paintings are unmistakably from that period. The old stretcher bars are nearly black with age. They were constructed with the lap-jointed corners common to middle-quality canvases of early Seventeenth Century Holland." Vladimir's voice grew louder, as if marshalling the evidence diminished his doubts. "Rembrandt painted on both linen and cotton canvas. These were the cheaper cotton, saved for the less important portraits.

"The canvas was ancient and crispy, dark with the decay associated with the impurities in cotton of that day. Cotton of that era had lignin in it from seeds and other debris. In time, lignin breaks down into acids. The acids attack the canvas, turning it brown and brittle. The canvas was stretched with the hand-forged tacks from that area and period. Lastly, the canvases have the original identification paper, ink on vellum, signed by Rembrandt, the same signature as on the paintings. Even more, in several letters in archives in Amsterdam, it was stated that the paintings of the van Gelden family—the so-called Night Portraits—were done in the latter half of sixteen thirty-two. Do you know the significance of that?"

I shook my head.

"Then I will tell you. When Rembrandt was in his early twenties, he signed his paintings with his initials RH. Around sixteen twenty-nine, he added an L to them. RHL stood for Rembrandt Harmenszoon Leiden. And in that same year, he expanded it to RHL van Rijn. Later, in the middle of sixteen thirty-two, he stopped that approach and began simply signing his paintings with his first name, Rembrandt. Except that—and here is the significance—the original spelling of his name was without the D. Rembrant. A few months later, in sixteen thirty-three, he added the D. No one knows why. For the rest of his life he signed his name with the D in the spelling. So there was only a short period at the end of sixteen thirty-two when he signed paintings as Rembrant without the D. This is the time when the Night Portraits were supposed to have been painted. And guess what? When the Night Portraits were finally discovered, they were signed Rembrant, without the D!"

"If you know that, then a thorough researcher would have learned it as well and made certain that the forgeries were properly signed," I said.

"That's ridiculous!" Vladimir shouted. "You think that not only might there be such an amazingly-talented painter who could paint a believable Rembrandt forgery, but that he would also know the peculiar history of the spelling of Rembrandt's signature? You think he would match up the spelling oddity with the time frame of the Night Portraits, a time frame that is known by almost no one? If so, you are as gullible as some of those patrons upstairs." Vladimir raised his glass, tipped his head back as if to stare at the ceiling, and drained the cognac in a gulp.

"You take the signature," he said, "and add to it the canvas and stretcher and tacks and provenance and the aged and crackled paint surface and the unmistakable painting style that Rembrandt used with his portraits, it's... Rembrandt's talent transcended the millennium. It's like Michelangelo or Da Vinci. Perhaps no one will ever again be able to paint like that. It's impossible to imagine that they are not the real thing!" Vladimir's thunderous voice echoed in the study.

Vladimir's argument was compelling. I was visualizing the Rembrandts in the Metropolitan Museum, perfect images over rough and imperfect surfaces. I recalled the old landscape painting in Kiyosawa's study, the darkened stretcher bars from centuries before, and how the painted surface was rough and cracked with age. I suddenly realized how the forgery was done.

"I'll tell you how Dr. Kiyosawa did it," I said. "He purchased a group of Flemish landscapes from that era. The paintings were by an artist of little account, sold in a group at an estate sale. Dr. Kiyosawa painted over them. First, a layer of rabbit skin glue, then oil paints, hand-mixed with hand-ground pigments to perfectly imitate the relatively coarse paints of the day as well as duplicating the colors of Rembrandt's palette. The original brush marks and the cracked surface paint left an embossing on the new paint above, giving it a head start on an aged appearance. But Kiyosawa mixed dryers into his paint, and within a week or so of completing each portrait, the paint had shriveled and cracked as it dried."

Vladimir's eyes once again showed doubt.

"I could show you Kiyosawa's studio. I could show you his materials. I could show you one of the old paintings that is left from the lot he started with. If you looked at the back of it, you would recognize the old stretcher bars and darkened canvas as a sister of the paintings you bought and sold."

Vladimir turned and paced away from me.

I spoke to his back. "The man who sold them to you is either the murderer, or he knows who the murderer is. I'm not after you. I'm after him. I'm trying to keep him from murdering the painter's daughter, who apparently knows something incriminating. If you tell me who sold them to you, I will go away and I won't bother you again."

Vladimir turned around and faced me.

"And if I don't tell you?" he said.

"If you don't tell me, I will publicize what I know, and your client will find out that you sold him a pile of well-painted fakes. I imagine the fallout from that will put you out of business and ruin your reputation."

"And if I am correct, and these paintings are the real thing? What then?"

"Then you can sue me, too. But it won't do you any good after the rumors and innuendo have destroyed you."

Vladimir swelled with anger, his chest expanding and his head rising an inch as he inhaled a huge breath into his giant chest. He held the breath. His face darkened, moving from the yam color toward eggplant.

I tensed my muscles, readying myself for an explosion of violence.

But it didn't come. Vladimir began a long exhalation, like a pressure valve releasing. His chest slowly fell and his color lightened. He walked over, picked up the brandy bottle, poured his snifter half full, then downed it.

"The man who sold me the Night Portraits is named Kelly Smith." Vladimir took several deep breaths. His voice wavered.

"How did this Kelly Smith contact you?"

"A crate arrived one day. I was going to refuse it. We can't accept unauthorized shipments. But the return address said Night Portrait Number One, care of van Rijn, LLC. It was too enticing to refuse."

"He sent you one without any payment?"

"The note inside said it was on approval, that Kelly Smith would be contacting me, and that if I didn't want it, he would send a call tag for its return."

"And if you did want it," I said, "you would pay for it, and he would ship the second one."

"Yes. It was a bold presentation." Vlad poured more cognac, took a sip. "But he knew I would be hooked from the moment I first saw it."

"How do you contact him?"

"I don't. He contacts me. All I have is the Beverly Family Bank in Santa Fe, New Mexico. I make the checks out to van Rijn, LLC."

"A limited liability corporation?"

"Yes," Vladimir sighed. "The shipments came from van Rijn,

LLC, care of a drop-ship company in Las Vegas. Of course, I was curious, so I did a little research. I read that New Mexico's state laws allow you to set up an LLC that hides your personal information. You can deposit the checks in a New Mexico bank, have the money wired to an account someplace else, and nobody can trace where it goes or who gets the money."

"A good setup for hiding," I said.

"Yes. I also called the drop-ship company, and they say a Mr. van Rijn delivers the crates for shipping. The address they had for him was the van Rijn, LLC in care of the Beverly Family Bank. This is the only reason I have some doubt about this man. But it is also perfectly reasonable to think that he merely wants to be careful to hide his newfound wealth. He doesn't want to be a mark."

"This newfound wealth. How much is it?"

Vladimir sighed again.

"I've paid him five hundred thousand for each of five paintings."

"Two and a half million dollars," I said.

"Yes."

"And you have sold them for much more."

"Yes. I have no complaints, except..."

"Except, what?"

"Except that I had to pay in advance for the last painting, and I haven't gotten it yet. The most important portrait of them all. The portrait of the entire family with the dead baby."

FORTY-EIGHT

I had Vladimir write down the address of the Beverly Family Bank where he mailed the checks to the van Rijn, LLC.

I told Vladimir that I would call him if I needed any more information, and that I expected that he would take my call. If I did not need any more information, he would not hear from me again.

He made a tiny diffident nod, an incongruous movement from such a large man.

The couple I'd seen going into the party walked out of the house behind me. We three turned the same direction down the sidewalk. To give them a little privacy, I walked at an angle across the street. After I was on the other side, the couple and I walked parallel paths, heading west toward Park Avenue. It had been raining while we were indoors, and the night air had cooled to a chill.

From across the street, I heard the couple laughing in musical tones, giggling in bursts, followed by hushed murmurs and whispers and admonishments to talk quieter, first from her when he mentioned a name, then from him as she forgot her own request and impugned the character of someone else. Their private post-party world was full of jokes and amusements about the people up in the loft, wry comments and insider understandings known only to their official Group of Two.

I heard few distinct sentences except one about a girl with yellow hair, which made me think of a poem in a book that Street had given me. It was a collection by a famous Irish poet that an Irish-Welsh-Scottish cop like me should have known, but didn't.

I glanced across the pavement and saw them arm-in-arm under the elliptical wash from a streetlight, bent a little forward as they walked this island of a million people but aware only of each other. He seemed to stare down at the sidewalk as her red high heels swung one after another into his vision, percussive, pointed, hot red repudiations of the damp cold mood that rose from the wet pavement. She turned her head sideways, tucking her face against his chest, her smile visible in the dark. They radiated closeness, a singular unit immune to the infections of the world.

I slowed and looked over as the syncopated clicking of her heels changed cadence and timbre. They had turned in through a small gate, and were walking up the steps of another large house with multiple chimneys just as at the house of Vlad.

The man slipped a key into the lock of a large door, and he let them into an entry half-filled by a huge crystal chandelier.

The street was now empty, and my footsteps were the only sounds that rose above the distant traffic on the north-south avenues.

Many times I'd walked with Street Casey over the crazy-steep hills in the postcard city 3000 miles to the west. We'd done drinks with appetizers and theater and dinner and post-dinner, single-malt scotch at the Top of The Mark, and then hiked with laughter and jokes and abandon back toward the big bed in our favorite old hotel. We always skipped the elevator with its intrusive passengers and walked the winding stairs, Street ahead of me in her black heels and dark nylons and little black dress. Those memories were carved into mental rock, never to be diminished.

But the precious nights with Street were always the exception. They reminded me that the rest of the time, she went home to her own condo, secure in her knowledge of her love for me, but equally secure in the rightness of her decision to live separately, to avoid becoming too intertwined lest, as one of the Irishman's poems described, things ever fell apart, and the center could not hold.

I'd spoken to her a couple of hours before, as she was on her way to Sea-Tac airport. Now, as I walked the Upper East Side, she would be looking down at the sparse lights scattered across the darkness of central Oregon, soon to begin the long descent toward Reno.

I visualized her jammed shoulder-to-shoulder in the human cattle car. I knew that she wouldn't chat much with the big, jocular saleswoman on one side. Nor would she trade many words with the young funny guy on her other side, the guy eager to try out some new lines on her and see what it took to get a woman ten years his senior interested in trying out his brand of excitement.

Street was like so many people are, doing her best to be pleasant when necessary, but more comfortable focusing on her work, solo projects outlined in her laptop, scheduled in her iPhone, and performed in her laboratory, complicated endeavors where human interaction was necessary but was not necessarily desired. Even more than me, Street lived alone, whether she was around people or not.

We were loners, she and I, she by choice, me by default. No doubt the Irishman had written a poem about that, too, but I hadn't learned it, yet.

As of the last several days, I'd learned that Leah was another loner, but I hadn't figured out whether she was in the by-choice or the by-default category.

She was out alone tonight on the 40-foot Ciel, anchored in an empty cove on a freezing mountain lake, the highest big lake in the northern half of the planet. Her boat would be darkened for safety. I imagined her down in the saloon, drapes pulled shut, two little votive candles her only light. Spot would be lying on the carpeted floor, elbows spread wide, holding his head high and watching her intently if he thought there was a chance of a treat, or flopped down to his side if he'd given up hope.

I didn't yet have a sense of Leah. Her loss of husband and father and the resulting terror so warped her demeanor that I'd had no chance of glimpsing her normal personality. She'd gone from being Tahoe's well-known TV talk show host, ensconced in the lively world of interviewing and writing and producing a popular show, to being reduced to hiding on a boat, grappling with major physical injuries and even larger emotional wounds.

Leah had told me that she was frightened. I'd heard the primal fear in her voice. It didn't take much thought to realize that having Spot at her side was the only thing that kept her from panicking.

They say we enter and leave this world alone.

What they don't tell us is that we spend a good part of the journey alone as well.

FORTY-NINE

According to the inscrutable equations in the airline computers, my morning plane out of LaGuardia made a stop at O'Hare in Chicago, then flew all the way to Las Vegas where I changed planes only to head back east to Albuquerque. Without a reservation, the car agency only had subcompacts left. So I scrunched into a plastic box sized for ballerinas, knees on either side of the steering wheel, head jammed against the ceiling.

At 5300-plus feet, the capitol of New Mexico is the highest major metropolitan area in the country. But it is so far south that it is warmer in the summer than Reno, which is 900 feet lower. The air conditioning in the little box wheezed as if it had asthma and had lost its inhaler. It puffed such a tiny stream of tepid air toward my sweaty face that if I'd held a candle in front of it, the flame wouldn't have been sure which way to bend.

The drive up to Santa Fe rises the better part of 2000 feet, but when I uncoiled myself from the car two blocks down from the Beverly Family Bank, the rising temps of late afternoon in the desert canceled out the cooling effect of the increased altitude.

The Beverlys were doing a brisk business inside one of the cookie-cutter brown adobe buildings just off Canyon Road. I pushed through the door into the refrigerated air and once again marveled that my home climate in Tahoe didn't require air conditioning except in the meat section of the supermarket for maybe a week at the end of July and another at the beginning of August.

A dozen and a half other people appreciated the chilled interior, most of them lined up in front of the teller counter, and some of them waiting over by a grouping of desks behind which sat loan officers, bankers, and other management types who looked like college seniors.

I went over to the ATM. My wait behind a large woman

with shopping bags hanging off each arm gave me a chance to surreptitiously study the various employees. I only glanced at the tellers as they didn't have the authority to help me. The rule in any bank is to focus on the people with desks.

By the time the ATM had coughed out some cash for me, I'd memorized all of the desk workers. I went out and waited in the plastic box, engine burning gas in a futile attempt to power the air conditioner. I tried to dream up a good con. I was a treasury agent. The Beverly Family Bank was, unknown to them, being used as a money laundry. Although our agency was concerned about the drug lord's money, our main focus was saving the children. I was working on the details of the story when the first desk boy came out.

I followed him. He drove a shiny Nissan a few blocks, jockeyed around a parking lot before he found a space, and trotted through the scalding sun into a Subway sandwich shop. I double-parked within view. Twenty minutes later, he came out, wiping his mouth with a paper napkin. He pushed the napkin into the trash bin, then drove back to the Beverly Family Bank and went back into work. The total desk-to-desk time elapsed was 27 minutes, and I knew from that alone that one day he would be the bank manager, and ten years later would either own a bank or would have graduated to the upper banking levels at one of the finance centers in a big city.

Back in the Beverly lot, I waited for the next desk worker. It was one of the women, the slim one who wore a blue-gray dress with a little maroon neck scarf that would keep her warm come Santa Fe fall, but in summer revealed that the indoor climate was, as always, excessively chilled.

She carried a big canvas satchel over her shoulder, and she ate little carrots out of a plastic bag as she walked in maroon pumps across the parking lot and got into a small, Chevy sedan. I followed her a good distance to the sprawling lot of an indoor shopping mall. I got out and walked behind her, staying back as she strolled through two stores, then went into the food court and on out the other side, not even glancing at the menu boards with the pictures of burgers, burritos, and bagels with cream cheese.

The carrot lobby should put her figure on billboards.

She turned into one of those upscale shops that only sell the goods of a single designer brand.

She stopped before a handbag stand. She looked at one of them, picked it up and handled it, lovingly caressing it like it was a newborn baby, like it held a million dollars in unmarked bills. Then she looked around, telegraphing her intentions like a five-year-old about to steal quarters out of the jam jar on the kitchen counter, thus handing me my opportunity as sure as if she'd handed me a silver tray with a card on it that said, 'Here's your entrée into my private life. Whatever you want is yours, my secrets, my confidences, or, if you desire, a look in my employer's computer.'

She slipped the handbag into her shoulder bag and quickly left the store.

I followed her outside into the parking lot. I held up my cell phone, which, I'd been told, takes pictures, although I'd never figured out how to use it.

"It's handy to have a video camera whenever you want one," I said as she was getting into her car.

She looked at my phone. "I don't know what you are talking about," though the alarm and worry in her eyes was obvious.

I pulled out my wallet, not to show her the boring investigator's license, but to flash her the 19th Century sheriff's badge I'd bought in a tourist shop in Virginia City.

It's amazing what a trinket of metal will do.

Her eyes widened.

"The handbag you slipped into your shoulder carryall. The designer tag on it carries a big ticket, right? Probably grand larceny. An end to your career. Long probation, if you have a good lawyer. Maybe some jail time, if you don't."

She swallowed. "What are you going to do to me?"

"I'm going to fry some big fish. You help me, maybe you'll be one of the fingerlings that slip through the net."

"I... I don't understand."

I walked over to her car. She was sitting in the driver's seat, the door still open. Her dress in the heat clung to her midsection, revealing the benefits of the carrot diet.

I leaned on the roof of her car, crowding her space.

"Your bank has a customer our agency is watching. We need his forwarding address."

"What do you mean?"

"The checks get made out to a company called van Rijn, LLC, care of your bank. Some or maybe all of them arrive by mail. Your bank periodically writes a check on that account and mails it to someone. Or maybe it is a direct deposit. We need to know the name and address on the account the deposit goes to."

The woman hadn't moved. Sweat had formed on her forehead and on her chin.

"And if I get you this information?" she asked, her voice quaking.

I held up my cell phone. "Then I hit the erase button. No one will ever know your secret vice."

Her eyes quivered with worry. "Do you really mean it? You'll let me go?"

I smiled at her, feeling, as I often do with thieves, that any empathy was misplaced. "You don't have a choice, do you?" I said. "You'll have to help me and take your chances."

I followed as she drove, excessively slowly, back to the bank. She parked in the far corner away from the other cars—already a self-appointed pariah—and made the long walk to the bank door.

I parked closer, and she had to walk past me. I rolled down my window. "Thirty minutes at the most, do you think?" I said.

She turned and, squinting into the sun, gave me an acid stare, so affronted by my presence that she shook, but whether by fear or by anger I couldn't tell.

"I don't want your hide," I said, "only the address where the checks get sent."

She narrowed her eyes and grappled in her bag. For just a moment, as she pulled out her name badge, her watchband caught on the purloined purse, and it came out, red velvet and sequins glittering in the sun. She shoved it back into the shoulder bag, punching it twice with her fist as if it were the devil rearing its head into her life. Her hands shook as she put on the badge. She was unsteady as she walked away, like someone who'd just been in a car accident.

The bank door opened as she approached—a customer leaving—and she rushed on through before it could shut.

I waited fifty minutes, and was considering going in, when she came out of the bank. This time her walk was less regal, her demeanor wounded. She angled toward my car. She limped a bit on her left foot as if something hurt, but I sensed that it was less a twist of the ankle than a pain in her soul. She came to the window of my car. She held a Post-it note that had been folded two or three times. "I have a bad problem," she gasped at me in a desperate whisper. "Please take this and go away. Please don't make my life worse."

"All I want is the address," I said as I reached for the paper. "No one will ever know where I got it." I started the rental car.

The woman staggered and leaned—almost falling—against the roof above my window. "I've been seeing a doctor. We're working on it. We've tried drugs. Nothing has made it better. But this... you could ruin me."

I unfolded the Post-it note.

"We don't mail checks," she said. "We wire the money to a bank account in Reno. I wrote down the number."

She'd written the name of another limited liability company, the Reno branch of one of the giant banks, and an account number.

"I'm the least of your worries," I said. "Forget I ever saw you." I shifted into drive and eased forward. Her sweaty arm squeaked on the roof as I pulled away.

I thought about the Reno bank account as I took the long downhill glide to Albuquerque. That it was next door to Tahoe would suggest that the person who sold Vladimir the paintings may have personally gotten them from Dr. Gary Kiyosawa. Maybe even lived in Northern Nevada or Northern California. But I didn't want to grant that idea too much credence. In a state with legal gambling and prostitution, businesses in Reno were accustomed to customers with large amounts of money, and they didn't ask as many questions as one would expect in other states. The person may have chosen Reno just for its business climate.

Reno was on Interstate 80, and it had an international airport. The person who presented himself to Vlad as Kelly Smith could live anywhere, even in New York. If he often flew coast-to-coast, he might find a Reno bank account combined with a New Mexico LLC very convenient for private business transactions.

All I had learned was that the person who sold the Night Portraits to Vladimir Petruschka had put some effort into concealing the money that Vlad was paying him. That the bank was near Tahoe wasn't even a second cousin to conclusive, but it was suggestive.

FIFTY

I had time to kill before my plane left Albuquerque. I got Agent Ramos's card out of my wallet and dialed his number.

His voicemail picked up. I knew Ramos was sitting at his desk, probably surfing online, or buffing his nails. But he was too important to be interrupted.

"McKenna calling," I said to the computer. "I've got a quid pro quo for you that you're gonna like. The sooner you gimme a call, the more likely you'll get a merit badge out of this." I left the Salazar Company cell number.

He called back when I was standing in line, boarding pass in hand.

"This is Special Agent Ramos calling," he said, his insufferable arrogance oozing out of the little holes in the plastic next to my ear.

"I've got a good-sized spider web for you," I said. "When you're done reeling it in, you'll have a whole range of goodies to unwrap. Money laundering, stolen art, racketeering, murder."

"The doctor who was killed?"

"Yeah."

"But you don't know how it connects, or you wouldn't have called me."

"Right," I said. "But I'm confident that one of the many threads on this web will take me to the guy who's trying to kill Leah Printner."

"The TV lady," he said.

"Right."

"You've still got her parked somewhere."

"Yeah. But I'm worried. The guy Diamond's sitting on isn't talking. I know he's hired meat. And his partner is still out there looking for Leah. She doesn't want me to get her a ticket out of Dodge, says if she stays hidden in the area, the killer will keep trying to sniff her out, and we're more likely to nab him. I think she's right about that."

"But he might succeed," Ramos said. He didn't sound unhappy about the idea. It would make me look bad, which he would like.

"What do you want from me?" he asked.

"I give you the spider web," I said. "It involves a limited liability company in New Mexico that sends money to another LLC in Nevada, which will have yet another cover. What I'm looking for is a human connection. Somewhere in the spider web will be a name or a real live business or an address that isn't a P.O. Box. When one of your people finds it, you give me a call."

Ramos didn't speak for a ten-count. No doubt wondering if he could get the info without having to work through me.

Finally, he said, "Deal."

So I gave it all to him. How Jimmy Jamaica led me to Vladimir The Career Launcher, his purchase of Dr. Kiyosawa's Night Portraits from a guy who called himself Kelly Smith, the $2.5 million Vlad had sent in half-million chunks to Smith's van Rijn, LLC at the Beverly Family Bank, which then wired the money to the bank in Reno.

Ramos said he'd look into it and hung up.

The plane to Reno takes no more time in flight than it takes to board and unboard, and I was in Jennifer's Toyota and heading back to Tahoe two and one half hours after I spoke to Ramos. I turned south out of Reno Tahoe International and called Street.

"I'm back in Reno. You got home okay last night? Catch up on sleep?"

"Yeah," she said. "Now I'm on Beaufort's Beauty with Leah."

"How'd you get out to the boat?"

"Jennifer called her, said she'd ferry me out in the runabout if Leah wanted company and wanted to meet me. Leah told her she was at Skunk Harbor. It was easy for Jennifer to find. You coming out, too?"

"As soon as I turn over some rocks, see what's underneath. It'll probably be after dark. I'll call before I come out, so you aren't surprised."

We exchanged some sweet talk, said goodbye and hung up.

I was heading south through Washoe Valley when my phone rang.

"Typical shell companies," Ramos said when I answered. "These guys, they think if they layer-up and lawyer-up, we won't be able to follow the money, and they'll be protected even if we do."

"You found out where it goes?"

"Not yet. I didn't say the process was fast. Unlike some rogues, we do these things the right way. Proper evidence, warrants at each step. We want convictions, not cowboy justice."

I let the insinuation slide. "You got something for me?"

"You wanted a human name. One of our men has a contact who's very good with computers. As you know, the expertise we can bring to a complex..."

"What do you have?" I interrupted.

I heard Ramos take a deep breath over the phone. "The Nevada LLC you gave me forwards funds to another Nevada LLC which banks at a multi-national investment house. We're investigating the disbursements. There is one name I'm prepared to give you. The Suzanne Veronica Hall Family Trust."

"And I find this Suzy where?"

"Nevada City. You got a pen?"

"Hold on." I pulled off onto the shoulder, found pen and paper. "Ready."

"The account only has a box number on it. But my guy is good. He dug up a physical." Ramos gave it to me. "Let me know what you find out," he said as if he were a general giving an order to a kid in boot camp. Then he hung up.

I had to drive another mile south to find an exit where I could cross over and head back north on 395. I went back to Reno, past the exit where I'd previously come out of the airport, and a couple miles farther north, I headed west on Interstate 80.

The afternoon rush-hour traffic was heavy, and I spent twenty minutes doing the slow-and-go before I got out to Verdi and began the climb up the Truckee River canyon. Like many canyons elsewhere, the relatively small flow of water in the river at the bottom is insufficient to have created the gorge. But during several ice ages, glaciers have dammed Lake Tahoe, raising its level as much as 600 feet. When the weather warmed, and those ice dams broke, the monster tidal wave of water that was released was more than up to the task of gouging out the river canyon before the water inundated what was to become the Reno area.

West of Truckee I followed the highway up the huge rock landscape that was scoured by glaciers. Once over Donner Summit, it was a quick trip down the west slope of the Sierra. I turned off on 20, followed the ridgeline down, and was in the picture-perfect town of Nevada City by dinner time.

FIFTY-ONE

Suzanne Veronica Hall lived a few miles north of the Yuba River valley. The number was one of many on a group mailbox that was four rows by five columns, and positioned so the residents could access their box from their car windows. I turned in and drove over a hill and through a dale. Her house was a large and newish two-story box, designed to look a little, but not much, like a Victorian. The box part was painted sky blue. The Victorian accents and trim were painted white. She had a sizable lot, maybe two rolling acres, and views of the other, similar houses in the development. Beyond, was the foothill forest, looking very attractive, but probably not attractive enough to avoid being leveled for future housing developments.

I pulled up as the sun was lowering into the thick air of the Central Valley down below, parked Jennifer's Toyota in the gravel drive, walked up onto the covered, wrap-around porch, and rang the bell.

A small dog barked, a young child yelled, a pleasant-sounding woman told them both to be quiet.

The woman who opened the door was in her late twenties. She wore jeans and a large, blousy short-sleeved shirt. It was designed to be tent-like, hanging out to hide some of the plumpness in her figure. Her thick hair, pulled back into a ponytail, was nearly the color of tomato soup, and she had fifteen thousand freckles to match. It had been a hot day down in the foothills, and despite the rush of air-conditioned air pouring out the front door, she was still carrying a flush, as if she'd been working in the heat. She held a Jack Russell terrier in her arms.

"Good afternoon, my name is Owen McKenna. I'm a private investigator from Tahoe. I'm looking into the death of Dr. Gary Kiyosawa. I wonder if I could ask you a couple of questions?" I showed her my ID.

"Doctor Kiyosawa? You mean, the same doctor as... Yes, of course, he must be. You obviously know of my connection to him, or you wouldn't be here." She blinked her eyes several times as if they'd suddenly starting stinging. "God, that's terrible that he died. We better talk outside."

A young boy ran up from behind her. His hair was so orange, the color reminded me of traffic cones.

"Mommy, my truck broke. The wheel came off my truck."

"We'll fix it later, honey. Go play with your other toys."

"Mommy," his voice whined.

"Mommy's busy. We'll deal with it later. Go and play."

The boy stomped away, his bare feet slapping the wood floor.

"At least he's playing with a truck and not watching TV," I said.

"I'm very strict with TV," she said. "Video games and computers, too. You watch the way kids stare at screens, it's like they're naturals for addiction. Even as a baby, if there was a TV in the room, Lenny couldn't take his eyes off it. So I make him ride his bicycle, play outside, do the kind of activities my parents did when they were kids. I actually had them make a list of what they used to do." She glanced at Lenny, who was now sitting on the floor with a pile of Lego blocks.

"We can talk out here on the porch," she said, shutting the front door to keep the cold shut inside.

We sat under the overhang on chairs that faced the lawn. The setting sun was still hot. The little dog panted in her lap. Six or eight bumblebees buzzed the explosion of Cosmos flowers that fronted the porch. Periodically, Suzanne turned around to look in the window and check on Lenny. Each time she looked through the window, the Jack Russell terrier looked, too.

She reached over to shake my hand. "I'm sorry. I'm Suzanne," she said, "although you must know that."

"Owen McKenna."

"I didn't know he died," she said. "I know he was old, probably in his seventies, but he seemed healthy. What happened?"

"He was murdered."

"Oh, God, I'm so sorry." The shock on her face seemed genuine. "Did you catch the killer?"

"No. We have a few leads, but nothing solid. I don't imagine you will be able to add anything to what we already know, but I'd like to go through the routine with you if you'd be so kind."

"Sure. Anything I can do to help." Then she got a worried look on her face. "You don't suspect me, I hope!"

"No. Of course, not. But Dr. Kiyosawa was very private. We're trying to learn more about his life through those he knew. So we go down the list and talk to everyone he had any contact with. You are on the list, that's all."

Suzanne nodded understanding. "Okay. Go ahead and ask."

"When did you first meet Dr. Kiyosawa?"

"I never met him, at least not in the normal way. The first time I ever laid eyes on him was in the courtroom."

I thought about it, trying to figure out how to play it. She assumed I knew what she was talking about. If I confessed to my ignorance, she might clam up. If I played along, she would think that I'd catch her in any lie, and she'd be more likely to tell the truth.

"How did he seem to you at the time?"

"Sad, more than anything. Even though my life as I knew it was destroyed, I felt sorry for him. I believe he was an honorable man. He could have walked away after the accident. But he stayed and tried to help Lance. I felt terrible when the lawyer told us that the driver didn't have insurance and that our only hope was the doctor's insurance company. It really was a double tragedy, us losing Lance, and the doctor trying to do something good, yet still causing Lance's death. I have to assume it nearly destroyed his life just as it did with my life. Emotionally and financially." She turned and looked in through the window at Lenny. "But now, things aren't so bad. Lenny is my world. I'm getting back on my mental feet."

"How long ago was it, now?"

"Lance died five years and two months ago. April thirteenth."

"Did you have any personal contact with Dr. Kiyosawa outside of the courtroom?"

"No. Our only contact was a joint letter he wrote to me and to Lance's parents. It was a heartfelt letter of apology. His pain was significant. Heartbreaking, really. If my life hadn't also been nearly destroyed, I probably would have written back. As it was, I'd just given birth, and I was beyond distraught. In the end, though, it probably helped me that I had Lenny to concentrate on. It probably lessened my pain."

"What about Lance's parents? Did they have any contact with the doctor?"

"No. Or at least, not that I know of. They were crushed, of course. Especially, Steve. Carissa handled it marginally better. Steve was the one who insisted on the lawsuit. I was too out of it to really give it much thought. But Steve pointed out that Lance and I had a pact of sorts. I'd be the mother. He'd be the income earner. So his death really was a terrible blow to my financial future. Steve said it was only fair that I be compensated. But I felt the court went too far. I thought that Dr. Kiyosawa's insurance and such was enough, that we shouldn't be awarded more because then he might be forced into bankruptcy. The legal remedy still seems wrong to me today. Just because you can do something doesn't mean you should. But I was young. I couldn't think clearly. I didn't have a sense of what to do. And my father-in-law is very persuasive."

"Did all the settlement go to you?"

"Most of it. I'm obviously quite well off now. Although if asked, Steve would point out that I'd be very rich right now if Lance were alive. Everyone agreed that Lance's company was going to be very successful. The venture capitalists had committed ten million for startup, and they made agreements to invest up to thirty million if Lance made his targets. Anyway, Steve and Carissa got some money for their suffering as parents, and I think a little also went to Charles, Lance's brother. Or maybe Steve and Carissa gave him some of their share. I'm not sure. He deserved whatever he got. In fact, in many ways Lance's brother suffered the most. While I had the baby to focus on, and Steve and Carissa had each other, Charles had nothing else. Charles was only one year older."

"Were they close?"

"Incredibly. When they were little kids they spoke to each other in a made-up language, the way twins often do. Then, as they got older and took Spanish and French in school, they talked to each other in Spanish and French, sometimes mixing the two, just so their parents and their friends wouldn't know what they were saying. They always did that, even as they got older. They kept their communications private. When Charles went to Stanford, Lance decided to go to Stanford. When Lance took up competitive cycling, Charles did the same. It was like that all their lives."

"Did they both study the same thing at Stanford? If so, one would think Charles might have wanted to step in and try to run Lance's new company."

"Oh, that's the one way they were very different. Charles studied literature, not computers. But the problem with literature," she continued, "is that it's hard to earn a living. So Charles tried a bunch of different things. He even studied acting for several years."

"Hard to find work as an actor," I said.

"He actually had steady work at the repertory company. Of course, it didn't pay anything to speak of. But the thing is, Charles specialized in such a weird corner of literature, he couldn't even get a teaching job. The acting was the best job he had going."

"What corner of literature is that?"

"Something like literature of the Middle Ages. I remember that he did his doctoral dissertation on Beowulf, which is some kind of epic poem. Whereas, Lance did his dissertation on nano-technology, which is a thousand times more useful in our modern world."

I barely heard the last part of what Suzanne was saying. "Did Charles ever mention Grendel?"

"The monster? That's funny that you ask that," Suzanne said. "Yeah, he often talked about Grendel. Wow, so you must know old literature, too?"

I ignored the question. I remembered that Lauren Phelter had a long career owning a repertory company in Marin. "When Charles worked as an actor, do you know where he went?"

Suzanne thought about it. "It was a place in San Rafael, up in Marin County."

"The North Coast Playhouse?"

"Yes, that's it."

"Where does Charles live?"

"Up until the accident, he always lived near us in Palo Alto. But after the accident, he kind of fell apart. Got a little strange, actually. He moves around in a sort of aimless way. We never know where to find him. Steve and Carissa keep asking me if he's called me or if I've heard where he is." She stopped and made a severe frown. "Hey, don't start thinking that Charles could have anything to do with the doctor's murder! That's not possible. He's the nicest guy. A real pure heart."

"I'm just collecting information. Do you have a picture of Charles?"

"It was just too painful to have my pictures around after Lance died. So I asked his parents to keep them for awhile. They're on a cruise for the next week, but I could call Carissa when they get back. I'm sure she would be happy to give you whatever you need. Wait," she said. "I just remembered his book. There is an author photo on it. I'll go get it."

Suzanne went inside the house and came back with a small-sized hardbound book. She handed it to me, the back cover facing me. On the paper dust jacket was a small black and white photo. It was one of those artsy portraits from the chest up that showed Charles facing partly to the side, the left side of his face completely in shadow. He had thick, dark, messy hair that went back as if he'd been in a windstorm. He wore heavy black-rimmed glasses. His face was mostly obscured by the glasses and the shadow, but it still communicated gravitas.

I tried to see the face separate from the clothes and hair. Nothing clicked. Maybe grease back the hair, and you could see a vague similarity with Leah's tormentor, Tom Snow.

I turned the book over. The title was:

ART CRITICISM
A Socratic Dialogue About Judgment and Censure
by Charles Hall, Ph.D.

"He studied literature and wrote about art?" I said.

"Charles is one of those real Renaissance men," Suzanne said with enthusiasm. "Art, literature, philosophy. He does it all. A real brain. Of course, you don't make any money writing books about art, but nothing about Charles was practical."

"I can't see much from the photo. How would you describe him?"

"Well, he was a year older than Lance, so he would be thirty-five, now. He's quite tall, six-one or six-two. Thin. But he's not a wimp. He's quite strong. He was good as a bicyclist. Won medals and everything. As you can see in the photo, he's got kind of a bigish nose. Lots of hair. My God, it goes everywhere. It's like an animal that he carries around on his head. Does that help?"

"May I borrow this dust jacket? I'll mail it to you later."

"I suppose."

I gave Suzanne a serious look. "If Charles should happen to call you in the near future, I was never here. You've never heard of me. Life has been the same old thing. Okay?"

She nodded slowly, worry like a dark shadow on her face.

I handed her my card. "Keep this where no one will find it. If you hear anything about Charles's whereabouts, call me."

I waited until she nodded again, then I left, mumbling thanks as I trotted off the front porch and ran to the Toyota.

FIFTY-TWO

I drove fast back through Nevada City and up to Tahoe. My thoughts were jumbled. I concentrated on what I knew.

A young man named Lance Hall died in an accident in which Dr. Kiyosawa apparently had some culpability. Lance was in the process of starting a valuable company. The family sued Kiyosawa for the loss.

Lance's brother Charles Hall took the loss especially hard.

He was an art expert at least to the extent of writing a book about art criticism.

He was a professional actor to some degree, and he could probably play the part of an art expert convincingly enough to persuade Vladimir to purchase what Charles claimed were the Night Portraits.

He acted at the North Coast Playhouse, the theater company owned and run by Lauren Phelter, Dr. Kiyosawa's landlord. Charles could have heard from Mrs. Phelter that Kiyosawa rented from her. Charles knew literature and was focused on Beowulf and the monster Grendel.

He was brilliant, and would be more than able to construct a complex financial mechanism for laundering a large amount of money from Vladimir.

Kiyosawa's culpability in Lance's death gave him motive.

I realized that I had no hard evidence that Charles was the missing shooter, or that he hired the killers. But I knew it just the same. The only problem I had—and it was a big one—was that I didn't have a clue about where to find him.

I pulled over and pulled out my travel kit with the little address book. I'd written Lauren Phelter's number in it. I dialed, then pulled back out on the highway as it rang.

"Hello?" Mrs. Phelter said in my ear.

"Owen McKenna calling."

"Are you in New York?"

"No, I got back a few hours ago."

"Did you learn what you wanted to know?" she asked.

"Yes. Now I have a question about your previous career, your theater."

"My career? Really. How strange. But go ahead."

"Do you remember one of your actors named Charles Hall?"

"Of course. He was with me for several years. Very talented. Scary smart. And entertaining. He could distract all the other actors from their jobs with his anecdotes about history. It actually got quite irritating. Even so, I was disappointed when he left. But then I sold the company to my protege shortly afterward, so he had to cope with finding a replacement."

"Did you ever have any contact with Charles after you moved up to Tahoe?"

Mrs. Phelter paused. "Actually, we did keep in contact for a time after I moved. Charles even visited me here at the house. It was actually Charles who referred Dr. Kiyosawa to me. He knew of the doctor in some way, but I forget how. Anyway, he sent me an email, included the doctor's number, and said that Dr. Kiyosawa had sold his house. Charles said that Dr. Kiyosawa was looking for a place to rent and that perhaps I should contact him. He said I could trust that Dr. Kiyosawa would be a good renter, quiet and reliable. How ironic that turned out to be."

"Do you have any pictures of Charles?"

"No. Of course, there were a thousand pictures of our plays. You could contact the theater and see about getting some. Why? Do you think Charles has any connection to this case?"

"Yes. Don't open your door without checking your peephole. If he should come by, don't let him in."

"But he and I are friends," Phelter said. "Of course, I would let him in."

"My professional advice is don't let him in."

"My lord. Will you tell me what this is about?"

"I believe Charles either killed Dr. Kiyosawa or hired him to be killed."

"No, it couldn't possibly be. Charles is not just some stupid crook. You must be wrong. He would never do such a thing."

"Just be careful," I said. We said goodbye and hung up.

I knew Street's cell number and was able to dial it while I drove.

"I'm coming up eighty from the foothills," I said when she answered. "I'll be there in another hour or so. I'm going to come out to the boat to talk to Leah and borrow Spot."

"A guess as to when you'll be here?"

"Nine. Nine-thirty."

"So it'll be getting dark. We'll be waiting, under candlelight only, so approach carefully."

"See you then."

I next called Jennifer and told her my plan so she wouldn't be alarmed when I was moving around her property as night was approaching.

She said not to worry and to stay in touch.

The rest of my drive I thought about the flamboyant Paul at Twin Peaks Art, who looked a bit like the book jacket photo, thick dark hair and a big nose. He'd spoken of his previous years acting.

The image of Paul morphed into Leah's stalker Tom Snow who, though more muscular than Suzanne had described Charles, also looked similar, with dark hair slicked back.

Of course, the most obvious suspect of all was the missing shooter who, while wearing a mask, had taken his comrade at gunpoint from the hands of the South Lake Tahoe police. We'd never even had a glimpse of him. He could be anyone. But most likely, he was the man on the book jacket, Charles Hall.

FIFTY-THREE

The late summer evening was turning to night as I pulled up to Jennifer's mansion. Motion lights came on as I put the Toyota into the giant garage, but I didn't see anyone through the lit windows of the house when I headed around to the lake.

There was no windscreen in the runabout. I stayed sitting so that I was behind the tiny support for the steering and shifter. The cold air of nightfall chilled me to the point of discomfort, reminding me that despite the long, warm summer days, the twin threats of nighttime mountain cold and the bitter cold water made a hostile environment. Tahoe sits a mile and a fifth above sea level, and its water comes from snowmelt. In the heat of day, a strong person could swim in the hot sun for possibly ten minutes before the cold sapped their strength. But at night, if a person had the misfortune to be dropped into the water, they wouldn't last more than five minutes before hypothermia destroyed the power of their muscles, and they sank beneath the waves. As several people learn every year, if you don't respect the cold, you succumb to it.

I came around Deadman Point after thirty minutes of steady droning through the night, and slowed the throttle down to the lowest speed where the boat would stay planing and not drop its stern down into a plowing position. There was nothing but darkness ahead. The black water stretching away from me dissolved into the blackness of the mountain above Skunk Harbor. I slowed further, scanning for the darkened shape of Beaufort's Beauty. I was beginning to worry when it appeared over on my right. I dropped the throttle to idle, and turned toward the shape, the steering nearly unresponsive at such slow speed. When I was twenty-five yards away, I shifted into neutral and, confident of my steering ability without power, I cut the engine. I coasted toward the boat, gradually aware of the dim candle glow coming through the cabin curtains.

I cranked the wheel, the runabout slowly turned, and its inertia brought the side of the aluminum hull alongside the port side of the sailboat. I caught the handrail, pulled the runabout back to the sailboat's stern, stepped out and tied a line.

Leah was holding Spot, keeping him from making a sound, as I came down the companionway steps. The aft cabin door was open. Street had put her bag and her laptop computer on the bed.

I kissed Street and sat with them on the settee. In his excitement to see me, Spot tried to jump up. He hit his head on the ceiling of the Ciel 40. Street poured me some wine. I gave them an abridged version of my trip to New York, my detour to Santa Fe, and my short visit with Suzanne Veronica Hall in Nevada City.

When I was done, I looked at Leah and said, "I asked you several times about any events in your life that caused friction, especially any situations that involved both you and your father."

Leah chewed on the inside of her cheek. Her frown was pinched, the skin bunching above the bridge of her nose. Her hands were in front of her on the table. Each had a vice grip hold on the other.

"I didn't... I've never been able to face what happened. It was horrible."

"I know that Lance Hall died five years ago, struck, I believe, by a truck. I know that the court decided that your father was somehow responsible. Tell us how it happened."

I sipped my wine, trying to act relaxed, trying to let some of the tension settle. But my stomach was churning,

Street did a better job than I did. She looked at Leah with obvious warmth and support.

We waited a long time. Street leaned forward and touched Leah's hands. "It's okay, Leah," she said in a soft voice. "Take your time."

Eventually, Leah spoke.

"I was in Berkeley visiting my father. He lived alone in his house near the university. I'd just started my TV show. Sometimes, I went into the Bay Area and stayed with my dad on weekends. We'd go to the Berkeley Repertory Theater, or the Oakland Art Museum, or take BART into San Francisco and see the ballet.

"It happened five years ago, as you said. It was about a year after dad retired. He and I were walking down a side street. There were two young children on the sidewalk, a brother and sister, maybe five and three years old. They were pushing an empty baby buggy, one of those fancy double ones with the large wheels that parents use to go running with their babies. The girl was trying to hang from the handle, and the boy was turning it in circles. They were giggling like you've never heard. We stopped and watched them.

"Right at that moment, a car jumped the curb and hit the children. Dad ran to them. While the boy had significant cuts on his face, the girl was hurt much worse. Severe head trauma, blood running out of her ears, eyes that wouldn't respond to light. Dad knew she would die if he couldn't get her to the Emergency Room in a minute or two.

"While dad worked on the girl, I yelled for help, screaming for someone to call nine-one-one because my dad didn't have a cell phone, and I'd left mine at his house. But no one heard me. And there were no cars coming down the street.

"Meanwhile, the woman who'd struck the children had tried to drive away. She backed up fast, went over the opposite curb, crashed over a parking meter and got stuck on it. She got out of her car and stumbled down the sidewalk, drunk. No one else was around. Dad said that the little girl wasn't going to make it. The baby buggy wasn't damaged too badly, so we put both kids in it. Dad pushed it, and we ran to the hospital which was a half-dozen blocks away.

"As we raced into the hospital parking lot, a young man stepped out from between two cars. The baby buggy struck him."

Leah stopped, her eyes tearing. She wiped at the tears with the heels of her hands.

"When the buggy hit him, the man tripped and sprawled to the side just as a van was going by. The van was going way too fast." She stopped again, taking deep breaths, her face contorted by the memory.

"The young man was hurt bad," I said.

She nodded and swallowed. "The truck ran over him."

Street rubbed Leah's hands as Leah breathed hard.

"The young man was on life support for a day before they disconnected him. He turned out to be a Stanford graduate student who'd recently started a promising Internet company. He'd gotten commitments for millions in venture capital. His business was the talk of Silicon Valley. But after he died, the money people pulled out, and the venture died with him.

The young man had been married a year. He was at the hospital because his wife was giving birth to their first child. Dad had explained right away that he had pushed the buggy into the young man, knocking him down. The driver of the van was poor and uninsured, so the young man's wife and parents filed a personal injury suit against dad. The story of the injured children, and the drunk woman who hit them, came out at the trial. But the plaintiff's lawyer kept pointing out that if the baby buggy had never hit the man, he wouldn't have fallen and died. In addition to the loss of a loving husband and soon-to-be father, the economic loss of losing a young genius businessman was huge. The jury awarded twelve million dollars to the plaintiffs."

"And your father didn't have that much liability insurance," I said.

Leah shook her head vigorously. "His personal umbrella policy had six million. He liquidated all of his various investments, which added another three million to what he paid. But that still left him three million short. And he was retired, with no income other than that from the investments that he'd sold. He had to file bankruptcy. Without money to pay his monthly bills, he eventually sold his house."

"Those payments to the victim's family, that's what you meant when you said he gave his money to charity."

Leah nodded.

We sat there, the air feeling close and heavy with the difficulty of life.

"What happened to the kids you pushed to the hospital?"

"The boy was okay. He had facial lacerations, but otherwise was fine. The girl had a crushed skull and a major brain injury. They performed three operations over several months. The last I heard, the girl is now in the third grade, almost completely healed. The doctors say that she is only alive because of the speed with which we got her to the hospital."

Leah looked up from the candles. Her forehead was furrowed with stress. In her eyes was overwhelming confusion and worry. And fear.

"We were just trying to help those children," she said. "The young man tripped after the buggy bumped him. It was an accident."

"It's not a likely motivation to push someone toward murder," I said. "And crass as it sounds, the payment of nine million dollars to the plaintiffs would usually take the murderous edge off someone's hurt and rage at losing a loved one. But not this time. The man's brother, Charles Hall, has raged for five years. He pushed your father to polish up his considerable art skills to paint some forgeries so that he could sell them and collect more of the debt that the court awarded. After your father delivered the last painting, Charles had him killed, or maybe Charles did the shooting himself. Maybe it was to prevent anyone from learning the paintings were forgeries. Or maybe it was the final punishment for your father's part in Lance's death. But it still leaves the question of why he wants to kill you."

Leah's face went blank, suddenly shutting down, checking out. She stared at the candles.

"Leah? Is there something you know about Charles Hall?"

She shook her head and stared at nothing.

"Have you had any contact with him?"

"No."

"Did you say or do anything at the trial or afterward that could have caused the family more distress?"

Another head shake.

"Any contact with the widow Suzanne?"

"No." Leah was a robot, on auto-pilot, tuning us out.

"Leah, think. He wants you dead. Why? There is a reason. Something in your past, something you did, something you said, something your father did."

Leah didn't respond. She was gone.

I decided to shock her. I slammed my hand down on the table, palm out, making a very loud slap.

"WHY!"

Leah jerked back. The candles bounced into the air. Only one stayed lit as they fell back to the table. Instead of the sudden tears I expected, Leah's eyes flamed with anger. Her outburst was explosive.

"Because dad didn't cause the man's death! I did! I was the one pushing the buggy when it hit Lance Hall!"

We were all silent. Leah cried.

"Your dad covered for you," I said.

Leah sniffled, wiped her arm across her nose. "My dad pushed the buggy for several blocks. But he went too hard. He started to stumble, and he collapsed to the ground. So I took over. I was pushing the buggy when we got to the hospital. I raced into the lot. But I did a stupid thing. I ran crossways through the parked cars. The lot was almost full. But I saw a place where I could fit through with the buggy. So I ran straight for the entrance, not seeing anything else, not looking for traffic. That's when Lance Hall stepped out. I didn't even know the van was speeding up behind me.

"When I hit the young man and he fell in front of the van, my father caught up with me. He bent down to help the man. He saw that it was no use. So he turned and took the buggy from me. He immediately told me in a harsh whisper that he was pushing the children when it happened. I protested, but he was very firm. He said his life was at its end, and my life wasn't even at its middle. He yelled it at me, if you can yell a whisper. He'd never sounded that way before. I was in shock. He took the buggy with the children and rushed it into the hospital.

"All this happened because of me, not because of dad. Lance Hall died because of me. Dad went broke and then died because of me. My husband died because of me. My face got cut up because of me." She began to sob, softer than before. She seemed to collapse inward, getting smaller.

"Who else did you see in the hospital parking lot?"

"I didn't see anybody." Her head was bent toward the table, tears running down the side of her nose. Her face had a big red blotch on it, as if wine had splashed across her nose and cheeks.

"Think, Leah. Try to remember every detail." I put the book dust jacket on the table, pointed to Charles Hall's picture. "Did you see this man? Was he there with Lance?"

"Maybe. Maybe not."

"Go there in your mind, Leah. I know it's painful, but visualize the scene. Where were the people?"

"I told you, I don't remember anything."

"Yes, you do. You just don't want to think about it."

"I can't! The children had blood all over them. And the man in the parking lot was... He was crushed. The van ran over his head!"

Leah dropped her head onto her arms and cried in great heaving, choking gasps, as if she couldn't breathe, as if the memory would strangle her.

Street reached across the table and rubbed her arms and shoulders.

"It's over, Leah," I said. "Lance Hall is dead. But the children are alive. You saved them. You can let yourself off the hook. Your father took the blame for running with the buggy because he was a loving parent. He knew your life was just getting up to speed. His action was noble and selfless, and it was exactly what he wanted. He wanted you to have a life. He would want you to get past this. Even Suzanne Hall is getting over it. You don't have to shut it out. You can think back on it. You can let yourself remember that day without beating yourself up anymore. If you do, something will come to you. Something that will help us find Charles Hall. If we can find him, we can save your life."

We three sat at the little table for several minutes, each of us silent. I assumed that, like me, both Leah and Street were visualizing the scene from five years before, the terrible chain of events in the hospital parking lot, events with life-and-death consequences. Events that set into motion the twisted world of the fictional monster from a thousand years before. Charles was tormented by reality and fiction alike, and Grendel lived inside his mind.

Leah lifted her hand off the table and pointed to Charles Hall's picture on the back of the dust jacket.

"I remember him now."

We all looked at the picture of the modern Renaissance man with the wild hair.

"He was there. He was with his brother Lance. So he must have known that I was the one pushing the buggy. When Lance got hit, after dad took the children into the hospital, this man knelt down on the pavement. He held Lance's crushed head and screamed. He shouted over and over." Leah stopped talking.

"What did he say?" I asked.

"I don't know."

"What do you mean, you don't know? Of course, you know. If you can remember him shouting, you can remember what he said."

I didn't realize that I'd been raising my voice to a near shout.

Street reached over and touched my forearm.

"I remember hearing him shouting," Leah said. "But I don't know what he said because he was speaking French. I don't know French, but it sounds like no other. He was shouting in French."

I stared at the candle flame. Hint of memory. Vague shape. Obscured in fog. The mirage took on a shape, then evaporated, then came back more clear.

"Does your laptop have a dictionary in it?" I asked Street.

"I think so, why?" She went into the aft cabin, brought it back, set it on the table.

"In the supplements, they often have small translation dictionaries," I said. "English to French, French to English."

"Yes." Street clicked and typed. "Here you are." She turned the laptop to me.

I scanned to the words, and there they were.

I slid off the settee and stood up, my head bent under the six-foot ceiling. I could feel my heart in my chest.

"What did you just realize?" Street said.

"I know who Charles Hall is," I said.

FIFTY-FOUR

I told them the gist of my plan. I needed Spot, so Street agreed to stay with Leah for safety. As Leah's time on the boat had expanded, the number of ways her location could have been leaked expanded as well. I was worried.

I gave both of them a quick security tour, concentrating on those items that did not seem like weapons. An intruder thinks about concealed guns and knives, but is unlikely to be very concerned about typically benign items. More importantly, the typical individual is not courageous enough to use most weapons. A person who could never summon the guts to stab someone with a knife, may nevertheless find the courage to smack an intruder over the head with a cooking pot. The low-tech weapon that gets used is infinitely more effective than the high-tech weapon that doesn't.

Below decks, in the galley, I pointed out the cast iron skillet. It was medium-small, perfect for someone of Street's or Leah's strength. I also pointed out the votive candles. After they'd been burning for an hour, they held enough hot wax to temporarily disable anyone by throwing it in their face. At the chart table was a pair of binoculars on its neck strap, which can be swung to devastating effect. Last and best, was the fire extinguisher. It could be sprayed several feet, and the canister is a great battering ram against a skull, or for crushing wayward hands on a table or against a doorjamb.

Topside was a safety oar. Swung or jabbed with good timing, it made a good weapon, and could even thrust someone overboard. There was also the boat hook, easy to get to, lightweight, yet strong.

The last item was in the former category of requiring guts to use. But it is one of the best weapons of all because it looks benign, and people, bad and good alike, don't see it as a weapon until it is too late. The lowly screwdriver with its thin shaft and strong handle fits in a pocket without the danger of cuts that accompany a knife. I'd found two of them stowed with other tools. I gave one each to both Street and Leah. Street slipped hers into the back pocket of her jeans. Leah set hers on the table.

I said goodbye at the transom.

"How long do you think you'll be gone?"

"Until midday tomorrow."

Street faced me in the dark. I couldn't see her eyes, but I knew that she was looking up at mine, wondering about this craziness, willing herself not to lodge protests about my plan, my work, my life. I was grateful for her reticence.

We kissed, and she said, "Be safe, Owen McKenna. I want you around in my old age." Then she turned and disappeared down the companionway.

Spot and I climbed into the runabout.

I didn't like taking Spot, but I needed him.

When we got back to the mausoleum, we trotted to the garage and Jennifer's Toyota. Our first stop was my cabin. I knew it might be under surveillance, but I needed some equipment. And if somebody were watching, either he was the man I was looking for, or he was working for him. It was too late for him to chase me when I was chasing him.

I grabbed the dark gray toolbox, which contained my lightweight leather gloves and an assortment of tools well-suited to taking apart locks I couldn't pick, removing hinges from doors and windows I couldn't pry open. Even my small folding saw with its carbide-tipped points would, with considerable effort, open a hole in a roof if necessary. I also had a set of picks, although I'd never had the delicate feel and touch necessary to be very good at using them. If there were an alarm, I might be out of luck. But the less sophisticated ones could often be breached, and I carried an assortment of wire, splicing clips, and tape. I changed into dark clothes and dark running shoes, grabbed a dark cap and left.

I drove with Spot counter-clockwise around the lake and got to Tahoe City, almost directly across from Skunk Harbor, at midnight. There were no lights to speak of across the lake at the northeast shore, and I stared at the blackness, imagining a tiny little floating container miles off in the darkness, its womb holding Street and Leah below the waterline, a couple of votive candles for light.

I found a dark place to park on one of the side roads. Spot and I got out and walked through the shadows toward the back of Twin Peaks Art. Except for a security light on a pole a few doors down, the back of the building was dark. We stopped next to a dumpster and a retaining wall and waited in the darkness. Spot sniffed the dumpster. I listened. The occasional sound of sparse traffic on the street in front of the building was the only human noise. Spot lifted his head and tweaked his ears as a coyote started yipping a quarter-mile distant. More joined in, and a cacophony of chirps and screams and yips filled the night. Then it stopped as if they'd all decided to finally agree.

"Okay, Spot," I whispered. I put my finger across his nose. "Stealth and silence is our motto." We walked out from behind the dumpster toward the back entrance of Twin Peaks Art. The door was heavy-gauge steel. When I got close I saw the smooth heads of a double pair of bolts that indicated there were brackets on the inside and a good-sized piece of lumber in the brackets. I was moving sideways toward a dark window when I heard a loud noise from inside the door. There was a scraping sound and then the thud of wood being tossed onto the floor. I pulled Spot farther into the shadow at the back wall of the building. A lock turned, rusty hinges made a loud squeak, and the door opened.

Light flooded into the dark parking area. Two figures came out. One had his arm around the shoulder of the other. Spot and I froze.

A man spoke, his voice loud, words slurred. "C'mon, man, you should try a lil' of that brandy. Just a lil' bit. It makes the most amazing fire inside. Warms you from your tongue to your balls. Wha'd'ya think, ol' pal, huh?"

They came farther out, and turned just a bit. There was enough light to see that Paul the art consultant had his arm around Jeter, the mentally-challenged man who did trash and other chores for Twin Peaks Art. Paul was steering him out into the parking lot against his will.

"I brought that hip bottle, right here on m'hip." Paul reached his arm toward his back pocket and the effort turned him and Jeter around like two dogs trying to chase one tail. Jeter's left foot flopped with each step.

"I don't like to drink, Paul," Jeter said. "I tried it. It tastes bad."

"Hey, if I like a lil' brandy, you would like a lil' brandy. We're pardeeing, right Jeetsie? We go way back, you'n me. We got history."

Paul steered Jeter around again and then toward the corner of the building. "C'mon ol' Jeetsie boy. Let's go out and see what's happenin'. We could go down to the lake. Go for a swim. C'mon, wha'd'ya think? It'll be fun."

I knew how this was going to end once Paul, the ex-actor with the thick dark hair, got Jeter into the water, so I took Spot and walked out.

"Paul, Jeter. Name's McKenna. We met in the store. This is my dog Spot. Got something I want to talk to you about. Inside." I held my arm out toward the open door.

"Hey, McKenna," Paul slurred. "I 'member you. You can come with us. It'll be a real pardee."

I stepped in front of them. "Time to turn around, guys," I said.

"Whoa, that's a big doggie," Paul said. "Maybe he'd like to swim in the water."

"Back inside," I said more firmly. I pointed toward the open door.

Paul and Jeter stumbled toward us.

"Spot, growl," I said. I touched his throat, the sign for sound.

He made a rumble in his throat,

Paul and Jeter jerked back.

Spot looked up at me for approval.

"Yeah, that's right," I said to him.

Spot wagged and growled some more.

"That dog is gonna bite," Jeter said, alarm in his voice. "We should go, Paul. That's a bad dog." His voice rose to a high pitch. His fear was palpable.

Paul was backing up, pulling Jeter with him.

"Inside," I said again.

They stumbled through the door. Spot and I followed. We were in the back of the frame shop. The overhead lights were off, but some task lighting shined on the worktables.

Paul still had his arm around Jeter's shoulders. He steered Jeter over to a shop stool near the chopper machine with the Hitchcock blades. "Here, Jeets boy, you take a load off. Paul's gonna say hi to this hound. Biggest damn hound I ever saw."

Paul came forward, listing to his right. It seemed that he was accentuating his impairment. He was angling for Spot, but Spot had moved away. Paul lost his balance and leaned toward a worktable for support. There was a machine for cutting circular mats. Paul grabbed the machine with one hand. Flopped his other hand down on the table. It landed on a stack of circular matboard cutouts. They slid. He lost his balance and almost fell to the floor before righting himself.

Jeter sat on the stool, both feet planted on the floor. He held his arms out toward Spot, fingers spread, palms facing out in front of him as if to ward off evil spirits. His eyes were fixated on Spot.

"Awe, Jeetsie," Paul said. "Don't worry about the hound. He's just a big ass hound, that's all. Right, Mc..., what did you say yer name was?"

I stepped between Paul and the back entrance, shut the door, picked up a 2 X 6 off the floor and fitted it into the braces on the door.

Paul looked at me, muscle tension pulling at the corners of his eyes. Then he was smiling again, the happy drunk.

Behind Jeter was a heavy plywood crate up on edge, the top of the crate leaning against the wall. The exposed side was open. Inside were foam inserts that lined the face and the edges of the big box. A large landscape painting with an ornate gold frame sat inside the crate. Nearby was a large sheet of white foam, cut so that it would cover the art and the frame, no doubt to protect it during shipping. Behind the white foam was the plywood facing to be screwed onto the front of the crate.

Spot angled over toward the crate. Jeter rotated to keep his outstretched hands between him and Spot. His eyes stared, his tongue moved back and forth in his open mouth. Spot sniffed the floor, raised up his head and sniffed the air.

I stepped sideways to where several heavy-stock aluminum rulers hung on a wall hook.

"I remember that landscape when it came in," Paul said. His words were excessively thick. He leaned against the table for support. "The painter's got talent, sure. But it looks cheap. It's like he was just trying to see how fast he could make a painting. Or she. Ha, ha."

Spot stopped in front of the half-crated painting. The landscape had a meadow filled with wildflowers and a mountain in the distance. Around the mountain were clouds, and the peak poked through them into the sunshine.

Jeter seemed less fearful now that Spot had moved past him and was sniffing the painting.

"'Course, Jeets likes it," Paul said. He glanced at the door again. "Don't you Jeets? You said it was pretty. That's okay. No offense, Jeetsie boy. I agree with you. It's a very pretty painting."

Spot moved his nose around the painting.

"Hey look at that. The dog likes art. Isn't that somethin'. Hey, Jeets boy. What's that customer's name you been makin' the crates for? The dog likes his paintings."

While they focused on Spot, I lifted a heavy-duty 48" ruler off the wall.

Spot moved his nose up the painting, then right, then stopped. He lifted his paw and swiped it down, ripping the painting from just to the left of the mountaintop down through the clouds and into the wildflowers.

Paul gasped.

Jeter inhaled. "Oh, no! That bad dog wrecked the painting."

"Good boy, Spot!" I walked over and pet Spot vigorously with my left hand, holding the ruler in my right. "You smelled the special paint." I let go of Spot, leaned on the ruler, grabbed the torn edge of the canvas and gave it a good yank.

Most of the landscape canvas tore free, revealing behind it another painting, this one exquisitely rendered in the style of Rembrandt. It showed a young somber family in a darkened room, father and mother on the left, boy and girl on the right, and, in the middle, lying on a small bed and lit from an unseen light, naked and angelic in death, the van Gelden baby.

"The last of the Night Portraits," I said as I turned. "Painted by Dr. Kiyosawa under threat of harm by Charles Hall. AKA Jeetsie boy. AKA Jeter Salle."

Jeter took several steps away from me, his awkwardness suddenly gone. He pulled a small handgun out of his pocket. He aimed it at me.

"Don't even think about moving," he said, his voice suddenly crisp, his enunciation clear.

"What?" Paul said, shock on his face.

"That a Colt Detective Special?" I said. "A thirty-eight caliber shorty is a long way from the fifty caliber cannon you've been using up until now."

Charles shook his head, grinning. "The fifty-cal stuff was just some unemployed chumps who did some target-shooting with a guy who had long hair and a harelip, and spoke with a Navajo accent. Let me guess. You figured out the name."

"Chuck Hall? Yeah. The verb chuck is Jeter in French. Hall is Salle." As I spoke, I concentrated on the periphery of my vision, memorizing positions of worktables and equipment. "Lauren Phelter told me that you were a good actor. So you used a Navajo disguise to hire the dirtballs to kill Kiyosawa and his daughter."

Charles grinned. "The long-haired wig was easy. But the harelip trick deserves a prize. A quarter-inch strip of linen, crazy-glued from the skin inside the edge of my upper lip and stretched up to the gum above. It holds up for hours. No one can see it and not think it is real." It was a boast. He smiled. He'd kept the secret a long time.

Paul was trying to speak, stammering, almost choking, shock in his eyes. "Jeets. I don't get it. I thought..."

Charles looked at him, then his eyes refocused on me. "Time for a swim." He waved the gun at me. "Turn around. Hands behind your back."

I turned.

"Paul," Charles said, "grab that packing tape gun. Tape his wrists."

"Why even bother with this last painting?" I said. "You've got your two and a half million from Vladimir, less whatever you paid Kiyosawa. The total amount of the judgement against Kiyosawa is mostly settled. You could have left. You're almost untraceable. Certainly no Russian gallery owner is going to figure out how to find you."

"I'm an honorable man," Charles said. "I make good on my promises."

Paul stumbled over to a shelf, got the packing tape gun and came over behind me.

With Charles at my back, I looked at Spot. I didn't know how to communicate without talking. So I gave him The Look. My eyes intense, like before he gets a treat or gets to go outside or gets to run.

Spot saw my eyes, stared at me, but wasn't sure what I wanted.

I made a tiny fast vibration-nod of my head, my eyes as wide as they get. I tried to look crazy.

Paul pulled off some tape. He grabbed one of my arms. I didn't know exactly where behind me Charles was. I hoped Paul was between us.

"And the boys with the big gun," I said as Paul carefully, with drunken precision, wrapped tape around one of my wrists. "They worked for cash. A promise of final payment when they finish the job," I said. "So what was the point of the Grendel T-shirts?"

"They sucked that up like it was some lost Native American Brotherhood of Grendel. I gave them the Beowulf backstory, and they bought into it with the same fervor that has kept it alive for a thousand years. Jesus, people are stupid. When I made up the T-shirts and started handing out crayfish claws, it was like giving merit badges to little boys with big guns."

"That's where the crayfish claw came from," Paul said. He was trying to get my other hand lined up for the tape, but he was struggling. "I found it on the floor. So I gave it to that woman who teaches at the atelier. She likes to draw dead animal parts."

"SPOT!" I yelled as I jerked back, spun and dropped to the floor. I hit Paul and he went down toward Charles. I shot my arm out, tried to catch the falling tape gun. As it slipped away, I used my fingertips to flick it up toward Charles's face.

Charles swung his gun down toward me as he fired. The muzzle blast flashed in my eyes as the round went high. The huge crack ripped at my ears.

I rolled and grabbed Charles's right ankle. Spot growled behind me. Charles had the rare, brilliant sense to resist the impulse to pull his right leg away. Instead he stood on that leg and kicked me in the forehead with his left shoe. I rolled away, blinded for a moment by the blow. Spot went over me and ran into Paul. I jumped up.

Charles saw Spot coming, took aim.

I grabbed the heavy 48" ruler. Swiped it in an arc. Brought it down on Charles's forearm.

He screamed. The gun fell to the floor and bounced over toward the big double-bladed saw. Blood immediately stained his sleeve.

I stood in front of him, the ruler raised, a Samurai sword. "Spot, no," I said. Spot stopped, turned and looked at me, confused. "No," I said again.

Charles panted. His lower lids raised up and covered the lower half of his irises. His upper lids were wide. He looked feral.

"People are hard-wired for symbols," he said. He was half bent, a hand on his wounded forearm. He leaned left, then right, his fight-or-flight response on high alert. Talking to try to distract me.

I kept the ruler raised.

"Give those guys crayfish claws, it's like they finally found meaning," he said. "They put chains on the claws and wore them as necklaces. Christ, if I'd called it the Grendel Church, they would have paid me instead of the other way around." He shot glances around the room, deciding when to make his move. "It's like giving 'I'm Jeter's Friend' cards to Paul and Vienna and half this town. You want people to believe you're helpless, hand out a dumb card and it seals their perception." He shifted to the left, closer to the saw where his gun had come to a rest.

I moved that direction, cutting him off. "But you screwed it up," I said. "My first impression was that Jeter wouldn't put in the apostrophe."

Charles's forehead creased for a moment, like a wrinkle in his confidence, then he recovered. "You're right. That was a mistake. I let the stress get to me." He inched to the side, away from the big saw and his gun.

I moved between him and the saw, ruler raised. "And your hired hand slipped up."

"That was a lucky move, McKenna, grabbing that guy at the window. But it doesn't matter. He doesn't know anything. He just thinks he had a mission, decreed by the Grendel Brotherhood. Do this job, and the mysterious Navajo guy shows up and gives him money. But the other guy is as devious and tenacious as a wolverine. He knows how to stay hidden. He's killed before. Real big on follow-through, he says. He thinks that when he finds and kills the lady, the money is his like some kind of Grendel magic. It's out of my hands.

She's dead. It's just a matter of time." Charles feinted left, then dove right and dropped down by the chopper.

I swung the ruler. It hit the chopper rail. Charles rolled to a moulding bin, grabbed a piece of gilded moulding as long as my ruler and thicker than a baseball bat. I was on him, sliced the ruler down onto his out-stretched ankle, aluminum against bone.

He screamed.

Spot growled behind me. I turned to see if Paul was coming for me. But Spot was only reacting to Charles's scream. I sensed movement from Charles. I turned back to see him swinging the moulding from a sitting position, aiming for a center field popup. I jumped back, but the big golden stick caught my thigh.

Pain shot through my leg. I hobbled back against the saw table.

Charles jumped up, his gilded moulding held high. He advanced toward me.

"Why Leah?" I said. I raised the ruler. Saber against club.

Charles's eyes went a little wild. I glanced at Spot. If I could get Charles to lose the club and go mano-a-mano against me, Spot would come to my rescue.

"Why Leah?" Charles said, raising his voice. He circled a step to the left, then right, like a boxer working in close. "She took Lance. She took the only person I cared about in the world. Lance was a wizard. He was smarter than me. Do you know what it's like to go through life where everyone you meet is incompetent?" Charles's voice was shrill. "Lance and I took refuge in each other. We were going to do great things. Leah Printner and her father killed my brother. They destroyed one of the great people. An innocent man with immense intellect and enormous future." Charles stared over my head, to my side, seeing another place. "Then the doctor recorded the whole story and gave it to his ex-wife. That would have been smart if he hadn't been so stupid to tell me. He thought he could threaten me?! I showed him that doesn't work."

"So you're Grendel? Getting your revenge on the good people? The power of the symbol, of the legend, you've bought into it too?" I saw an opening, swung the ruler.

Charles was too quick. He thrust the moulding out like bunting the ball. My ruler hit wood. Golden chips of plaster flew like sparks. Charles rotated. He swung the moulding in a big arc, going for a home run.

The moulding was too heavy to stop with the ruler. I jumped backward. The moulding swished in front of my face, skinning my nose. I fell back against the worktable.

Charles dropped the moulding and dove for his gun.

I grabbed the circular matboard cutouts and spun sideways, firing them off like Frisbees toward Charles. The cutouts separated in the air, three arcing disks with sharp beveled edges. One of them hit the side of Charles's temple, drawing a bright red bloodline up to the corner of his eye as if it had been a scalpel.

Charles shook his head. I ran toward him. His hand was closing on the gun as I kicked it out of the way. Charles was on his knees. He picked up the big moulding and stabbed it up into the air. It caught me under my jaw. I stumbled back, vision fading, holding out my hands to break my fall. I caught the platform of the chopper machine with my hands as my knees collapsed.

I saw a blurry movement. Charles dove across the floor. Pounded the heel of his hand onto the chopper's footswitch. I realized too late that my left hand was in the wrong place. The blade shot down and chopped off a quarter inch of my little finger. Blood spurted.

Charles was finally away from his gun and his moulding.

"Spot!" I yelled. "Take him down!" I fell sideways, turned toward Charles, pointed at him. "Take him down."

Spot was unsure. The man was already down on the floor. Spot grabbed Charles's leg. A tentative hold. The man kicked at him, the wrong move. Spot bit harder and snarled. Charles kicked again. Spot clamped down and did the earth-shaking growl, shook the leg like a rug. Charles screamed and writhed and stopped kicking.

I was dizzy from the blow to my jaw. The frame shop was on a giant platform machine that tilted it to the left and then forward. I tried to straighten up, pitched toward one of the worktables. I caught myself, my hand smearing a blood trail across the surface. The lights were on a strange dimmer. Everywhere I looked was a black area surrounded by dim light. Spot's growl was loud, but it came and went in my ears.

I sagged to the floor. Put my head between my knees.

The lights surged back up. Spot's growl went back to the loud setting. I felt the blood pulse where the tip of my finger used to be.

I looked for the packing tape gun. It was next to Paul who cowered against the wall. I knee-walked over and picked up the tape gun. Pulled off a piece and wrapped it around the end of my finger. Blood still pulsed under the clear tape. Pulled off another piece. Made this one tighter. Got my right hand into my left pocket where I had the Salazar company phone. Dialed 911. Told the Placer County dispatcher where to send the cops.

FIFTY-FIVE

Spot and I spent a few hours at the frame shop, talking with the Placer County Sheriff's Department personnel. They took both Charles and Paul in, saying they would get a statement from Paul after he sobered up the next day.

While I was talking to the sergeant, the local doctor came. He fished my fingertip out of the chopper cutoff bin and, being an old-fashioned, sensible guy, agreed with me that we didn't need to throw all the new fancy surgical techniques at my situation. The bone portion in the tip had shattered, and it was just too small a chunk of finger to bother trying to reattach. So he did the cleaning, trimming and stitching repair work on site while I talked to the cops. The repairs weren't pleasant, but it was nothing compared to the BAM of the blades and the whoosh of compressed air and the squirt of blood.

Spot and I were back in my cabin by four in the morning. It seemed unnecessary to wake Diamond and Street and Leah and Mallory to fill them in on my frame shop adventure, so I took another one of the pain-killers the doctor had given me and was able to get a few hours sleep.

Diamond woke me with a phone call. "Heard from Placer County. You got the guy who ordered Kiyosawa's murder."

"Yeah, but he says the order on Leah still stands. I believe him. The other shooter is out there somewhere, looking for her, trying to uphold the honor of the Brotherhood of Grendel. Any ideas?"

"I was going to ask you that," Diamond said, his voice dejected, "and tell you that we found the body of an older woman. ID says Regina Kiyosawa."

"The doctor's ex-wife," I said. "Leah's mother."

"Right."

"Cause of death?" I asked.

"Not sure. The body's decomposed enough that we can't see anything obvious. I tried to get hold of Street to ask her to do a time-of-death analysis, but she doesn't pick up. The ME wants to move the body."

"Street's with Leah on Beaufort's Beauty," I said. "I'll call her. She can probably be there in a couple of hours. Is that soon enough?"

"I'll try to hold them off," Diamond said.

"Where's the body?"

"Come over Kingsbury Grade and back down a few miles. You'll see our vehicles."

"Is this where the kid referred to Miner's Gulch, where the guys were shooting the big gun?"

"That's how we found her," Diamond said. "We hiked up where the kid said. Lot of flies and such buzzing not far from the trail. That's where the body was."

"I'll be there with Street," I said.

I hung up, called Street, told her Diamond wanted to talk to her, and asked her to be ready to leave.

Spot and I made good time getting down the mountain and over to Jennifer's. We went around the giant house without stopping to knock, got the runabout out of the boathouse and pulled up to Beaufort's Beauty about 45 minutes after I spoke to Diamond.

I tried to keep explanations brief, told Leah I'd get back to her later that day, and left Spot with her for protection.

When Street and I were far around Deadman Point and I knew that our voices could not carry to Leah, I gave Street a quick version of the night before, then told her about the body Diamond had found. Her face got very serious.

"We'll have to stop at my lab, so I can get my sample kit," she said.

I nodded. We rode the rest of the way without talking, the roar of the runabout's outboard filling the space around us.

Street got her VW bug out of Jennifer's garage, and I took Maria's pickup. We pulled into Street's lab at the base of Kingsbury Grade twenty minutes later. She ran in and came out with a large plastic toolbox. We left her car at her lab. I drove up and over the grade and partway back down, and pulled over near six Sheriff's vehicles, all with their light bars quietly flashing.

A deputy took us up the trail to where the crime scene process was under way. Diamond met us at the yellow tape. Street pulled out her surgical mask and gloves, put them on and went on through the trees to where the body had been dragged and hidden.

"She needs to look at maggots, right?" Diamond said to me.

"Collect them, yes."

"The body looks to have been here quite a few days. You think she'll have a chance of finding any?"

"I don't know," I said. "I'm sure she'll find something informative."

"I forget how the time-of-death thing works," Diamond said.

"It basically gets down to judging the time elapsed since death by how much the maggots have grown. She preserves some maggots to stop their growth. She raises others to adulthood to see what kind of flies they turn into. Once she's identified the various species, she can compare how developed the maggots in the body were with the known development course of the particular species. After she takes into account recent temperatures and some other factors, she can estimate when the body was dumped."

"Because mama flies are very good at laying eggs as soon as an animal or a person dies, right?" Diamond looked nauseated at the thought.

"Right."

Diamond shut his eyes for a moment.

He turned and pointed up the mountain. "The canyon the kid described is up over that ridge. Pretty good place to shoot. No one to hear or see."

"Except kids."

"Good point."

"Find any evidence?" I asked.

"Not much. Guys might be lowlifes, but they pick up after themselves."

"No shell casings?"

Diamond shook his head.

We went over the case for close to an hour. Street came back through the woods, carrying her toolbox. When she got halfway toward us, she stopped, took off the mask and gloves, stuffed them into a plastic bag, jammed the bag into her pocket. Her movements were jerky. Angry. As she came closer to us, I could see her jaw clenched, but her eyes were hidden behind her sunglasses.

We left Diamond and his crew in the rising summer heat and headed back over the summit and down to her lab. I dropped her there, lingered at her office door before I left.

"It doesn't get any easier, does it?" I said. I touched her cheek.

She took off her sunglasses and looked at me. Her jaw muscles bulged, little hard swellings interrupting the thin, fragile, beautiful jaw line below the acne scars. Her eyes were moist, but no tears fell.

She shook her head. "No it doesn't."

FIFTY-SIX

I went back home to my cabin. My finger was throbbing. I took another pill. Stood at the window. Outside, the sun was brilliant. But the forest looked dark and foreboding. My thoughts were darker. I stared into the woods, watching the deep shadows under the heavy tree canopy. I watched for movement, watched for surveillance. Watched for a shooter who knew that I could take him to Leah.

Watch for Grendel.

The phone rang. It was the Placer County Sheriff's Department with more questions. An hour later, I was on the phone to Mallory. An hour after that, I was talking again to Diamond. And after that, Street.

My whole day went like that. By early evening, I still hadn't eaten, still hadn't talked to Leah. I didn't want to tell her about her mother. I didn't want to explain that even though I'd caught Charles Hall, the original shooter that Hall had hired was still after her, working to earn a pile of cash, striving, in some twisted, sick way, to honor the memory of a fictional monster from a thousand years before.

I finally made a sandwich and ate it standing at my kitchen sink. Then I called Street and asked if she would come with me back out to Beaufort's Beauty and help me talk to Leah about her mother.

We met at Jennifer's gate. I punched in the code and Street followed me down the long and winding road.

The sun was just slipping behind the mountains across the lake. The clouds above took on dramatic highlights, brilliant pink on their western edges, dark gray on their eastern sides.

We pulled into the garage. Jennifer came out to meet us. She asked about us, about the case, about Leah. We tried to sound upbeat and evade most of her questions. Jennifer was brilliant and wise, but she was still a kid. And it's hard to tell a teenager about bodies and maggots and amoral sickos who will shoot you for cash and then feel proud that they've been initiated into a group of men who think it's cool to worship a monster that tore its innocent victims apart and ate them.

After we talked in the driveway for awhile, I stepped aside and called Leah to tell her that Street and I were on our way out to visit.

After five rings, the Salazar company voice mail system kicked in. I left a short message and hung up. Maybe Leah was in the head, and the phone was in the forward cabin, too far away to hear.

I went with Street and Jennifer into the house. Jennifer had made fresh bread and wanted us to take some out to Leah.

Five minutes later, I dialed Leah again.

She still didn't answer. I left a second message, telling her to call immediately.

I turned to Jennifer. "Have you heard from Leah?"

"Yeah, I called her this afternoon. She was fine. She said that the sun was really hot, so she mostly stayed below decks."

"She say anything else?"

Jennifer shook her head. "Not really. She said there had been people at the beach all through the morning. But everyone had left in the early afternoon. She said Spot was kind of antsy, so she was thinking she would take him to shore in the dinghy a little earlier than normal."

I nodded as I called a third time. When I got the Salazar voice mail again, I hung up.

"She could be topside," Jennifer said, "with the phone down below. I've done that. The waves lapping at the hull make it very hard to hear a phone down in the cabin."

"I've called three times. Spot would have heard it. When a phone rings, he lifts his head and cocks his ears toward the sound. Leah would have noticed."

"Maybe she's already taken Spot to the shore for a quick run before it's totally dark, and she forgot to bring the phone in the dinghy," Street said. "When she gets back and picks up the phone, she'll see the message indicator. She'll call you back."

"I can't take that chance. I'm worried. I'd like to take the rocket. Is it fueled up?" I asked Jennifer.

"Yes," Jennifer said. "Let me get the key."

We ran inside. Jennifer got a key ring out of a desk drawer in the study and handed it to me. "I should tell you that my neighbor said the rocket is a little twitchy up around sixty or seventy. So be careful not to turn too hard. It could flip."

"Got it."

"Should I come with you?" Jennifer asked.

"No. You should stay here in case we miss Leah in the dark. She could have dropped her phone in the water and decided to come this way. She'll need company."

"Be careful," Jennifer called out as Street and I went out the kitchen door on the lake side.

We ran down the lawn to the boathouse. I switched on the light.

Compared to the runabout, the black and red speedboat glistened in the light like a pointy spaceship ready for launch. It was shaped like a cigarette race boat, only on small scale, maybe 26 feet long, with a large prow and a small cockpit to the rear. It sat in the sling of an electric boat hoist, its keel three feet above the water.

I found the hoist switch. A motor and winch lowered the boat into the water. The hoist sling continued to sink into the water so that the boat's prop could clear it.

The boat rocked as we jumped into it. Street sat in the left seat. I turned on the engine blower, then found the buttons on the remote I'd been carrying. The garage door rose above us.

The rocket's controls were simple, with a keyed ignition, and a throttle/shift.

I started the engine, and it rumbled a deep growl. I turned on the running lights, shifted from neutral into forward and eased the boat out of the boathouse and into the dark evening with the last remnants of sunset light leaving the clouds.

Boating rules require no-wake operation near shore, but I didn't have time. I punched the throttle forward. The engine roared and the boat accelerated like a fast car, barely plowing the water before it jumped up into a planing position. The speedometer climbed to 30, 40, 50 and then 60 mph before I eased back on the throttle and put the speedboat into a big sweeping turn to the right to head north up toward Skunk Harbor.

The gale that came over the windshield tore at our hair, but we barely heard the wind roar over the powerful engine.

The bright lights of the South Shore grew more distant as we raced north toward Cave Rock. The dark horizon on the north side of the lake showed a twinkling line of lights that stretched from Incline Village on the northeast, around to Tahoe City over on the northwest. In the distance, up on the mountains above and behind Tahoe City, were the lights of Squaw Valley, showing where the aerial tram climbed the big cliff to the High Camp complex 2000 feet above the lake. The tourists sipping cocktails around the pool with the snow-filled cirques making an amphitheater above had no idea that the great dark lake down below held deadly secrets that connected to a poem written a millennium before.

Street and I said nothing as we shot by the dark hulking mass of Cave Rock, the rocket's engine sounding powerful enough to fly. We continued up past Glenbrook, around Deadman Point at high speed, and on to Skunk Harbor.

I slowed to about 20 mph, still on plane, but just barely. We stared through the darkness toward the area where Leah was anchored. I flipped on the rocket's spotlight. Street and I stood up as I trained the beam across the water in a slow sweep, back and forth.

There was no flash of reflected light from the Ciel's reflectors.

We continued in toward Skunk Harbor. When we were two hundred yards offshore, I cut the throttle, and the rocket dropped off plane and settled down into the water, coasting at idle. I kept shining the light back and forth, but still we saw nothing of the boat. Maybe my sense of location was off. I'd never come in so fast. I widened the arc of my sweep. Out toward the center of the lake. Back toward the shore. North up the beach, then back down the beach. The light swept across the crescent of sand. Over the ghostly stone house with the missing windows. On to the rocks that curved out to Deadman Point.

Nothing. The Ciel was gone. Leah had left. I made another pass with the spotlight, just in case we'd missed something.

I was about to turn it off when Street grabbed my arm.

"Owen!" she said in a harsh whisper. "Point the light over there! Near the stone house! Something's moving!"

I swung the light around. Nothing stood out. No movement.

I moved the light over the house. The dark windows looked like vacant eyes. Again nothing.

Street's hand tensed on my arm. "To the left!" she whispered.

I angled the light.

There it was. A motion in the trees. White. And black.

Spot came around the far end of the house and trotted down to the beach, his eyes flashing as he stared into the spotlight beam.

FIFTY-SEVEN

I pushed the throttle forward. The rocket rumbled as the boat thrust forward. The prow lifted up as we plowed water. Thirty yards from the beach, I pulled the throttle back again. The prow dropped, and we coasted toward the sand. I activated the lift on the stern drive to raise the prop, then shut off the engine.

"It's us, Spot," I said. But he had already picked up our scent from the onshore breeze and started to do the little bounce of excitement on his front legs.

The boat eased toward the beach, then ground to a stop as its deep-V hull knifed into the sand. I climbed out of the cockpit onto the prow and jumped off onto the beach.

Spot was ecstatic, jumping on me, then racing around the beach in an ellipse, jumping on me again.

I rubbed his head. "Where is Leah, boy?" I said, empty words in the air. But even as I thought they were useless, I realized that Spot's behavior did indicate where she was.

As if reading my thoughts, Street said, "Why do you think Spot is still here? Why didn't he run away? He could have headed south, headed toward the scents that he knows."

"Yeah. He could have run through the forest. Or run up the mountain to the highway above. But I think the fact that he didn't suggests that Leah headed out toward the middle of the lake."

I let go of Spot, walked into the water, which felt like ice as it filled my shoes, and grabbed the boat. I pushed the boat back until I was up to my knees. When the hull was freed from the sand, I rotated the boat, bringing its stern toward the beach.

"If Leah had taken the boat either north or south," I said, "Spot would have seen which way she went. He would have followed along the shore. But he must have stayed because Leah was heading straight out into the lake."

Street turned and sighted out toward the dark deep water.

"Even then," she said, "he would have run out onto Deadman Point. That would have brought him closer to her as she left."

I looked left and right. "Then she must have gone to the northeast." I pointed. "Toward the lights of Squaw Valley."

Street looked across the lake, then turned back toward me. Her features were shadowed, obscured by the distant lights across the lake.

"Any idea why Leah would ditch Spot and head across the lake?"

I nodded in the dark. "Yeah, and I don't like it."

A moment later came the sharp, deep crack of a far-distant rifle shot, followed by the trailing whir of a high-speed round knifing the air across the water.

FIFTY-EIGHT

"Spot, come!" I said.

He trotted into the water.

"Up into the boat!" I patted the gunwale.

Spot jumped his front paws up onto the edge of the boat. I got my arms around his abdomen and lifted. He scrabbled over the edge into the cockpit.

I pointed the boat toward the deep water. I gave it a shove, then boosted myself up onto the transom, stepped on the stern drive and climbed into the cockpit.

I jumped into the seat and started the engine.

Street already had Spot lying on the floor as I pushed the throttle all the way forward. The rocket roared and nearly leaped out of the water. The bow rose up, obscuring our view, and then dropped down as we shot onto plane. The boat accelerated like the racing machine it was, the speedometer needle arcing through the numbers. I shut off the running lights, and we went dark, a roaring black arrow flying across the dark water.

The chop on the water was slight, so I didn't ease back on the throttle until the needle crossed 70. Much faster and it felt as if the tiniest wave could send the boat into the air.

From the sound of the rifle shot, I guessed the shooter was at least a few miles out onto the water. But sound can do funny things as it carries across the surface, confusing one's perception of both distance and direction. Sound on water usually makes things seem closer than they are. So I kept the speed up for a couple of minutes. I figured the shooter was still motionless. Either he would continue shooting, or he would wait, silent, listening to our progress. If I stopped, I could train the spotlight carefully and search for the light-bounce off the Ciel's reflectors. But then he would see that our light was stationary, and we'd be an easy target. Better to keep moving.

I picked up the spotlight as we sped across the dark surface, the boat making a steady but powerful vibration as it roared beneath our feet. I shined a jerking beam across the water. Back and forth.

Street leaned over and spoke directly into my ear, her voice loud enough for me to hear, but not so loud that it could penetrate the engine roar and be audible across the water.

"What do you think happened? Why is someone shooting out on the water? Are they shooting at us?"

She pulled her mouth from my ear and put her own ear in front of my mouth.

"I don't think so. The bullet goes two or three times faster than sound. If he were aiming at us, we'd hear the sound of the round before the crack of the shot. My guess is that Leah took Spot ashore in the dinghy. Spot jumped out and ran down the beach. The shooter was in the trees downwind, so Spot didn't smell him until it was too late. The shooter probably ran out, carrying his rifle. He jumped in the dinghy and grabbed Leah. He throttled up the outboard fast, and got them into deep water before Spot could get to them. The man took Leah back to the Ciel, hauled her aboard, lifted anchor and started the sailboat's engine. They towed the dinghy and drove the Ciel out into the middle of the lake where it is very deep. Now the man is out in the dinghy with his rifle, shooting high-powered rounds into the Ciel, just below the waterline."

Street tensed. She spoke in my ear.

"He's trying to sink the sailboat?"

"That's my guess."

"Then Leah is trapped aboard?"

I nodded.

Street tensed at my side. While the boat roared like a race car, I was only aware of her silence.

"Can he really do that? Sink a boat with a rifle?" Street asked.

She put her ear at my mouth.

I didn't know what to say other than the truth.

"With that rifle, yes. Each round will go all the way through the boat, shattering two big holes in the hull. It won't take long."

I sensed Street go limp. She slowly sagged over into the left seat, then put her knee on the floor, bent down and hugged Spot.

FIFTY-NINE

We'd raced ahead for another minute when I saw a reflection as I swept the spotlight across the water. I brought the beam back, and there was the Ciel, far away, looking helpless as it sat alone in the middle of the dark lake. It was hard to see, but it seemed to sit low in the water. I pulled the throttle all the way back. The rocket slowed and settled down into the water. I couldn't focus on anything as it rocked for a few moments. Then my beam again found the sailboat. I was about to scan to the side, looking for the dinghy, when a light flashed in my peripheral vision to the north.

I kept the spotlight on the Ciel. Half a second later came a splash of water near the boat. Two seconds later I heard the loud rifle crack.

I drove through the dark toward the sailboat, approaching on the side opposite from the shooter. With luck, we'd have a moment or two when the shooter would not be able to see us. I spoke to Street as we approached.

"I'm going to jump off as we go by. The shooter will be able to see our boat through his scope. We can't be sure that the sailboat will block his view. So I want you to keep driving this boat."

"Can't you just grab Leah and pull her onto this boat?"

"I assume she's tied up. Probably down in the cabin. It may take me a minute. We can't take the chance that the shooter hits this boat."

"What if I do it wrong?" Street said, her normal confidence wavering. "This speedboat is very tippy."

"Don't worry. You don't have to go real fast, just be unpredictable. Make a swerving path. Every few seconds, shine the spotlight on the sailboat. When I wave, come in across the stern. We'll jump on board, and then you hit the throttle."

I thought about what the man's reaction would be.

"As soon as he sees what we're doing," I said, "he might come this way."

"What do I do if I see him?"

"If you see him coming in, keep weaving, so it's hard for him to take aim."

As I said it, I knew that it would be easy for the shooter to hit a target as large as the speedboat, even if it was weaving. I might be sending Street and Spot to their death. I couldn't tell Street to do something so dangerous without a warning.

"Even if you weave," I said, "he could still hit you."

"But the only way for Spot and me to be safe is to leave. Then you and Leah would die for certain. Even if you got out of the sailboat before it sank, or before he shot you, the water of Tahoe is so cold, you'd die of hypothermia. I'll do as you say."

"You're tough," I said.

"Earlier you said that his kind of gun would shoot all the way through the boat."

"Yeah."

"So if you and Leah are down inside, a bullet could hit you. It could already have hit Leah."

"Yeah," I said. I hadn't wanted to say that I was afraid that he'd already killed Leah, and that shooting and sinking the boat was only to put her grave at the bottom of the lake, 1600 feet deep, where it would never be found.

Street made a motion for us to switch places.

"I'll take your place at the wheel so you can jump off as we approach," she said.

I moved out of the seat and crouched behind it. Street sat down, put her left hand on the wheel and her right hand on the throttle. She slowed as we approached the sailboat. It sat even lower in the water, listing toward the port side.

Street came alongside the stern. I jumped aboard as another light flashed in the distance.

"Go!" I yelled.

Street hit the throttle. The rocket roared as I felt a terrible thud below me, below the water line, the sickening sound of a heavy round ripping through the boat, stopped by nothing. A moment later came the deep crack of the shot, the sound lagging behind the much faster bullet.

As Street and Spot raced off into the night, I moved toward the dark companionway that led down to the cabin.

"Leah?" I called out. "It's Owen. Where are you?"

"There was no response. I half-jumped and half-slid my way down the steps into the dark saloon, landing in deep ice water that was two feet deep on the starboard side and probably four feet deep on the port side.

I flipped on the interior light switches, but the lights didn't come on. Probably a round had struck some wiring.

"Leah!" I shouted.

No response.

I felt my way through the dark to the aft cabin on the port side, opened the door, sloshed my way into the deep water. I reached around under the water, feeling the bed, feeling the floor with my feet. I tried to be quick, but I had to be thorough. I didn't want to make a return trip to any corner of the boat.

Leah wasn't there.

I came out of the cabin, swim-walking my way through the deepening water.

There was an explosion of sound that came from all directions at once. Another round had perforated the boat from starboard front to port rear. The boat listed more. The current flowing from the saloon felt like a whitewater stream.

"Leah," I yelled again.

The silence was interrupted only by the swirling gush of water coming into the sinking boat. I felt around all corners of the galley, then turned across the boat and opened the head. I pushed my way inside, felt the dark corners with hands and feet.

Nothing.

I pushed out, turned aft and felt through the shower stall. It was empty as well. I went forward into the saloon.

The dining table on the port side was under water. I knew the table base would be a handy mooring to tie a person to. So I dived under water to make my explorations. I felt around the table post, and lifted up the lids to the stowage lockers under the settee cushions, which had already floated free. I found nothing but the gear and supplies we'd previously stashed for Leah.

I came back up to breathe in the shrinking airspace, gasping for air, shivering in the ice water that was Tahoe in the summer.

Using my feet and hands while mostly keeping my head above water, I felt around the chart table and the desk.

The forward cabin was last. The door was shut tight and the latch was jammed. Maybe from water pressure. Maybe from structural damaged caused by the high-powered rounds. I kicked and pushed and pulled at the door, shouting Leah's name. Eventually, I got it open.

I pushed into the forward cabin. The water was five feet deep. To breathe, I had to jam my head against the ceiling. I felt the boat shifting, prow moving down, water deepening. I took a deep breath, then submerged and swam underwater. The bed held nothing, the corners of the cabin were empty, the little settee was undisturbed. Back up for air, I had to turn my head sideways. The water had come to within eight inches of the ceiling. I felt claustrophobia grip me as if I were trapped in a cave that was flooding.

Another round exploded through the boat. The shockwave might have blown out my ears had they been under water. I submerged again and pushed my way out through the cabin door. The water in the saloon was at the ceiling on the port side. I hugged the starboard side, keeping my head in the airspace, trying to breathe, trying to think of what I'd missed.

The starboard settee.

I submerged and felt my way around, into the lockers below the seats.

The boat was empty.

Maybe he'd already sunk her body. Sinking the boat was only to destroy evidence.

I came back up for air.

Another explosion. A rush of water.

The boat made an alarming shift to the port. I'd seen pictures of sinking boats. It was the last roll before it submerged beneath the waves.

I was rushing back up the companionway steps when I heard a moan.

From where?!

"LEAH!!"

I spun around. I jumped back down into the water.

What had I missed?

I turned a full circle, my head against the ceiling, breathing the last of the air.

The large wet locker behind the shower!

I pulled the locker door open.

Water swirled through the cabin. There didn't seem to be any air in the wet locker.

"TAKE A DEEP BREATH, LEAH!" I shouted in case she could hear me, in case the wet locker hadn't yet completely flooded.

I took my own breath and submerged into the freezing black liquid. The door to the wet locker felt small and I swam through it, my arms reaching out, flailing through the space.

My hand brushed fabric. I kicked forward. My arms landed on flesh. I moved my hands, exploring. I had her arm. I pulled but she didn't come. She was tied somehow. I felt down to her hand, which was behind her back, one wrist tied to her other. Her hands were immobilized, but not tied to anything else. She was held in place some other way.

She could help if she had use of her hands.

I got out my pocketknife, felt for the blade. I slipped the blade between her hands, poked the tip under the line and sawed away from her hands, hoping not to cut her in the dark.

A line cut and her hands came apart, but the cord stayed tied around one wrist. Good enough. At least she could move them. But she didn't. She was unconscious and under water.

On her way to drowning.

I put the knife in my teeth and went over the rest of her, looking for where she was tied.

It was like frisking a suspect, only under freezing water and in a darkness so complete that there was nothing but black.

I went down her body to her legs. Followed one to her foot, expecting her ankle would be lashed to a tie-down loop or something. It was free. I went down the other leg. It was free as well.

My breath was running out, lungs burning for air.

I pulled her arms again. Again, she didn't move.

I pulled on her leg and her body floated up, legs out, her head still near the wall of the locker.

Her head.

I reached up and felt her head. Then her neck.

She was lashed at the neck, held tight against something solid, a pipe, or something structural. A heavy line was tight around her flesh. I put the tip of the knife under the line, pushing the back of the blade against the flesh of her neck so I could get the knife under the line.

This time the line was thicker and required more sawing.

Another explosion came through the boat. Hammers to my ears. My head felt like the explosion was internal. I felt a rush of dizziness. Up was down and right was left.

Concentrate. Hold my breath. Saw the line.

SAW!

The knife popped through the line. Leah was free. But she was a dead weight.

The boat began to roll back to starboard. It felt as though it had righted itself as I pulled Leah's limp form through the wet locker door and into the saloon.

I realized what had happened. The last of the air had left the perforated boat. It was now sinking. The heavy keel weight was pulling the boat down fast, leading it like an arrowhead, keeping the boat relatively level as we plunged toward the bottom.

My ears squeaked as the pressure mounted at an alarming rate. I felt dizzy. The small space made it difficult to swim while holding Leah. I held her with one arm, pulled at the water with my other. Two kicks and we were up the companionway.

Somehow, I expected to rise out of the dark cave-like saloon into the light of normal night. But it was just as dark.

Water rushed by us as I hoisted Leah out topside. I pushed free. The sailboat plunged on down below us.

A mast stay cable smashed down onto my forearm, which was holding Leah. It cut into my arm muscle and dragged us down with the boat. I let go of Leah's arm, reached around the cable and grabbed her again. The boat accelerated away. In the cold darkness I felt a rush of water movement, a glimmer of doom as the top of the mast glided by fast, a silent scythe in the night. Then we were finally free.

But how far below the surface, I had no idea.

My breath was gone. Black spots of fading vision replaced the blackness of underwater night.

For a moment, I was aware of swimming, of pulling Leah toward the unseen surface. It was too dark to see the escaping bubbles as my lungs gave out. Was I even swimming up? Or was I swimming sideways? Then, as my brain began to shut down from oxygen starvation, I floated away.

I was a five-year-old child, in a lake in New Hampshire. One of my Boston uncles had taken me to his cabin. He'd thrown me off the dock in good fun, not realizing I couldn't yet swim. I'd moved my arms and feet in an instinctive dog paddle, a feeble muscle memory with antecedents in the womb. The dock was above, the water was only a few feet deep. My uncle's smiling face shimmered through the waves. But I might as well have been in interstellar space, so distant did my uncle seem.

Then the dock became a boat and my uncle morphed into a dark image of Street leaning over the edge of the boat. Uncle's smile became Street's grimace of terror in the night, and she grabbed at my shirt with one hand and at Leah with the other. She was shouting at me, her words a screaming torment of despair. I floated helpless, coughing water, trying to breathe, having no success.

But somehow Street got Spot to clamp his jaws onto Leah's jacket and hold her while Street focused on me, tugging and yelling and crying.

An explosion opened up a hole in the rocket's hull, inches from my face. Maybe that hastened me getting a frozen leg hitched up over the gunwale. Street screamed louder, shouted instructions, told me to move now!

She pulled on my arm, and gradually we got me rolled over the gunwale and flopped into the boat, a worthless lump of hypothermic flesh. Then came another explosion as a round impacted an unseen part of our boat, and I had the surreal thought that the shooter's giant rifle was a single-shot bolt action that took a long time to reload.

Maybe it was that sudden realization that gave me hope, gave me motivation to move. He couldn't pepper us with rounds because his gun required reloading for each bullet. And aiming from a floating, turning dinghy was very slow at best. If we could act fast enough, maybe we still had a chance to survive.

I tried to get up, but I couldn't stand. I rolled onto my belly, telling myself which muscles to contract to get me up onto my hands and knees. Gradually, I crawled next to Spot. I lay my chest on the gunwale. The boat tipped dangerously to the side. Street leaned in as well. We three pulled on Leah. The boat was about to capsize.

We got Leah's upper body over the edge, and then finally pulled the rest of her inside the cockpit.

Street told me she had to attend to Leah and that I had to drive. She had to shout. She had to help prop me in the seat. I could barely move. But I leaned against the steering wheel with my unresponsive body, while Street pushed the throttle forward.

The boat surged forward in a big arc. Street reached the wheel and tried to turn us straight. But my arms slipped through the wheel and I couldn't find the muscles to sit back and pull them out.

Street struggled with me and with the boat, and by the time she got me out of the way and sitting back in my seat, we'd come around from south to west and were heading toward the lights of Tahoe City.

We both saw the flash of light at one o'clock. Or two o'clock. It was hard to tell. Street made evasive turns to port, then starboard. I flopped back and forth in the seat, unable to hold myself steady. I could only watch as Street made a third quick turn and put the boat into a hard cut as she pushed the throttle forward and tried to escape the man in the dinghy.

But he appeared in front of us, driving the little outboard as fast as it would go. Street turned to starboard as he went to his port, both trying to avoid a collision. They both turned back, unable to anticipate the other.

The man had only two seconds to decide that we were going to collide. He jumped into the water just before the rocket hit the inflatable dinghy broadside.

Street cut the power and our boat coasted to a quick stop, the crushed dinghy dragging beneath us, hooked on the stern drive. In the sudden silence, I heard the rush of water streaming into holes in the hull of the rocket. Street shifted into reverse, and we backed off the ruined boat. Without air, the dinghy had no more buoyancy, and the weight of its outboard engine quickly dragged it and the heavy rifle beneath the waves.

We could have stopped and picked up the man. But I was hypothermic, and Leah was unconscious. The man would have had no trouble overwhelming Street and then tossing us all overboard and making his escape.

Street shifted back into forward and raced past the man who was now treading water in the middle of the giant, black, freezing lake. We left him alone out in the Tahoe night, knowing that in a few minutes, his muscles would seize up, and he would join the dinghy and Beaufort's Beauty on their long trip to the bottom of the tenth deepest lake in the world. Street put the rocket into one last turn, turned on the running lights, and faced us toward the South Shore, fifteen miles distant.

She yelled in my ear as the boat roared forward.

"See that group of lights on the South Shore? That's near the Timber Cove pier. Steer toward that. Do you hear me, Owen? Steer toward those lights. And keep the speed up. We're taking on water. If we stay up on plane, maybe most of the holes will be above the water line."

So she left the controls to me.

My head lolled. My vision went bleary. My left arm kept slipping off the wheel. I started to revisit places in my distant past. Then my head would jerk, and I stared at the out-of-focus lights in the distance. Eventually, I warmed up just enough to bring on shivering. Violent shivering. My body jerked as if to break its own bones.

I focused on driving the boat. My shivering increased. When I was a bit more conscious, I too sensed that the boat was getting sluggish as the bilge filled with water.

I eased the throttle forward and the boat roared and lifted a little higher in the water as the speed climbed up to 50, 60, 70. The engine shrieked its high RPMs. The boat vibrated on chop that felt like concrete washboard. Now and then, the boat left the surface, and the washboard was replaced by a glorious, smooth glide through space. Then came the hammer-slam of contact. The boat made little whippy motions side-to-side.

I glanced behind me many times, seeing short, freeze-frame visions of Street in the running lights, bent to her task, a woman who, despite occasional fears and insecurities, was a person in whom enormous competence trumped all other manifestations of her personality.

My freeze frame movie showed the full course of treatment, from pressure on Leah's back expelling water from her lungs to CPR. And later, after Leah had coughed up water and gagged and coughed some more, Street got some of Leah's wet clothes off and some of her own dry clothes off. Street got down on the cockpit floor next to Leah, with Spot on the other side, and a jacket and a blanket she'd found piled on top of them. Leah slowly warmed from the adjacent bodies and appeared in the dim glow of the running lights to be sobbing incoherently. Through it all, Street got a 911 call off on her cell, and the ambulance was waiting as I came in to the South Shore a dozen minutes later, too fast, skipping over the tips of the waves. I throttled back too late, steered away from the pier at the last moment, and rammed the rocket directly onto the sandy beach. We jerked to a fast stop.

I pulled myself to a standing position so I could help Street. I let go of the steering wheel, fell out of the boat into the cold shallow water and passed out.

SIXTY

This time they kept Leah overnight in the hospital, but sent me home to Street's condo. I was under strict orders from Doc Lee to spend an hour in a hot tub while Street fed me wine.

In the morning, Jennifer stopped by to visit, riding her bicycle all the way up the busy highway from the mausoleum.

Street and Spot and I were out on Street's deck as she pulled up.

"Still don't have your driver's license?" I said.

"I take the test for the third time next month. Until then, Marjorie is helping me practice."

"I could help."

"Are you kidding? I talked to Street on the phone. She told me the whole story. My God! She said you crashed the rocket straight onto the beach last night. And it's full of bullet holes."

"I'll take out a second mortgage and get a part time job. Two or three centuries from now, I can buy a new rocket and a new sailboat and a new dinghy."

"I didn't say you had to pay for it. All I said was you might not be the best role model for someone learning to drive. Anyway, face the reality. I could never spend all my money even if I devoted my life to it. And seriously, I would trade anything I have for two of my best friends. I was terribly worried when I didn't hear from you last night! I paced the old mauseleum for hours."

"Never pace on our behalf. Save it for important stuff like your next driver's test."

Jennifer sat down on one of the deck chairs. Spot rolled to his other side, and stretched his head to put his chin on Jennifer's lap. His ear stud sparkled in the sun. Jennifer hugged him. "I'm so glad you're safe," she said.

Street and I were drinking coffee. I poured a cup for Jennifer and handed it to her.

"I can only drink that stuff if it's loaded with sugar and chocolate and whipped cream," she said.

"Go ahead and try it," I said. "It's Street's special brew. Gotta take it black to appreciate the flavor."

Jennifer took a sip and almost gagged. "Bleah! If drinking that is what it takes to be an adult, I don't ever want to grow up!"

The sun was high and burning hot, and I couldn't get enough of it. I'd just put my head back when I heard a vehicle pull up. I opened one eye.

Diamond got out of his cruiser. "Street. Jennifer." He made a hat-tipping motion without the hat.

"Any word on Leah?" I said.

"She's gonna be okay. She's tough, that one." Diamond looked at me. "I figured you'd be out of commission for a bit, so I told her about her mother. Figured you wouldn't mind."

"Thanks. How'd she take it?"

"She just gave me one of those sad forced grins and said that she had to start over, that everyone in her family is dead. But she didn't cry. At least not while I was there."

Diamond squinted out toward the lake. "Then I got a call from Washoe County. This morning a hiker on the Tahoe Rim Trail phoned in from up by the Mt. Rose Highway. Found a body in the Tahoe Meadows. Looks to be the stalker Tommy Snow. Like Leah's mother, the cause of death hasn't been determined yet." Diamond turned to Street. "It's Washoe County's jurisdiction. They didn't mention whether they want your consultation services."

"Maybe they can do this one without me," Street said.

Diamond nodded. "I haven't told Leah about Snow."

"It can wait," I said.

We were all silent. Diamond walked up onto Street's deck, sat down sideways on the top step.

"So we may never know who took the long trip to the bottom of the lake," I said.

"Maybe we will," Diamond said. "We found a black Chevy Silverado pickup parked in the woods off the highway on the mountain up above Skunk Harbor. It was stolen in Santa Cruz. The lab guys found powder traces all over the inside, as if the suspects had fired their rifle out the window. So we confronted our prisoner, told him what we knew, that the guy who hired him was in the chicken coop, that his shooting pal was at the bottom of the lake. He broke. Started squawking and hasn't stopped. He gave us the pal's name. A drifter from Montana named Denton Pillary. We'll check it out."

I nodded. One of the tree shadows had begun to encroach on my sun, so I shifted my chair to move back into the heat.

"We found this under the floor mat. We're guessing it belonged to Leah's mother."

Diamond handed me a little rolled mat, about a foot long, and festooned with sparkling green beads at the ends.

"Inside the roll was one of those plug-in computer memory chips," Diamond said. "Turns out Dr. Kiyosawa had made a long recording about how Charles Hall got him to make the Night Portraits. The doctor said he was going to hide the recording as leverage against Hall in case he didn't keep his end of the bargain. I guess that didn't work out."

I untied the string and unrolled it. Once flattened out, the outside showed an ornate, embroidered flower. Inside, was an assortment of artist's paintbrushes. They were held in place with looped threads. Behind the brushes was white liner paper that made it easy to see the size and shape of each brush. The brushes were lined up in order of size, from a quarter of an inch in diameter down to micro-tiny.

"Leah's mother's brushes," I said.

Diamond nodded.

"Leah will appreciate it. Have you heard when she is to get out of the hospital?"

"Later this afternoon."

"Thanks. Mind if we give this to her?"

"That's what I was thinking. Adios. I gotta go."

Diamond drove away.

Street was admiring the embroidered flower on the brush holder. "It's a lotus blossom. Maybe this was a kind of salve for Leah's mother. The modern world was probably just too frenetic for her."

"What do you mean?" I asked.

"You know about that?" Jennifer said to Street, excited. "Cool." Jennifer turned to me. "It's part of Greek myth. Homer wrote about it in the Odyssey. When Odysseus was trying to get home from the

Trojan Wars, he came upon the lotus-eaters. They were a dreamy, happy, contented people all because they ate the fruit of the lotus."

Street was looking at the embroidery up close. She frowned.

"What?" I said.

She turned the brush holder over. "These threads in the embroidery. See where they're tied off in these little micro knots? A bunch of them have been retied."

"How do you know?"

"The knots were probably untouched for decades. They would have faded over time. Now, if you look very close, you can see that all the little fade marks have moved, and next to them are bright little marks. The unfaded threads that used to be on the inside of the knots are now on the outside of the knots."

"I can't see that close."

Street handed it to Jennifer.

Jennifer nodded in agreement.

A couple of hours later, we left Jennifer's bike at Street's condo, piled into Street's VW bug and drove to get Leah at the hospital. Leah sat in front, and I drove, while Street, Jennifer and Spot crammed into the back of the VW, possibly a new record for VW rear-seat occupancy. We took Leah home to her little house that the cleaning crew had cleaned up, but which was still messy. Street made tea, which she poured into mugs with kanji characters on them. We all sat at the little kitchen table. I gave Leah the brush holder.

Leah was very strong.

She held the brush holder to her chest like it was a baby. "I always heard how my mother said that if her brushes were safe, she'd be safe."

She unrolled it and touched the brushes with her fingertip. "I'm going to think that wherever she is, she has found some safety."

We pointed out the new knots on the brush loops.

"What do you think that means?" Leah asked.

"Just a guess," I said, "but it looks like those knots are for the threads that hold the brush loops. We're thinking that the paper liner was not an original part of the brush holder."

Leah stared at it.

Then she rushed over to one of the cupboards below the kitchen counter, pulled out a sewing box, and dug through it. She found a tweezers and a tiny pointed, hook-type tool.

She tried both on the knots. The hook tool worked best.

She sat down at her desk and pulled the desk light over so it shined up close. It took ten minutes for her to untie the knots. One by one, the loops that held the brushes came free. With all the loops and brushes gone, the liner paper came away.

It was actually two small sheets of paper. They were worn and creased, and full of little holes at the edges where the loop threads had been stitched through.

Leah stared at the top piece for a long time. She stood up from the desk, brought it over and set it on the table so we could see.

It was a watercolor showing Leah standing and painting at an easel.

The watercolor was rendered in an exquisite style, a soft technique that depicted only a few very fine details and highlights, yet somehow created the essence of the artist at work. The picture showed Leah's concentration, her immersion in her work, the essence of her creative energy.

The painting was masterful in that it showed the real Leah as her mother had no doubt seen on TV. Yet it left out the unknowables such as what Leah's subject was or how she painted.

In one of the corners of the watercolor were some tiny kanji characters.

Leah was over at a pile of books that had been dumped out of her bookshelf by the burglar. She found a volume and brought it over, flipping through its pages. It looked like a reference volume for kanji characters.

She stopped on a page, studied it, turned to the index, flipped through to several other pages, compared the illustrations to the kanji characters her mother had put on the watercolor.

Minutes went by as Leah tried to figure it out.

Eventually, she shut the book and spoke.

"My mother obviously did not speak or write Japanese. But maybe my father helped her when they met. As best as I can understand this, these kanji characters mean, 'Love and art are the only parts of life that matter.'"

Leah picked up the painting and looked at it again.

"What was the other piece of paper?" Jennifer asked.

Leah went back to the desk and picked it up.

"It's a note from my father. 'Dear Leah, If you are reading this, then something happened to me. As you know I'm not much for words. I prefer to communicate with paint. But I want to say that you are a very good artist. I've left you an annuity that should allow you to paint full time. Dream big, my little Leah, dream big, and you could go to the stars.'"

EPILOGUE

Two months later, I left Spot at my cabin with Diamond in charge. Which meant that my wine cabinet and my microwave would both be in disarray when I got back. A reasonable trade to avoid the kennel. Spot liked visiting with a hundred dogs. But he had trouble doing the duckwalk to get through the low kennel doors.

I picked up Street at her condo at the bottom of the mountain, took 50 up and over Echo Summit and down the American River Canyon to the Central Valley.

"What ever happened to the last Night Portrait?" Street asked.

"Paul, the art-consultant-for-life, didn't want anything to do with it. So he gave it to me. I gave it to Leah. It's hanging in her living room. However, it's a pretty dark piece, with the dead baby in it. So she's thinking of giving it to the Atelier Olympia. They can put it with their other studies."

An unusual weather system had pushed in from the Pacific making it misty in the valley. When we went over the coastal range and into the Bay Area, I expected fog, rain, and worse and regretted that I'd once again forgotten umbrellas. Instead, we drove into one of those spectacular afternoons where the landscape glowed, and the visibility was fifty miles.

We took the Bay Bridge into The City. The skyscrapers shimmered in the unusually hot summer sunshine. Hundreds of sailboats speckled the blue water of The Bay. Over by the Golden Gate, an improbably large tanker cavorted with a cruise ship. Some kind of air show was taking place over the water just off Fisherman's Wharf, five biplanes weaving smoke trails into an elaborate design.

Street and I found a parking garage off Leavenworth and walked down to our hotel on Post. We checked in and changed out of our jeans. Street had explained to me that black was the perennial color of choice in the upscale urban art world.

"But the female Collectorati in New York all have a splash of color somewhere on their persons," I said. "And the male Collectorati periodically wear an extravagant gray to demonstrate their liberal attitudes toward clothing."

Street frowned. "Sounds like New York has lost its edge."

"Tell that to a New Yorker," I said as I pulled on navy Dockers and a navy flannel shirt, then added a red tie. I traded my canvas sneakers for my only pair of shoes that were actually made of leather, brown fading toward tan.

Street looked at my unblack clothes. "I guess you've lost your edge, too."

"That's not what you said the last time you put on those clothes and then promptly let me take them off."

Street was buttoning up slim-fitting black pants. She pulled a loose black sweater over her black tank top, the spaghetti shoulder straps of which just peeked out from under the sweater.

When she slipped on her black sling-back shoes with the spiky two-inch heels I said, "Maybe we should skip the opening, order in champagne, and work on my edge. I could practice removing those heels."

Street's lips and eyes hinted at a smile that would have made Da Vinci send Mona Lisa back to the modeling agency. "Maybe later," Street said.

We ordered Anchor Steams in the bar off the hotel lobby. I drank mine down while Street sipped hers like it was dangerous, and then we walked across Union Square to the gallery.

The address on the invite was a building on Geary. Glasser Price Gallery was on the fourth floor. We heard harp music as the elevator door opened. The crowd was large. The men wore black jackets. Some had narrow black ties to accent their black shirts and pants, while some went casual and skipped the ties. The women wore evening gowns. Black. The only color in the room other than my clothes was the wine. Everyone held a glass, nine reds for every white.

"I hate these things," Street muttered.

"I suggested an alternative."

"You know what I mean. We need to be here, and it's always worse for the artist, but everybody just makes small talk. Nobody looks at the art. I'll feel better after I've started on a glass of wine."

I left her at the entrance, muscled my way toward the wine table and returned with two glasses of a Central Coast Pinot. We clinked glasses and made a circuit of the perimeter of the rooms, stopping to admire each painting.

Leah's works were spectacular, hung in a single row that stretched around the two main rooms of the gallery. They were small landscapes, California hillsides with complex drapery of Black oak following the gullies and arcing across the crests. Some of the scenes depicted spring, the grass cool and green and soothing. Some were during summer when the grass turns golden and the oaks take on a darker hue, making calligraphic patterns across the hills. It took me a moment to realize that the tree patterns looked like kanji. It was one of those exciting discoveries when the viewer realizes that the artist is doing something in addition to simply making gorgeous images. It wasn't a sentimental thing, nor was it a clever camouflage trick. It was instead a subtle, subliminal quality that informed the work and hinted at deeper meanings. Perhaps one could read them if one knew Japanese.

"These are beautiful!" Street said, her voice hushed.

"Yeah," I said.

"It looks like most of them are already sold." Street pointed at the red dots to the right of each one. "Here's one that isn't. 'Two Hills With Creek.' It's so intimate, almost as if the creek is hiding from the world. Do you see that? Or am I making it up?"

"I see it."

"I'd like to buy it and this one, 'Dancing Oaks.' Owen, can you find the gallery director? I'll wait here to stake my claim."

The woman in charge was over by the wine table, chatting up an elderly couple who looked like they owned Nob Hill.

I walked up. The woman looked at my clothes and gave me a small patrician grin that reminded me of Lauren Phelter, the landlady who brought us into Leah's life. "Excuse me," I said. "To whom shall we speak about acquiring a couple of paintings?"

Her smile broadened. "I'd be glad to help you, sir."

I led her over to where Street stood protectively in front of the paintings.

"I'm Owen McKenna, and this is Street Casey."

"Lara Buchanan. Very pleased to meet you both. Oh, good

choices. 'Two Hills' and 'Dancing Oaks.' Strong images with a delicate theme."

I said to Street, "I'd like to add a third to your collection. Would that be okay?"

Street grinned. "Wonderful."

"Can you suggest a companion piece that is still available?" I said to Lara.

She glanced around and gestured across the room. "See those two, second and third from the left? One is 'Three Hills Shining,' and the other is 'View From Below.' Either would be good, but I especially like the oak patterns in 'View.' It would go well with these two." She pointed at the oak patterns, moving her finger up and down and sideways.

"More kanji," I said.

Lara Buchanan raised her eyebrows. "You noticed. Very good. Leah doesn't want us to mention that aspect. She says it is something for the viewer to come to over time."

We went over to a built-in desk in the corner of the room and made the arrangements. Lara thanked us and said she'd call us when the show came down in three weeks. Then she put red dots to the side of our paintings.

The crowd had thickened toward the proscenium between the first and second room. We pushed our way into it. Once through the archway, we saw Leah at the center of the throng in the second room. She stood tall and elegant in a dark green dress with glinting silver thread sewn into it. More Japanese patterns. High heels showed under the floor-length gown.

Leah's hair was pulled up and back in a tight bun. Jennifer had paid for reconstructive surgery on her ear and scars. The scars were still fresh, but already the result looked much more natural. She could once again smile without the skin pulling down on the corner of her eye.

But a couple of smaller scars still remained, the skin around it was leathery, and no one would ever mistake her fabricated seashell ear for a normal one.

Yet Leah wore no special makeup to obscure her scars. In her ears were sparkling diamond studs that drew attention to the sides of her face. The one in her rebuilt ear caught in the track lighting and threw colored sparklers throughout the room.

Dramatic as her dress and earrings were, Leah outshone her outfit. She grinned as she spoke and she gestured with her hands, long fingers outstretched and expressive. She tossed her head back when she laughed. Her smile grew wider still as the delicate muscles in her throat worked with the robust laughter.

For the first time since meeting her, I could picture the previous Leah, charming and animated on Tahoe Live, as captivating as she was beautiful. Now she was arresting and beautiful once again in spite of the injuries, because she knew this was her moment, and she inhabited it like a movie star, proud, effervescent, vivacious, pleasantly full of herself and her big night in the spotlight.

We hovered close, and our brief turn with Leah eventually came.

"Leah," Street said. "Your paintings are wonderful! The sun on the hills is so warm. I adore them." She made no mention of our purchase.

"Thank you!" Leah hugged Street. "And thank you so much for coming." Leah turned and looked up at me. "And you, Mr. Owen McKenna..." She gave me a two-handed shake, warm and long, then hugged me. Her smile was luminous, her eyes crinkling.

Her radiance dimmed for a second and she bit her lip. "I did what you said and decided to be who I am, no cover up. I made some bad mistakes, but I'm putting them behind me. And I'm an artist, not a model. I don't care about TV anymore. It doesn't matter if I'm not perfect. I'm just lucky to be here. If you and Street hadn't..."

I interrupted, "But you *are* perfect, Leah Printner. And a great artist as well."

She paused, her eyes searching mine. Suddenly the smile was back in full force. She put her index finger to her lips, kissed it, reached out and touched my lips. Then a group of seven or eight people swooped in and surrounded her, calling her name, shouting praises above the din. Leah was swept away.

Street and I left and got into the elevator.

Street spoke first. "She shows how to do it, doesn't she?"

"Reinvent yourself?"

"More of a total renewal. When something really bad happens, when the dam bursts and you're swept away and lose everything you thought you had. She shows how to pick yourself up and start all over again."

"Good lesson," I said.

"About what we can do if we can find the strength to try?"

"Yeah."

We pushed through the lobby door and walked out into the vibrant city that pulsed with life.

About the Author

Todd Borg and his wife live in Lake Tahoe. To contact Todd or learn more about the Owen McKenna mysteries, please visit toddborg.com.